I0668734

DREAM CASTERS
LIGHT

BY

ADRIENNE WOODS

Dream Casters Light The Dream Caster Series 1
Copyright © 2015 Adrienne Woods
Illustration: Joemel Requeza

If you purchased this e-book from anyone other than Fire Quill Publishing
or a licensed FQP reseller, you should be aware this e-book is stolen
property.

This e-book is a work of fiction. Any references to historical events, real
people, or real locales are used fictitiously. Other names, characters, places,
and incidents are the products of the author's imagination, and any
resemblance to actual events or locales or persons, living or dead, is entirely
coincidental.

Fire Quill Publishing
www.firequillpublishing.com

All rights reserved, including the right of reproduction in whole or in part
in any form.

All graphics and text associated with Fire Quill Publishing.
Formatting by www.firequillpublishing.com
Manufactured in South Africa.
First Fire Quill publishing edition May 2015
ISBN: 978-0-9946641-3-6

DEDICATION

To my best friend of twenty years Vinique, her family Graig
and my two beautiful Monkeys, Ashton and Leighthan. Thank
you for your love and support and for the inspiration behind
Dream Casters. Love you lots.
Adrienne

OTHER NOVELS IN THIS SERIES

OTHER NOVELS BY ADRIENNE WOODS
THE DRAGONIAN SERIES

TO FIND OUT MORE VISIT
www.authoradriennewoods.com

CONTENT

ACKNOWLEDGEMENT

First and the most important, as always, thanks is to our Father in Heaven, for blessing me still every day, without Your guidance, I wouldn't have done or finished with another novel if You were not involved in this every day. You are my purpose of life and I will love You till the end of time.

Then I would like to thank my extraordinary proof readers, you know who you are, for your valuable input, patience and willingness to delve into another one of my worlds.

For the endless support of my family; My husband Heinrich and two beautiful daughters. I would be lost without your loving support and your ability to keep me pursuing a new project each and every time.

A special thanks to my wonderful editors, Hillery, you are still a true Paegeian, and now a true Reveran citizen as well. Your love for beautiful words has given yet another project the wings it needed to soar. Monique and Zoe, have become true citizens too, and your insight to the words on these pages made Chastity and all her friends so much more entertaining, and a big thank you for polishing my work to perfection.

To my cover artist Joemel. You nailed this one 100 percent and I'm in awe of your talent and how better you get with time. You were able to reach once again into my imagination, capture, and re-imagine a world I thought only I would ever see. Because of your passion and skill my book will be judged by its cover for sure.

To my publishing company, Fire Quill, for giving a home to my all my series and to the best team I ever worked with. Helen, Gerald, Sandra, Carlyle, Monique and Kelly, Hillery and Zoe, you are all stars for making my novels reach much further then I dream for.

Last, but not the least, a big thanks to my fans. I hope you are going to love this new story, be open mind please as its completely different from the Dragonian Series. I will always, always be grateful for your love and support.

Lots of love

Adrienne Woods

PART I

CHAPTER ONE
THIS IS ME

TWO SETS OF FOOTSTEPS MADE BARELY A SOUND ON the rough and weathered wood as they walked across the bridge that led from Main Pacific to the Glands. The streetlights were dimmed as dusk began to settle and last vestiges of light from the setting sun were fading to night. The lumbering clouds were moving in, blocking out any light from the two moons that shone overhead, even the stars seemed less bright dotted across their velvet backdrop. With his golden dust Graig Chen could conjure and wield anything by simply believing in its reality. If he wanted it to be real, it would be.

The Reverse was the most painful thing either of them had ever experienced, but Liam, a healer and Graig's only confidant, had promised him that they would be able to live in the Domain like normal

Nomads, humans.

Graig and his pregnant fiancé, were fleeing from their home world in secret, having no other choice if they desired a normal life for their unborn child.

They knew neither of their families would ever understand, even though it had been his grandmother who had always said, *the heart wants, what the heart wants.* How could he have known that his heart would want a Shadow Caster, and not just any ordinary Shadow Caster. She was special, or at least her family was. She was expected to uphold the family line with her offspring, Graig knew that did not include carrying the child of a Light Caster.

The two lovers could never live in peace, not since the balance between good and evil inside Revera was thrown into upheaval. There were only two choices for casters like them, either light or dark. The balance could not accommodate a person containing both, so for his child's sake they had no choice but to leave Revera and live like normal humans in the Domain, or what humans would call reality. He'd found a perfect place, one he'd made sure no one would ever find, not even his two best friends.

They knew about the relationship, they'd been there when he'd first laid eyes on her, tried to talk him out of it, to forget the blonde bombshell that would only cause him darkness and misery, but without her his life would be spent in darkness and misery.

Her silver blonde hair and bright blue eyes had done him in, if only he'd seen the bow that she'd aimed straight at his heart. If it hadn't been for his love when the arrow hit, and for Liam, a healer, he wouldn't be in his current predicament; trying to get him and her off this dimension; a world that most people would call make-believe, but Revera was far from that. It was the world of dreams, and Graig was a Level Four Caster whose mission was to retrieve others living in the Domain out for Selene, their only live Somnium. It was on one of these very missions that he had met the love of his life, the one woman he couldn't live without, and he didn't care if she had black dust, he didn't care that she was a Shadow Caster, or what some would call a nightmare wielder. Yes, those horrible dreams that leave you paralyzed with fear are actually wielded by Casters, not some grave impression of one's subconscious. They are responsible for doubts and forgotten dreams. She was his nightmare, and a nightmare he was prepared to die for.

He knew deep down that she would never survive living in Revera and he was unable to cope with the Oblivion, wherever it was. Oblivion was the realm of the Shadow Casters, created when Selene cast out Magdelena, the very first Shadow Casters, who was the third Somnium, as a consequence for the death of her brother, Darius, the second Somnium. Magdelena had no realm to call her own, so she created Oblivion by focusing her hatred toward Selene, a world that could exist inside Revera, far from Selene's sight. For years, Selene tried to find it, but as long as the Sodivic bloodline flowed through Shadow Caster's veins, Oblivion would never be found by a Light Caster.

Sodivic blood was the key to Oblivion's secrecy, and Magdalena's family line. There were many Sodivic's since the dawning of Oblivion but Magdelena reigned over them all. Graig had met many Sodivic's on his quests, each meeting always ending up in a bloody mess, and in all the years he had encountered them, not one had ever shown any kind of mercy or remorse. They were sadistic and couldn't be reasoned with. He had been taught from a young age, if you see a Sodivic, you kill it. That was the number one rule taught to the Level One Light Casters.

His fiancé was the only one that proved his theory wrong. Over the past century, their bloodline had been busy dying out, leaving her one of the few powerful Shadow Casters left.

Graig would pay dearly for loving her if her father ever found them, and he couldn't even think about what would happen to the unborn child she carried.

Graig squeezed the hand that was resting tightly inside his own grip as they neared the end of the bridge.

"We're almost there, my love. Not much longer."

"You're sure nobody followed us?" Her eyes were wild, searching everywhere in the darkness.

"I'm sure. Besides, they won't be able to see us." He opened his hand, just to make sure she hadn't forgotten what he was, and threw more golden sand into the air, shielding them from anything that tried to follow them.

Then he heard it. A crunch. He stopped abruptly and she slammed into him. One second of doubt was all it took to break the spell, and before he could realized, they were surrounded by Nimgolians, the biggest and most wicked shadow hounds imaginable. They were evil, and reminded him of a Rottweiler that had chased him one time in the Domain.

Dogs could always see them, whereas humans couldn't. He had always assumed the dust worked differently for animals. He used to toy with them, he'd told Zac once it was a good work out, before hitting them with a dose of dust that would kick them out for at least half a day. Against these hounds, however, his golden dust didn't just put them to sleep, it put them to sleep forever.

"Take my bag," Graig spoke softly, reaching out his hand.

"I'm not leaving you. I can fight."

"These are your family. It's enough that you have to know that they will die, I'm not going to let you kill them."

"I don't give a shit, Graig. You are my family now, you and bean, nobody else."

Graig smiled. Ever since they'd found out that she was pregnant, she'd called the fetus, bean. Spinning her in his arms, he gave her a hard kiss and handed her a Celestial—an oval shaped gel pendant that would take her and the child to their safe haven, in case he didn't make it—and a small green bag filled with his dust. "Just in case," he spoke, swallowing the lump in his throat.

"There is no in case, you make it, you hear?"

She planted a hard passionate kiss on his lips. The kind that filled him with confidence, he had no doubts, not even in that second, that would have given away their hiding place.

"Vinicola, are you sure you want to do this?" One of the Shadow Casters mounted on the back of a hound, growled. His voice made Graig's skin crawl. Everything about them screamed evil. How that power ran through this beautiful creature standing fiercely next to him, was beyond his knowledge.

Graig surveyed the Caster before him. His hair was wild, hung to his shoulders, and was pure white, just like his love's. He must be her family, but how close he didn't know. Yet, the man didn't look anything like her. He was big, had broad shoulders, and was dirty.

Vinicola laughed, the laugh that Graig hated. It didn't sound anything like her, but it was the only language she knew to speak, a sound that told them if they killed her, they would feel her father's wrath. This was purely a retrieval mission, but it was a wipe out for him. "Sibian, you can tell him I'm done with Oblivion, and nothing you do will ever drag me back to that wretched hell-hole you love so much."

"Your mind seems a bit clouded, dear," the Shadow Caster said. "Let me refresh it." He lifted up his hands and let his dust flow freely, and four more Shadow Hounds appeared out of his dark sand.

Graig whipped his bow from his shoulder and started to shoot invisible arrows that would take shape through his golden dust.

The hounds that were hit fell into useless heaps of black sand. Vinicola ripped off her whip that had been secured around her waist, and did the same. The other hounds exploded into the sky, but they weren't destroyed, they would re-emerge a couple of minutes later, whole once again.

It was useless for her to fight, she only gave him a couple of minutes as she was still one of them, even though she'd made the choice to leave in her heart.

Graig made sure he used all the minutes she gave him and when it was time for the full on fight, they both took on two at a time.

He conjured his sword for full-on battle and started slashing away.

"Graig!" Vinicola's voice yelled in panic. When he

found her she was captured, with a huge Shadow Caster's arm around her neck.

In those few seconds he felt defeated, their plan was ruined and he knew he wouldn't get a second chance with her.

As he stood there, an axe hit him straight in the back, the dark sand ripping his veins inside his body apart. It hurt like hell, and he could feel his golden sand starting to seep out of him. Vinicola's shrill scream pierced the night air around them.

He wasn't going to survive this, but he'd made the choice for the love of his life and their unborn child.

He took a Celestial out of his pocket— stood up with a mother of an axe still inside of him—and mustered all the strength he had. He had only moments to act before the others would come, or worse, take her away.

He threw the Celestial hard on the ground near her feet and yelled the word "San Francisco" as loud as he could. In an instant, a bright light blinded all the Shadow Casters and he watched her close her eyes tightly.

Vinicola knew what to do and he watched as she, and the Shadow Caster who had his arm around her neck, disappeared.

The Shadow Caster would die. His DNA wasn't attached to the Celestial, and he wouldn't make the trip. He had won. Just then another object sliced through his neck and he fell on the floor, the last images he saw was a body without a head before everything went black.

SIXTEEN YEARS LATER

"CRAP, CRAP, CRAP," WHERE THE ONLY
WORDS THAT left my mouth as I took each painful
step. Rollins knew just how to give ballet lessons that
were straight from Nick's pit. A stabbing pain ran up
my calf and I had to stop as it went into a spasm. *That
should teach me to be late for class.*

If it hadn't been for Clare Bean—yep, her surname
was Bean, which led to plenty of teasing when she was
little—I would've been on time. I would've had that
extra ten minutes to stretch.

We had always been friends, Clare and I, since we
were crawling around in diapers. Her house was a
couple of houses down from mine and our moms were
all too happy to bring us over for play dates. But since
Ass and Abs, Taylor Winchester, had come into the
picture, Clare had gone all gaga and friendship didn't
seem to mean a thing to her anymore.

At first he hadn't been too bad. He'd always had a
thing for Clare, but a month ago at his party, we'd been
sort of trapped in the basement alone for a couple of
minutes and he'd declared his 'undying love and
affection' to me. Me, Chastity Blake, or just Chas as
my friends call me, let me rephrase, as my friends used
to call me, as I'd rejected his affection, using finger
quotes. Every girl my age knew what guys, especially
the ones that looked like Ty, meant when they declared
their affection to you.

Clare was my best friend, what else was I supposed
to do? I'd thought the idiot would feel like stinky feet

and forget about it, but no, he thought that I should be taught a lesson, and told Clare that I'd made a move on him. She'd actually believed the dog.

Now for the past four weeks I'd had to endure their humiliation on a daily basis. First it was the posters on every locker with guys names crossed out. The entire baseball team from what it looked like, and the heading was *Chastity Blake's To Do List*.

It was so lame, but coming from her, it hurt. It hurt a lot.

I thought everyone would forget about that in a week, but they didn't and more rumors were added on.

Then came the exploding paint in my locker. I struggled to get the red paint out of my hair and had walked around with it for an entire week. My mom almost had a heart attack though, acting all strange and was ready to pack up and leave.

Today, they locked me in the girl's bathroom. I crawled out the window, which wasn't easy, and that was why I was late today.

Still, I tried to ignore it, even though it came from my best friend. Standing up to them would only cause more shit.

As I kept walking, the fork in the road came nearer. One path led through the city. Five traffic lights with many twist and turns flashed though my head. The other road led past the lake. No traffic lights and it was a shorter route, but my mother disliked me taking that one. Still today was the perfect day to make an exception.

I chose the lake and started to think about my crappy situation again and regret of telling Mom not to pick me up from ballet, really started to bite me in the ass.

Literally. It was like a tiny stabbing jolts of pain on my bum that ached with every step I took.

The next couple of years of school would probably suck if there wasn't an end to Clare's pranks soon and my father, sorry, step-father, Tim "the military man" Swanson, wasn't going to move just because of the social life epidemic I was experiencing.

I never understood why Mom had married him. There wasn't a time that I couldn't remember Tim not being in our lives, but she was so different from him. She was a free spirit, loved to paint and for some reason she had a thing about dreams. Since I was little, she's always asked me what I dreamt about the night before. It was creepy to people that didn't know my mom but it didn't bother me much.

Tim was easy to sum up. It was always 'YES SIR!' and 'NO SIR!' although he didn't like the 'NO' very much, and loved the 'HOW HIGH DO YOU WANT ME TO FREAK'N JUMP' type of thing. Our relationship never used to be like that, but the older I got, the harder he became on me. Mom stood up for me a lot though, but I hated that they ended up fighting over stupid things I didn't really want to do.

So lately my relationship with the only dad I knew was everything except the relationship a father and daughter should have.

Other family, I don't have them. It was always just Tim and her.

As I pondered my lack of family, something to the left caught my eye. It was parked right in front of the lake and my entire body felt as if someone had pulled a plug and let all the air out. It was Ty's pick-up, and I knew who else would be with him inside it.

When noises from Derek Benson came, I knew it wasn't just the two of them, but the entire freak'n football team. They sometimes came here after practice and right now, I wished that I'd taken the other stupid road.

I watched as Clare's figure jumped off his truck. She wasn't as tall or as lean as me, thanks to the 50 % Asian blood that flowed through me, but she was not chubby either. She was of medium build, not that there was anything wrong with it.

Here we go!

"Oh look, if it isn't the baseball team's slut," Clare shouted loudly and everyone turned and laughed. If these were strangers that did this, it would've been different, but they weren't; they used to be my friends. We used to laugh together, make jokes at the table and even pass notes around in class. Even Nicole, who used to make up the rest of our little trio, had her nose in a teen magazine and pretended that nothing was about to happen.

I knew I should've just walked away, but today was different. I was tired, I ached from head to toe, I was in my still in my darn tutu, I'd just pulled my pants over my leotard and exchanged my ballet shoes for sneakers. I really didn't have the time for her little charades of insecurity.

"The baseball team? Really? Now we know who has all the intellectual stem cells between the two of us," I said and carried on walking.

"And who has all the grace and beauty," Clare chirped.

"And also a shallow mind." I couldn't help myself. This is what happened when I started. It was like my mouth had its own passageway straight to my brain and I couldn't do anything to switch it off.

"Oh, yeah, shallow minded. At least I know what loyalty means, bitch."

I laughed again. "Loyalty. Can you even spell it, Clare?" Instant regret jumped through my core. Hurt rose briefly in Clare's eyes but vanished just as fast. She was dyslexic and I had been helping her with words ever since we were just tiny little things running around.

"I know how to spell slut, bitch, and skank."

"Well, sorry to burst your bubble, sweetheart. I never did anything with Taylor, but wait, I tried to tell you that, and you still believed the son of a bitch."

"That's a lie, Chas," Taylor said. "Seriously, you really expect people to buy that? I know what the guys in the locker rooms are saying. I'd never be with someone like you."

Clare gloated as she looked with admiration at Taylor and the entire group laughed.

"Yes, Chas, why didn't we ever get to see some of the action the baseball team got?" The blond guy with the dark eyes was inches from me, tugging at my tutu.

"I don't know Jake," I slapped his hand away, "probably because you've taken too many hits on the football field and can't even multiply two and two anymore."

Jake laughed.

Suddenly, I was shoved from behind, and I stumbled forward. My backpack flew from my shoulder and fell hard on the road. I got up and when I turned around, Clare's face was inches from mine. "So what, the guys are below your standard, is that it?"

"Yes," I said. "It's exactly that. I've been trying to tell you that, but for some reason it doesn't want to sink into that closed mind of yours."

"Stop saying that. I'm not stupid," Clare yelled and shoved me again.

"Then what are we doing, Clare?" I yelled back. "We've been friends for ten years, ten years and you go and believe biceps and abs."

Clare shook her head with her arms folded across her chest and looked the other way.

"I would never do that to you, but it doesn't matter what I say, your mind was made up the minute that idiot felt like a rat and crawled back to you."

"That is not what you said that night at the party." Taylor had that smirk plastered on his face. "The night you decided to try and have all this." His hands ran up and down his body as if we needed direction.

"Seriously?" I started to laugh. "It just shows you how well you really knew me if you think I was going to fall for a tool like you. Screw you, asshole."

"In your dreams."

"Lame comeback," I said as I pulled my backpack over my shoulder and walked on.

As I started to walk, it seemed like today might just be my lucky day, that they were going to leave me alone and let me pass, but as I walked past the second tree, Derek and Jake, both linemen, blocked my view.

My heart beat slightly rose but now wasn't the time to show them a hint of fear. They were like a pack of wolves, looked like animals and thrived on fear. "Get out of my way Tweedle Dee and Tweedle Dum."

They laughed. "Make us," Derek sneered. Now I'd heard some rumors about him, and none of them were any good. Stealing his mother's pills and drugging girls to have his way with them was the highest on that list.

"C'mon guys, let the skank go," Clare said.

"They won't do anything, sweetheart. They're just messing with her a bit," Taylor said softly but not softly enough. I could hear the giggling coming from Clare. *How could she enjoy this so much?*

"Fine, just don't do anything I wouldn't," Clare yelled.

"Then it looks like I'm screwed." *Seriously, keep your freak'n mouth shut.*

Derek and Jake started circling me as if I was a piece of meat. I closed my eyes as my heart started to thump inside my chest. Run and their fun would begin, and I was no animal.

I opened my eyes and more members of the team joined in. Some of these guys had really been my friends, or so I'd thought. One of Derek's wing men, Mark, a guy with really short hair that looked like he had giant's DNA flowing through his veins, came close and sniffed my hair like someone that had to be locked up. I turned around and glared at him. He just laughed and backed a bit off.

"That is enough!" Nicole finally said as she put her magazine down and came closer.

Tommy, a red head who was an extra on the football team, grabbed her.

"Let me go, you idiot," Nicole yelled at him and he laughed. "Clare, make them stop for crying out loud. It's Chastity."

"Good, maybe it will teach her to stay away from her best friend's boyfriends."

"She didn't do it," Nicole said. "Taylor is a douche."

"Stay out of this Nicole!" Taylor yelled. "Before I tell Clare about your little schemes."

"What schemes?" Clare asked, but I blocked out the rest as the ogres were really starting to freak me out. Would they really do that, and if they did, would Clare and Nicole really watch as they took their turns?

"Ooh, look, I wonder what the little ballet princess is hiding underneath those slacks of hers." Derek touched the hem of my slacks. I slapped his hand hard, and more of the guys started to touch me.

"Get the hell away from me."

"Clare, make them stop!" Nicole yelled again.

"No, she deserves it."

Those words angered me as my heart beat faster. I thought I was close to passing out as my head started to spin, instead I felt loose, soft grit inside my hand, and there was a lot of it. As I rolled the material around my fingers, it felt as if the entire world stopped for a second, or just slowed down.

I could smell Derek's smoke breath close to me, it stank and I felt the soft warm breath of Sam, another idiot on my face.

A mixture of cologne overpowered me as the four guys stood really close to me. Their hands touching my arms and clothes.

Then I saw the grit in my hands again. It was soft, not like sand, and it had a light golden color to it.

At once the slow motion stopped and I threw a handful of the stuff, hitting Mark full in the face. He crouched and tried to get it out his eyes. I felt more sand in my hand and Jake was next. I didn't know where it came from or how any of this was even possible, but right now that didn't matter. As I threw a handful at each and every one of them, a refill was waiting patiently in my palm.

Derek was next and before I knew it, all the boys were coughing and crouching down. Then one by one they fell over, in a fetus position with eyes closed and soft snores coming from their lips.

Clare and Ty ran to the guys and crouched down. Ty felt for a heartbeat, but from the sound coming from their lips I knew they were still alive. I waited for men with cameras to jump out from behind the trees, yelling GOT YOU or something but it didn't happened.

The fear on both Ty and Clare's faces were real.

"What did you do?" Ty yelled.

"Nothing they didn't deserve!" I yelled back hoping he would just back the hell off.

"You're a freak!" Clare yelled, and stormed at me. More sand accumulated in my hand, but to me, she was still my best friend, one whose mind had been closed by the idiot that was busy running away.

I opened my palm and let the grit fall to the floor. A breeze picked it up and blew it softly into Clare's face.

She stopped in her tracks, give a huge yawn and lay down on the ground.

Was she sleeping?

I looked at my hands. The grit was gone, there weren't even traces of it inside my palm, nothing made sense.

"Just go," Nicole said as she crouched down next to Clare to investigate.

I stood still as a statue trying to process what was happening to me.

"Chastity!" Nicole yelled again. "Go!"

I looked down at Nicole. My legs finally started to

move into the direction of home, and grabbed my backpack that had fallen on the turf.

I reached the city of Chicago fast and almost ran into a police officer that was chatting to one of the waiters. Guilt over what I'd just done was evident on my face so I ran in another direction.

"Hey, you there, stop!" He yelled.

I didn't listen and he chased me for a couple of blocks but he had probably had one too many donuts on a daily basis and couldn't keep up. I took so many turns down back alleys that when I finally stopped I had no idea where I was.

I breathed hard, trying to catch my breath and looked back at my hands. The was still no trace of the grit. It had just vanished. My heart beat fast again and cold sweat dripped from my temple as flashes of ogre-like bodies, almost the entire football team, falling down right after I threw the grit at them came to mind. Coach was not going to like this, and how was I going to explain any of it to anybody?

What the hell did I just do? I glanced at my hands one more time. *What the hell was happening to me?*

CHAPTER TWO
LOST

I'VE LIVED IN CHICAGO ALL MY LIFE AND I
HAD NO idea where I was. The buildings all looked the
same, foreign and it felt as if I'd been transported to
another place, far, far from home.

My phone had broken when Clare shoved me and it'd
fallen to the ground.

It was in the front pocket and I knew Tim was going
to kill me for ruining my first phone. The black screen
had a huge crack and the phone didn't even try to turn
on.

Eyes scanned me up and down as I wondered through
the city, wearing only my tutu over a pair of slacks. I'm
sure I looked like someone who'd just escaped from the
loony bin. Walking into another alley, I removed my
torn tutu and walked with the thing in my arms. When
the sun started to set, fear got hold of me.

It was funny how strange people get. They knew that

I was lost. The fear was evident on my face as I walked in circles, because I could've sworn I'd passed the laundry shop on my left half an hour ago, yet none of them stopped to ask if I needed any help.

Soon I found a bus stop and plunged down. Traffic was jammed and I just wished that by some miracle I would find my way home tonight.

As I sat, my eyes caught the bruise on my arm illuminated in the lamplight. It was in the shape of finger marks and I couldn't recall who'd given it to me. It had been Derek or Mark.

The bruise was turning purple now, but the only thing I saw was the soft golden grit-like dust leaving my hands as I threw heaps and heaps at them, behind my closed eyelids. *Where did it come from?*

My mind was seriously going on a trip and I started thinking that maybe Derek slipped some of his mom's narcotics inside my glass of juice at lunch and this was the result, but when I pinched myself, it felt real.

"Meow," a cat close by said as it jumped onto my lap.

"Shades?" I stared at the cat with huge eyes. It looked like her, she had those two round markings around both her eyes and raven black fur with a grey bushy tail. The markings around her eyes were what gave her the name, because it looked like she was wearing sunglasses.

I liked to think that Shades was mine, but she wasn't. Tim was highly allergic to cats. She was a stray and would come to my window every night begging for a bowl of milk and a warm place to sleep. She'd been my secret keeper for the past year and I didn't know what I would do if the cat ever got run over by a car or got hurt.

It felt nice seeing a familiar face, even if that face belonged to an animal.

"I'm so dead. Tim is going to kill me." I looked down at the cat with both my hands cupping her cute scrunched up face gently. She was a Persian, and I couldn't understand how she could be a stray.

"It was Clare and her gang, look." I showed her the marks on my arms and she stared at them. Yep, she really did. That was why I felt I could tell her anything. She always acted as if she understood everything I told her. I blabbed the whole story as she was nestling herself on my lap. When I was done she opened her eyes and just gave me that look, the one that said, "Don't worry, everything will be okay and that Clare is a bitch". I giggled at that thought.

Shades jumped off my lap and stretched. She looked back at me and started to walk further down the street.

"You're just going to leave me here?" I yelled after her as she ran past people's feet. She turned around and came back.

Okay, that was freaky.

I just stared at her as she rubbed herself on my leg and looked at me again. She started to walk again and something inside of me said that I should follow her.

I knew it was silly and I felt extremely stupid as the cat led me through dark alleys and rushed down some stairs. There were plenty of homeless people sleeping below the streets. Fear crept over me as they stared, but they stayed on their cardboard mats. I even climbed through a gutted window and was back on the street.

Chas, you're stupid, the cat has no idea what you said.

Still, It was better to be with someone familiar, even if that someone was Shades, than being alone with strangers looking like I was crazy. Guess talking to a cat furthered that possibility.

We turned so many times and walked a block or two before she made another turn. It felt like hours and it was finally starting to sink in that this cat had no idea where she was going. She was probably looking for her next meal.

Suddenly, she stopped and didn't want to go any further. I crouched down and blew out a huge gush of air. It was dark and the only lights that shone were from the street lights. I picked up the cat and held her close to my face while scratching her ear.

"This was stupid, huh? I shouldn't have followed you," I spoke softly, close to her ear.

Shades stared at me as if she was chirping something at me and I giggled and looked around.

I saw Ms. Botty's flower shop and I stared at the cat. My eyebrows knitted as I looked at Ms. Botty's flower shop again.

Ms. Botty's flower shop was two blocks from where we lived. Mom purchased flowers once a week from her.

"Thank you, you genius," I kissed Shades on the neck and the cat jumped out of my arms and ran in the opposite direction of my house.

I giggled, this feeling was so strange. Mom was never going to believe that a cat brought me home, or maybe she would, she was a bit fruity and believed all sorts of crazy things, but Tim wouldn't. He was the realistic type and would probably give me the worst beating for scaring Mom like that.

My heart jumped into my chest. Tim had only given me a hiding once. He was from one of those families that believed that you should bend the tree while they are still young. Mom didn't like it one bit and I could still remember the huge fight they had that night.

I stopped for a second when I saw three cop cars in our driveway.

My heart pounded. What the hell was I going to say? I didn't even have a story and telling them the truth would win me a straitjacket for sure.

I couldn't think of anything and lying was just going to end up biting me in the ass. I wasn't a liar. The one time I had lied, I found out that I was really crappy at it, and decided to only speak the truth as best as I could. But this time the truth was insane. Nobody was going to believe me.

I closed my eyes and opened the door. A familiar smell lingered in my nostrils. It was warm inside and I felt like crying as I'd really had the crappiest day ever.

Mom gasped as she ran to my side and folded her arms around me. We looked nothing alike. She was a red head with beautiful blue eyes and very sensitive skin. Me, I had dark, shoulder length, raven black hair with high cheekbones. I assumed I must look like my father, who I knew was Asian as it was clear in my appearance.

"Where the hell have you been?" Tim screamed and rushed past three cops who were taking a statement in our living room. "Do you have any idea what you just put your mother through?"

He was right, my *mom*. Why would he care?

I hated crying and tried really hard not to, but the tears won the battle as my mother hugged me again.

"She is safe now, Tim. I'm sure whatever Chas went through, she'll tell us after she's taken a bath."

"Vinique! That's it? That's all you are going to do?" Tim yelled some more with his hands in the air. He was beyond pissed off.

"Don't push me today, Tim!" my mother yelled. "I had a really shitty day." She'd never spoken to Tim like that before, or glared at him like that. It wasn't like her.

Tim grunted and the lamp on the table was smacked down from its spot and smashed onto the ground.

"Mr. Swanson," one of the cops said. "You need to step out of the house for a second."

"No, I'm fine."

"Is everything okay, here?" The lady cop asked.

"We're fine," Mom said with the sweetest smile she could master. "My daughter is safe, that's all that matters. Thank you so much for coming out. You are free to leave."

Mom still had her arms around me. She'd never been this upset before and I really felt crappy.

The cops just watched us for a couple of seconds and then the lady cop smiled. "Okay, if you need our assistance, just call us again."

"Thank you again, all three of you and don't worry. We are perfectly safe." Mom tried to alleviate their worries and the cops left.

Tim stared at both of us. I hid my face in my mom's shoulder, but I could feel his eyes on me, glaring into my soul. With huge strides he left and went to the basement, to his man cave.

I jumped as the door of the basement slammed hard behind him.

Mom kissed me again and led me up the stairs and

into the bathroom. She didn't say a word, didn't ask a question, just opened the taps.

"What happened, Chas? Where were you? Why didn't you phone? Do you have any idea what you put me through today?" She was close to tears.

"I'm sorry, Mom. It was Clare and the gang again," I said and start telling Mom everything. I even showed her that my phone had cracked when Clare pushed me. She wasn't happy about that either. I told her as much as I could, except the part where soft, golden brown dust-like grit had emerged in my hands out of nowhere and made my opponents fall asleep…..it sounded so crazy.

Mom caught sight of the bruises on my arms as I was still busy telling her what happened, sort of and I thought she was going to explode. "What is this? This is going too far, Chastity. It's me and that school tomorrow."

"Please Mom, don't. You're only going to make it worse, I'm begging you."

"Chastity."

"Please, I'll be fine. I found my way home, please."

Mom just gave me that look. The one that said she knew that I was in terrible danger and couldn't do anything for me as it was my battle to fight, not hers.

"Fine, but one more incident Chastity Blake, just one more, and I'm marching down to your principal, you hear?" she said and hugged me again.

"I'm going to make us something to eat." Mom finally gave me a soft smile, with a worried look, and left the bathroom.

I wasn't even hungry, just so tired, but the bath was working its miracle.

My mind skipped through the events that happened

this afternoon and lingered on Shades taking me home. It was her road, but it'd done the trick. I was home and all thanks to a cat.

Nothing made sense. It was impossible, and yet it still happened. Fear of tomorrow, not knowing what Clare and her gang was going to tell everyone knotted my stomach. I never hated school like this before, and for Clare to believe that scaly bastard over ten years of friendship, hurt a lot. I wasn't even into jocks. Yes, their pecs and beautiful features were nice to look at, if only they were smart. Most of the jocks I knew were idiots and did dumb idiot things like drinking and smoking and showing off their talents in front of girls like Clare. She was smarter than that and it hurt that she was so blind to Ty's dog manners.

I was more fascinated with the minds. The geekier they were, the better, if only you could take their minds and put it into someone like Ty, then his rumors could've been true, and the sad part of it was that Clare knew that about me. She knew everything about me, except what I'd done today. I hadn't even known that myself.

She was right, I was a freak and every time I closed my eyes I saw her crouching down next to Mark, yelling those words at me.

After the bath, mom and I ate alone. Tim was still in his man cave, either trying to cool down or trashing the place. It was probably the former because no sound came from the basement. He had a temper but always tried to keep it at bay. Mom had this calming demeanor, she could calm anybody down.

"Is that all that happened today?" Mom asked. I just stared at her. At times I swore she could read minds.

That she knew the truth about me. It would freak her out, even if I was her daughter. No normal human being would understand. I didn't even understand it.

I nodded. "Can we please just not speak about this Mom? I'm really tired and just want to go to bed."

"Okay, baby."

I poured a glass of milk and heated it up slightly. I did it every night and wondered if my mom knew about Shades, if she did, she didn't say anything. I took a can opener and hid it inside my bathrobe pocket when she wasn't looking. A tin of tuna from the cupboard also went in there when Mom went to Tim's man cave. Shades deserved it tonight.

"Good night," I said as Mom came back. "Sorry about today. I didn't mean that."

Mom wrapped me in her motherly arms again. "Of course you didn't. I'll get you a new phone tomorrow and pick you up."

"Mom!" I groaned.

"No Chastity, that is not negotiable."

"Okay," I said and ran up the stairs to my room.

I sighed as I closed the door behind me and took a breath. I was in my sanctuary. A place where my bookshelf was stacked with novels. My desk was always tidy and my computer had been off for the past four weeks. I only used to chat to Clare at night, so I didn't need it anymore.

I walked over to the bowl that was in my room and opened the tin of tuna, pouring some milk into another.

I fell onto my bed and just lay there. My mind was clouded with thoughts and I kept staring at my hands, trying to find holes or something that could make today's events possible, but there was nothing.

I knew it hadn't been my imagination.

It couldn't have been.

I flinched as the cat jumped and my small 'forget-me-nots' planted in a small grey pot fell to the floor.

She meowed, apologizing about her not so gentle entry as I jumped out of bed to save what I could, and stared at my door, hoping Mom or Tim's super hearing hadn't heard it.

Then I put the plant into the empty milk glass and stroked Shades on her fluffy head. She was really such a beautiful cat.

She must belong to someone, she wasn't skinny, and she had a beautiful coat.

I crawled back into bed and when Shades was done with her milk and tuna, she came to join me.

She kneaded the spot for a few seconds before she lay down gently with her little paws stuck underneath her. A loud purr escaped her belly and I smiled.

This was home, and I was safe tonight.

I FELL ASLEEP FASTER THAN I THOUGHT I would. Guess it was the fatigue that had finally caught up to me. At first it was normal. I dreamt about absolutely nothing. The sound of a trashcan's lid falling woke me up. My eyes flew open and I closed them again, opening them slightly.

My heart beat a thousand beats per minute as I realized I wasn't inside my bed anymore. I wasn't even inside my room, or my house.

I was lying on the hard, cold floor of an old sewerage that clearly wasn't in use for sewerage purposes anymore. It smelled like pee and rotten dustbins. It was gross and made me wanted to gag.

A brown piece of cardboard that smelled worse than feet covered my body and I shoved it off. I was still wearing the clothes I'd had on today. The tutu was all ruffled up and torn. The one side bent into the shape of my body as I slept on it.

No, this can't be.

I sat up straight and thought hard. The cat had gotten me home. I'd seen my mom, I'd taken a bath. What the hell was I doing here then, sleeping inside the tunnel like a homeless person?

I jumped as I found a couple of other bodies lying on the other side of the tunnel.

I didn't remember who they were or recall meeting them, but since I was here, I clearly had.

I looked at my arm. The mark was still there and I hovered to pinch myself.

If I felt this, I'd know I was awake, and that this was real. If I didn't feel this, I was just going to crawl back under that stinking cardboard and wait for my alarm clock to buzz.

Still I didn't want to pinch myself. I didn't want to find out. I closed my eyes and did it.

The pinch was real. My eyes shot open and I was still inside the tunnel.

Rats rushed by me and I shrieked. I thought the bodies would wake up, but they didn't. They just stayed there, motionless.

I saw another rat and pushed my knees to my chest.

I frowned and as I looked again, I opened my eyes wider to make sure I really saw it and that it wasn't my mind playing tricks.

There was clearly something off with the rat. From

the front, he was fine, but the back. You couldn't see the tail or feet. It was surrounded by dark smoke.

He scurried away, deeper into the tunnel and another couple followed.

I looked again.

All of them had this dark cloud of mass following them.

My heart beat again. Something wasn't right with this place.

I looked around again, touched myself and squeezed softly. *If this place is real then where the hell am I?*

CHAPTER THREE
THE INITIATION

A NOISE DEEP DOWN IN THE TUNNEL
clanged loudly. I got up and heard the crunching sound
of glass underneath my sneakers. The stench forced me
to inhale through my mouth but the taste it left was ten
times worse.

A cold breeze in front of me screamed opening and I
just had to get out of here and hopefully find my way
home. Still the funny looking rats made me wonder if I
hadn't already lost my mind and was stuck somewhere
inside four, white padded walls.

More rats rushed past me, all of them minding their
own business, but the black mass was following them
like a shadow. It was creepy and made my skin crawl.

I found the opening and started to search the wall
praying that there was something lodged inside that
would support my weight. My hands found a beam. It
was really far from the floor, but I just had to get my

foot on there. I needed to get out of this abandoned sewerage tunnel.

After half an hour struggling, I finally managed to push myself up and found another beam close by. It was some sort of a ladder, and I found one beam after another. In less than a couple of minutes, I found myself out of the tunnel.

It smelled worse than inside. A strong breeze made it hard to breath, and I took off my knitted ballet shirt that covered my leotard and wrapped it around my head.

My scent lingered heavily on it and it smelled ten times better than the air.

I tried to see through the wind and nothing made sense. I had no idea where I was, nothing in front of me looked familiar. To be honest I didn't even think I was in Chicago anymore.

The buildings were dilapidated. Structures that were once stores, were torn to the ground. Rubble was strewn everywhere and there wasn't a sign of another living soul.

Loneliness crumped my chest. I was struggling to breathe as it was but this heaviness made it ten times worse.

Dreaming popped into my head, but there were no way that dreams could be this real. To feel the wind burning your skin, drying it out in mere seconds, the cold brushing against my body. I started to shiver and knew I had to get out of the cold, but where to? I had no idea.

A ripple of golden dust twirled around me and flew in a golden stream in front of me. My first instinct told me to follow it. It flew over a street lamp that lay on the asphalt. I climbed over it and ran to keep up. It flew around the corner, and I saw more destroyed buildings. The cars were rusty, with no doors or tires.

I didn't know what had happened here, or even where the hell I was.

I jumped around as a cold finger traced down my back. I could feel eyes on me. Who they belonged to I had no idea but the chill, the kind that flows through your core and makes you shiver from within, told me that they didn't belong to anybody good.

Through the corner of my eye the golden trail flew into another old building. There was a faint light coming from inside and I ran as fast as I could toward it. There were people there. I didn't know whether they were good or bad, but the thought of not being alone was better than the feelings I'd had a couple of seconds ago.

I could tell the structure used to be beautiful. It had two golden lions molded inside the wall. Part of the one lion's head was broken off and the other one had plenty of soot over it.

I found the outline of a reception inside. Around it were crates and lots of steel tables stacked against one another.

Further down past the reception I found a fire that burned behind something that used to be a couch. It was what made the faint light, but there was nobody in sight.

The trail of golden dust drew a direction line in mid-air and a knowing feeling told me that it was where I should go.

The trail flew forward and down another opening that led into the ruiend wooden walls.

Although I didn't understand the golden dust and I really didn't like this situation, I had a feeling I could trust it to get me to safetly inside this nightmare.

I crawled down the opening. It was pitch black and my heart beat a notch faster.

There was no sign of the golden trail. A horrible laugh broke the silence and my first reaction was to get the hell out of the wall, but then my eyes caught the golden trail again. It lit up the wall in the distance and it was the only light. I rushed to it again and followed it.

The laughter came again. It sounded mechanical and I was scared out of my mind when a clown figure came into sight.

It wasn't real, it was plastic and I reached out to touch it just to make sure. He let out another laugh and I jumped back a couple of paces. I caught the golden trail in the distance again and ran to keep up.

With the eerie clown behind me, I could face whatever lay ahead.

This was one of the reasons I hated stupid clowns.

More rats squeaked below my feet and I danced like a show pony as I could feel them inches from my shoes.

I hated how my heart jumped a million beats per minute—or so it seemed—and the inky black darkness blinded my sight. I didn't like watching over my shoulder every five seconds either. Someone or something was not far behind me. I could still feel its eyes on me and I just wished that I could get out of this place, wherever this place was. Still I followed the golden trail and it led me straight to the end of the alley.

It stopped and started to swirl around in an oval shape until it became a solid golden circle. I found myself staring at it, I was mesmerized and couldn't stop looking.

Then it stopped and landed on what looked like an altar. Faint light started to glow and the altar became alive.

It looked like an old mirror that was formed in the shape of an eye. The mirror was the inside of the eye.

It became brighter and brighter until my reflection was caught in the mirror.

I tried to turn around and run away but when I glanced one more time, my reflection just stood there, as if it was someone else. She kept staring at me, she wasn't afraid and told me to wait.

It was so freak'n creepy.

My feet were nailed to the floor and I couldn't move.

My reflection started to narrow, as if something invisible was closing in on the sides. It changed the shape until it resembled the pupil of a snake's eye.

The outline of a woman appeared inside the pupil. I could see her hair flowing in a path of wind. The strands were long and liquid. I knew it wasn't me as my hair was cut in layers that only reached my shoulders. I stared at it as I couldn't do anything else.

The same golden dust-like grit from this afternoon emerged inside my hands again and ran down to the ground. I stared at it. This was anything but normal. The color of the sand had started to change slowly into a darker brown. It kept changing until all the light gold was gone, gradually turning darker and darker, until it was solid black. I didn't understand any of this, and I didn't know what it meant.

A shrill noise came from the eye, and I covered my ears with my hands. More grit accumulated in my palms and I could feel it flow into my ears. It hurt like hell and in a panic I screamed.

The grit flowed through me and it felt like it was embedded under my skin, I scratched at myself trying hard to get it out.

Then a horrible ache jolted through my head. The sand flowed all the way to the pit of my mind. I let out another scream as everything just burned.

A hand grabbed my shoulder, and I turned around. When I tried to get away from it, it only clutched my shoulders stronger, speaking softly to relax my beating heart. I struggled to focus on who it belonged to. My eyes watered from the pain the sand had caused and it made the figure blurry. It was taller than me and the deep sound of its voice told me it was male. The force of his grip around my wrist somehow broke the spell that held me to the spot in front of the eye.

I could move again and the further I got from the eye, the less my head hurt. I had no choice but to trust whoever he was, and get away from this insanity.

He pulled me up the opening through the wall, the way I had come a couple of minutes before, and found the area with the small fire again.

I started to cough uncontrollably, like I couldn't breathe and more sand came running out of my throat. It started to become less and less, until there were just specks of black sand clinging to my skin and clothes.

I tried to shake it off, wary that it might be dangerous, but it stayed there, like a part of my leotard. I'd never felt this dirty before.

"Here, drink this. It will make you feel better," he said and a silver flask came into view. Tim had a similar one, but he hardly drank out of it and just kept it as some sort of souvenir.

I looked at the hands that held it, they were covered with dark leather fingerless-gloves. When I saw his face, I thought it was Ty, but when I looked again, it wasn't.

His hair was dark, and cut into that scruffy hairstyle Ty had, his eyes were dark too. I gazed at him and noticed a pair of full lips, sun-kissed skin and an Enrique Iglesias mole above his lip.

He took a pair of glasses from his pocket and put them on his face. He was the most beautiful creature I'd ever seen and it seemed my dream guy had just turned into a reality.

He wore a leather jacket and dark leather pants with the coolest black boots. He was at least two heads taller than me and had broad shoulders and long limbs.

He spoke again, this time in Spanish and when I didn't answer, he chose another language.

I finally realized what he was doing. "English, is fine. I'm American."

"So you do speak. For a minute there I thought I had to sign," he said with a hint of a smile tucking at the corner of his mouth. He pushed the flask, still in his hand, a bit forward and this time I reached out and took it.

"Thanks." The word barely came out and I took a sniff at the opening of the flask. It smelled like alcohol, the 83 percent kind. "What is this?"

"It doesn't matter. In the Oblivion it's the only piece of sun you will get. Now drink."

"The Oblivion?"

"Drink," he ordered again without answering my question and I took a sip. It burned all the way down and I started couching again.

"Yeah, it's another thing you'll get eventually used to down here."

I handed the flask back to him. I wasn't planning on staying here. A cold breeze brushed up behind me and I rubbed my arms, trying to will warmth into them, but it didn't help. My hands were freezing too.

The guy immediately took off his jacket and put it over my shoulders. "Here, it will keep you warm. Where are you from?"

"Chicago," I said as I knew I wasn't in Chicago anymore.

He gave me a crooked smiled. One that reached his eyes. He was damn perfect. "Ahh, the windy city."

I huffed, wanting to smile but not here. I didn't trust anything around me.

"I'm Leigh, short for Leighthan." He let out his hand and stared at it and then back at me. "And you are?"

"Chas, short for Chastity."

He looked at the floor and his lips curved upward. "Like chastity belt?"

Why is that the first thing that always popped into everyone's mind when I introduced myself. It made me smile and I nodded.

"Yeah, like chastity belt." I blew out a gush of air as if it was going to help and wished that it would get rid of this feeling, but it didn't. No matter how many breaths I took or how many I let out, the feeling didn't want to go away. "So what is this place?"

Leigh raised his one dark eyebrow. "You don't know about the Oblivion?"

"The what?"

"The Oblivion, you know the other side of Revera."

I just stared at him.

Both his eyes rose slightly as if a light bulb finally lit up. "You don't know anything, do you?"

"Clearly not." I said a bit more sarcastic than I wanted to.

"So you have no idea what you are?"

"What I am? Other than my beautiful complexion and raven dark hair," I joked. Stop it Chas. This wasn't the place to make stupid jokes. "No."

"You are a Dream Caster, or by that black sand all over you, I'll say a—"

A loud clucking noise on the other side made both Leigh and I jump, interrupting his explanation of what I really was.

Leigh crouched immediately down, grabbing my hand and pulled me down with him. By the way the fire reflected on his face, he looked anxious, alert. "We have to go," he said and searched with his free hand behind him, picking up a black bag that made me think of a golf clubs and something that used to be a bow, it was missing the string.

It didn't make sense why he would carry that with him, if he had no arrows to protect us.

I tried to look at what had made that sound and saw nothing but shadows. I was pulled down again, behind the used to be a couch.

"What are you—"

"Shush, you don't want to be found by those things out there."

"There is nothing –"

"I said shush," he whispered and gave a stern look that lasted only a couple of seconds before he peeked past the couch again.

He took a couple crouching strides toward the door that I'd entered through earlier.

A huge clang echoed through the entire building or what was left of it, and I saw the lead pipe I'd kicked by accident.

Leigh jumped straight up, grabbing my hand in his tight grip. "Run!"

My heart thumped heavily inside my chest as we aimed toward the exit and just as we almost made it I saw it. It was a giant-ass Rottweiler, but it wasn't a Rottweiler at all. It had the same structure as the rats inside the tunnel.

Leigh pulled his bow in front of him, the one with no string. We were so screwed. Yet he still released an invisible arrow. Loon!

I gasped as golden sand emerged out of thin air, forming a solid golden arrow.

I knew that sand, I'd seen it this afternoon for the first time, only his was much brighter.

The arrow struck the beast in the head and it exploded, falling into a heap of black sand.

Leigh grabbed my arm this time, and shoved me toward the exit as I just stood there in place gawking at the scene before me.

"Move!" He yelled and I ran through the exit. We were outside again, and running through the dark and disgusting smelling streets toward the end. We turned around another corner and found a heap of bricks that used to be a wall, and ducked.

"What was that!"

"Nimgolians. Where there is one, there are bound to be many."

"Nim what?"

"A shadow hound."

"Wait, you mean more are coming?" I needed to know.

Leigh grabbed my chin softly. His glasses were resting on the middle of his nose, and I raised my gaze to look at his. "Just calm down, okay. I'll get us out of here."

I somehow knew that I could trust him. I mean if he wanted to kill me, he would've let demon smoky do the job.

He gazed one more time around the corner, and then he pushed me right up, took my hand in his warm one and ran in the opposite direction down the street.

We ran until we found an old merry-go-round. All the horses had started to lose their paint. The eyes looked scary and I jumped again as lights came on and a very old carousel tune started to play. It was very slow at first, as if it was operated by batteries, but it grew into a stronger tune, one I used to love, but never would ever again.

My heart bounced inside my chest as Leigh darted past the carousel and through another structure. We hid behind something that look like a shell.

The carousel died and everything became so quiet that the only thing I could hear was my own breathing. His was extremely calm and I wished I shared the same confidence as him, but I didn't. I was beyond scared.

When the shell structure started to move, and lights came on close by, I understood where we were. It was an old theme park, one that hadn't been visited in years.

We ran again and exited through what once was a gate. By now the entire theme park was alive, letting those Nim-monster things know we were here.

I'd never ran like this before and I was glad for Rollins' ballet classes.

We finally found another deserted street and Leigh slowed down.

I didn't like this one bit and kept looking over my

shoulder as I tried to keep up with him.

"Why are we stopping?"

"We lost them, don't worry, I think it's safe to take you to the Celestial."

"The what?" I felt like an idiot as nothing made any sense that left his mouth. "First the Nim-things, now Celesians…"

"A Celestial. It's like a porthole, back to your world."

"Back to my world?" I couldn't grasp any of it, even if I wanted to. If this wasn't my world then what was this.

He handed me the flask again and shoved it in front of me. "Just drink, it does help, believe me."

I did what he asked without smelling it this time.

It burned again and I handed the flask back to him. Why I took another sip, I didn't know. I knew how strong that stuff was but it was like I expected something completely different.

Leigh's eyes still searched everywhere as he walked fast toward the edge of the street.

I pulled the hoody of his jacket over my head to retain more heat.

"So you care to tell me what I am?"

"You are not from your world, Chas. You are what people would refer to as Dream Caster, the kind that can wield dreams."

I squinted again at him. I knew the term wield, any idiot would know what that meant but putting it together with dream was something that didn't exist.

"You want to tell me that I'm like a modern day Sandman? Or in my case woman?"

He looked at her through narrow eyes as his

eyebrows knitted together. "I'm not familiar with that term. What is a sandman?"

"You know, the guy that throws sand in little kids eyes to make them fall asleep?"

Leigh chuckled softly. "That's absurd! Why would anybody throw sand in somebody's eyes to make them sleep? Wouldn't it burn the shit out of your eyes?"

My entire body felt as if it was inflated, which wasn't a bad thing as it was doing something else, than being afraid.

"Never mind."

"Dream Casters, we are responsible for Nomad dreams."

"Nomad?" I asked again.

"You know, folks that can't weave dreams."

"Okay, so I'm a dream weaver, or Caster whatever, yay me."

"It's what I said."

I sighed, I wasn't going to get anywhere with this guy.

We reached the end of the road and a huge square with a dried up fountain stood heavenly in front of us.

More ruined buildings and half a statue of someone must have been important long ago stood right on the opposite side of the square. I realized that I hadn't seen one tree in this place, or anything that used to be a tree. "What happened here?"

"Nothing happened here," he said. "It has always been this way."

I shook my head. My breathing became heavy again. I had to get out of here, wherever here was. I couldn't be stuck in this place forever. I had to see my mom again, and I'd even settle for Tim.

Leigh stopped dead in his steps and I walked three steps more and turned around to see what was up. His eyes were gazing everywhere, turning on one spot slowly as he kept his gaze on so many things. I did the same, but saw nothing. Still it creeped me out as I knew things that had the ability to turn into dark dust when golden arrows struck them hid somewhere inside these buildings.

Then just like earlier, it happened again. A dog appeared out of thin air right in front of us, ready to pounce and once again, one of Leigh's golden dust arrows hit him straight in the head. More came, and I felt as if I was going to throw up with all the adrenaline rushing through my veins. More arrows flew in the air and more monstrous beasts exploded and fell into heaps of black sand right in front of us.

Leigh grabbed me around the waist and pulled me behind him as he killed another shadow beast that was inches away from me with a golden object in his hand. It disappeared just as fast. I tripped over a stone and scraped my knee as Leigh killed another three shadow dogs. I found one inches away from Leigh. "Five o' clock," I yelled and just like that, he drew out an invisible sword from his sheath that emerged into a solid blade just as he struck the beast in the chest. Black sand wash over him and he shook it off with a couple of body shakes.

It stopped, but I could feel more were waiting in the dark for the right moment to catch us off guard. I could sense it, could feel the darkness pouring out of this place.

"Chas," Leigh said without lowering his bow, "are you okay?"

"I'll live," But I didn't know for how long. I didn't say the last part out loud and felt his hand pulling me up by the arm.

"It's almost time."

"Time for what?" I said in a high-pitched voice that I didn't mean to. I guess my nerves were on their last.

"For you to go back."

Okay, I remember something like that. It had to do with the Seletine-something that was some sort of a porthole. I was ready for that.

"In about a minute a light will show itself," he carried on. "Whatever happens you make sure you get your ass to that light, before it disappears."

"What will happen if I don't make it?"

"Then you will be stuck here," he said in a tone as if it wasn't a big thing at all."

"Got it," I said. "Get my ass to the light before it disappears." I just have to make it.

He smiled slightly. "And remember, you can always choose."

"Choose, what?"

He didn't answer, as he drew back his bow and shoot another arrow at a clouded figure. A bright light appeared on my far left, just like Leigh said it would.

"Go, don't stop for anything. I have your back."

"What about you? Will you be okay?"

He chuckled, killed three other beasts in a matter of five seconds and drew back the invisible string. I knew it carried another invisible arrow that will appear as a golden arrow when it mattered. "I'll be fine. Just go." He released the arrow and it turned gold right before it hit a dark beast in the shoulder. "Go!" Leigh yelled again.

"Thank you," I yelled as I ran for dear life. I was after all depending on a light. I prayed it was home, my bed.

From the corners of my eyes, I could see two dogs on both sides were heading straight for me. I wasn't going to make it, but I had to try. Images of plans formed in my head of how I was going to slip past the dogs and I sprinted like never before. Miss Haly, the athletic teacher at school would've been so proud of me. I was finally giving it my all.

The shadow dog pounced straight for me, and I crouched as I waited for its bite or whatever these dogs did. Sand covered my body and I saw a golden arrow glinting inside the sand. It disappeared and I got up and ran again. The other dog was a few paces from me. My legs burned and my lungs felt as if they were on fire. The other shadow figure came in fast and nipped with long sharp claws at my leg. I cried out in pain and watched blood oozed out from four long vertical claw marks that could've easily took off my leg. Still, I got up and leapt for the light. The beast followed and exploded as light engulfed us. The pain seared through my entire body and I only realized then that I still had Leigh's jacket around my shoulders. I jumped up, cold sweat rolled down the side of my face.

I breathed fast and heavy, I looked around and I was back inside of my room on my bed. I was wearing my nighties again, and my hands, they were clean. I felt a bit sweaty but I was clean.

It was just a dream, the voice in my head said, *but why is my leg still aching?*

I pulled down the covers and found four gashes running down my leg. My covers and pj's were soaked with blood and my leg hurt more than I'd ever thought it could. *How could this be possible?*

CHAPTER FOUR
UNINVITED GUESTS

THE NEXT MORNING I TOOK OFF THE bandages. I'd put on the night before. It was clean, my leg was clean and the marks the shadow hound left were gone. *Did I just imagine that?*

I ran back to the kitchen where the front loader held all my bloody linen and found Mom cooking up a storm. I glanced at her and then at the washing machine spinning the bed linen soaked with blood.

Mom followed my gaze and stared at the laundry spinning in the machine too. "Are you okay, sweetheart?" She asked with concern pulling the corners of her eyes.

"I'm fine," I gasped. I was shocked, felt as if I was busy losing my mind and I turned around walking back to my room. I struggled to shake last night's events from my thoughts. I could still remember every single thing that happened in that place. Dreams were not like that. You usually only remembered a fragment of what you dreamt about, not everything.

I also knew I wasn't imagining the blood and the pain I'd been left with when I woke up in bed last night. I distinctly remembered the blood and the strong iron smell that lingered for hours in my room after I changed the bed linen and cleaned up my wound with whatever was in the first aid kit.

I even struggled to sleep because for some reason I could still smell the blood, imaginative or not, the smell was real.

I got dressed as I thought about Leigh. If he'd gotten away from those shadow dogs I didn't know, but I hoped that he was okay, and alive. I would really like to see him again and thank him properly for saving my ass.

When I got back to the kitchen a plate of bacon with eggs and toast waited for me at the breakfast nook. Mom didn't say anything as she read the newspaper with a cup of coffee almost touching her lips.

I took a seat behind my plate of scrambled eggs and bacon. One look at it, or sniff, and my stomach started to turn and I got up, ran to the toilet and puked my lungs out.

Tears lingered in my eyes as I bent over the toilet again. Emotions of fear and shock of last night's events were turning the inside of my gut in turmoil.

"Honey, what's wrong? You know you can tell me anything." My mom's voice came from the door.

Not this time, Mom. "I'm fine." I couldn't tell my mother about that dream. She would think I was crazy, even though she had always asked about my dreams, this was different.

I finally came out of the bathroom. "I've got to go. I'm going to be late for school." I picked up my backpack, which was where I left it last night by the door.

"You want me to drive you?"

I looked at my mom, and smiled. "I'm okay, mom. Really. I just got lost yesterday, that's all."

"Okay, sweetheart," Mom came over, gently stroked my face and gave me a kiss on the head. "Be safe, I'll see you this afternoon and then we can speak about your dream last night."

I just stared at her. *How did she know?* I shook my head. Mom always wanted to know about my stupid dreams, it was my paranoia that had gotten the best of me.

"Bye," I said and walked to the bus stop with thoughts of Shadow hounds and the most badass, geek beauty I'd ever met.

ON THE SCHOOL BUS EVERYONE MINDED their own business. Nobody even glanced my way, *why should they, Chas?* I whispered inside my head. I was sure after today the bus driver would probably never let me on his bus once Clare and the gang told everyone what I'd done yesterday at the lake.

There was no sign of Clare, Ty, Nicole, or any of the guys when I found my locker. Scared of opening it, I closed my eyes and took a deep breath.

Don't have a heart attack, don't have a heart attack. My hand lingered on the lock and I opened it quickly.

Nothing came, no explosion of some sort that would cover me with a liquid stickiness, no booby trap, nothing.

I took out the books for the first three periods and shoved them into my backpack, fast. When I shut the locker door, I jumped as I found Clare leaning against the locker beside mine. I closed my eyes and wanted to tell her to take a hike when she opened her mouth.

"Relax, scared-y pants," she smiled. "Where were you this morning?"

I frowned. "This morning?"

"Yes, Ty and I went to your home to pick you up, but there was absolutely no answer. Did you take the school bus?" she said with slight confusion on her face as if the school bus was drenched with the plague or some other deadly disease, and started to walk in the direction of our first period.

She stopped and turned around.

"What are you waiting for?"

I closed my eyes and pinched myself. No I was definitely awake. I looked around, waiting for any of the others that might jumped out behind a closed door or something.

"Chas, what is it with you today? You're acting really weird." Clare came back and spoke softly as concern was evident on her face.

I'm acting weird?

"I'm fine, I just don't feel so well. It must be the fusion my mom tried last night," I lied.

"Fusion? Since when does your mom cook fusion?"

"She's trying new things."

Clare laughed and I couldn't help but to feel as if we'd just picked up where we'd left off four weeks ago before the Ty incident.

I followed her into the Science lab and we split up to

join our respective lab partners.

Through the entire class Clare was sending me notes, made faces behind Freddie's back, which I didn't like because he was one of my favorite geeks, but I smiled. Something was definitely not right with this picture. Whatever it was, I didn't care. I had my best friend back, even though she'd acted like a complete bitch these past four weeks. If she was willing to forgive and forget everything, then so was I.

The school bell rang and Clare waited for me to pack up. "So when did we start on molecules and mass?"

I looked at her. Science wasn't Clare's thing either. She was more of the P.E. Queen. I just giggled.

"I know, it all goes so quickly, right?" I said.

"Way too fast for me." We split at the end of the corridor. "See you in P.E.," she yelled and went the other way.

"See you," I spoke softly.

It was weird, seriously weird and although I wanted to trust it, I couldn't. I froze as I thought about yesterday. She called me a freak and today she was all best buds with me again. Something was going to happen in P.E., I just knew it.

In P.E. they chose teams again for the volleyball game. One team belonged to Clare, the other Beatrix.

The first name Clare called was mine. Everyone's eyebrow rose and some even gasped. Clare just shook her head as I moved forward slowly. Beatrix called her first name and it was back and forth until we made up two teams. Then we started playing against one another. I wasn't good like Clare, but together we made a killing team. It was just like the old times where she would yell in codes that none of the other girls – except me –

understood and we won the game by ten to five.

We high-fived each other every time we scored and when the bell rang again it was break.

I wanted to break from her when I saw Ty and Derek.

"This guy is seriously making my blood boil," Clare said and I just rolled my eyes. He kissed her softly as I walked past.

"Hey, Chas. So did you think about my offer, yet?" Derek asked.

"What offer?" It came out harsh.

"Wow, a snake spat in your milk this morning?"

Clare laughed. "Ignore him Chas." She grabbed me by the elbow and moved with me to our regular table. "She's not into Tweedle-dums like you, Derek."

The guys laughed and took seats around our table.

I huffed and pinched myself as they spoke to one another about another party at Ty's house. He threw them every time his mom and dad went away on a couple's retreat. Ty and Clare actually became a couple at one of the parties we were accidentally invited to. Everyone except me was excited, just like the last time.

I pinched myself again. Still awake. I had a really weird feeling and couldn't help but watch over my shoulder every five seconds.

Nicole walked with her tray to our table and even she acted as if yesterday or the past four weeks never happened. We were like one happy family again.

The entire day it felt as if I was stuck in the twilight zone, but I had to admit, it was one of the best days I'd had in a long time.

When the final bell rang, I walked fast, scared that maybe the entire day was meant to gain back my trust and that a horrible prank would blow up in my face.

That Clare had told them to mess with my mind and act like nothing bad had happened and then boom, reveal the unexpected.

She caught up with me at the main door.

"Hey, where are you off too?" She put her arm around my neck and walked with me down the stairs. "Seriously Chas. Speak to me, spit it out. What is it with you today? You're really starting to freak me out," she looked worried. Clare wasn't someone that had a skill for pretending and she definitely sucked in Drama and in school plays.

"Nothing. I just had a bad dream yesterday."

"About what?"

I sighed. "It doesn't matter, it was just a stupid dream." I smiled and hugged her back. "I'm sorry about today. I promise that tomorrow I'll be myself again."

"I'm going to hold you to that. You coming with us?" She asked as Ty appeared out of nowhere."

"Can I give it a miss? My mom is picking me up today. Bonding time," I lied if they were trying to lure me to the big thing.

"Sure, say hi. And Skype with me tonight. Same time?"

I nodded and ran to the parking area where all the parents were waiting.

"Bye, Chas." Derek yelled as he was running toward Ty's pick up. I waved, sort of and walked on again.

WHAT THE HELL?

I pinched myself for the gazillionth time today and still it was just as painful as the first one this morning.

My mom's SUV was nowhere to be found and I almost changed my mind and ran back to Ty's truck when I found her climbing out of a Porsche SUV... Did

I mention Porsche?

I knew something about today was wrong. There was no way that we could afford that on Tim's salary.

I walked to the SUV, not knowing how I should act and smile. But Mom didn't share my enthusiasm and just ordered me with a shaky voice to get into the car.

I did and found two men dressed in white leather. I felt like I was being sucked into a different zone, like in The Matrix. You know, the movie where Keanu Reeves couldn't be more yummy?

One sat in the front, behind the wheel, and one in the back. Mom climbed into the front after she closed my door.

The guy behind the steering wheel started the engine and I stared at my mother, who just looked out the window. I had no idea who these men were and glanced at the one next to me. He gave me a sweet smile.

When we got to the house, Mom plunged herself down on the couch, without saying a word. The two men stood, neither of them sitting down.

"Can anyone please tell me what is going on? Mom, who are these people?" I didn't care about manners anymore. This was the last straw and I was freaking out.

"Please, Chastity. Sit down." The one guy with the blond ponytail that had sat beside me on our way here said. He couldn't have been more than three years older than me.

"No! I'm not going to sit down. Who are you?"

"My name is Kale. I'm a Seeker and we know what happened yesterday."

My face went all numb and my mother just looked at me with concern in her eyes.

"You came because I got lost?" I played the dumb

card but the look on both their faces told me that they were referring to what happened before I got lost.

"We know, Chastity." The other one spoke. He was slightly older than his buddy, maybe early thirties, late twenties and had dark, raven black hair with dark brown eyes. It wasn't Leigh though.

"I don't know what you are talking about."

"You're playing that card?" Kale said with a hint of a smile.

I didn't want to say this in front of my mother. But the look on her face said that they'd already told her.

"She doesn't even know what you are talking about," Mom finally said something.

"Ma'am, we've already explained it to you. As unbelievable as it sounds, it's real. Your daughter was never supposed to live in this world."

"Wait, what?"

"You are a Dream Caster, Chastity. Your mother has no recollection of any of this. So we believe that your biological father was one of us. It sometimes happens – more than our kind likes – but you are technically part of our world and need to come with us."

"What, are you insane? I'm not going anywhere with you guys."

"It is not safe here."

"I can take care of myself."

"We aren't speaking about you. We are referring to the normal people. It is not safe for them to have a Dream Caster that has no idea what she can do, running free in this world." The dark-haired grouch said.

Mom still kept quiet. She just stared at me.

"I'm not going to leave my mother. I…"

"You have no choice. We would take care of your

mother, it would be as if you never existed."

"What?" Both mom and I said.

"It is for the best."

"You can do that?" I asked, sounding shocked.

"We already did, with your opponents of yesterday. It wasn't easy, because we couldn't erase everything. So we just erased a little," Kale explained.

So that was why Clare and the others were acting so strange. None of them remembered what had happened the past four weeks.

"Is it true, Chastity?"

I looked at my Mom. The fact that I'd lied to her was making me feel like a dog. "I didn't know, mom. How was I supposed to tell you that sand appeared in my hands when they wanted to attack me? I didn't even know if it was real or not."

"Oh, it's real," Kale said with admiration in his eyes, on his entire freak'n face. Mom shot him a glare.

"Sorry," he spoke softly with both hands behind his back.

"I'm your mother, you could've tried."

"Then what, mom? Would you seriously have believed me? I knew what it sounded like."

My mom just shook her head with her eyes closed. Yeah, it sounded crazy and she already struggled with believing it as we spoke, even with these two men that looked like they'd stepped out of the Matrix movie, standing right here in the middle of our lounge. It was hard to believe.

"Where is it you want to take her?"

"To where dreams exist. Revera. You can't follow, which is why she has to come with us. Nomadic minds don't see any of it, and it would be as if you are stuck in darkness. It's not a place for normal humans, like yourself, ma'am."

"I told you my name is Vinique," Mom sounded angry. "Can she come back if she doesn't like this River-place?"

"Revera, and no. It's a one way ticket I'm afraid." The dark head spoke again.

"No," Mom said. She was adamant as she got up and started to pace.

"Ma'am," Kale said. Mom shot him another look. "I mean, Vinique. I'm afraid that no is not an option here."

Mom started to laugh. "You're just going to take my daughter against my will?"

I didn't like that.

"It's law."

"It's not the law, we live here. Here it is called kidnapping. If you don't know what that term means, I have plenty of dictionaries that can break them up for you."

"Your law doesn't matter. The child belongs to Revera, to her father. She doesn't belong in your world."

"I don't care, she is my child. I carried her for nine months." Mom started telling them about everything. How she'd sat with me when I was sick, when I broke my leg falling off the sleigh when I was five. She told them everything, and they listened.

"We understand that you have a connection…"

"Connection. Listen to the way you speak. I love my child. She is not going with you. That's it."

"Then you give us no choice."

Golden sand appeared out of the dark heads palm. I knew what he was going to do. He was going to erase me from my mother's memory.

"Wait!" I jumped between my mom and the dark head's sand. "I'll come with you, just don't use that on my mom, please. I'll speak with her. Just give me a couple of minutes, please."

Both of them are looking at me through narrow eyes. "Please, just let me say goodbye."

"Chastity," Mom started.

"Not now, okay? Please, Mom. I don't want these men to make you forget me. Do as they say," I whispered.

"I would never forget you, no matter what they say they will do."

"They can, mom. Clare and Ty, all of them forgot about the past four weeks. It was wonderful," I spoke. "They will make you forget that you even had a daughter. Please."

My mom finally nodded with tears in her eyes. "Can I at least help my daughter pack?"

"Of course," Kale spoke and the other one wanted to say something. "Not now, Duke. Let them say goodbye."

Duke grunt, and stormed out of the house.

"Sorry, my partner isn't used to human conversation. He still has plenty to learn. Take all the time you need, but know that running away..." he smiled. "I'm sure you get what it is I'm trying to say."

I nodded and watched him walk out the door too.

I led mom up the stairs. She looked defeated and I hated the silence. I hoped that she wasn't afraid of me.

When we entered my room I gasped as I found another Mom on pilot-mode sitting on my bed. I wanted to yell but the Mom behind me covered my mouth with her palm.

My eyes were huge when I stared at her.

"It's okay, Chas. Don't scream otherwise they will know. I'm going to take my hand off your mouth. Not a peep."

Her entire demeanor changed and she scared me a bit. I nodded. When she drew her hand back I ran to my mom sitting on my bed. She didn't even look at me.

"Mom," I spoke softly and shook her gently. She didn't move.

"What did you do with her, who are you?"

The fake rolled her eyes. "Chas, it's me. The dummy is not real, she will take my place for a few hours, giving us plenty time to get away."

"Take your place? I don't understand."

"Why didn't you tell me about last night's dream?" She didn't look heartbroken anymore, she looked pissed off.

Then it hit me. I never told her or anybody about last night's dream except Clare, sort of. "How do you know about last night?"

"If you'd told me, we would've been miles away from here now, Chas. I wouldn't have had to use your father's sand to conjure her." She pointed at second Mom's figure who was still sitting on the bed. My father's sand….nothing made any sense.

I looked through the window where the SUV was parked. Duke was standing against the SUV with his arms folded. Kale was speaking to him softly.

"I don't understand. It was just a dream, Mom."

"It was far from a dream honey."

I froze.

"Why do you think I kept asking what you dreamt

about all the time?"

I shook my head. Staring at the floor. *It wasn't a dream?*

"Chastity?" Mom shook me softly.

"I don't know. I thought you were some spiritual freak."

My mother's posture slumped. She sighed and closed her eyes. "A spiritual freak."

"Yeah, you know someone that think they can detect your future out of your dreams," I yelled at her softly so that our two guests couldn't hear. "Mom what is going on, please?"

"Later, we've got to get out of here, now."

"Didn't you hear what Beavis and Butthead said? We can't leave. They'll find me."

"No, they won't. Just trust me."

"What about the dream?"

"I'll tell you later. Now go pack light. One backpack, Chas. We don't have time for anything else."

I nodded and my mother left. I shoved in a lot of underwear, a pair of jeans, track suit pants, stepped out of my pumps and into my sneakers. I grabbed two black t-shirts and a hoody.

I stared at the mom on my bed. She looked just like the one that'd left my room a couple of seconds ago.

This was so weird.

I couldn't shake the feeling of last night's dream from my mind and how the hell my mom knew about all of this. Was she just pretending downstairs not knowing, and if so, why? Why didn't she tell me any of this?

I found my real mom running up the stairs, not making a sound, but she looked everything except my mom now. My mouth gaped as I just stared at this woman in front of me. She changed her skirt, with her camisole and knitted top and pumps for something that resembled Beavis and Butthead outside, but completely black.

Her red hair was taken up into a bun.

She had a black backpack over her shoulder. Crazy scenarios filled my mind as mom walked past me and she smiled slightly as she closed my gaping mouth.

"Let's go," she said, and as she walked past my room she spoke softly – I couldn't hear what she'd said – and closed the door. We walked all the way to the back to the hall, toward her and Tim's room. I just stared at her.

Mom turned around. "Chastity! Come."

I did what she said as she pulled down the string that hung from the roof. The attic's ladder pulled down and she helped me climb up it.

It was dusty and dark and I had an urge to cough but I knew if I did, Beavis and Butthead would hear us and all our plans would be ruined, so I breathed into my arm and hope that my scent would take away the old dusty smell.

When my mother's body emerged, she pulled up the ladder. It was pitch dark, and I couldn't see a thing in front of me. A couple of seconds later the light went on. I jumped because I hadn't even heard my mom walking past me. How the hell had she become so quiet? Who was she?

"Mom, you're scaring me. What are we doing up in the attic."

"You'll see. Trust me."

I nodded. Even though I had no idea about this side of my mother. One thing I knew was that I could trust her, she was my mom, even though she resembled a modern day Sarah Connor.

"Mom, is it true what they said, about my father? Does this have anything to do with him?"

"Yes, and no," Mom spoke fast and soft as she opened the lid of an old black chest.

My eyes grew as she took out a bow similar to the one Leigh had carried with him last night, just very modern. I found myself at once in front of the chest. "Where did you get this?" I touched the bow softly. It was missing the string.

"It was your father's," she said as she took out a couple of other items. An old green coin bag with golden symbols on them.
A knife with a black hilt and a whip that was looped up. She added it to a sheath she was carrying around her waist and hid it with her leather jacket.

I just stared at her. I couldn't believe that was my mother.

"Don't look at me like that. I had to do what I had to do. Giving you a normal life, meant letting go of mine." She touched my cheek softly. "I'm still your mother."

"Yes, a mother who has a kickass side to her," I said.

She laughed softly. "That's my girl."

"So I take it we're not leaving with Beavis and Butthead?"

"No."

"Mom, how do you expect to get past them? Unless you know Kung Fu or something."

"We are not going past them." My mother had a glint in her eye, something I'd rarely seen when she played with me as a child. She smiled and took three small oval devices out of the chest. They were a soft grey with a mushy gel substance in the middle.

"What's that?"

She pulled out a side lever of the chest and ten guns lay in their matching sockets.

I gasped softly. I only saw Tim's gun once, but it wasn't as beautiful as these. Mom took all of them out and placed it into a big black bag. There weren't any bullets but something told me that she didn't need any bullets. Her golden dust would make them appear out of nowhere.

"Vinique," one of the guys from the SUV, called and Mom's head shot to the entrance of the attic. I pictured them finding the other mom, sitting frozen on my bed. I didn't know if she was still in a trance or not but when she started to yell at them and I heard Duke's voice cussing, followed by hollow sounds of footsteps, I knew that they bought whatever fake-mom said to them.

"We've got to go. Now."

I followed my mother's gaze to the door that led to the attic. "How the hell—"

A buzzing noise came from the wall of the attic and my head shot back. My mother stood right in front of it.

It was the same light from yesterday, the one Leigh told me to go to if I wanted to get back to my world. The light formed a vortex. I couldn't stop looking at it. It was so beautiful.

It got bigger and bigger. My mother reached out her hand to me. "Trust me."

I hesitated for a few short seconds and then took my mother's hand and nodded.

She smiled.

The following words that left her mouth didn't make any sense. The only thing I got was the word Montana before she jumped into the vortex with my hand firmly inside of hers, and the last thing I remembered was a huge bright flash.

CHAPTER FIVE
THE CABIN

EVERYTHING SPUN FOR THE NEXT COUPLE of seconds, my body, my head, even my stomach. When I felt like barfing, I landed with a thud on hard surface with my face in the dirt.

I spat out a few leaves, ground and twigs out of my mouth. My chin ached and when I touched it, my fingers were covered blood, but not so much that I needed a transfusion.

My stomach was still turning and I crawled on all fours to the nearest tree and threw up.

"Chas," My mother's warm hand touched my back and took my hair out of the way so it wouldn't get drenched with vomit.

"Please tell me this is a dream and you're waking me up to go to school." I pleaded, ignoring the horrible swirling in the gut of my stomach.

"I wish it was that easy, honey. We're safe for now, but they'll come again."

I opened my eyes as I smelled something horribly sweet like chocolate. "Here, eat this. It helps with the after effects."

It was dark, almost black. "What is it?"

"A piece of pure chocolate, the kind you've never had before."

I took a small piece and bit hard. It was sweet and bitter at the same time, but she was right about the effect rushing from my body. I took another bite and kept it inside my mouth this time, until it completely melted away.

The spinning subdued and you wouldn't have known that we'd just gone through a carousel out of hell and landed into the middle of a forest.

Looking up, I saw tall, high trees surrounded us.

There wasn't anything for miles or a road in sight.

"You feeling better?" my mom asked and I knew she wasn't just talking about my injuries or my stomach. She touched my chin softly. "I'll fix that later."

I nodded.

"Take two more minutes. I've got to find out where exactly we are." She took out a map and started looking at it intensely while I took another breather.

"So who were those men?"

"They are Selene's Seekers. People that find people like us in the Domain."

"The Domain?"

"This world, Chas."

"Are you a Seeker too?"

She smiled. "Not entirely, but sort of."

"Then why are we running from them, mom?"

"It's one of those things that you'd need a cup of coffee and I'd need a brandy to discuss."

A brandy? "You never drink."

"You make me sound like a saint. Believe me, your father was the saint. Not me."

I couldn't believe that. Everyone that knew Vinique Swanson-Blake knew she had a kind heart. She loved animals just as much as I did, she worked at charity funds to help the poor, even threw out my old clothes to give to the homeless children. She was a saint.

She looked around, gazing at the map every five seconds.

"So what, are you in some kind of trouble with them for leaving with me?"

Mom just smiled. I hated this small gesture that answered absolutely none of my questions.

"Mom!"

"The clone kept me and Tim from danger, for now. Those men are far gone by now, baby. We can discuss all of this later, right now I need to get us to the cabin first."

I looked around. "What cabin? All I see are trees." I turned my head and looked around some more. "And more trees. Look …another tree."

A giggle escaped my mother's lips. "Nice to know you are turning into your old self again. Let's go."

We picked up our bags and I followed her as we walked past more trees.

We walked for hours, the trees were really starting to make me feel claustrophobic and extremely small, not to mention how many boulders we had to cross, and two streams. There was no way there was a cabin anywhere.

Birds chirped and I looked up. The trees almost

blocked the sky, but not entirely. I skipped over another boulder that was in my path and ran up to stay close to mom's pace. Another thing, she'd gotten really fast.

A huge electric noise filled the air and my mother flew backwards as she connected with it. I screamed and ran where my mother's body had landed. She was lying with her eyes closed.

"No, no, no." I repeated fast as I touched her body to wake her up. "Mom," I yelled.

I shook her some more, she didn't even stir. I laid my head on her chest. She was still breathing and her heart was still beating, so I could rule out death.

"Help!" I cried out, but it only made the birds fly away. I cried out a couple more times, but nobody answered me back.

"Wake up, please." I shook her again. "I can't do this alone. Please."

She didn't respond and I knew we were so screwed. Who knew what sort of animals were going to wake up when the sun went down and see us as an easy meal.

I didn't even know how to make a fire or anything. How was I going to defend us from anything? I grabbed my mother's bag.

These don't work with bullets you idiot.

I tried to make my sand emerge again, but nothing happened. I was really scared and it had worked yesterday. Why didn't it work now?

I shook my mom again. "Please wake up." I felt like crying, like that day I'd lost my mom in the shops. It was so scary and although I was really small, I still remember that. Tim found me and it was how the two of them met.

The incident from yesterday came next. It seemed so

far away now, but it wasn't. It was real and those men had erased my best ex-friend's mind to think that she was still my best friend. What did a complete mind sweep looked like? Would it have worked on mom, since she was one of them?

My backpack was much softer than my mother's and I placed it gently underneath her head and sat down with my back resting against the nearest tree.

What the hell happened to her? I tried to see if I couldn't see the magnetic field that caused her to be in the state she was, but there was absolutely nothing. No buzzing noise, nothing.

Then my biological father made his way into my thoughts too. I knew absolutely nothing about the man. The only thing I did know was that he was Asian. Mom didn't like speaking about how they met, but they made one hell of a stunning looking kid. One that had mom's blue eyes and dad's raven black hair with slightly narrowed eyes.

I pulled my hoody closer as a breeze brushed through the trees. I could be glad that it wasn't winter, because if it was, we would've frozen to death right here on this spot.

What my mother had said made me wonder about a lot of things. She said that Dad was the saint, she wasn't. Mom was always the one who wanted to keep peace between me and Tim. She'd never say a bad word or gossip about someone. How could she not have been a saint? What was her past like and how did my real Dad fit into all of this?

To be honest, I used to think the other way around. Like dad was some sort of Chinese drug lord and that mom desperately tried to hide from him. It was one of the reasons that explained why she never wanted to answer my Daddy questions.

Did we have money stashed somewhere? I shook my head. I didn't know why I'd even thought about that. But it saddened me that I really didn't know anything. It was unfair. My entire life had been a lie, my mother should've said something.

My mind wandered back to last night's dream. I remembered what Leigh said. He'd told me that I could choose. Choose what? Not to be on the run, this life. Nothing made any sense. Mom couldn't die right now.

Suddenly, she grunted and started to stir. I crawled back to her side.

Then finally her eyes flung open. They looked bewildered and she jumped up with protective hands over me as she realized what had happened. Shock and surprised reflected back as she noticed the trees again.

"We're alone." I said.

Mom still looked around. "What happened?"

"One minute we were still walking and the next you somersaulted back in the air and landed right here. You were out for two hours."

"Two hours?"

I nodded. "I was scared mom."

She grabbed me tight and held me against her chest. "I'm okay for now. I think I found the cabin."

I pushed her gently back to see her face. "What, where?"

A smile appeared on her face, and she pointed into the direction we were heading a couple of hours ago. "Right there."

I looked. Squinted, and shook my head. "Mom, there's nothing there."

A heartfelt laughter left her mouth, and she got up, and crouched down next to her bag. "There is nothing there, yet."

She pulled two black gloves over her hands, and picked up the green coin bag with the golden symbols on it. I just stared at her with eyes filled with questions and curiosity.

Mom took out golden sand. It was just a pinch and it shined like golden diamonds on the black gloves. She walked a couple of paces toward the place that had injured her badly.

"Mom, be careful, please."

She stopped and blew the dust gently from her glove.

At first nothing happened and then something started to appear. It was hard to explain.

I thought about an artist painting and how his paint brush formed outlines on the canvas first. This wasn't exactly like that, but as close as I could get to what I saw.

The roof of the cabin appeared first and it was like an invisible blanket was being pulled off the rest.

I just stared at the cabin and heard mom giggle. "I knew it was here somewhere." She looked at me and closed my mouth softly. "I'll explain everything. Come."

We walked up the steps of the cabin. It smelled like wood, like pine.

"No, key?"

"It doesn't need a key, sweetheart. Oh, shoot." She turned back and walked past me again, took out another pinch of sand out of the bag and placed it into a small pot that hadn't been there a minute ago.

"Oh, shoot," I said in a sarcastic tone. She looked

back at me. "Yeah, you're really badass, mom."

She laughed and nudged me inside the door playfully.

The cabin resembled any cabin. It had a small lounge, a table with chairs right opposite a small kitchen and stairs that led to hopefully two rooms with a working bathroom.

I put my backpack on the couch while mom put hers on the kitchen table and walked into the kitchen and started opening every cupboard. She took out more of the golden sand from the green coin bag and blew a bit softly into each cupboard before she closed it.

Curiosity killed the cat, or in this case made me bolt to the kitchen to see what she was doing.

I opened the one cupboard she was done with and found it stacked with food. Every cupboard had different types of food. Pastas, cereals, rice, cookies, chips... you named it, it was somewhere in one of these cupboards.

I found a bottle of brandy in Mom's hand and a glass in the other. "You want that cup of coffee now?"

I stared at her and back into the cupboards. "Mom, what is this?"

"Coffee it is then."

"I don't understand. What's in that bag? Magic dust?"

"Something like that." The kettle boiled and I just stared at the food stacked in all the cupboards.

Mom never liked junk food, but here it was, junk food, upon junk food, and more junk food.

"Mom?" I looked at her who already had a glass of light brown liquid mixed with a couple of ice cubes in her hands. "This is really starting to freak me out.

What's going on? Why did we have to run from those people if we're like them? And how do you know about my dream?"

She just gave me a sad look – it was laced with guilt – that much I could tell.

She didn't answer and turned around when the kettle finished and poured hot water in a mug with a spoon's handle sticking out. I watched her take out a jar of milk from the fridge.

I found myself in front of the fridge as she closed it and opened it again. A gasp left my mouth as food stacked for at least fifteen people stared back at me.

"This is nuts."

"Come sit with me and we'll talk." Mom pulled out a chair at the small table made for four.

I blew out a gush of air and went over, pulled out the chair opposite Mom and plunged down. The cup of coffee stood right in front of me, steam wafting from it. I wasn't really even in the mood for one, but if coffee was the only thing that would make her talk about all the paranormal things that had been going on these twenty-odd hours, then I welcomed the coffee with open arms.

My mother let out a huge breath before taking another sip of her brandy.

"Before we begin, I need you to answer me one thing, Chas."

I nodded.

"What color was the sand in your dreams?"

CHAPTER SIX
THE TRUTH SUCKS

"WHAT?"

"The color of the sand, Chas. The sand coming from your hands?"

I closed my eyes and shook my head. "How in the world do you know what I dreamt about?"

"Chastity, I need to know. It's very important."

"No, mom. I need to know what the hell is going on."

"Fine!" she sighed again. She pulled her black glove resting on the table back over her hand and pick up the small green bag – was far from a coin bag – opened it and took out pure golden dust again. It sparkled, and the contrast against the black glove made the sand even more sparkling. "This belonged to your father," she said as she played with the golden dust with her index finger. She smiled at a memory forming on her mind and then it disappeared with another sigh.

"What is that, Mom?"

"Sand, golden sand that has the ability to do whatever you want it to."

She looked up from the dust in her palm at me and smiled.

"Sand that can do what?" I said, knowing that it wasn't as farfetched as it would have been a day ago, I'd witnessed it myself at the lake and saw how she'd stacked the food cupboards filled with goodies in a matter of seconds. Even Leigh told me what I was, but I really thought that it was just a dream. The image of Derek and Jake falling flat on their faces, snoring jumped into my mind. "Wait. Sand as in sleeping sand?"

"One of the things they can do."

"So what, you guys ware like the Sandman?"

Mom laughed. "Sorry," she said. "The Sandman is just a kids version of what we used to do, or let's say he used to do. What the Seekers said are true. Revera does exist and it's real."

"Mom, you know how crazy this sounds, right?"

"I know." She smiled.

"So what is it exactly we can do?"

"That's a lot to explain with one cup of coffee. But I think the basics are needed. We are what people would call Dream Casters."

Leigh told me the same and here my mom was confirming it. I wasn't crazy. "That I got from Beavis and Butthead."

Mom laughed. "Chas, they are far from Beavis and Butthead, that I can assure you. They are very smart and they will send others more scary than them soon."

"So the place they spoke about, it's real?"

"The dream world, known as Revera, yes. It's real. For many millenniums, Revera was peaceful. It was ruled by three Somniums. They were what you would call the royals of this world, the best at everything, almost like gods. Magdalena Sodivic, Darius and Selene Faline. They were siblings. Then one day Magdalena's sand turned dark. We don't really know what caused it, but it started to have a different effect on Revera. Some of the smaller towns started to disappear and the Faline's knew she had to be cast out. It only aggravated Magdalena more that they didn't understand or try to understand and help her figure out how to control it, and she became so angry that her dark sand became stronger. To make a long story short, Revera was almost destroyed and Darius sacrificed himself to overpower Magdalena. She disappeared and through her bloodline, the Shadow Casters were born."

"The Shadow Casters?"

"Who do you think creates all the bad dreams sweetheart? Doubt? Lost dreams?"

"You mean like nightmares?"

Mom nodded and she placed the golden sand back into the green bag.

"What does any of this have to do with my dream?"

"When Dream Caster children turn sixteen, they became Initiates. It always starts with the dream. The dream reveals what color sand you will have, and a couple of days later, it will start appearing."

Couple of days later... I didn't say it out loud. I got up and started to pace around. Leigh said that I could choose. This must be what he meant.

"What is it Chastity?"

I shook my head. "I was in a bad place, mom. Everything was dark, smelled awful, there was no sign of anything alive."

Mom's facial features changed and she looked sad, defeated. "It's the Oblivion."

A small smile played on the corner of my mind. "Yeah, I know. Leigh told me."

"Leigh?" she asked. "Who's Leigh, sweetheart?"

"The guy, in the dream. He helped me escape, kept a lot of Shadow dogs from me."

"No," Vinique shook her head. "The Initiation dream is something you have to go through alone."

"Mom, if I had to do that alone, believe me, I wouldn't be here today."

Creases between Mom's eyebrows appeared. She thought really hard about something. "It doesn't make any sense. Did he tell you who he was?"

I shook my head. I wanted to tell her he was hot, but it didn't seem like the right time.

"There were Nimgolians?" Mom asked another question.

"Are those the animals that turns into heaps of black sand when you shoot them?"

Mom nodded.

"They weren't the friendliest puppies either."

"Tell me about the dream." She didn't smile or giggle at all.

I closed my eyes and started to tell my mother everything. It was so vivid, I could still see it playing like a movie behind my closed eyelids. I stopped with the white light that appeared in the middle of a deserted square with millions of Shadow hounds that tried to rip out your flesh if they could. "My leg was badly injured when I woke up. I tried to clean it but my linen was soaked with a lot of blood. It's why I chucked it in the washing this morning. When I woke up again, it was gone, which only freaked me out more."

"Why didn't you wake me up, sweetheart?"

"And tell you what?"

"The truth. I would've never sent you to school this morning and Beavis and Butthead wouldn't have found us either."

"So why is it bad that they know about us?"

"They're like your father, good. Their dust is golden and they're the only ones welcomed inside Revera. The Oblivion is no place for a Dream Caster, it was no place for a baby either."

"A baby?"

She smiled. "Seventeen years ago a Shadow Caster fell in love with a Dream Caster. She almost killed him, and he would've died if it wasn't love at first sight for him. His friends took him to a healer, and they saved his life, but he couldn't stop dreaming about this girl." She got up and went to the kitchen as she kept telling the story.

"One day, he got his chance. She, on the other hand was surprised that he was still alive, but there was something about this guy that took her breath away. He wasn't like the other Light Casters. He was kind and thought twice about who he killed." She came back with another drink in her hand and looked at me. "In Revera, they teach all the Level One Light Casters about what they should do when they come face to face with a Shadow Caster. Destroy." She looked back at the ground. "It's been a war that will never be won. Still this Dream Caster went out of his way to be with the Shadow Caster. They would meet in secret and they fell in love. She fell pregnant and was scared of what Selene and her father would do with the fetus, so they tried to escape Revera." She had tears in her eyes, something Chastity didn't understand. "He didn't make it, but she found a way out. He made sure of it, before he died."

A tear rolled over her cheek and a horrible feeling made me feel as if my air pipe was going to close. "Mom, what aren't you telling me?"

Mom looked at me. "Remember when I told you that your father was the saint?"

I nodded.

"I was the Shadow Caster."

OKAY THAT WAS SOMETHING I SHOULD'VE seen but for some reason I didn't. The story about my parents was a typical Romeo and Juliette story, the only difference was that Juliette fell pregnant in this one and she couldn't die with her love because of her unborn baby.

We sat at that table, just staring at one another. I tried to make sense of this. Mom was a Shadow Caster. Something I knew wasn't good. "Your father was so excited when I told him that I was pregnant, but a day later he was crazy with paranoia. Not knowing what you will be, or how we were going to raise you in Revera, so we decided to raise you in the Domain. It wasn't easy because nobody could see Dream Casters in this world and we had to go through a lot of pain in order to become what people would call normal."

She didn't make sense at all, speaking about becoming normal and being invisible was kind of confusing so my mind skipped over that part and lingered on another.

"So I take it I'm not Dream Caster material?"

"I didn't think you were going to become one, that is why I didn't want to raise you like one." She gave me another guilty look.

"So, I'm half good, half evil."

Mom shook her head. "In Revera, there is no grey area. It's either black or white. Good or evil, Chastity. That's why I asked you what the color of your sand in the dream was."

"Black is bad, isn't it?"

Mom hold out her hand. The black glove was off and I just stared at it. Then a swirl of black sand started spinning like a whirlwind in mom's palm. "I came from a very dark bloodline. One that would never forgive me if I ever had to return to the Oblivion."

I nodded. "That's why my sand in the dream was black, wasn't it?"

Vinique sucked in a breath. Tears filled her eyes and then she closed them. She bit hard on her lower lip and I knew it was to keep the tears from rolling down her cheeks.

"But the sand at the lake was gold."

Vinique's eyes flew open. "What happened Chas?"

"I'm sorry I lied. I did get lost though, but it was because of me turning into some sandy freak."

"Tell me everything and don't leave a single detail out," Mom said and led me over to one of the couches. We took the love seat and I started to tell her everything. How Clare was still mad at me and what happened that day at the lake.

"Derek really scared me mom, and then..." I took a deep breath. " I thought my heart was going to explode, and I found golden light brown sand in my palms. I didn't know where it came from or anything and when

Mark went for me, I threw it in his eyes. Derek and Jake were next, and the sand just kept coming."

"They all fell asleep?" Vinique asked.

I nodded with a slightly raised, worried eyebrow.

"And you're sure your sand was gold in color?"

"It doesn't look like Dad's but I'm pretty sure."

Mom sighed. "That's good."

"Leigh said I can choose. What did he mean?"

"I don't know this Leigh you are talking about, but I'm grateful that he was there to help you through this."

"Could this dream maybe be about you and Dad? Telling me that I am sort-of both."

"I don't know, baby."

"Then how did he know, Mom? What did he mean by choosing?"

"I don't know."

"You think it's what he meant?"

"Remember there is no grey in Revera. Only black and white. You can't tell anyone Chas. I don't know what they would do to you if they found out, but from the look on your father's face and the way he acted after the excitement of the pregnancy was over, it's not good."

I sighed. This was all so confusing.

"Can you show me your sand?" Mom asked.

"I don't know how to, Mom."

She smiled. "Close your eyes and listen to my voice."

I did what she said.

"Imagine yourself in a field with flowers. You are lying on your back and soaking up the sun."

My eyes flew open. "Seriously?"

"Do as I say. Close your eyes."

"Fine." I closed my eyes again and think about the

field with the flowers again. I imagined myself lying between tall grass with little purple flowers around me. The warmth of the sun started to make me feel tired, lazy.

"Clouds are busy moving in front of the sun, feel the slight change in temperature." Mom's voice carried on.

For some reason I imagined them dark. Images of the oblivion flashed in between the vision of me lying in the field, feeling lazy.

My heart started to rise.

"You hear a sound, it's not the wind."

It was a deep growl that I heard that night. It belonged to a shadow hound. My eyes flew opened and I found myself stranded in my vision. The clouds were dark, only a few of the sun beams streamed through them. The wind was blowing like mad. I couldn't hear mother's voice anymore and for some reason I was searching, scanning the grounds for …Leigh.

Something on my left caught my eye and my body swung around. I stared into the slobbery mouth of a huge beast, with long canines and black beady eyes. Low growls came from him and then he took a step toward me. His eyes didn't leave me once. They were locked on mine and I took a step backwards.

Black smoke overpowered his back legs and they moved slowly up towards his front and then his entire face disappeared as the smoke came toward me.

My heart rose faster and faster and the sand appeared in my palm again. I looked down. "No!" It was pitched black, just like the hound.

The smoke came closer and closer and I crawled backward, until I found no more ground. The entire place that was once beautiful turned into soot and burned down trees. It was dark and black, and I struggled to breathe again.

I had absolutely nothing to fight against the dark that was trying to consume me, only the dark and black dust. Dust I didn't want.

The hound jumped out of the black dust like smoke and I screamed.

"Chastity!" Mom's voice yelled and my eyes flew open. I was back on the couch. My hand trembled softly and I pulled them through my hair.

Heaps of sand were on the couch, making me jump up. Her eyes still reflected horror as she stared at me.

"What happened?"

"I don't know. One second you were still talking to me, the next I was there, literally." I spoke fast without taking my eyes off the couch filled with sand. Light golden sand.

"That would explain the sand. It comes when you're scared. We should try to make it come from will."

"Mom," I said. "My sand was black."

Mom got up too and flung her arms around me. "It doesn't matter. You're sand is gold. Which means when they find us, they'll take you to Revera."

"When they find us? What do you mean?"

Mom let go of me and she backed a couple of inches away to look at me. Both her hands gripped my shoulders. "They will find us. It's just a matter of time. Your father's sand will protect us for now, Chastity, but it'll run out and that's when they'll come."

I just stared at her. I didn't like that one bit. We would get separated and I would be alone. "So what are we going to do, Mom?"

"We're going to train. You need to know how to

wield your sand freely, without fear, you need to learn how to wield the things you need from the sand, and how to fight when danger comes."

"Fight?"

"How do you think your father and I met? We were both Guardians."

"I thought you said you were Dream Casters."

Vinique laughed. "All of us are, but we are trained in the thing that we shine the most at. And what our family does best, is fighting, Chastity. We are fighters."

CHAPTER SEVEN
THE ART OF WAR

MOM HADN'T BEEN JOKING WHEN SHE SAID WE WERE fighters. The first day when she showed me what it was she could do, I almost wanted to run away.

I always thought that Tim was the dangerous one in the family and if anybody wanted to harm us that he'd have chopped and kicked the living daylight out of whoever thought about it. If anybody told me a week ago that my mother would actually do the kicking, I would've laughed in their faces.

Now, it was a different story as she showed me moves where her hands broke through a block of concrete and kicked through wooden beams that splintered in half, daggers thrown into a target board, breaking targets with a long whip, things that would take me a lifetime to master. Not to mention how she wielded a weapon from her dark sand. The knife felt real, all the details were sculpted into the hilt. It even had a red ruby right in the middle of the hilt where the blade started. Something that I wasn't good with at all.

"Chas, again!" Mom yelled as my golden sand was strewn all over the place creating long lines without a hint of a weapon or anything that resembled an object. It was just sand.

"Mom, I'm tired."

She crouched next to me where I was kneeling on all fours concentrating hard on my golden sand. "You've got to concentrate, want it with your heart, mind and soul or you're never going to wield anything."

"Do you cast dreams like this too?"

Mom nodded.

"Can you show me?"

Mom's eyes open wider. "NO! That I can't and won't do. I've told you before, Shadow Casters only create nightmares, the worst kind. What humans usually see is only about twenty percent of the real thing. It is why dreams have always been so vague. If you have to witness it as I would create it, it would be the full dose, it's worse than Oblivion."

"Then how am I going to learn?"

"Revera will help you with creating dreams. I can't." She gave me a stern look. "I can only help you with this, Chastity. Now again."

I closed my eyes and thought about wanting my sand again. It was difficult, I struggled the first time with it, but I had to admit that the more I tried it, the easier it got. I saw it flowing freely in my mind, imagined its touch against my hand, the slight warm temperature, its golden color. Then I felt it flow freely, accumulating in the palm of my hand. I let it pour into a heap on the ground until there was enough to create something from it.

"Now imagine a dagger. See the sharp blade, the hilt."

I saw the picture as I stared at her sand. "I got it."

"Now concentrate on the detail. What does the hilt look like? Does it have a ruby, on it, snakes twirling around it?"

I liked the snake idea and imagined two snakes twirling around a copper hilt. I imagined what the leather on the hilt looked like. The soft touch with a suede feel to it. Two lines appeared again, but not a hilt.

I lost the picture in my head and took a deep breath. "This is hopeless."

"No, it's not. But maybe you're right. If you're getting tired there is no way you are going to conjure it. I suggest a two hour nap, Chastity."

"Seriously?"

Mom gave me her a typical mother's look. "Sleep, now."

My body slumped as I got up from the ground and walked back to the cabin. I slouched all the way to my room that was on the upper level and fell onto my bed. Nowadays it felt as if I could sleep for an entire month. Two hours was nothing.

For the last few weeks, ever since Mom told me what we were, nothing was fun anymore.

I would start off with a two mile run at dawn, followed by a big breakfast of bacon, eggs, hash browns and toast. Then it was an hour of martial arts, an hour of kick boxing and another hour of weapons training. Lunch would follow after that and then the rest of the day was practicing with my sand. My mom was a drill sergeant straight from hell.

Sometimes I wished that the people would just find

us, but the minute that thought formed into my head, I felt guilty. It would mean Mom would disappear. I couldn't imagine life without her but I know I wouldn't be able to survive in Revera knowing that Mom was trapped in the Oblivion, which is where they would take her when she was caught.

The plan was simple: when the men came, my mom would pretend she was my kidnapper. I didn't look anything like her. Thanks to my father's strong Asian complex that shone through me.

All of a sudden I didn't want to think about that day anymore, so I closed my eyes and cleared my mind.

Since my Initiation dream, I hadn't dreamt of anything else. Mom couldn't explain to me who Leigh was either. Light Casters, that young, wouldn't be able to go to the Oblivion, unless they belonged there – and judging by Leigh's golden sand, he was no Shadow Caster.

What he meant by me being able to choose, could only mean one thing: I could become a Light Caster. But why would my mother tell me that there was no grey area? That you are what you are?

In my case I was both. Dad was a Light Caster, a Level Four, as mom had said, which was the highest level Dream Casters could achieve, unless you were one of the Somniums —and Selene was the last one.

When my eyes opened again, the sun had started to set. It didn't matter whether it was light or dark, my mom would still carry on with training. At least I wasn't as tired as I'd been a couple of hours ago. I thought about just lying in bed, pretending to be asleep but then her voice jumped into my head, explaining how important all this was going to be if I was going to survive in Revera. I had no choice.

I rolled off my bed, and got up. My body felt stronger from training day and night, the muscles in my arms and stomach had started to cut nicely. I didn't look like a dancer anymore, but more like some sort of gym junky.

I opened my door and the smell of meat filled my nostrils. Ahhh. Stew.

Mom paraded in between the pot on the stove to the cupboard, with a glass of whiskey in her hand while music played softly in the background. I'd never seen her drink so much in my entire life, but then again, I never knew my mother was such a badass too.

She looked over her shoulder as I entered, and gave me a loving smile. "Good, you're awake. Hungry?"

"Starving," I said.

"Grab the plates, food is almost ready."

I did as she told and picked up two plates and placed them on the counter by the gas stove.

In a couple of minutes both plates were filled with a heap of rice and stew covering the entire plate. Another thing that had change ever since I started with this intense training was my appetite. I'd never eaten this much in my entire life. You'd think I'd have picked up a couple of pounds, but it was just the opposite. I'd shed a couple of pounds and all I picked up was muscle, lean and strong. I couldn't wait for the beach.

My mother took my hand and closed her eyes.

"Father, bless our food which we are about to eat and although we know that danger is near, keep us safe, Amen."

I opened my eyes. "Bon appétit."

"It looks delicious." I sounded ravenous and started to dig in.

Mom just stared at me as I shoved lumps of food into my mouth every five seconds.

"Easy tiger, the food isn't going to run off your plate."

Her comment made me giggle as I imagined grains of rice and blocks of beef growing little legs and running off my plate. "I'm just so hungry."

"Then eat more fruit, Chastity."

"Bleh."

Mom shook her head. "You are the only teenager I know that doesn't like fruit. Everyone else loves at least two or three different kinds."

"Not my thing. I hate the sweet taste they carry."

"It's healthy sugar which your body needs too."

"Chocolates are also healthy."

Mom rolled her eyes, it made her look ten times younger than she was.

"Can you at least tell me what I'm going to go through when they come?"

"I told you before, you act like you don't know me, act scared, like I put you through hell."

"Mom, you are putting me through hell."

Mom chucked her napkin at me. "Not that kind. Like I just kept you here against your free will." I gave her a raised eyebrow look. "Don't comment on that, please."

I laughed.

"I wasn't talking about that. I mean, tell me about Revera."

She put down her knife and fork and leaned back in her chair.

"The small bit I saw of Revera was breathtaking. Your father used to tell me that anything was possible, it's a place where dreams come true."

"It sounds like Hollywood."

Mom laughed again.

"Not that kind. The kind that makes your dreams literally come true. Light Casters have the ability to wield their own happiness."

"Then why did you guys leave?"

"Because the love we shared wasn't allowed in Revera. Even if I stopped, one Shadow Caster inside Revera would destroy it completely the way Magdalena almost did so many years ago."

"That is so unfair. I mean, you guys didn't choose to love one another, it just happened. Sometimes I don't know if I want to go to Revera."

"And live a life running from them? It's not the kind of life I want for you, Chastity."

Silence filled the dining room for a few minutes.

"How many will come, Mom?"

"I don't know. It won't be the two from before and I'll have to disguise myself as I'm sure Beavis and Butthead already told Selene about you and that you got away. It would be a team of elite Pursuers, and they usually travel in groups of about five, maybe six." She took a deep breath and smiled softly. "Your father used to be the leader of his team. They would go on many missions and quests for Selene. When guardians graduate, they have to prove themselves first so they get to guard the edge of Revera, all the escape routes, be on guard and watch out for Shadow Casters that try to enter Revera. It's not easy but now and then they would find a way."

"How did you and Dad meet then, if your love wasn't allowed?"

A soft smile broke on her face. "It wasn't always

easy but your father used to wield a place. It didn't hold very long, only a couple of hours or so."

"A couple of hours or so?"

Vinique laughed. "You haven't been in love yet, sweetheart. So a couple of hours feels like nothing if it's spent with the person you love."

I felt sorry for her. She really hadn't had a chance at all to be with Dad and be truly happy. To think that he'd given up his life so that his family could escape.

"You never even got a real chance with him, did you?" I spoke softly.

Mom just smiled. "I did. You. You are in so many ways like him. Smart, stubborn and you follow your gut, not to mention you inherited his humor and the ability to say exactly what's on your mind."

"That's from him? I thought it came from you."

We both laughed and finished our meal. As I finished my glass of Coke, Mom put the dirty plates in the dishwasher.

"You ready?"

I got up and walked to the kitchen. "I probably don't have a choice, so yes, I'm ready."

Mom grabbed me playfully with her arm around the neck. "If only your will was connected to that mouth of yours, this would've been so much easier."

We practiced till late that night. I tried so hard, but the only thing that appeared were the two lines. It was followed by plenty of tries and plenty of frustrated grunts. I really wanted to do this, but for some reason I just couldn't get the picture that was inside my head to appear from my golden sand.

Mom glanced at her watch and sighed. "I think it's time to do our runs, make sure the shield is holding, and call it a night."

I looked with worried eyes at her. "How much do we still have?"

"Not a lot, enough to last at least another day or two, three at the most."

"Then I should try a couple of times more, Mom."

"You're tired, Chas. It shows in your sand."

My gaze snapped to my sand. It still looked like sand and still had that light, brownish gold color.

Mom giggled and gently lifted up my chin to look at her. "You're producing less and less. Take it from me, you need your rest. Tomorrow is a new day."

"Can we try something else, tomorrow?"

"Sure, what do you suggest?"

"Instead of drilling me like Major Pain, can we start with this, and finish with the physical stuff?"

Mom squinted, her eyebrows knitted together as she took in what I suggested. "That might be a good idea."

We walked back to the cabin to get Dad's sand that was hidden inside the gold and green bag.

Once Mom had slipped on her gloves, since the dust would turn black if she made physical contact with it, she gave a tiny bit to me. I couldn't stop looking at the last piece of magic coming from my father. It was like pure gold and glistened inside my palm as the light from inside hit the small specks at the right angle. It was so beautiful. I cupped it safely with my other hand, careful not to lose one speck, and went back outside.

The perimeter was all around the cabin. About five feet from the cabin were small pot-like objects which contained a little bit of dust. I started re-filling them and Mom did the same, starting from the back of the cabin until all the pots were filled. I still had a bit left and placed it gently inside the green bag again.

"Why wouldn't my sand work?"

"It's not powerful enough yet, sweetheart. But it will be, one day." She smiled and wrapped her arms around me again. I could hear Mom's heartbeat. It was steady, familiar and it made me feel safe. I couldn't imagine what life without her would be like, not to mention spending it in another world, one where make believe still existed.

"Go, take a bath and sleep. You need your strength for tomorrow."

I planted a goodnight kiss on Mom's cheek and ran up the stairs. The cabin sure was a magical one. When Mom mentioned that we were going to train with weapons and learn how to do kata's and other phrases I didn't even know how to spell, I had no idea where we were going to find the space to do it.

Mom refused to go into the forest, behind the shield and there wasn't enough space to learn all this inside, or so I'd thought. But when she threw some of Dad's sand and said a small incantation, another thing I'd never heard her speak before, a door appeared right in the wall.

When I opened it, everything we needed was right in front of me. It almost reminded me of the gym at school. There was a track, which I used for running two miles every morning, and a lot of targets and weapons hanging against the wall. A blue mat where Mom taught me how to punch and kick took up most of the space in the inside of the track. Bright lights lit everything up and three ropes dangled from the roof where we became well acquainted as I was drilled up and down them.

I remembered how my mouth gaped and my mother

had to literally closed it for me. If there was one thing I'd learned that night, it was how powerful Dad's sand truly was.

I imagined night after night what kind of life we would've had if he was still alive. Would we still have been on the run now, or would he have protected us from this life? I would probably never have known who I was.

If my father was like my mother, trying to keep Revera away from me and vice versa, he would've done everything in his power to keep us shielded, just like Mom did now.

Tim started phoning a couple of days ago. Mom just gave me a worried look. "The dummy disappeared," she said. It was all she said. She'd had to do what was necessary to keep him safe so she never answered any of his calls. He must be going crazy with worry at this stage, probably thinking she'd left him after nobody found me. I thought that it would be a wonderful experience since I wasn't a big fan, but felt quite sorry for the big guy. He might not have loved me very much, but I knew he adored my mother.

After the bath I crawled straight underneath the covers and switched off the nightlight. The stars shined brightly through the window and the moon lit up the lower part of my bed. It sure was peaceful here in the cabin Dad owned. I wondered if Revera was in the sky like the books and movies about Sandman explained.

I closed my eyes and played with the tear-shaped pendant that was around my neck. I pictured my parents dancing a slow dance in the lounge right after he came to tuck me in. Okay, so maybe I would've been too old to be tucked-in, but it was something I'd never had from any male figure in my life. At least he'd have been here tonight. I imagine them kissing, even though it would've grossed me out, but it would've been what Mom needed, what I'm sure she still longed for. She would've been happy and wouldn't have to pretend that I was enough.

Then I thought about Shades. I wasn't there anymore to give her the daily bowl of milk and I hoped that she was fine. I really missed our strange conversations.

I closed my eyes and said a soft prayer and with that, fatigue washed over me and I fell asleep.

CHAPTER EIGHT
MY SAND

THE NEXT MORNING I DIDN'T START OFF
with my two mile run after a bowl of muesli and berries
topped with yogurt. I hated the berries but didn't want to
pick them out of the yogurt. So, I had no choice but to
suck it up and eat them. My strategic plan was to close
my nose and swallow it whole.

After breakfast we went straight to the back and
started practicing on making the dagger appear out of
my golden sand.

I'd seen Mom do it so many times. She didn't even
have to imagine it anymore. She just believed that it was
there and it was.

She told me that the first time was the hardest. Once I
saw and touched the weapon I wielded, the second and
third became a lot easier and it carried on until it
became like breathing. It had something to do with
feeling the object you wielded contained. Once I felt it, I

would know it was real and that it was possible.

I took a deep breath before I stared at the heap of sand right in front of me.

The picture of the dagger formed in my mind. I could see the silver blade glistening and the snakes around the hilt. I even managed to put a ruby inside the middle, just like the one Mom's dagger had.

"You got it?" Mom whispered.

I nodded, holding on to that image.

"Now make yourself want it with everything in your ability, Chas. Think of a scenario where you might need it, a scene, even if it isn't real and make it real inside your mind. Then conjure it."

I never imagined it like that, and maybe Mom had something here. So I went deeper into my mind. I went back to the day Mom wanted to see my sand and focused on that awful burned down place that used to be a field with purple flowers. I found it faster than I thought I would. I breathed in the burned air and heard the crunch of the grass that was blackened underneath my shoes. The soft growl was right behind me. Slobber ran down my shoulder and I knew the Shadow Hound was hovering over me. He would be huge and I would feel helpless, but not this time. I had something to fight back with this time, I just needed to conjure the stupid dagger.

I turned around and found his drooling mouth inches from me. His teeth were big and his breath was foul. The black smoke behind him started to consume his body again, until the hound disappeared completely. The darkness crept forward, wanting to consume me. My heart didn't bounce like a bird that was trapped inside a closed room anymore. It was ready, ready to be strong and fight back, ready to trust my sand.

I wanted that dagger so much, I could see it, I could feel it and then I saw the heap of golden sand right next to my body. I looked at it for a fraction of a second and back at the hound.

Mom gasped and everything disappeared right in front of me. I was still in the backyard of the cabin, surrounded by huge trees.

I looked down at my sand and right in front of me, lying in my sand was the dagger, I couldn't believe it. I ended up staring at it, the same way Mom was staring at it. I'd finally done it. I conjured the dagger out of my sand.

Mom picked up the dagger as if it was about to break into what it was made of, but it looked solid. It looked just like the one in my mind. It's hilt had the ruby right in the middle with the two snakes twirling around it. The blade was silver. I touched it softly but pulled my finger back and put it quickly into my mouth. It was flaming sharp and a small cut with blood oozing out of it was evidence that the dagger was real.

"You did it!" Mom yelled with excitement as she enfolded me with both her arms.

"I freak'n did it. It's so awesome. I told you this would work."

"Yes, you did, smart ass. Now go hit the track."

My face fell. "Really?"

"Track, now."

Loud music blared from the speakers as I ran my daily two miles. I was suited up with a device to count my steps, calorie loss, everything, as if I had to lose weight, but for some reason it was important to Mom, so I obliged.

Then after my two mile track it was rope climbing. I hated it in the beginning, it always felt as if my arms were going to break off afterward, but after doing this every day for the past few weeks, it had really become one of my favorite things to do. I climbed the rope like a tiger and once I touched the roof, I would slide down. My leather gloves protected me from the rope and Mom just looked at me as if I hadn't just broke my own personal record of yesterday.

After rope-climbing it was a gazillion pushups and sit ups, working out my arms, abs and back. Lunges helped to get my legs stronger and getting my butt firm.

Then it was time to recite what I would say once they came.

My mother would escape the same way we came here - through a Celestial orb. She constantly wore one of those devices on her for when that day came.

I looked at it every night. It was the same thing that Leigh had spoken about in my dream. It was dark grey and had an oval gel substance in the middle. It looked just like a funny looking object with a sticky back that would attach to any wall, door, tree, whatever you could think of and then it would magically activate. The orb let you jump through worlds and from place to place. An excellent getaway tool.

They would come soon as Dad's sand was almost finished. It was the only thing that protected this cabin from the real world and from the other Dream Casters, good and bad.

"When they come, what will you do?"

"Act like a victim." I spoke like a soldier, these questions had been had been drilled into me so many times.

"If, by some miracle, they tie me down, what will you do?"

"Nothing, I won't yell out for you, I won't cry, I'll do nothing."

"If they tell ask you who I am?"

"I'll tell them I don't know. You kidnapped me while I was on the run after the day my sand came, I haven't seen my mother since, and that you tried to change me. Will they really believe that?" I stared at my mother.

"The Shadow Caster's believe that if they can get close to Light Casters when they are your age, they might be able to change them to fully dark by influencing their beliefs."

I could feel my frown knitting both my eyebrows together. "You mean like brainwashing them?" I couldn't imagine what person in their right mind would like to go and live in the Oblivion by choice.

Mom smiled. "Something like that."

"Will they do the same to me, if the Shadow Casters find us first?"

"I doubt that. I haven't used my sand beyond the wall for a long time, they can only track other Shadow Casters when sand has been used, and new fresh Dream Caster sand, no matter the color. We've been practicing a lot with yours so I doubt that if you used it behind the shield that they could detect it easily."

"But the Light Casters would."

She nodded. "Those Seekers didn't come for me that day, Chastity. They came for you. You were not ready which is why we left them there. I'm sure that Selene already knows about you and about me. So if you ever meet her, which I'm sure you will, just keep to our story. That a woman with blonde hair found you and that she tried to change you, but you don't know how. The less you tell them what you know, the better. If they know that you have the Shadow Caster's blood inside of you, Selene will cast you out."

I nodded. "What if I can't do this? What if I screw up? If anything happens to you..." I couldn't think about it.

My mother smiled lovingly back at me. "If you can't watch, roll yourself up in a fetus position and look away Chas. I can get myself out of any situation, but I doubt that I could get your ass out of Oblivion. I'll try my best, but..." she shook her head.

"Then I don't have a choice. You can't go back there."

Mom took my head softly in both her hands and kissed me on my head.

"If there is any chance that they realize who I am, they would say stuff Chas, stuff that used to be true, horrible things. But know that I changed the minute they laid your tiny body inside my arms."

I grabbed mom tight around her neck. "Promise me you'll be okay?"

"Chastity, I'll be fine, as long as you promise to keep the golden sand and never show them the black."

I pushed her away at arm's length. "But I don't have black sand, Mom."

She stared at the ground and the expression on her face told me that she was hiding something.

"Mom?"

"You could still get it." She turned her back to me and fiddled with her fingers.

"How?"

"Your dark side can trigger it, Chas. You need to be

super careful. Any sign of weakness, anger, frustration, anything that can open your darkness, can bring on the black sand."

I gave an unbelievable laugh. "You never thought of telling me this earlier? Mom, what if…"

"Shhh, don't think like that. If you feel frustrated, or angry, just walk away, Chastity. Until the anger disappears. Don't ever wield your sand if you're not sure about your emotions. It has to be good, in every way before you wield something."

"I don't understand. I didn't feel good when I used my sand on those assholes at the lake."

Mom smiled. "That's a good sign, but you need to be careful, Chastity."

"Dad was a Light Caster. Why didn't his sand ever change dark when he fought against you guys?"

"Because he was a Light Caster, he was fighting against the evil, not with them. We are not sure what you are yet. You could be either. If the Shadow Casters get a hold of you, Chas!"

"It won't happen."

"Just be careful. You only get one chance in Revera."

Mom glanced at her wrist watch. "I need to get some lunch into that stomach of yours. Pack all the weapons away and meet me in the kitchen."

I watched Mom as she left. I hated this feeling of not knowing what was going to happen. Were we going to still have tonight together or not? I sighed and bent from the waist down to pick up the first weapon. It was a cross bow. This one had small arrows that had the ability to shoot out one after the other in less than five seconds. Mom didn't need the arrows. She wielded her black sand and hit all bull's eyes. I, on the other hand, was lucky if my arrows appeared, not to mention hitting the target board.

I truly hoped that Mom was right that it would become easier now that I'd wielded the dagger.

I picked up the next weapon, a whip. It was another of Mom's favorites and I learned the past few weeks that it was the main weapon she used to fight with. My father had had his bow. I could just imagine how he had used it, shooting out bright golden arrows at those nasty dogs. I made a mental note of asking Mom how the Shadow Casters managed to wield them. It must be from a lot of hatred.

I picked up something that reminded me of small daggers. It came with a wrist glove which you pushed the daggers inside and when you needed it, you just flicked your wrist in a sideways movement and they came flying out of the glove. It was a really cool weapon.

I placed all the weapons in a small chest. It wasn't the one that had been hidden in the attic for years, but it was very similar.

Once the room was clean, I went to the kitchen. Mom was busy making her famous mustard and cold meat sandwich as I plopped onto the nearest high chair. I watched her add the mustard and pickles onto the sandwich.

"Can I ask you something?"

Mom looked up. "Shoot."

"Where do the Shadow Hounds come from?"

She huffed and a small smile appeared on her mouth. "Nimgolians. They're not as vicious as you think, Chastity."

"They're not?"

She shook her head "We each get one on our tenth birthday. They're these small puppy whisks of dogs, beautiful."

"You had one too?"

"I did. She was a gentle creature and most of the time was misunderstood."

"Why do I get the feeling she no longer is?"

"My father killed her when he found out about your dad."

"What?"

"He thought it would be a way to make me fear him again, but he was wrong. I hated him more than I feared him."

"Why do they seem so vicious then?"

"Because they feed off fear. We're not afraid of them because we nurture them from puppies. Light Casters always have that fear inside of them when they see them. As you know, they aren't your average-looking dog and I don't think the disfigured face and huge teeth help them much with gaining trust from the Light Casters."

"So, basically, they're like real dogs?"

Vinique laughed. "Basically, but they can do vicious things if their Shadow Caster orders them." She took out a couple of plates and handed them to me to set the table.

"But where do they come from?"

"We have shrines inside Oblivion. They're like a Level Four Light Caster but dark. Her bloodline are the only ones that can wield them. Mine was wielded by a woman called Seamora. She didn't like being a Shadow Caster and when she wielded Kiara for me, she put a lot of love into her. She also put a bit of mischief and too much energy, but overall it was the perfect recipe for a Shadow Hound."

"Can Light Casters tame them?"

"If they can look beyond the darkness and evil emanating off them, I don't see why not. But then again, the Light Casters have their own animals."

"They do?"

"They are called Anitules. Their Casters are known as Tulas, a very old name for someone gifted to bond with Anitules. If I remember correctly, your father had an eagle called Lima, who would come to his rescue whenever things got out of hand."

My eyebrows knitted as I thought about that.

"What is it, sweetheart?"

"Why wasn't he there that night, when you needed him?"

"Because Lima would've killed me."

"But he was just an eagle."

She laughed. "Animals in Revera are not like the animals we have here, Chas. They are huge, so big that Casters can ride them. Lima was a giant eagle."

"What?!"

"He showed me a picture of Lima once, he was a beautiful creature."

"Did he die too?" I had to know.

She shrugged.

"So the Light Caster animals are just like the Shadow Caster animals."

"You are one smart girl."

"What can I say? I guess I get it from both my parents."

Mom bumped me softly. "Eat your sandwich, smart

mouth."

We dug in and I had to say, it was the best sandwich I'd ever had. I enjoyed every single bit of it, up until Mom told me to finish my milk because we still had plenty of training to do.

Training carried on until late in the evening. Around nine o'clock, I watched Mom part with the last bit of my father's sand. She stood outside the cabin with a blanket over her shoulder, just staring out into the woods.

It couldn't be easy on her, knowing that she didn't have anything that strong of Dad's with her anymore. That thought and watching her just standing there brought tears to my eyes.

They would come, any day now. My mother had spoken so many times of this night. The night that could be our last. Still, it didn't matter how many times she spoke about it, trying to get me strong for this evening, I wasn't ready to part ways with her. There was still so much I needed to know, but she said I knew enough. I would learn the rest in Revera and the less I knew now, the better off I would be when they did come.

THE NEXT DAY I FOUND A PLATINUM
blonde at the table, reading from a newspaper.

"The color suits you," I smiled down at her and plunged myself onto the opposite chair.

She smiled. "They say a change is as good as a holiday. In my case it's probably something like 'time to find your old self again'."

I laughed. My mom was a natural platinum blonde, Tim used to joke about that on numerous occasions, but she refused to go back her normal color. Now I knew why. She was unrecognizable as a red head.

For the next two days we talked about so many things. We actually spoke about boys and it was sad not knowing if my mother would ever get to be there when I was grown up and ready for them.

Still, the drilling about what I had do when the Pursuers came, got worse. It became an hourly thing. I could even say it in my sleep if I had to.

I woke up and stared at the morning sky filling the room. Every day now, I thanked God for another morning with my mother. They were getting short now. Breakfast was the best time of the day. Mom would talk to me about so many things, about how I'd changed her and the full life I'd given her. I knew she wasn't ready to let me go either. She wanted so much more than just fifteen years, but the cards weren't in our favor and the minutes were precious, we didn't know how many more we would share together. I began to understand what she meant by a couple of hours spent with loved ones felt like nothing.

At ten, I would go about my wielding lesson. We didn't do it outside anymore and did it inside the fighting room. She was right. The more I did it, the easier it got. It wasn't as hard as the first time, I didn't even have to imagine the Shadow Hound anymore.

When I opened my eyes, my dagger was lying in the heap of golden dust. I had three daggers now, all locked up inside the chest. They didn't vanish like Leigh's had in the dream which was another good sign. Strong blood flowed through my veins.

"Tell you what," Mom said as she walked over to the chest. "Let's try this with a bow."

"Mom!"

"You're ready, Chas. It's not so hard." Mom had an overexcited tone to her voice as she ran to her room where she kept Dad's bow.

I giggled as I watched her exiting the door. She came back two minutes later with Dad's bow wrapped in a blanket.

The minute she placed his bow without the arrows or string in my hand, I started to second guess myself. I'd only seen it once, from Leigh inside my Initiation dream. He was really good. But I know I wasn't ready for this.

"You can do it, sweetheart. It just takes practice. Imagine yourself pulling back the string and imagine the arrow."

"That's a lot of imagining, mom."

She chuckled as she stood right behind me and I pulled the imaginary string of the bow back. "Take a deep breath, visualize the arrow, feel the strong grip of the string. When you are sure you've got it, release."

I closed my eyes and imagined what my arrow should look like. I put strain on my arm and pretend it was a string that couldn't move back anymore. Then I imagined Leigh, the way he'd released his arrows and they magically appeared in thin air. Long, pointy, golden arrows. I let go and opened my eyes immediately.

No arrows.

"It's okay. Try again." My mother smiled and I raised the bow to my shoulder again.

After the umpteenth time, when my shoulders ached and I couldn't pull back the imaginary string anymore, I lowered the bow.

"I can't do this anymore, mom."

"You have to try, Chas. I don't know how much time I have left."

"Mom, I don't feel my sand. I think I used it's quota for today." I gave a small chuckle, but didn't get the same response from mother. Mom just stared at me with huge round eyes. "Mom, It was a joke, unless—"

"It's not that, Chas. They're here."

PART II

CHAPTER NINE
PARTING WAYS

"WHAT DO YOU MEAN THEY...NO!"

"When other Light Casters are near, Initiates, or Level One Casters feel a bit drained, which stops the sand from flowing naturally. We didn't train enough today for you to feel so tired Chas."

"Are they in the house?" I didn't want it to be today. I still needed to know so much more.

"Close your eyes."

"Mom, I'm not ready."

"Neither am I." She stroke my face gently. "But we have no choice. Now close your eyes and do what we practiced."

"What if we just stay here?"

"They'll find us, Chas and the plan will be ruined. I can't go back to Oblivion and you won't survive there either. Now do as you're told."

I closed my eyes and knew that Mom was going to

scratch herself on her face to make it look natural. I took the deepest breath I could master and screamed.

I opened my eyes as Mom put a thick rope around my wrists behind my back and a bandage over my mouth. I couldn't help but give her a look of fear. What if I screwed up and give away the fact that she was my mom?

I watched her make the transformation, her eyes became dark, black and an ice cold finger traced down my spine, making my skin crawl. Millions if goosebumps rippled on my arms. She looked like pure evil and I closed my eyes, trying to remember her beautiful blue eyes. I knew they'd had to change to play her part. To make her role in this convincing and become the Shadow Caster she once was.

The door to the arena flew open, but it wasn't an arena anymore. It was the inside of a huge closet.

"Found her!" A woman with a pale complex, wearing white clothes with a short haircut that fit with her outfit yelled.

She grabbed me around my arm and pulled me gently out of the closet. The bandage over my mouth disappeared instantly.

"Where is she?" A male asked. He was huge with raven black hair tied into a pony tale. He wore red and white leather paints and had a pair of sunglasses resting on his head. His jacket was pure white, just like the woman who'd ripped of the bandages covering my mouth.

When I didn't answer, he switched over to Mandarin.

"English is fine," I whispered.

"Your name?"

"Chastity Blake."

"Where is the Shadow Caster?"

"The Shadow what?" I said, just like my mother had drilled into me. I know nothing. The man gave me a blank stare before he nodded once. A couple of other guys, one wearing a cowboy hat, and two dark men with long coats resembling Ponytail's, which was called Tom, gear, started moving silently in the cabin. All of them had weapons in front of them. The cowboy was walking in front with a huge crossbow while the other two held guns.

A small Asian dude walked in and stayed closed to us.

"Do you know what you are?" The woman asked.

I shook my head.

Why hadn't I sticked to my mother's version,? She'd drilled it into my head over and over and asked *what*, the way I had that night when Leigh asked me the same question.

"Why was this woman after you?" The woman asked again.

Fear crawled into my gut and I couldn't answer. Where was my mom? I remembered looking at her and when this woman opened the door, she was gone.

"I'm not going to hurt you. I promise." She gave me a soft smile.

"A couple of days ago, my hands were covered with sand…without me picking any up." My tone was shaking, breaking up, and I sounded scared. It sounded like I didn't make any sense. I looked at both of them, her and then the Asian dude as the woman exchanged a look with him.

The ponytail came back down the stairs and stopped in front of us. "What was the color of your sand?"

"What do you mean, what color? The color of sand. It was light brown."

"Golden," the woman asked again and I nodded. "She's one of us, the Shadow Caster was trying to change her."

"How do you know this woman?" Ponytail asked again.

"I don't. She took me while I was on the street in Chicago. I woke up here."

"Where is she now?"

A loud, breaking noise from upstairs made me scream. *Don't do anything, you know nothing*, Mom's voice yelled inside my head.

"Fox, get her out of here, now," Ponytail yelled as one of the dark men came tumbling down the stairs and landed face down on the carpet. He didn't get back up. The cowboy and the other guy was still upstairs. I had no choice but to follow the woman that looked like a white mouse.

"It's going to be fine. I promise."

At the door, I was pushed out of the way and I watched as one of the sofas crashed into the door inches from us.

"Stay here, don't move." The girl, who I assumed was called Fox and not rat said as she went after her team members.

I peeked around the corner and saw Mom's black dust in the form of the whip, her favorite weapon. She was really good at fighting against all of them. Bodies wearing white flew a couple of paces away and then I heard that same buzzing sound that I had heard that day in the attic, and by the shouts and fists hammering the floor, I knew she had escaped the same way we'd came here. She was safe.

"She's just gone," the Asian man that crawled from under the table said, sounding a bit annoyed.

"You know who that was?" Ponytail asked.

"Vinicola? It can't be," Cowboy dude said with a bad Texan accent. *Vinicola, Vinique.*

"No, John. Vinicola disappeared a long time ago."

"I remember. You don't have to remind me of that night," Cowboy said and then he looked back at me. "The question is, why'd she try to recruit this one?"

They all stared at me.

"Are we talking about *the* Vinicola?"

The woman slapped the Asian dude hard on his back. "Henry, there's only one Shadow Caster who can handle a whip like that, and it's Vinicola."

The cowboy dude laughed.

"It's not funny. Selene is not going to like this one bit. Knowing that the Shadow Caster who killed one of her best Light Casters is back..." Ponytail shut all of them up. "It'll be on us, all of it." I wanted to smile. My mother was famous and the Light Caster Ponytail was speaking of, could only be my father. By the look on these people's faces, my mother wasn't just famous, she was very dangerous too. Then Ponytail walked toward me with huge strides.

"Your sand?"

"Tom," Fox said.

"Fox," his head snapped back at hers. "Remember who's in charge here. You had your chance."

"I'm just saying, she's been through enough."

"Still we have to make sure that she wasn't turned." He stood right in front of me and started putting his fingers on my lips to look inside my mouth. I pulled away hard, pushing his hands away.

"Tom!"

"Your sand."

I shook my head. I wasn't in the right place to wield it now and Mom did warn me about what could happen if I wasn't in the right place. "I don't know how to make it come."

"Your sand," he said again.

The woman's hand grabbed him gently by his arm. "She doesn't know what she is yet. She can't even wield her sand properly, just take her to Revera."

"You know we can't take her there if she's a Shadow Caster."

"She's only a child." She grunted back at him. "I don't care who's in charge. This is still my team and I say we take her back to Revera."

The two of them stared each other down.

"You heard Fox, Tom." The cowboy said and touched my arm softly, guiding me toward the exit.

A grunt escaped Tom's lips and he pushed past Cowboy and me to get out first.

Outside, two huge SUV's were parked on the grass. *What was it with these people and SUV's?*

They looked similar to the SUV Beavis and Butthead had driven that day when they'd picked me up from school.

They were big and black with tinted windows. Inside was all black and leathery and I took a deep sniff as the scent of new car still lingered in the air.

Cowboy climbed in after me and Fox opened the opposite door. I knew I was going to be smashed in the middle like a piece of ham between two slices of buttered bread.

Tom slid in behind the steering wheel and the Asian dude called shotgun, while the other two guys took the first SUV.

Tom spoke in some code over his ear and mouth pieces that were still attached to him, and the only thing that I could make out was that the SUV in front of us was going another way, and of course over and out.

I caught Fox's eye just as we drove off, and tge rat-like woman gave me a soft smile.

Cowboy, on the other side of me, slid his hat over his eyes so that just his nose and mouth stick out.

Something told me that this was going to be a long ride.

"So," the Asian dude turned around his seat to look at me. "You talk the talk?"

I frowned and looked at Fox for some indication to what he was talking about.

"Mandarin," she said.

"Oh, no." I shook my head. "I don't speak Mandarin, or Cantonese."

Mr. Sandman, a very old song that used to be one of Mom's favorites played over the radio. The Asian dude smiled at Tom as he turned it slightly louder. "I like this tune."

Fox smiled and stared out the tinted window shaking her head softly while the Asian man kept singing softly along with the chorus.

I huffed as the words of the giddy song filled the car. The reality was so far from what the woman was singing about. Mr. Sandman was indeed a fairy tale version parents told their kids to help them have sweet dreams, but in reality, there was good vs. evil, both badass at fighting with weapons and sand that appeared from deep within when they needed it.

They were Casters, and that was something I didn't know if I was cut out for or not.

THE RIDE TO WHAT TOM WAS REFERRING to as thePassageway, was far from the cabin in Montana. It was hard for me not to cry. I didn't know if my mother was safe or not and being stuck with people I didn't know made the situation even worse.

I was scared and thought about the past couple of weeks. My life had turned from jealous girls and abs and asses to golden sand and wielding weapons.

The only one who spoke to me was the Asian guy. His name was Henry, and he was as geeky as they get. Still he didn't speak Mandarin or Cantonese. He didn't even have an accent. I didn't ask him what his age was, as I silently wished for him to just shut the hell up.

I didn't know what he was doing on this mission, he didn't look like the fighting type. He'd been sitting in a corner, or underneath a table, way out of danger while the others were fighting against Mom.

The curves of my lips turned up slightly every five seconds or so as he kept speaking. Henry carried on babbling like a little schoolgirl until Tom literally growled at him. He turned around after rolling his eyes and everything became silent again.

The SUV turned into a very small town. It was dark but you could still see some light around the edges of the sky. It lit up the dark streets where most of the street lights were out. The only ones that worked were right in front of places that were still open.

I turned my head and looked past Fox. A port which

still operated had about ten or twelve boats bobbing in the water and a lighthouse shone in the background. The wind blew against the car as they came to a halt at the stop sign.

I didn't see a beach, just pebbles and rocks where the water crashed against land.

The SUV drove slowly down the street again, past a convenience store and a pharmacy. A hardware store and a small diner stood on the other side of the street.

Tom kept on driving the speed limit as I looked through tinted windows, this time, out of Cowboy's window, as he was still sleeping. The soft snores that he let out told me that much.

By the second stop sign, Tom turned left and the road carried on for another couple of miles. When they finally came to a halt and Tom switched the engine off, I could see the outline of what looked like another lighthouse. This one was badly in need of some TLC.

Fox reached over me and give Cowboy a hard shake. "Wake up, we're here."

My head snapped to Fox. "Where is here?"

"The Passageway," Tom snapped and I lowered my head. I didn't like the demeanor and vibe that was emanating off of him. I knew that whoever Tom was, he didn't like me at all.

"Don't worry about Tom," Fox spoke softly. "He's like that around everyone." She winked which made me smile. I liked the rat. I could tell that she was a really good fighter and for some reason used to be this team's leader. I really wanted to know why she wasn't the leader anymore.

Tom looked around fast before he opened the old creaking white door to the lighthouse.

"After you," Fox said and I took a deep breath. I had no idea how an entire Passageway was going to fit into a lighthouse that looked as if it was held together by termites holding hands, but I followed Tom and Henry none the less. We climbed the wooden stairs that looked as if they were going to snap in two at any second.

I tried to sidestep every hole and crack I could see inside the steps, and hated how much noise they were making.

"Phil," Tom said softly and Henry's laughter came out in a mocking tone right in front of me.

As I mounted the last couple of steps three men appeared. A man in his mid-forties with a huge stomach and bushy eyebrows shook Tom's hand and gave Henry a slap shake.

"And who is this?" he asked as he looked at me.

"This is Chastity Blake," Fox said and winked at me.

"Chas, meet Phil. He is the Tector, the guardian of many entries that lead to the Outer and Revera."

The Outer? I had no clue what she was talking about but I smiled. Still, a bit unsure about all of this as my mind couldn't comprehend how on earth the Passageway, whatever that was, fit into this old lighthouse, but then again, I still struggled to accept that whenever I was angry or scared, gold sand sprouted from my hands which could actually make other humans sleep or hurt ones that weren't from this world.

"By that cut on your face, I would say this wasn't as easy as you thought, hey John?"

Cowboy chuckled. "We managed fine, old man."

Phil smiled, stared at the door he was guarding and pulled a huge bundle of keys from his pocket.

"Is it true that Vinicola is back?" Phil asked softly

but I couldn't hear Tom's reply. I only knew that he spoke about me as Phil's eyes lingered on me for a couple of seconds. He finally went back to his task and the keys rattled again until he found the right one.

He opened the door and we all stepped inside and started to cough at the dust that had accumulated over each and every object that was in the small room. From what it looked like there was a couch with a dirty old garment covering it, a cupboard and a mirror. I gave Fox a look that was filled with questions, the most important one was what the hell were we doing here?

"Think it would kill you to dust now and then?" Tom asked and Henry laughed.

Tom shot him a look. "I can't wait for you to hoot again."

Henry slapped Tom on the shoulder and I thought that maybe this dude really had some sort of death wish or something. "You love me, admit it."

But Tom just shook his head and cleared his throat. He walked up to the mirror, picked a rag up from the floor and wiped it sort of clean.

Tom took out a marker and started drawing signs on the mirror. Plenty of squares, circles and odd triangle shapes. When he finish drawing in a circle shape around the mirror, he tapped softly in the middle. A soft buzz came from the mirror and then it seemed as if the mirror shuddered slightly. The dust fell off the mirror and it cleaned itself. I had to open and close my eyes, because I thought I was dreaming. Yet, after everything I'd learned the past few days, I knew dreams were as real as you and me.

We all stood back waiting for the process to finish and when the shapes Tom drew on the mirror started to move around and formed a huge symbol in the middle of the mirror, the substance turned from glass to a jelly, watery substance.

"Ready Chas?" Fox asked me.

I gave her the look. The one that screamed that I would never be ready for this shit, but I guessed I didn't have a choice so I nodded.

Phil slapped Henry hard on the back which made me jump. "Time to squawk again my boy."

"I don't squawk," Henry said in a slightly dull tone and turned to look at me. His smile reached his eyes again. "See you later Chas." He winked and ran straight for the mirror.

The minute he dove through, all sorts of colors came sprawling out. It was simply stunning and I couldn't help myself as I watched in awe as bright yellows, pinks, purples, blues and slight reds flashed past me.

"Don't take too long, Fox," Tom said before he disappeared through the mirror too.

"You want to go next?" John asked us, and Fox nodded, before she looked at me.

"Chas, it's the only way to enter through to the Outer."

"What is the…"

"Shush, I'll explain later. Right now, you need to pay attention. Just hold your breath as you go through the mirror. Close your eyes. Although it may feel like you are going to suffocate, know that you are perfectly fine. Tom and Henry are waiting on the other side. The fog is cold, so brace yourself. But only for a little while."

I just stared at her.

"It's the only way."

"Fox?" John asked.

"John," Fox cut him off.

"Now close your eyes and take a deep breath."

I did as she said, while looking at John. *What did he want to say, when she cut him off like that?*

I didn't look, although I was dying too, but my fear of losing my eyes or whatever was way too big to peek.

My finger touched the mirror. It felt cold as my arm reached further inside. The freezing temperature almost felt as if it was burning into my arm, into my bones and when pain started to emerged, I grunted and pulled back.

A hand connected hard with my back which made me fall into the mirror. A horrible, excruciating pain tore through my flesh, and everything I was.

My heart beat so fast as I crunched down on my teeth. A deep grunt from within made this feeling seem ten thousand times worse.

Then the same stabbing pain I had only experienced once before, inside my Initiation dream when I was standing before that mirror, made my skull want to snap in two.

I couldn't take it anymore and clutched my head and screamed. The freezing fog immediately engulfed my screams and ran its course down my throat and into my lungs. Pain and a fright I'd never experienced before overwhelmed my entire existence and nothing I did, made any of it easier.

I couldn't cough, even though I tried with all my might. It felt as if the fog just pushed itself inside of me, and we weren't a match at all.

Then the pull came and my body connected hard with the surface. I coughed, gasped for air, and screamed one last time before all the pain just disappeared. Like none of it had happened at all.

Tears were close by, even though I felt that they were a sign of weakness. Maybe I was weak, but at that moment I didn't care.

I couldn't open my eyes to find out where I was, and I just lay on the cold hard floor.

My hair and clothes were wet, I didn't jnow why because I couldn't feel any water, just a freezing pain. My heart beat so fast it was the only thing I could hear.

"Chastity," Tom's voice finally got through and I could sense a figure kneeling beside me.

"Open your eyes!"

I did and saw a pale white hand touching mine. Even though I was staring at his hand right on top of mine, I couldn't feel it and it was a very strange sensation.

I lifted up my stuffy head, looked up at him and stared with knitted eyebrows at his huge figure.

A big, grey owl flew past him which caught my eye and I looked at the hopeless bird trying to find a resting spot.

What was an owl doing here?

I thought it was strange that after what I'd just gone through, that was the number one question on my mind.

Forcing my gaze from the owl, I found us stranded inside a cave, with no openings, only walls and walls, with this gooey substance pooling at my feet. The bright light from the substance made my eyes hurt and I looked away, but not before I saw half my body still drenched in it. I couldn't feel its cold or the wet anymore, only the cold of the hard surface.

I slowly pulled my legs from the liquid that surrounded us inside the cave.

I looked again, looked back at Tom, while my heart

started to beat faster again. *This couldn't be happening.* My eyes had been closed, I was a thousand percent sure of it.

Then why cant I see color?

CHAPTER TEN
THE OUTER

FOX AND TOM CAME WALKING OUT OF THE bright lake a couple of minutes later. Both their coats were drenched and judging by the grunts coming from John, he didn't like being wet.

"Is she okay?" Fox asked as she passed Tom and walked to where I'd stationed myself against the wall of the cave.

"You should've mention the Clencing to her, Fox."

"She wouldn't have gone through that mirror, Tom. I did what I had to do."

Tom shook his head. It was the only compassion he'd shown me since we met.

"Chastity," Fox said and kneeled before me. "I'm sorry. I…"

"You should've mentioned something. I could've prepared myself for pain. I thought I was going to die."

Fox closed her eyes. "Would you truly have gone through if you knew what waited for you Chas?" She asked and opened her eyes again. Her hand touched my arm, yet I still couldn't feel it. I just stared at her hand. *What did they do to me?*

"What is this place, why through the mirror? What is the Clencing he spoke about?"

She looked over her shoulder at Tom, who glanced down at his watch. "We have time," he said and she nodded.

"The Clencing is a process that all Dream Casters must go through. It doesn't matter whether you are light or dark. It strips you of your human DNA, the thing that makes your body yours, and reprints another, and that is why there is pain. We can only be seen by other Casters inside the Domain, Chastity. Humans aren't able to see us. They don't see our dust, they only experience what we wield for them. The Clencing is a must, and one I'm not very fond of."

"So my body is no longer human?"

"It is, it's just not human to the Nomads."

"So what am I back in my world?"

"Inside the Domain, you are invisible."

That hit me quite hard, and I don't know why I felt as if I'd fallen asleep and woken up inside one of my novels. "So what, next you are going to tell me that Jace, Clary and Edward Cullen are real?"

She squinted slightly. "I don't know who you are referring too."

"Of course you don't," I said and got up from the cold floor. I huffed slightly. The funny part of not being able to feel was that I could still feel the cold, not on my skin, but deep inside of me, as if it had made a home in my bones and organs. It was the only thing I could feel and I wondered if there was any warmth that would make me feel human again. Scratch that, I wasn't human anymore, well not to humans that is.

This really sucked so much.

"Look, I had no choice."

"Yeah, I heard you the first time," I sort of snapped at her and wiped my hands on my wet soggy jeans.

I found John hitting his hat a couple of times against his leg.

"You okay?" he asked without looking at me, as I stationed myself near him.

"I'll live," I huffed again. Still making jokes, and not knowing if any of it was real or not. "So what now, we tap our heels or something and say Revera three times real fast and poof, we're out of here?"

John smiled.

"It's not the Wizard of Oz, Chas. It's Revera and we are not going to Revera just yet, we need to make a stop at one of the Compounds in the Outer."

Again that name, what was the Outer?

I knew I wouldn't get the answer from him. "Then how do we get out of here?" I looked at the ceiling which was still pretty dark, but the bright light from the mirror liquid made the cave wall slightly visible. "Cause I hate to break it to you, Cowboy, but there is no sign of a door or anything."

"We don't use doors to get into the Outer." Fox walked toward us. "But you are going to have to experience a bit more pain, Chas."

PAIN…AS IF IT WAS MY BEST FRIEND ALL
of a sudden. Pain that Clare had caused me for four weeks, pain of losing my mother and lying about it,

pain. It was constantly around me and I hated the existence of it so much that I wanted to puke.

What pain, Fox didn't say. I guessed she didn't have the stomach to explain it to me.

The only thing I figured out was that the cave worked like a clock as Tom kept gazing at his watch, an action that was really tugging on my nerves.

Then a slight rumble came. The cave shuddered slightly but not to the extend where loose rocks fell to the floor. When it stopped, Tom walked into the other side of the lake, held out his arm and whistled. The owl came and landed on his arm.

For some reason I'd forgotten about Henry. He'd disappeared through the mirror with us, but the only person that had made it out was Tom and this owl.

Then what Phil had said jumped into my mind. *It's time to squawk again…I don't squawk, I hoot.*

"Henry is an owl!" I yelled which made all of them look at me as if I was crazy. Tom shook his head, the owl hooted while Fox and John laughed.

"He's an Anitule, which mean that in the Domain he transforms into a human. Anitules are very sacred to Light Casters."

The name I'd heard before but I pretended it was foreign. I remembered what Mom had said about her Shadow Hound, or what they called Nimgolians.

"Fox, we have to go," Tom ordered and Fox pulled me by the arm. A grip I still couldn't feel.

We walked into the lake again. "Take a deep breath, Chas."

"How big? How long are we going to be under?"

She sighed, "See this is what I was talking about. We don't have much time, Chastity, now take a deep breath."

I took a couple of deep breaths and watched how Tom and the owl disappeared into the water. How could an owl swim? It didn't make any sense.

"We need to go, now." She gave me a motherly look and I nodded. I shook off the fear of going through excruciating pain again, and walked into the lake as fast as I could. My jeans instantly became heavy as they connected with the wet of the substance.

I dove in and swam a little with my head above the water. The bright light from the water made me close my eyes. Then I took a mother of a breath and dove down.

I didn't open my eyes but felt a current guiding me to where I needed to go.

Then I started to turn in the water like Leigh's arrow had that night in the dream where we'd met.

I turned so fast that I didn't know what was up or down anymore.

I connected with something hard, and I felt the dull pound inside my head just before an excruciating pain jolted though my mind, but for some reason I didn't lose consciousness. I couldn't feel the pain on the outside, but inside my skull it was burning like fire.

The silent grunt didn't help, I lost my breath and twirled into the water for a long time.

No end was in sight and I knew for sure that this time I was going to die. My lungs started to burn, in need of air that would never come. My muscles ached from twirling around like a piece of crap flushed down the drain. I felt like crap, the worst kind.

Memories of my entire life flashed through my mind. Mom was constantly in them. Clare too, the

Clare who used to be my friend. We laughed at something funny. Then other memories, one of me as an adult, the future of what could've been. I was happy, I'd found someone and we walked hand in hand. I couldn't see his face but I knew I was extremely happy.

The pain wasn't that hard to deal with anymore, now that I knew I wasn't going to make it.

My mind started to shut down, memories disappeared until there was nothing but the dark.

VOICES IN THE DISTANCE SPOKE. I COULDN'T HEAR what they were saying, they were so far away.

Then I heard my name.

"Chastity?" I heard it again.

Water spilled out of my mouth and I coughed. "She's coming to," Fox said. "Give her space, John."

An owl hooted, and for some reason it sounded relieved.

"Chastity?" Fox voice was softer. She didn't yell it anymore.

I opened my eyes. They burned, and I closed them again. I'd never felt so tired in my entire life.

"Don't sleep, wake up," Fox said a bit harder this time and I opened my eyes partially.

"I can't," I croaked out. "So tired."

"I know, baby, but you need to wake up."

"Fox, she almost drowned, she must be exhausted," John tried.

"She needs to stay awake, just until we reach the Compound then she can sleep as much as she wants," she said to John. I could swear there was a cuss word in-between that sentence but I didn't care anymore. Heck, ever since I came to this world, a part of me just wanted to cuss the whole time.

"Now, wake up." A hard slap connected with my face. It brought back pain with a snap of a finger.

"I'm awake," I said, my eyes still burning like hell. Both their figures were blurry, but to my surprise color came through.

John picked me up.

"John, she needs to stay awake," Fox grunted at him.

"I heard you the first time, she'll stay awake. I'll make sure of it. But she is exhausted Fox, she's been through hell and back. A little compassion won't hurt anyone."

Fox mumbled something and it felt so good in John's arms that I really just wished I could sleep.

"Chastity," he shook me and my eyes flew open again. Tom mumbled something from the front and I could see small lights mounted to the ceiling passing us every five seconds.

John's eyes looked down at me every five seconds too as he walked extremely fast.

A door opened and I closed my eyes again as a cold breeze rushed over my body.

"Chastity, wake up."

"I'm awake," I grunted.

"Then open your eyes. I know you are tired, but you need to stay awake just a couple more minutes."

Voices, loads of voices, like we were in a crowd appeared. Then cars made it in there too. Curiosity of where we were now grew and I opened my eyes again. We were in some sort of city. The people were minding their own business and the city sounds lingered in the back.

No one asked if we needed help. I knew that it must have looked strange seeing the four of us with a wet owl on a man's arm, drenched in wet clothes. I knew we were wet, I could hear the slof, slof, as we walked, still, nobody offered to help.

I opened my eyes again as John shook me like I was a rag doll.

"If you close your eyes one more time, I swear I will make you walk the rest of the way."

"I'm awake, I promise," I croaked softly again.

The bright lights of the building that we walked under didn't help much with my burning eyes, but I had no choice, as I knew the minute John would put me down, I would fall flat on my face and snore.

Hooves galloping on the turf made me turn my head and I saw a horse with one of those carriages couples like to take.

A park was on the opposite street.

It didn't make much sense as I could swear this was the Domain. It looked like a city back home.

"Where are we?"

"The Domain, but it's part of the Outer too."

I shook my head slightly, which brought on a horrible ringing sound. "It doesn't make any sense."

"It doesn't have to now. Just concentrate on staying awake. We are almost there."

"Where?" I asked.

"The Compound. There is a healer and he will take care of you, Chas, but you need to stay awake."

"I'm awake," I whispered again and felt the urge to close my eyes once more.

I did, and to my surprise, opened them again five

seconds later.

We were past the city lights now. Most of the sounds of cars and galloping hooves with strangers just walking by were gone.

I kept staring at the stars. They were so bright and I wondered why I never stared at their beauty before now.

We passed through a big old steel gate that made a horrible squeaking sound and trees blocked my view from the stars.

A hard knock on a door came from in front and then a woman's voice acknowledged Tom as she opened the door.

"We've got her, but she almost drowned in the Lining," Tom spoke fast.

"Come in, come in." The woman's voice was full of alarm but still sweet.

The warmth came first, it caressed my skin and it felt wonderful.

"Chastity." John shook me one last time.

"I'm awake," I said but I didn't open my eyes. Screw him, I was where he said I needed to be and I could sleep.

"Put her on the couch, I'll get Elliot," the woman said.

"Thanks Ginny," Fox spoke and I felt the soft couch on my back and the softness just urged me to drift away again.

A LIGHT SO BRIGHT SHONE IN MY EYES.
I hated it and disliked whoever was disturbing my sleep pattern.

Then it disappeared slightly, as I could still see the

blotch of bright behind my eyelids.

"There is no damage," A manly voice said. "Get her upstairs, the first room on the left and leave her be. She'll be fine."

"Thanks, Elliot," Fox said.

I felt myself being carried up a staircase and placed down on another couch.

"Scoot," Fox's voice came again. "Thanks, John."

"Hey, you did nothing wrong. There is no other way to Clence."

She huffed. "Yeah, I know. Still it doesn't help with the crappy feeling about all this."

"Fox, she'll be fine."

No reply came and then I felt her shaking me softly. "Come, Chas. You can sleep as long as you want to but we need to get you out of these clothes."

"Can't you just use your sand or something to cast a drying spell?"

Fox giggled. "Unfortunately it doesn't work like that. Now sit up, let's get these wet clothes off you."

I did what she said, or tried to do. Still I couldn't open my eyes.

Shit, I'd never felt this crappy before. My stomach turned, my head spun and it felt like I was coming down with a fever.

She tugged and pulled on my hoody, then my shirt and pants were next and I hated that she pulled off my underwear too.

I was completely vulnerable and couldn't even lift a finger to help myself.

I'd never experienced being tired like this before. Not even after Rollins' worst ballet class, and she was a master at giving those.

When a warm garment fell softly over my body, and a bed underneath, I didn't wait to feel the covers being pulled over me.

This was it, I couldn't stay awake another minute longer and I drifted away faster than counting to three

CHAPTER ELEVEN
THE COMPOUND

I TOOK A DEEP BREATH AND THE URGE TO stretch had me lifting my arms above my head.

It felt good.

Mom was probably cooking up a storm this Saturday morning….then it all came back to me at once.

There was no Mom, or home. The last thing I remembered was being carried by John, somewhere safe…the Compound, wherever that was.

"Two days, that is a record, Chastity," a voice to my left said and I found a man, in his late forties, maybe early fifties with blonde hair sitting near me. He had soft blue eyes and a slight scar over his left eyebrow.

He sat casually in a chair with a newspaper in his hands and black framed glasses resting on his nose.

He took them off and put down the newspaper.

"Usually when your kind come to us, they sleep an

entire week."

"Wait, I slept for two days?"

He chuckled.

Yeah, I usually pondered on the not-so-intelligent questions. But I couldn't help it. I was wired differently and the smallest, unimportant things usually come up first.

"Are you sure you don't want to sleep some more? You've been through a great deal."

"No, I'm fine. I don't think I've ever slept like this before." I pushed myself up straight.

My muscles were still sore, as if I'd just done a million different types of exercises.

I looked around. The room had a very old ambience to it. The walls were brown, the lighting was in a form of a chandelier and the bed was posted, with white embroidered linen.

"Where am I?"

"You don't remember Fox and the rest bringing you here?"

"Vaguely."

He smiled softly. "My name is Elliot. I am the Guardian of this Compound inside the Outer."

My head started to ache just listening to the foreign words again.

"What is the Outer?"

He leaned forward in his chair and rested his arms on his knees. "The Outer is like a barrier between the human world or Domain like Reverians like to call it, and Revera. Lots of things happen in the Outer. We deal with many Shadow Casters and we keep the Domain safe as well as Revera. Nobody can go to Revera without going through the Outer."

"So this is like an invisible world inside the world?"

He smiled again. "Something like that. We like to teach in the field, it will help you understand it better."

Teach? Nobody said anything about classes.

He got up and took a couple of steps toward the door. "You are safe here, Chastity. I'll send Stacey up with a fresh pair of clothes."

"Thank you," I whispered still dumbfounded about the whole teaching thing and what he'd meant by *teaching in the field.* I watched him leave.

Oh crap, crappy, crap, I hope he wasn't speaking about facing Shadow Hounds and their Casters.

My mind only thought about that for a long time. If I had to face Shadow Casters, would my sand turn dark? Mom never mentioned anything like that and I hated not knowing what it was I should do.

A girl with dark brown hair and the brightest pink hair piece I'd ever seen walked into the room. She was all leather, leather pants, with a leather vest over a pink t-shirt.

"Hi, I'm Stacey, I bet you have plenty of questions huh? It's not like we get a lot of Diddles. No, Casters are usually born in Revera and we chose the crazy of it all," she spoke extremely fast.

I shook my head. "Diddles?" It sounded like someone that was extremely shallow.

She giggled. "A word I came up with for someone like you."

I raised my one eyebrow.

"You know, that had no idea what they are until they are told."

She wss clearly a huge morning person which I wasn't, and seemed to babble a lot.

"Here, Elliot asked me to bring these up for you. We're more or less the same build, they might be slightly long. It's a mission to find something that fits my length."

"Thanks," I took the clothes that she handed over to me.

"So, Fox told us that you were kidnapped by a Shadow Caster, and not just any Shadow Caster. You get that she's one of the deadliest out there, right? I wonder what kept her away for so long, we always thought she'd died the night Graig did."

Graig. Was that my father's name? I could've sworn Mom mentioned someone like that before. It slipped out once, a long time ago. It had to be.

The girl was still babbling. "That must have been horrible. Do you know what she wanted with you?"

I shook my head. I didn't want to speak about my mom again, to lie to all of them.

"It's so weird. We all thought Vinicola was dead," she babbled on and I wondered if she ever stopped. "And then she made her appearance just like that. You can be so glad Tom and Fox found you. Vinicola is not someone to mess with. Shadow Casters can do serious damage to a new Caster, for some reason they think you guys can be persuaded to turn dark, which is actually silly…" she stopped in mid-sentence and looked at me who just gawked at her. "I'm sorry. I know I can be overwhelming. Believe me, it's a curse." She giggled at her own little joke.

I smiled, not knowing what to say and knowing *it's okay*, would just give her the right to carry on, and it was the last thing I wanted her to do.

"I'll leave you be. When you're ready, just follow

the steps, through the hall on your left and last door is the kitchen."

A sarcastic *wow* was all I could think when she left the room. I did not want to know what she was like on a mission. How did they keep her mouth shut for more than five seconds?

I got dressed and followed the steps down like she said.

Three hallways were right in front of me.

For some reason I couldn't remember which one she said I should take and no sound came from any of them, so I took the one that was right in front of me.

It was slightly dark, and had plenty of portraits of people wearing clothing from different eras.

There was even one of Marie-Antoinette. I knew it was her because we'd done an entire history lesson about the woman during the French Revolution who wanted to give her starving people cake instead of bread.

Benjamin Franklin also made his appearance.

What was royalty and a Founding Father doing amongst them?

I opened the door that was at the end of the hallway and found a huge library with plenty of books open on one of the tables.

I started to page through the first one.

It had an old smell to it, and when I lifted it up to see it's cover, the title was barely legible.

"It's the Book of Nightmares," a voice said from behind me.

It didn't belong to Elliot, but to another blonde guy that could easily be his son. He was wearing a jeans with a Metallica t-shirt and his hair was as messy as it could get.

I stopped looking through the book and folded my arms in front of me.

"Name is Max, you must be Chastity."

"Chas is fine," I replied. "I couldn't remember which hallway to take, sorry."

He chuckled. "I don't blame you, Stacey has that ability to make you so confused that you don't know whether you should go up or down."

I giggled.

"You rest well?"

"Yeah, thanks."

"Good. I promise you, you're going to need all of your strength."

He walked toward the door and the vibe he gave told me that I should follow him.

He took me straight to the kitchen and disappeared again.

Fox looked up from her plate of eggs and gave me a huge smile. "Two days, that must be a record."

A woman with shoulder length, red hair giggled. She was slightly older than Fox and really pretty and friendly too.

"Welcome to the Compound, Chastity. I'm Ginny, come sit and have breakfast."

I smiled at her. No need to introduce myself it seemed all of them already knew who I was.

I took the space right across from Fox.

"What happened? I told you to take a deep breath."

"Something hit me on the head, and that was when the breath disappeared too."

"I'm so sorry about what happened, Chas. I…"

"It's not your fault, Fox." Elliot had just walked into

the kitchen.

"Still, she could've died and it would've been on me."

"No, it would've been on Tom. They aren't your team anymore. You need to let that go."

She huffed and smiled. "They will always be my team Elliot, no matter what Selene says or does to punish me."

I didn't like the vibe that was starting to form.

"She's just worried about you, this is not a punishment, Fox."

"Then why does it feel like that?"

He smiled. "Maybe it's something you can take up with her when you return to Revera."

She sighed. "Yes, sure." She dug into her scrambled eggs again just as Ginny put a plate of toast, eggs and bacon in front of me.

"Where is everybody?" I asked.

"Tom and Henry are training with John and Margot. Max, well he is always doing his own thing, and Stacey…" Fox shook her head which made everyone laugh including me.

"You need to get used to Stacey, Chas. She has the tendency to get extremely excited over the smallest things," Ginny said, putting it lightly.

"She's nice," I replied and put a fork full of egg into my mouth.

"So how long before Chastity can go to Revera?"

"What, I have to stay here?" It slipped out and Fox gave me another guilty look.

"The Compound is also a training facility, Chas. Remember what I told you in the room."

I nodded and kept quiet. I didn't know who knew

what and if this was going to be my new home, I didn't want to make trouble for anybody.

To be honest, I felt like an orphan, being chucked from one foster home to the next, but I kept my mouth shut, thoughts to myself and ate my freak'n eggs.

"As long as it takes, Fox. Chas need to be ready on all levels before she can join others her age inside Revera. Otherwise…"

"Yeah, I know. She won't make it."

I didn't like that at all.

Nobody but myself will decide whether I'm going to make it or not.

THE REST OF THE DAY I WANDERED around the house like a lost cat. I found the training room, if you could call it a room. It was more like a hall, where Tom, John, Henry and the girl named Margot were training.

It was hardcore stuff.

To see John and Tom in action with Henry attacking Tom's attackers with his beak was brutal. It made me think twice about moving to Revera and I wondered if it wouldn't be better just to off on my own.

Believe me, that thought had come up a couple of times, but when Shadow Hounds and Dark Casters entered my thoughts, not to mention the Oblivion, it disappeared.

I wasn't ready to take all of this on by myself, and guessed I needed the help of these people if I wanted to get better with trusting my sand and developing my skills.

I watched star-struck at how Henry's owl figure got

bigger and bigger after Margot found a way to get him off her.

She turned around and got such a fright of the oversized bird that was almost her size that she stumbled backwards.

All of them laughed and Tom helped her up. "Don't ever turn your back on an Anitule, Mar."

"Got that," she said without taking her gaze from Henry.

Tom blew his golden sand in Henry's face and the owl shrunk to its normal size again, hooted once and landed on Tom's arm.

After that, I got pretty bored. Nobody even noticed I was there so I walked through another passage and found the entrance. I looked at the couch and remembered the first night they'd brought me here. I knew it must be the couch that Ginny had ordered them to lay me down on.

The door of the Compound opened suddenly and three boys about two years younger than me walked in and started to spray graffiti on the walls.

I just stood there and gawked at them.

"Hey," I yelled at them and wanted them to stop but they paid no attention to me whatsoever. "Hey!"

My hand moved through the one boy and touched the other's shoulder. He jumped a couple of paces, dropped the can and ran. The other two followed them.

"Come back here, you need to clean this up." I ran after them and when the door shut behind them, the art disappeared from the walls.

Ginny started to laugh behind me and I turned around.

"I don't get it, there were..."

"That's what makes the Compound so much fun," she answered simply with a huge grin on her face. "They see a very old house, and not all of this. It's the best disguise in the world for the Compound." She looked at me with soft eyes, and her smile softened slightly. "We experience this so many times that we don't pay attention to it anymore. Sometimes we see them, other times we don't." She kept staring at me and her face became slightly more serious. "What I never experienced before is what just happened with you and that boy. How did you manage to touch him, Chas?"

"What!"

"You touched one of them. Why do you think he ran?"

"I...don't know." It must be the shadow inside of me. Something I desperately didn't want anybody to find out about.

"It's the Clencing," Elliot came out of nowhere. "I doubt that we will see them again," he joked. "Chas's print will stabilize and then she will be completely invisible. It's only a matter of time, don't worry about it." He kissed Ginny softly on her temple and she turned around and walked away.

I didn't like that either. It was as if she could see straight through me, knew that it was a dark trait and hoped that I would confess.

Elliot lingered for a couple of seconds more and then he smiled as if he knew my secret as well and walked away. I went to my room for the remainder of the day.

I didn't know how I was going to stay here with people that dealt with Shadow Casters regularly. It wasn't safe for someone like me.

At dinner we had to listen to Stacey's babble again

when a horrible alarm went off. Fox grabbed my arm without saying a word, while the others went in the opposite direction with Tom and John on their heels.

"What is going on? Why did that alarm go off?"

"Shush," Fox said and as she shoved me inside my room and locked the door behind us.

All the windows disappeared instantly and blended in with the walls.

"Fox, what is happening?" I whispered.

"You are safe in here, Chastity. The Compound takes care of their owners."

"That's not what I wanted to know! Please, tell me." Adrenaline rushed through my veins.

"What did Elliot mean this morning when he said you spoke about it in your room?"

"It doesn't matter. If you want me to live with these people I need to know what the hell is going on."

"Chas, it's a Shadow Caster. The Compound is like a huge gate between Revera and the Domain. If someone enters who is not from the light, those alarms go off."

"So Shadow Casters are trying to get into Revera?"

She nodded. "They have been for years. The only way they will succeed is if a Light Caster in the Outer allows them."

This wasn't good. "Are they going to fight?"

I was worried, what if it was my mother that was desperately trying to get me out of here.

"Yes," she said and just stared at the door, or where it used to be.

I sighed. I really didn't like this place much.

WE WAITED FOR WHAT SEEM LIKE

forever when the windows and door finally reappeared Fox went to the door.

"Stay here," she said.

"Like hell I am."

I didn't care, I could protect myself, I knew the basics.

"Chas you don't know what those Casters want. You were with one, they might have followed us here and are looking for you."

"Then leaving me by myself is not the right thing to do, Fox."

"Okay, fine, but you stay close, you hear?"

I nodded.

The first thing we heard when we opened the door was a scream filled with agony.

We both rushed to the room it came from and found Max, the boy I'd met earlier in the library, sprawled over the bed.

"Max, I'm so sorry," Stacey babbled at his side. "I didn't see the second one, I'm so sorry."

"For once in your life, just shut up," he said through clenched teeth. There was a cuss word in between that sentence and Stacey got up and ran to Ginny who folded her arms around her.

His torso had black veins running across it and Elliot's hands lit up with bright light as he moved both hands over it.

"What happened?" I whispered to Fox without taking my eyes off Max.

He cussed, cried, and cussed some more.

"Hold him," Elliot said as he started to squirm on the bed.

John and Tom grabbed him and pushed him down

onto the bed.

I couldn't take the screams coming from his lips anymore and went out of the room.

Stacey followed me and we sat against the wall right outside Max's room.

Stacey hit the back of her head against the wall. "I didn't see him, I should've seen him."

"Hey, calm down okay. What happened? Was it Shadow Casters?" *Duh, what else could it be.*

She nodded. "It was Level Four Casters. If Tom and John hadn't been there, we wouldn't have made it. Something's not right."

"What do you mean something isn't right?"

I hated asking all these questions but I hadn't been there and I needed to know, it was the type of person I was.

She turned her gaze toward me. "Level 4 Casters are the highest any Caster can go. They're just below Somniums. Two of those Shadow Casters were Level Four."

"And…"

"You don't get it. Level Four Casters don't waste their time with the Outer, they usually go directly for Revera."

"Elliot said the only way…"

"It's not the only way. Only a very high level Caster can find a way into Revera without going through the Outer."

"Then why do Shadow Casters even waste their time with the Outer, why not go directly for Revera?"

"That is exactly my point, Chas. We know of four Level Four Casters in the Shadow World. One is Crane, who is like the Lord of Oblivion, and then there's

Elody, but she never comes here, it's beyond her to fight, but it doesn't mean she doesn't like to torture light Casters to get what she wants. She's just as evil. The others are Vincent and Samual, and both of them were trying to get into the Outer.

Oh shit, they were after me, but what would Level Four Shadow Casters want with me? It really didn't make any sense. "You think they were here for me?"

"I don't know. They never go for a Light Caster who just discovered what she is, that's a job for a Level Two Caster."

"Then why?"

"I don't know..." she cut me off with a grunt.

"Oh come on, I can see it in your eyes. You do know, you just don't want to tell me."

She just stared at me for a short few second. "Fine, I think it has something to do with the woman that kidnapped you. Vinicola is Crane's daughter. For years she didn't make a single peep and then all of a sudden she shows up with you, trying to recruit."

I gulped hard, but was glad that the hallway was slightly dark.

"So they were here for me?"

"They must have been. We have to find out why Vinicola wanted you so badly, and why she sent her brother to find you."

CHAPTER TWELVE
TESTS

I STRUGGLED TO FALL ASLEEP AND FOUND MYSELF sitting on the ledge by the window. I stared outside not knowing how long I was going to be able to see color again, and lost myself in the beauty that was before me.

The Compound soared high into the sky, funny how it didn't feel this way, but here I was, staring on a park a couple of miles down and small buildings that made me miss home so much more.

Max's cries eventually died and it turned out that Elliot wasn't just a doctor, he was what Reverians would call a natural healer. You needed to be gifted for that and he drew the dark the Shadow Casters had left in Max's body out with his light.

Then the thoughts that had haunted me all night emerged again.

So I have family, but not the kind anybody wanted.

I didn't know Mom was sort of royalty in Oblivion and that the Lord of that awful place, Crane, was my grandfather.

I'd always wanted one, but I doubted that he would've been the old, friendly pappy that taps on his lap for you to crawl up and sit on. I used to envy the girls back at school when they complained whenever they were forced to visit their grandparents over the weekend.

I had an uncle too, whether it was Samual or Vincent I didn't know, but I had an uncle who had a heartbeat.

Still, Mom left them for a reason, and Stacey was right, we should find out why they wanted me.

If half and half didn't exist inside Revera then coming face to face with these people wasn't an option. They would kill me.

This knowledge brought on more fears.

How did they know about me?

Did they have Mom?

I didn't want to think about it, she couldn't live in the Oblivion. Still, how they had found out about me made me worry a lot about her safety.

Then I saw it. It was as if it knew I was worried. Rays of golden sand filled the night. It flew around the buildings and went into each and every window. I smiled and knew what it was. They were dreams being casted. A huge yawn played on my mouth.

Hopping off the sill I crawled into bed and fell asleep faster than I expected to.

At first I was just sleeping, dreaming of nothing and then I was in the woods. My dreams felt so real now, something that I'd only experienced once. The day of my Initiation dream.

Orange light in the distance and the clutter of a fire made me want to go investigate. I found Leigh stoking the fire with a stick.

A jolt of happiness rushed over me as he was perfectly fine, not a scratch or a lost arm from the night of my Initiation dream. I remembered his jacket but I found him wearing it which was so weird.

He smiled as I reached him. The glasses on his face made him look extra mysterious, it made my stomach flip a couple of times.

Why was he here, again, inside my dream? I didn't know the answer but one thing I did know, I suddenly didn't feel as alone as I had earlier.

"Thank you again for the other night."

He just smiled.

I looked around. "I'm afraid to ask where we are."

Leigh chuckled. "No danger tonight, I promise, just a chat, a really important one, Chas."

I nodded. "I guess you heard about earlier tonight. Do you know why they came?"

He shook his head.

Okay, I thought and sank down on the log opposite Leigh. "What's up?" I said a bit too over excitedly which made Leigh smile, but it disappeared just as fast and he kept staring at the fire which started to freak me out a tiny bit.

"Leigh?"

He sighed. "It's about tomorrow and what follows. I don't know how to warn you any other way than through dreams as they monitor me through the Virtual Realm."

"The what? What Virtual Realm?"

"They haven't told you about that yet?"

I shook my head.

"Tomorrow they are going to start with tests and training, some of them are through the Virtual Realm."

He looked at the fire. "Elliot will tell you it's to know where to place you inside Revera, Chas, but it's not. What happened tonight makes this even more crucial for you. He ponders on a lot of things. Deals with plenty of Shadow Casters. I know what I saw in that mirror Chas. Your sand is not light, it's dark."

"But you said I can choose."

"You can, you just have to be careful. The tests are created to make sure you are not a Shadow Caster."

My throat became dry and I swallowed hard. "My sand is golden in real life, or here in the dream world." It sounded so stupid and so ironic.

"I know, for now, but your sand will show its true color in these tests. You need to learn how to wield your golden sand without using a hint of dark emotion Chas. Bad moods and fear turns Shadow Casters."

I closed my eyes. I was so screwed. There was no way that I was going to be able to hide my dust from these people.

"It's not that hard to hide it. Just take these tests as they come and don't try to face anything. They will teach you later how to deal with Shadow Casters, these tests are not the way. So don't try to overcome them. Just give in to whatever they are going to show you, run, if you must."

"Run?" I said with slightly raised eyes. "That's your master plan?"

"Casters will fight, and if you wield your sand it will be dark, Chas. Don't fight otherwise they will chuck your ass into the Oblivion and believe me it is not a place you want to be."

"How do you know all of this?"

I could see his Adam's apple bobbing slightly. "Because I helped create the Virtual Realm, these tests."

I gaped. "You created them?"

He gave me a look of shame, I could tell he wasn't proud of it. "I had no choice, Chas. It was the only thing I could do."

"Are you going to be in them?"

"I am, but you won't see me, or hear me. Any slight interference from me and they will start digging. You don't want them to dig either."

I thought about all of this, and again felt completely and utterly alone. I had nobody here.

"So they're prepared to lie to me? Fox and John, even Tom?"

"They have no choice, they are following Selene's orders."

A small sarcastic laugh escaped my lips. "The more I hear about Selene, the more I don't want to meet her."

Leigh gave me a stare filled with warning. "Don't ever say that out loud, okay. She's not what you think she is, she's not bad she's just extremely paranoid in her own way, especially when it comes to the safety of Revera. If she picks up anything from you Chas, she will do whatever is in her power to choke the darkness out of you. You are not strong enough to handle that termination. You need to learn first."

"Fine, then give me something more. What am I going to face in these tests?"

He shook his head.

"You've got to give me some sort of a hint, Leigh."

"I don't know. There are over a million tests, Chas. It

could be anything," he said. "They are real, you won't even know that you are in one."

"Then how the hell am I going to know that these test are over, and not some other creepy test to only try to trick me more? I need to experiment with my golden sand, if I can't do it in these tests...." He got what I was saying. It felt hopeless. They could book my corner in some rundown building as I knew I was going to the Oblivion. It was set in stone.

"Chas, you need to trust your instincts."

"Trust my..." I giggled sarcastically. "My instincts tell me to run, Leigh. Ever since that day I got my sand, it's all they've been saying to me. How am I going to trust that or anyone else in this place?"

"You can trust me."

I just stared at him. He had been in my Initiation dream when I needed him and he was here now, warning me about things I didn't even know were going to happen yet.

"I'll do what you asked, but I don't like running away; it's lame."

"That's not what these tests are about. Facing your fears comes later."

"Oh yeah, when? In another virtual test, as if they are real the way you say they are, I won't even know the freak'n difference."

"Calm down, Chas. If you aren't sure, don't wield your sand."

"I'm not sure half the time, Leigh and we are still in the Outer, not in some virtual program."

"I know you feel defeated Chas, but you can do this. I know you can."

"So you keep saying," I mumbled softly. "Anything

else?" I didn't want to sound annoyed but I was. I should've been grateful to Leigh as he was really doing me a favor and took a huge risk warning me about these tests.

"Nope, that's it."

"Why are you doing this? Helping me with everything?"

"You seem like the kind that needs all the help she can get, Chastity."

I huffed, and took a deep breath. "So I guess a thank you is in order?"

"Not at all. We have a lot in common, even if it doesn't look like that now. Revera may be a dream world, but I can promise you nothing about Revera is a dream. Not all of them can be trusted, so be careful Chas."

I nodded.

We sat there for a while, just staring at the embers of the fire that were flying through the sky.

"Can I ask you something?"

He nodded.

"Who are you, do you live in Revera?"

He smiled. "You could say that."

"Please just give me a straight answer," I begged.

"Let's just say that I have limits to where I can run around and play."

"Who created all of this, me, you?"

"The same person who created all the Nomads."

I huffed. I didn't even want to start thinking about that part as I doubted that God would create anything like this, but then again, He has a funny sense of humor and it seemed to come to light on a regular basis lately.

"Can I go? Apparently, I have a big day tomorrow."

He smiled again which made my stomach flip. Why I had a thing for guys in glasses I would never understand. But Leigh was far from a geek, he was a kick ass heart-throb with very bad eye sight.

"Sure, and please be careful. The Virtual Realm can't harm you, but act like it can, okay."

"That is if I know it's the Virtual Realm." I got up, and brushed down my ass to get rid of the loose pieces of wood that were stuck on my jeans.

"Oh, before I forget, if you see the cat, keep your mouth shut."

What cat? I turned around but Leigh and the fire had disappeared.

I OPENED MY EYES AND FOUND MYSELF BACK IN MY bed. The sun was starting to light all the objects that were stacked against the wall. The shadows weren't so dark anymore and I tried to fall asleep again, but failed miserably.

At six thirty I sat at the breakfast table, alone. Leigh's conversation from last night replayed inside my head. I had no idea how I should let things happen or run away if I couldn't handle it. That wasn't who I was and it conflicted with something Mom had drilled into me in that short, almost three weeks, we'd spent together: To face your fears and fight. We were fighters.

I wondered for the first time in a long time about my real dad, who he was and what his plan was for us. Apart from what Mom told me, the little she shared and the reputation he had with Fox's team wasn't enough to help paint a picture of him in my mind.

He would probably have found a way to hide us from Fox and Tom and I wouldn't have had to face any of this.

I jumped as both Ginny and Margot walked into the kitchen. Ginny wore a pair of Capri jeans and a flowery top. Margot wore skimpy denim shorts with a pair of army boots and a tight t-shirt.

"Did you have a wonderful rest, Chastity?" Ginny had a sweet tone to her voice and for some reason I couldn't imagine her lying to me later in the day.

I smiled back politely. "I did, thank you." Urg, I sounded like a morning person.

"Hungry?" she asked, walking over to the oven that was stationed in the far corner of the kitchen.

"Starving," Margot said with a slight grunt as she played with a crystal that hung from her neck. The thing was beautiful, it had so many colors in it and I couldn't stop staring. I saw Margot stop fiddling with it and found her staring back at me. I looked back to the table.

Ginny looked at me and raised her eyes softly and plastered on a fake smile. Leigh said to trust my gut, and my gut said it was fake.

"Is Max going to be ok?" I tried to break the silence.

"Yes, he will be up and ready to face another day in a couple of days. Elliot is really good at what he does."

"That's good to know," I said softly.

"So," Margot said and looked at Ginny whose back was to us. "The number one question is what were Level Four Casters doing here?"

My gut didn't like her tone.

"Margot, Elliot said to leave it alone."

"No. I want to know, 'cause I can promise you they

don't need the Outer to get into Revera, Ginny."

"I said leave it alone." Ginny's tone was filled with warning.

"My brother almost died last night. I need to know what she is." She looked straight at me, my gut said that she was going to leap and kill me with her bare hands. *Run.* "Are you a Shadow Caster?"

I just stared at her. Nobody had ever asked me that straight, not even Leigh, although he knew what I was.

"Margot, that's enough. If you can't play nice, I suggest you leave the kitchen, now, before I call Elliot."

She hit her fists on the table, pushed herself up and walked with huge strides out of the room.

Pretend Chas, just like Mom said, the voice inside my head said. "Is that why they were here, for me?"

"Don't worry about that Chastity. We don't know for sure, but Fox think it's because of the woman that kidnapped you. She's quite important in the Oblivion. Maybe they just wanted to find out why she felt the need to try to recruit you."

"I'm sorry about Max. I didn't want anybody to get hurt." I got up, feeling guilty about almost killing a boy only slightly older than me.

"Chastity," Ginny called but I didn't stop. I headed straight back to my room.

I paced up and down for a long time. Trust your gut was what Leigh had said, but my gut was all messed up. It told me to run, it still did, and I didn't know who to trust.

I closed my eyes and saw my mother. Not with her platinum blonde hair and dark, dark eyes, but with her beautiful red hair and bright blue eyes. She twirled a piece of my raven black hair that hid my face and placed it gently back behind my ear.

You can do this, honey. Trust your instincts, they are stronger than you know.

My eyes flew open. Her voice sounded so clear, so real, as if she was right here.

Tears welled up in my eyes. I never thought that I would miss her this much.

My instincts were strong, I'd known it all along, I just needed the confirmation of a voice I completely trusted.

Leigh was right, I could do this.

CHAPTER THIRTEEN
A RUDE AWAKENING

AROUND EIGHT THIRTY FOX KNOCKED ON my door.

"Ginny told me what happened, are you okay?" She sat down on my bed.

I nodded.

"Margot isn't one of the most pleasant little creatures out there. She's realistic and really cares about her brother."

"Yeah, I got that."

"Hey, Max is going to be fine."

I nodded again and smiled.

"Then stop sulking and wipe that guilty look off your face."

"What guilty look?"

She gave me a side glance. "Chas, I carry that same look every time something goes wrong. I'm a pro at detecting guilt."

I giggled. Still, the fact that she would lie to me soon

made me feel as if she was going to rip out a knife from her side pocket and stab me in the gut.

"You need something in that system of yours, food preferably and Elliot needs a word."

She got up and walked to the door.

"Fox?" I asked and she turned around

"What is it Chas?"

"Why do you think the Casters were here, last night? Margot asked me if I was…." I couldn't say the word.

"Margot is just a silly girl who believes in silly objects. That pendant she carries around her neck?"

I nodded.

"She believes that it actually has the ability to show her when a Shadow Caster is near. Don't worry too much about what Margot says or thinks. I can promise you that girl has no idea what she wants and changes her mind on a daily basis."

Her face said it all. The way she looked at the carpet. "To answer your question of why I think Level Four Shadow Casters were here," she said, and took a deep breath. She looked at me again and smiled. "Let's not go there, okay. I'm sure they won't come back any time soon."

I nodded and let her leave.

I went back down to the kitchen and Ginny gave me a motherly smile.

"Come sit, I'll whip you up some eggs."

I did as she asked and took a chair close to Elliot who was reading today's paper.

He finally put the paper down as Ginny placed a plate of food in front of me.

"Sorry about Margot this morning. I promise you she will be dealt with."

"It's fine, really. I just haven't been asked directly if I was, you know, part of the other team."

He smiled, carrying a look as if he wanted to ask that too and that was my cue to start digging into my plate, ignoring the stare.

"What you see with Margot is what you get. She's like an open book, but Max, he is the total opposite."

"Good to know."

"But I'm not here to speak about Margot and Max. I'm here to talk about today's events."

Here it comes, the lies.

"We have to start with training you soon and with that comes a couple of tests, Chastity. Some in the form of a lot of questions you need to fill in and others through a couple of tests in the Virtual Realm."

I swallowed my eggs and looked at him. "What sort of tests?"

"It's not that important, but they were created to help us find out where you belong inside Revera."

I nodded and stared back down at my plate. I'd known that answer, that lie, was going to come, still I'd silently wished for another, one that would prove I could trust these people.

"Okay, just as long as they won't be about math, I suck at math."

Elliot laughed as Ginny sat down with a cup of coffee in her hands.

"I'm sure they won't be that difficult."

I finished my breakfast quickly and went back to my room.

I was disgusted with his lies; Leigh said it would happen, still, I didn't want it to be true, because that would mean that they really would try to trick me into showing my true nature.

At half past ten, Fox knocked on my door.

I'd been staring out the window for the past half hour and trying to clear my thoughts about what lay ahead, to keep calm and to not wield my dust.

"Are you ready?" Her head peeked inside my room.

"Sure, let's do this." I smiled and followed her down the staircase again. "So what sort of test will it be today?"

She squinted. "If I remember correctly, the first one is the most boring you will ever experience. A lot of questions. So I guess you'll be fine."

I giggled. Fox wasn't a good liar, so I doubted that it was a lie. She usually looked away when she didn't want to lie.

"Okay, boring questions it is."

We took the passage on the right, I'd never been down this passage and we stopped before a room with a solid steel door.

"I thought you said it was questions only?" I looked at her and back at the door.

She giggled.

"It's the room where all the tests need to be given Chas. Don't look so worried. Just answer the questions truthfully, they really do help in placing you inside Revera."

"Okay."

She pulled the heavy door open and I found a grey room. There were no windows, only grey walls and a desk right in the middle.

"Elliot will be with you in a minute."

I nodded and watched her leave again.

I didn't like the grey room and my gut was telling

me to run away.

Concentrate Chas, no running. You've got to face this, but not face-face this.

I sighed again and jumped slightly as Elliot opened the door and came in.

He flopped a stack of A4 paper on the desk with a pen. "Plenty of questions Chas." He looked at his watch. "It will take you almost half a day to finish all of them. When you are done, press this button." The button was red, like it would set off an alarm and he smiled. "Answer them truthfully, please. That is all I ask."

I nodded again and watched him close the steel door behind him as he left.

I threw myself onto the chair and looked at the stack of paper. There were at least a thousand questions to answer, if not more, and I took the pen and started reading the first question.

Name? Surname, age, year you were born. I scanned the page and turned over to see what was on the next. Five pages, asking me questions about myself, what did I want to become. *I didn't have a clue a couple of months ago, and now I am even more clueless, so good luck with that one.*

Questions about my home, where I grew up, my life with my mom, what happened that day etc. were typed out on countless numbers of pages. The sooner I started, the better.

I filled in each question as honestly as I could. Even the ones that were a lie, the ones that Mom and I rehearsed so many hours a day, that I was sure if they asked me a few months from now, I would still be able to recite what I wrote down.

It took me an entire hour just to fill in a hundred pages. By the second hour, my wrist began to ache and I had ink all over my palm.

By the third hour, I couldn't feel my hand anymore from all the writing and by the fifth hour, life came back and an ache stronger than before was lodged inside my wrist. My handwriting became all scribbled and I doubted that Elliot would be able to decipher anything.

When I filled in the last question, my stomach growled.

I needed food and I needed it now.

I pressed the red button and the door automatically released. When I found the kitchen it was deserted and I made myself a huge BLT sandwich.

I had to admit, it was weird not hearing or seeing anyone and I started to wonder where all of them were.

I walked up the stairs and went to my room. I opened the door and closed it behind me.

I stared out the window. The sky looked absolutely stunning with colors of light gold, orange, and a slight pink showing it was twilight.

I turned around and my heart stopped for a few seconds. I cupped my mouth and the last piece of sandwich fell to the floor.

I wanted to scream, but I didn't.

Tom, Henry the owl, John, Fox, Elliot, Ginny, Margot and Stacey had been executed and crucified against my wall. Long, rusty nails pierced their hands and feet as they were splayed like a horrible, grotesque painting. Blood was spread all over the walls and ran down in rivulets, soaking the carpet. I stared, frozen in horror and shock as I took in the scene before me.

Fox grunted, she was still alive and I ran to her body.

"Who did this?"

"Where is Max?" she asked.

"Max?" I asked and a tear rolled over my cheek. This cannot be happening. "Fox who did this?"

"You were safe in the test room, they came back. Chastity you need to find Max. He could still be alive. You'll need him now more than ever."

"No, I need you. Let me help you." I touched the huge nail inside her hand and she yelped.

"You can't save me, get Max, and get the hell out of here," she said through gasps and heavy breathing.

"Where are we supposed to go, Fox? I can't leave you."

"Get Max," she ordered again. "I'm not going to make it, Chastity, just get Max and get out of here."

I nodded as tears rolled down my face.

"Good girl." She smiled and breathed out her last breath.

I sobbed softly. *Why did they have to bring me here? Get Max. Shit, now I have to find him too.*

I wiped off my tears and opened the door to my room.

The hallways looked dark and creepy and I found Max's room faster than I thought. I opened the door slowly and found him still lying in his bed.

I closed the door, locked it behind me and went over to his bed.

He still had a pulse and he breathed. *Signs of life, check.*

I shook him slightly but no sign of waking came from his side.

"Max," I cried softly. "You need to wake up."

I shook him again, this time slightly harder and he

jolted upright, grabbed me around the neck and pressed a knife against my throat.

"Calm down, it's me, the new girl," I yelled.

He took a few seconds to register. His body was soaking, and hot, like fire. He still had some black veins running over his arms and torso.

"It's me, Chastity, please I don't want to die," I begged again.

"What are you doing here?" he asked and let me go.

I stroked my neck from his grip and took a couple of breaths to calm my beating heart. Then the tears started to flow.

"Chastity, what are you doing in my room?"

The doors and the windows of his room disappeared instantly. The Shadow Casters were back. Fox said that they won't come back, still they did, more than once.

What did they want with me?

"What the hell is happening?" Max stumbled to the spot where his door used to be, feeling for a knob, as if it was still there but just camouflaged.

"Stop, please. We're safe in here," I begged him.

"My family needs me," he grunted and felt for the knob again.

"They don't, they're dead."

His entire body froze.

"I'm so sorry. I was busy with the test. I don't know what happened. I found them inside my room staked to the wall. Fox told me to find you, she said you would know what to do."

He didn't even move.

"Max, please. I'm scared and I don't know where to go from here. We need to stick together."

He shot me a look. "Why did the Shadow Casters

come, Chas? They're Level Four. It doesn't make sense. Ever since they brought you here, all this shit is happening."

"I know, okay? I'm sorry."

"Stop saying you are sorry and tell me the truth."

"I don't know what the truth is," I yelled back at him. "All I know is that for some reason a Shadow Caster kidnapped me. I didn't know who she was until recently. She's some big shot's daughter inside the Oblivion. Please, that's all I know."

He walked over to me. "If you lie to me, I swear I will kill you myself." The cusses were there, in between all those syllables and I'd never heard anybody cuss as much as Max.

"I'll take the knife from you and kill myself."

He narrowed his eyes and then looked away. "Margot?"

I shook my head.

He nodded a couple of times and clenched the side of his torso again. I shifted my body under his weight and helped him back to his bed.

"I'm no good like this Chas. Elliot wasn't done healing me properly," he said.

"Well, then we need to find another healer and fast. We're inside the Outer, I'm sure there is a healer somewhere that can help you."

He laughed. "You make it sound as if they are around every corner." Another couple of cuss words worked themselves into that sentence and I rolled my eyes.

"Do you have to cuss so much?" I asked.

"We are living in the Outer, not your ideal world to grow old in Chas. Oh, wait, I forgot, there aren't a lot of us here that grow old period."

"I see sarcasm was bestowed on you as well. Now lie down." I helped him onto the bed and he winced some more as I sort of dropped him.

This seemed like a hopeless case.

"So what do we do?" I asked after a while as I couldn't come up with any sort of plan. To think I wanted to run away. I wasn't going to make it very far.

No reply came from Max, and I found him sleeping again.

"Max," I whispered and he opened his eyes. "What do we do?"

"We wait, Chas. There isn't much we can do now if the door or windows don't show themselves."

"Are they here?" I asked again.

"Stop with the gazillion questions please, you are giving me a headache."

"Fine, so we wait."

Hollow footsteps walked up the stairs and Max's eyes flew open once again. He switched off his night light and the room was pitch dark. The beat of my heart, I was sure Max could hear, was loud.

He got up real quick, that must have hurt, but he didn't make any sound of pain. I could hear his breathing around the room, but what he was doing I had no idea.

The Shadow Caster's footsteps creaked loud in the hallway. They were parading, speaking in a tone of voice that made my insides crawl. I didn't like the pitch of their voices.

What they were saying sounded foreign and I'd never been so scared in my entire life. This topped my number one spot, whatever it was.

I closed my eyes and pulled my legs to my chest,

rocking on one spot, trying to take deep breaths and calm myself down.

Then something neither of us expected happened.

The windows and door appeared while their voices were still speaking. I got up, and looked at Max.

A bright light filled the room and I had to shut my eyes for a second. It came from a Celestial that was attached to the wall.

The words coming from Max's mouth were more or less the ones that left my mom's mouth that day in the attic.

The only part I understand was North Dakota before he grabbed my arm and pushed me through the Celestial just as the door to Max's bedroom opened.

Chapter Fourteen
Guild and Strength

A STRONG WIND PULLED BOTH OF US INTO the Celestial. I felt the same force from the first time I'd taken one with Mom. It was a feeling of turmoil, like I'd gotten thrown into a blender on high speed, and then we landed with a thud. My chin ached and I spat out fine red sand.

The world still spun heavily around me and I would give anything for one of those dark brown chocolates just to feel normal again.

When the carousel spinning finally stopped, I picked my head up and saw Max's body a couple of feet away from mine.

I crawled over to him as fast as I could and lay my head slightly on his chest

He was still breathing, then he gasped hard and sat straight up, taking in our surroundings through alert eyes. A painful grunt escaped his lips as he clenched his body.

"Are you okay?" I asked as he moan and cussed.

He finally nodded as he spat out some saliva. It was mixed with red, not a good sign.

"How about you?" He looked up and his eyes lingered on my chin. It burned as his fingers touched the scrapes softly. "We'll fix that soon, but we need to get off this road."

I nodded, got up and helped him up as well.

He limped with half of his weight pressing down on me, and I thanked the heavens for the farm house that was a couple of miles down the road.

I didn't know if these people would be able to see us or not, and to be honest, for the first time, I wished that we could be invisible and just lay low without them knowing that we were there.

"So what now, do you have a plan?"

"Sort of." He spoke fast and soft, still looking around.

He didn't go directly for the farm house, and I got a bit scared as a large dog came straight for us.

He barked like crazy, and didn't want to stop.

The door of the farm house opened and a huge farmer walked out.

"Jay, quiet, you silly dog."

"He can't see us?"

"No, but the dog can," Max said and limped toward the barn with the dog barking still behind us.

"Will he attack?" I asked looking over both our shoulders.

"No, he just barks like he has no idea what he's looking at."

"You've experienced this before, haven't you?"

"What, getting chased by dogs in the Domain?" He

smiled. "All the time. It's quite fun if you don't feel as if a train has just smacked into you."

Still the dog kept barking, even though the owner told him numerous times that there was nothing out there.

"I don't like this, make him stop," I begged Max.

"I can't, not with John Boy watching."

I smiled. I knew who John Boy was, it was an oldie about a farming family and the oldest son was named John Boy. It was one of my mom's favourite shows and she even bought herself the DVD box set to watch them over and over again.

The dog went for us a couple of times, but he didn't attack, just like Max said.

When we reached the barn, we opened it and went inside. A couple of minutes later, the dog's crazy barking stopped as both of us just lay on the hay.

"So, what now?" I asked again.

"Rest Chastity, believe me we are going to need it."

I sighed. I didn't like not knowing if we were going to be safe inside this barn or not and hated the silence.

"Why here?" I asked. "North Dakota?"

"There's a Compound close by. I've only been there once with Elliot. I'm sure I can find it again. James is the Guardian of that Compound and he'll get word to Selene about our safety."

"Our safety?"

"I doubt that they know about the Compound yet. But when they do, they'll destroy it. It's what happens to Compounds when their inhibitants die."

I began to finally realise just how dangerous it was to live inside the Outer.

"So Margot was your sister?"

"Yes."

"Older or younger?"

"Five minutes older and she never let me forget that."

I looked at his figure lying next to me.

"She was your twin?"

"That would be correct once more."

"I'm so sorry, Max."

"Yeah, I know. You've said so many times. Now can you please shut up so I can get some sleep."

"Sorry, I'm just nervous."

"You are safe for now, Chastity, get some sleep."

I smiled at him, wishing I could believe him but my gut was still all over the place, yelling at me to not believe anything that lived inside the Outer.

I closed my eyes and my mind wandered to Fox's body staked against the wall as if she was some sort of rare butterfly species.

Tom and John, even Henry the owl. The others I didn't know as well as Max did, but it was hard to get over the fact that Fox wasn't there anymore.

Crickets were chirping away as if they were on steroids. It was a sound that would drive anyone insane, and I fell asleep faster that I thought would be possible.

"CHAS! WAKE UP." MAX YELLED AND MY EYES FLEW open.

He was standing right in front of the barn, trying to block the entrance with all his strength. The door was making a huge racket and at first I thought it was the wind, but when another blow made the door crack, I knew that it wasn't the wind, it was something huge, something with teeth and acid saliva, something really bad.

I got up and ran toward him.

"Get me that beam, the one over there."

I followed his gaze and saw the wooden beam to my right, on the ground.

It was quite heavy but I guess with all the adrenaline pumping through my veins it wasn't as heavy as I thought it would be.

I put it against the door and Max moved it into place while still keeping the door closed.

"We need to get higher up, there."

I turned my gaze and found a second level closer to the barn's roof. My eyes trailed quickly down in search of a ladder and found one against the wall.

"Go get the ladder and stack it against the side of the wall so we can get up there.

"Okay." I ran over to the ladder and dragged it back to the wall so we could get safely up.

"Climb!" Max yelled.

"What about you?"

"I'll be right there."

"No," I went back to Max and leaned against the door with all my weight. "You go."

"Chas," he protested.

"Max, I'm the best chance for us to both get safely up there. You'll never make it to the ladder in one piece. Not in the state you're in. Now go. I'll be fine."

He stared at me and finally nodded as he pushed himself to his feet and limp-ran toward the ladder.

Without his weight, I had to use all of my strength.

I moved a couple of inches forward with every push the Shadow Hound gave from the other side of the door.

When the wooden beam started to crack, I knew it was time to make my way to the ladder. Max was halfway up.

Another blow came and it left another crack.

I closed my eyes and prayed some more, but nothing helped. The hound could smell my fear from behind this door and he knew that this was an easy meal.

When Max's feet touched the floor of the upper level, I pushed myself away from the door and ran as fast as I could.

The door smashed into a million pieces and one of the wooden pieces hit me straight in the back. I stumbled and skidded onto my stomach. I was covered with straw and my body ached again from new scrapes that covered my arms and legs.

"Get up!" Max yelled.

I pushed myself up and flew into the air as the dog's paw connected with my body.

I smacked hard against the barn's wall and a couple of shovels and garden tools fell to the ground, inches from my body.

"Use your sand, Chastity!"

I grabbed a shovel instead.

"Use your sand, a shovel isn't going…" Max didn't even finish his sentence as I swung the shovel toward the dog and it connected with his face.

The blow vibrated through my body. The Hound growled at me first and then it snorted before it turned and yelped.

It worked, the dog turned around and ran out of the barn like a deranged puppy.

Max just stared at me and stared at the yelping hound who was already a mile down the road, then back at me.

"How did you do that?"

I shrugged and waited for Max to climb down.

His gaze still lingered on me as I went to pick up a spade, and shoved it into my back pocket.

He found a huge bale of hay and fell backwards, covering his eyes with his hands.

I went to sit next to him and just stared at him. "I thought we were going to be safe tonight, Max?"

"I thought so too. We need to go, before more hounds come," he said and pushed himself up from the ground.

I got up too and followed him

It was funny how none of the racket woke anybody, but then again we were still in the Outer and they were inside the real world, or Domain as they called it. We were invisible to them, and they couldn't hear or see Casters at all.

Still it was pretty weird as I knew that tomorrow the farmer would see the barn and I doubted that he would rule it out as a strong wind.

We escaped through what used to be the door and part of the wall and started to move in the opposite direction.

My gut was yelling now, telling me not to run, but how did I tell that to a Caster who lived in the Outer when I hadn't even reached Level One?

It felt like forever when we finally reached tall trees and Max told me to climb.

We found two branches high enough from the ground that were thick and strong enough to carry our weight. It was our bed tonight, which once again made me feel like I wss stuck inside one of favorite novels.

But this was far from a novel, it was real and a measure that would keep us safe for tonight.

"Give me your hoody." I took it off and threw it one branch down to where Max was.

He started to rip it into shreds. I just gaped at him.

"I'll get us some supplies tomorrow, but right now, you need to secure yourself to that tree. It's the only way you will be able to sleep tonight."

He started to tie the long shreds together and made some sort of rope before tossing it back to me.

I tied it around myself and around the tree and had to admit, Max was really smart, or maybe he loved to read too.

He did the same with his shirt.

"Try to sleep, Chastity," he said one last time before a soft snore fell from his lips. He must've been so exhausted.

I stared into the sky.

The stars shone like small sparkling diamonds tonight, the moon was full and there were absolutely no clouds in sight. There were so many stars that it was hard not to look.

I didn't know what tomorrow was going to hold but I knew one thing for sure, I wouldn't be able to make it without Max.

We just needed to find this Compound fast and hopefully it would have a healer, just like his old Compound had.

He needed the healing badly.

I closed my eyes and hoped that tonight I would dream of Leigh again. He could tell me where exactly the Compound was and I knew that he would.

Max snored harder and I huffed. A part of me

wished that I had his confidence in his dust, but I didn't.

The shovel had worked, even though Max had stared at me as if he hadn't expected that outcome. It was plain and simple, if an object hit you hard in the face, you would feel it, even if you were an oversized dog from Hell.

Then it hit me. I can be okay in this world, without letting anybody know what I desperately try to hide.

I didn't have to experience it with my sand, but I definitely needed to learn how to fight with other weapons, even with Mom's training, I needed more. I need to be stronger, better, faster if I was going to survive this trip.

Leigh was right. I would be able to do this, even though he'd been referring to a test and this was the real world, but he was right.

I should trust my gut.

CHAPTER FIFTEEN
DEAD AND ALIVE

WE HAD BEEN ON THE RUN FOR THE PAST weeks. Max got better and better as the days progressed. To my surprise he was a healer in training and was only supposed to observe Elliot. He'd never used his healing abilities himself, up until now. It was amazing to watch him heal himself every night. His hands would light up as he touched the slight dark veins the Shadow Caster had left him with a month ago.

We were supposed to be safe by now, but he couldn't locate the Compound, so we had to make a move for another, in Mexico.

I'd always wanted to go to Mexico, but never thought in a million years that it would be while I was on the run.

Still, Mexico was quite far and I thought we would never reach it in this lifetime.

When we weren't stowaways on a truck going in that direction, we would camp for the night, either in someone's garage or a building that wasn't in use anymore. There were plenty of those around after the recession.

The trees were also our sanctuary and I had to admit, I felt safer up in one than I did on the ground.

Max wasn't so bad either, but I got what Elliot said about Margot and Max, how the two differed from one another. Max only spoke when he needed to, which was usually at our training sessions or when he didn't like the way he felt toward things. Guess Leigh wasn't lying when he said that Casters had to trust their gut as Max's led us away from so many dangers.

I sighed as I thought about Leigh. I hadn't dreamt of him the past three weeks, which made me worry a bit. Why had he stopped looking out for me now?

One way that Max differed from his sister, was that he was extremely polite - that was if you didn't mind the cussing through all his sentences. Margot had the tendency to speak her mind, not caring how rude she sounded, at least when she'd been alive.

A horrible feeling crept into my gut just by thinking ill of her. She was dead and her soul should rest.

We didn't just run, Max taught me to fight with anything that was worthy to fight with and we stole an aluminium baseball bat from one of the sporting goods stores we passed during our first week. The thing had become my best friend ever since, but it wasn't the only stuff we took from stores. He grabbed food daily and clothes too. We both had backpacks filled with stuff we needed. We had to survive and although I didn't like it much, I understood why we had to do it.

The bat was a bit heavy in the beginning but with the two of us practising our swing shots it became lighter and lighter. A part of me was dying to try it out on a Shadow Hound, but that was a really small part.

We also did a lot of fighting against each other, sparring was more like it and he was quite surprised at how fast I picked it up, well he thought I was a fast learner. I didn't tell him that Mom had drilled me for three weeks before Fox and her team found us.

Fox. My heart still ached when I thought about her and their bodies stacked like that on the wall. It haunted my dreams daily.

Still, Max was a master when it came to Martial arts, Judo and Taekwondo and I saw my ass each and every time I tried to do one of the things Mom taught me.

It always led to Max finding a way to get me strangled up in one of his super grips which I couldn't escape, no matter how hard I struggled. I thought I would never be able to get out or dodge one of his grips, but to my surprise that day came too.

Running hills toward our next destination was his way of getting me fit, which wasn't that hard as I was already fit, thanks again to my mother's drilling.

Still, it was like it wasn't enough for him. He didn't like that I wasn't ready to practice with my sand and taunted me about that every day.

I gave him many reasons why I wasn't ready and my last reason made him back off a bit.

I told him that I needed to control my emotions first before I was going to start experimenting with my sand. I didn't want to turn dark, although he didn't know that little fact about me, and argued on numerous occasions that I wouldn't turn dark as my sand was golden, I wasn't ready to take that chance and put it to the test.

I learned a lot about surviving in the Outer with Max and I didn't know what I would've done if he hadn't made it.

It was no surprise to me that he'd had to do this before.

It was how they ended up at Elliot's Compound.

They used to be bigger, but three of his Casters died the night they found Max and Margot.

His situation was similar to the one we were in now. His dad used to be a Guardian of another Compound. It wasn't a big Compound and it was hidden, or so they thought when three Shadow Casters killed both their parents as they tried to enter Revera.

Max and Margot got away, the Casters got into Revera but didn't make it very far as Revera's Guardians found them and ended their lives.

I learned a thing or two from Max about the Shadow Casters. He had dealt with so many of them in his short life.

Where the Shadow Casters only had about four Level Four casters, Revera had a couple of hundred.

I wanted to know how it was possible for Revera to have so many Level Four casters and the Shadow casters so few and the reason was simple. Inside Revera every Guardian can reach a Level Four, where in Oblivion you have to be born from a special line.

It really made me think about Mom again and why my uncle was attacking the Compound, time and time again. He was looking for me. I was 100% sure about that fact now.

Was it to kill me? I didn't think so anymore.

If only special bloodlines can become Level Four

Casters, they were desperately in need of me, but that also meant that they must have found Mom. How else would they have known about me? It wasn't a wonderful thought to ponder on.

Still I was lucky to report that there were no more Shadow Hound incidents after that night at the barn, but I didn't know how long it was going to stay that way.

"Chas." Max shoved me hard and I opened my eyes. "Let's go," he said and jumped off the still truck.

We constantly hitched rides, it wasn't that hard since we were completely invisible to the owners and it was the best way to stay off the Shadow Casters' radar.

I picked up my backpack and my baseball bat and pulled it through the straps.

The huge "Mexico" sign was right in front of us and we walked past the cops, through the border without being detected.

The dogs barked like crazy but that wasn't exactly new.

I'd gotten used to being invisible and it was quite awesome to be hidden to the rest of the world, especially when you were on the run.

The sky was turning orange and a soft pink with dark edges and I knew that we only had an hour or two at the most left in this day.

Max didn't say anything and we hopped onto another pickup that was parked just outside the border.

Ten minutes later we were back on the road.

Around seven, we jumped off again. It was a small industrial part of Mexico and to be honest I didn't like the vibe that surrounded us. My gut differed on a daily basis with Max's now, but he'd done this kind of thing before where I hadn't.

The streets were extremely dark and eerie and I just wished that Max loved the city as much as I did, but he had this paranoia of us being detected too easily by other Shadow Casters in cities.

"Elliot told me once about the Mexican Compound. It's the biggest Compound in the Outer and also the strongest. If they let us in, we might actually be okay, Chas. We can finally get word to Selene that we're okay."

"You think she sent Casters after us?" I asked for the gazillionth time.

"I told you before, I'm sure she did."

"Then why haven't they found us yet?"

"We're always on the run. How do you expect them to find us? We never stay in one place more than two days."

It didn't make sense to me. I mean these people had gadgets, most of them I didn't even know about, and they couldn't find two Casters on the run?

Max took all the back roads. Some of the small convenience stores were still open, but most of the little streets were dark.

We passed a couple of factories. They were huge and it took us a quarter of an hour to clear a street.

Adrenaline constantly pumped through my veins and I was on edge the whole time, just scanning the buildings waiting for the day Shadow Hounds and their Casters were going to attack.

I pulled my hoody over my head and had to run-walk to keep up with Max's huge strides.

It was a miracle that he'd found a way for us to stay safe this long.

I started to understand why the life spans of the

Casters living in the Outer were so short.

I slammed into Max when he just stopped in the middle of the road. I could tell that he was on alert. Something caught his attention and I can't say how many times his gut had gotten us free from situations that could've turned ugly.

I listened too, real hard, and closed my eyes. Took in the sounds around me, trying to turn them softer, until I found what it was he was hearing, just like Max had taught me over the past few weeks. He was a great mentor and taught me a lot about surviving in the Outer, especially when you are far from your Compound. Still we needed Compounds. They were our safe havens and we needed our rest just like all living things.

I finally heard it. It was the snarling of hounds and shrill and sadistic laughter. I snapped out of it. I knew what laughed like that and I wanted to get the hell away from there as fast as I could.

"No, Chas. There's someone in there that desperately needs our help, a Light Caster," he said with eyes closed. He was still in the zone, fine tuning his hearing. "They might be from the Compound. It's our duty to help them."

"You're kidding me, right?"

"No. You want good food and a warm bath every night, this is your chance, the only one we might get."

I pulled my face, took out my baseball bat and nodded. "Fine, you sold me on the hot bath."

His lips curved slightly and he walked across the street. I was right behind him and wished that by some miracle there wasn't a full on battle going on in there.

We slipped through an opening and crawled behind

huge crates.

The warehouse was big, most of the equipment was gone, but there were still mouldings in the floor that had been used to keep the machines in place.

I peeked to see what it was we were dealing with.

Three huge hounds were clawing at the wall. They made low growling sounds. For some reason it reminded me of a dog and cat game. The cat was hiding inside the hole in the wall, and the dogs were desperately trying to drag it out.

Max lifted two fingers, with the sign for North East.

You sure? I mouthed and he nodded.

I took a deep breath.

Three hounds and two Shadow Casters, that didn't sound right, usually there was a Shadow Caster for every hound.

One of them laughed again, egging one of the dogs to get it, whatever it was.

I hoped Max was right, that it was a Light Caster and that we weren't going to put our lives on the line for a stupid cat or mouse.

I hated how sadistic this all was and that these Casters got high on fear.

Max drew a shield and a couple of knives from his dust and nodded his head.

He jumped up from behind the crate and I saw how three of his knives left his hand really fast.

"Now, Chas," he yelled and I ran as fast as I could with my bat clutched inside my hands toward the group of hounds.

The one hound turned his gaze around and my bat connected hard with his ugly mutt.

He didn't yelp like the one that attacked us inside the

barn had, no this one turned to dust.

The second one jumped on me, pinning me and my bat down.

Slobber ran over my face and my heart beat so fast that I didn't know if I was going to live another day.

One of Max's knives hit him and a ton of black dust showered on top of me.

I rolled backwards the minute I was free, pushed myself up onto my legs again and shoved the bat hard into the gut of the last hound just as it was making its leap.

He too turned into a heap of dark dust.

A black arrow hit me in the leg and I screamed, as my body connected hard with the ground.

It went straight through my leg and I kept staring at the black arrow side.

I grunted through my teeth and a couple of cuss words made their way into my ranting, trying to dampen the pain.

It didn't work this time.

Max had killed one of the Shadow Casters and the other one fled.

"Are you okay?" He came back, kneeling right next to me.

"I have an arrow sticking out of my leg, does it look like I'm okay?"

"We need to get it out, Chas." He started pulling and I screamed more.

The pain was excruciating and I couldn't handle it anymore, but still I refused to give up and die. I was too young to die. I had to survive. Had to.

It hurt even more when the arrow was out and Max tore one of his shirts in his backpack and wrapped it tight around my leg.

"We need to find a healer fast, Chas," he said. "There's no way I can heal this." He sighed. "Why didn't you use your dust?"

"The baseball bat worked, didn't it?"

"About that," he said softly.

"What about it?"

"I've never seen a Caster kill a hound just by hitting it with a bat before."

"Sand works for you, bats are my thing."

He chuckled. "You'll even joke in death, Chas. Just hold on, please."

"I'm not going anywhere. It's just an arrow," I said and tried to control the pain that was eating through my leg.

He crawled over to the spot and started to speak softly.

"Please tell me that there's someone there and that I didn't get shot for a piece of meat."

Max chuckled. "Casters are Nimgolians' meat, Chas. Especially one as delicate as her."

"It's a girl?"

"Yes," he said and started to speak in what sounded like Spanish, fluently. Golden dust emerged from his hand, a sign that he could be trusted and the little girl crawled out.

She couldn't have been older than six and had beautiful dark curls with soft brown eyes.

They grew when she saw me, and Max spoke to her in Spanish again.

"What is she doing here?" I asked through heavy breathing.

"I don't know, but we need to find her parents, and

fast too, just stay here." He picked up the girl and started to walk with her outside the factory.

I heard the sound of cars pulling up, their tires screeched to a stop.

"Max!" I tried to get up, but my leg was aching so badly. He wouldn't be able to fight off more Casters by himself.

Spanish words flew loudly through the air. A vigorous conversation was taking place outside.

Everyone was speaking at once and I wished that I could understand this stupid language. Then the little girl spoke, really fast and I understood the word Pappy, it was a known word in all the languages of the world.

The conversation grew softer and I could hear Max's voice speaking alone.

A couple of seconds later, three huge guys entered the factory with Max and rushed straight to me.

"It's going to be okay, Chas. Just hang on. They're from the Compound. The girl we saved, her father is the Guardian of their Compound. She got lost when her mother went to the market and they've been searching for her for five hours. We saved the Guardian's little girl. Everything is going to be fine."

"Would you please just stop babbling like a girl," I grunted and he chuckled again.

They lifted me up and it felt as if their hands were spiking into my body. I grunted and bit hard on my teeth as they walked with me out of the factory.

I closed my eyes and only felt the hard surface of what I assumed was the back of the pickup.

More people got on with me.

"Just hold on, Chas. They have a healer back at the Compound."

He spoke to me the entire way, begging me to stay awake, but I couldn't.

I tried to lift up my head to look at my leg, but it was so heavy that I couldn't. It spun like crazy too.

My body felt as if it had been chucked inside a pit of fire. Everything was so hot.

I saw my hand, it blurred out as if the Caster's arrow was poisonous and I was starting to experience the side effects.

My hand was black, not like Max's chest, it was completely black.

I knew that I wasn't going to make it to the healer and that this was it. I was going to die.

"I'm so sorry Max," I breathed out and could hear him screaming, begging for me to stay awake, followed by sobs, but I couldn't hang on anymore.

My breathing stopped completely and everything went black.

I WOKE UP WITH A JOLT AND LOOKED around the room.

The walls were grey, there were no windows and I was sitting at a desk with white pages full of questions.

The page number read 25.

I knew these questions, I filled them in before.

For some reason I was back at the Compound, Max's Compound.

I looked over my shoulder and found the steel door with the red button.

Then it screeched and opened slowly.

My heartbeat started to rise. *What was this? I died a couple of seconds ago, and ...*

A figure walked in and I stared at his face. Nothing

made sense. I'd seen all of them staked against my bedroom wall. They were all dead.

Then how the hell could Elliot be standing right in front of me?

CHAPTER SIXTEEN
THE TRUTH SUCKS EVEN MORE

"TEST!" I YELLED AT ELLIOT AFTER HE explained to me that the past three weeks me and Max had been through was just a freak'n test inside the Virtual Realm.

"Chas, calm down."

"Don't tell me to calm down. I saw all of you dead, hanging from my wall like bugs." The heartache of losing Fox and all her team members, of how bad I'd felt having to tell Max his sister was dead. *Max?*

The thought pushed me over the edge and I started to cough uncontrollably. Gasping for air as more thoughts of *What if I'd used my sand* appeared.

"Chastity, calm down." Elliot's arms were around me. "Deep breaths."

I'd never felt so betrayed. I knew that they would lie to me, but I never thought that they would've gone this far, to use the Shadow Casters being here that night to make me feel that their deaths were all my fault. It angered me.

I pushed Elliot away from me and swung at him hard. My fist connected with his jaw and he even spat up a bit of blood. Virtual test or no, I knew how to throw a punch thanks to Max.

"Where's Max?" I spat the words at him.

Elliot wiped the blood from his mouth with the back of his hand. My nostrils flared as he just stared at me. "He's in his room, just give him some time. The Virtual Realm takes a lot from you, especially the amount of time you guys spent in there."

"Did he know that it was a test?" I was afraid to ask that question but I had to know.

Elliot didn't answer, he didn't need to. The look on his face said it all.

I stormed out the door. Funny how I didn't feel this fatigue Elliot spoke about. I rushed up to Max's room and was glad that I didn't find any of the others who were supposed to be dead, along the way.

I barged through his door without knocking but stopped. He looked like shit.

"What is wrong with you?" I asked.

"Nothing," it barely came out. "It's normal, you on the other hand…" he smiled.

"This isn't funny, Max. If you didn't look like hell I would've beat you silly until you did."

"Calm down Chastity. It was just as real to me as it was to you. But seriously, can I have some of your mojo, please?"

"Screw you Max. You knew it was a test. I didn't." Tears formed in my eyes. Why, because I was beyond mad. Mad at all of them, all of them lied. I never thought that Max had it in him to actually do this to someone on his side, but I guess I didn't know him so well.

I turned around and walked away.

"Chas, wait."

I didn't. I found my room, opened the door and glanced over at the wall all of them had been stacked against.

Whenever I closed my eyes I could still see it. See the pain on Fox's face.

I shook my head. It wasn't real.

I shut my door loudly and turned the key to lock it. I didn't want to see any of their faces for the next few days and fell on top of my bed.

Sleep came much faster than I thought. I was sure that I would toss and turn, but I didn't.

When I opened my eyes again it was dark. I hadn't moved from the position I'd fallen into on the bed, and when I lifted up my head, my muscles ached.

I slowly got up, took a shower and wanted to go back to sleep, but my grumbling stomach disagreed.

Outside my room I found the hallways half lit up with small dimmed lights moulded into the ceiling.

My eyes narrowed as I passed Max's room. I was still so furious with him that it turned my stomach into knots and a nauseated feeling overwhelmed my entire body so badly that I had to stop, lean against the wall and take a couple of breaths.

I found the kitchen a couple of minutes later and went straight for the fridge. Inside was plenty of food, a half-eaten roast and lots and lots of condiments.

The ketchup and mayonnaise caught my eye and I grabbed both bottles as my stomach grumbled again, with the dish of leftover roast.

My heel connected with the fridge softly and I heard it close.

My need to find white bread was just as alarming as the need to get something into my stomach and I started to break off a huge piece of roast with my fingers and chuck it into my mouth. I'd never experienced hunger like this before. I mean, we'd eaten inside the Virtual Realm, but still, I was so hungry that I couldn't stop feeding my face.

Bright light filled the room and I turned around to find Elliot standing in the doorway.

Livid was an understatement of how I still felt.

I looked away without saying a word and went back to looking for bread. It didn't have to be white, but white would be awesome.

He walked up to me and reached over to open one of the cupboards. To my surprise he pulled a loaf of bread from the cupboard.

I knew I should've said thank you, but I didn't want to so I just started making my sandwich.

The fridge opened again, and he took out a glass. I watched him out of the corner of my eye, pouring the milk and then he moved it slowly in my direction.

"I know you are still upset, Chas, but I had no choice."

"You had no choice," I barked softly and stared at him.

My anger didn't want to dissipate as I thought about it again. "I thought that I died."

"I know, but you did brilliantly inside that test."

"Yeah, I'm still trying to figure it out how that test helped to show you where I belong."

He looked away. I was certain that he would come

out with the truth, telling me what these test were really created for.

"It's simple, you're a Guardian, Chas."

I huffed, shook my head softly and grabbed my sandwich.

"We need to speak about the test. It's quite important, Chastity."

It felt as if someone had pulled an invisible plug from my back. My body deflated with a sigh.

"Please."

I didn't say anything, walked back to the table where he'd made himself comfortable and sat myself down and looked up.

He looked at me for a couple of seconds before he opened his mouth to speak. "What you did in those tests, I've never seen any Caster doing that before."

"I did plenty of things in that test, so you need to be more specific."

The corner of his lips slightly curved, which pissed me off even more. This was all a big joke to them. It wasn't to me.

"You killed not just one, but two Shadow Hounds with a bat. How did you do it?"

My left eyebrow rose slightly. "I swung extremely hard at them."

What else did he want me to say?

"You misunderstood my question. Shadow Hounds can only be killed by a Light Caster's sand. You didn't use your sand at all. How did you do it?"

"I don't know. I just did."

"What were you thinking when you did it?"

"That I didn't want to die. Seriously, it's not a big deal. It worked."

He sighed. I knew he was getting frustrated with my answers. It wasn't what he wanted to hear. I didn't know how I did it. I couldn't explain this to him at all.

"Why didn't you use your sand?"

There was the million dollar question. What he wanted to know.

"I don't trust my sand. Ever since I came into Revera, all I hear about is how Light Casters can turn dark when using their sand with the wrong emotions. I didn't want that to happen."

He shook his head softly, like he was amused by my answer. "You've been misinformed Chastity. Only the ones with the Shadow inside their genes can turn dark when they wield their sand and their emotions are wrong."

I didn't say anything and a part of me was just so tired of hiding who I really was. Then my father jumped into my mind, whoever he was. Mom said he was one of Selene's best Guardians. He was a Level Four and from the way his sand glowed brightly in the darkness, he had to be really strong. His blood flowed through me too. "So sue me. None of you ever thought to tell me that before you shoved me into that test. If I'd known that I could've relied on my sand, believe me I would've used it."

I got up, I was sick and tired of him trying to make me confess what I really was. I grabbed my sandwich and my glass of milk and went back to my room.

I devoured my sandwich and drank my milk. I felt sleepy again after my meal and crawled underneath the covers.

This time I tossed and turned. I couldn't fall asleep as I kept thinking about what Elliot had said. Nobody has ever killed a Shadow Hound with only a bat.

I remembered what Max had said after the Shadow Casters vanished. He told me that he'd never seen that before himself. Why was I so different? Was it because I had both good and bad flowing through my veins?

I closed my eyes and could feel myself drift away when my door opened. My eyes flew open and I wanted to kick myself for not locking the door.

I found Leigh making himself comfortable on my bed.

"They didn't teach you how to knock?" I snapped at him too.

He smiled, thought it was funny and shifted his glasses up with his finger and just stared at me.

"I know you're upset Chas, and I wish that I could've warned you, but he gave me no choice."

"Gave you no choice?" I asked not knowing what he meant and then it hit me. Leigh created all of the tests inside Revera. "You created that test, didn't you?"

"I tried to talk him out of it, really, I did, but the guy can get seriously paranoid Chas. And he pondered on the reason of why two Level Four Shadow Casters came into the Outer." He sighed. "I told him two weeks inside a test could not be good for the two of you, but Max volunteered. It was either him or nobody, Chas."

"Wait, what?"

"You were supposed to do that test alone. When Elliot told me what he was planning, how he wanted to play it, I begged him to at least give you someone that could help you through this. Max immediately volunteered."

"Why use the Level Four Shadow Casters?"

"He wanted to know if there was a connection,

maybe something that you knew. Not using your sand, that was brilliant."

"I followed my gut, like you said. So that's why I never dreamed about you."

A huge grin appeared on his face.

"I didn't mean it like that," I said and giggled softly.

"It's cool, I like spending time with you. You are different."

"Tell me about it. Is it true what he said, that nobody's killed a hound before with a baseball bat?"

"Now that was pure genius."

"Answer my question, Leigh."

"Yes, it's true." He smiled which quickly turned into a sigh. "It's also another thing I wanted to talk to you about. He needs a reason for why you are able to do that, Chas. Elliot is the type of person that doesn't let go of things like that."

"Well, I don't have anything. I don't know how I did that. I just really didn't want to use my sand and I guess it must have somehow transferred over to the bat, I don't know."

He pulled his mouth upside down. "That is actually a brilliant answer. Next time tell him that theory. You don't want him to mention this to Selene."

Leigh got up from the bed.

"You're leaving already?"

He laughed. "I can't help it, Fox is about to wake you up. Got to go."

Fox is about....

My eyes flew open when a small shake against my shoulder made my entire body move.

I found her face with snow white spiky hair inches from mine. Guilty looks didn't suit her.

"Stupid questionnaire?" It hurt like hell that she'd betrayed me too and she sighed.

"I had no choice, Chastity. I thought it was going to be a small test. I only discovered afterward what it was Elliot did. I was furious, believe me. No Initiate has ever spent that long inside the Virtual Realm. Anything could've gone wrong."

"So who do I have to thank that it didn't?"

"Nobody. You got yourself out of there without any damage."

I took a deep breath and pushed myself into a sitting position. I wasn't nearly ready to get out of this bed but something told me that Fox wasn't here to just come and say sorry and that she didn't have a choice.

"How did you…"

"I don't know." I didn't even let her finish the question. I knew what it was and remembered what Leigh said. "I'm sorry. It's just frustrating that everybody asks me the same thing, and I don't have the answers. I guess some of my sand got transferred into the bat. I really don't know, Fox."

She stared at my bedding, and I could tell that she was really thinking hard about what I'd just said. "It has to be."

"Anything ever happen to anybody else like that?"

"Not exactly, but the woman that kidnapped you, she had a whip that more or less worked the same way, so I guess it's a trick that not everyone knows how to execute correctly."

"A trick?"

"Technique, I like to call them tricks." She slapped her legs hard and pushed herself from the chair. "You need to get ready, Elliot thinks it's safe for you to meet

205

Selene."

"Wait, what? I'm going to meet Selene, already?"

Fox smiled. "That was the deal Chas. You get one test, and one test only. You passed. You're going to meet Selene."

CHAPTER SEVENTEEN
THE GUILE

ALL THE MEMBERS OF THE ORIGINAL TEAM were ready to leave with me.

The goodbyes were really awkward since I was still upset with everyone at the Compound.

Max looked better. He wasn't so tired anymore and tried one last time to apologise.

"Chas." He took me aside while Tom was speaking softly with Elliot.

"What do you want?" I looked at the wall.

"I had no choice. I couldn't tell you that it was a test, but I couldn't let you do that alone either."

I remembered what Leigh said.

"What do you mean?" I squinted, pretending that it was the first time I'd heard about this.

"I volunteered when Leigh got worried about this test he had to create for Elliot."

I nodded. "So what, you expect me to say thanks now?"

"No, I just want you to find it in your heart to forgive me. Virtual Realm or not, we've been through all of that and I really got to know the type of person you are. Apart from Margot and Stacey, I don't have a lot of friends. It would be nice when you are done being pissed off with me, if we could hang out some more."

I smiled and shook my head. "I don't think that I will come back to the Outer soon. You know where it is I'm going, right?"

He smiled. "Margot and me are joining Revera soon. We've got training positions at the Institute. Something that happens from time to time. Our experience is needed when it comes to training new Guardians. Elliot thinks a change of scenery might be good for the both of us."

"Perfect, then I'll guess I'll see your mug soon." I turned around. It was the best see you later he would get from me.

I knew this was childish, my behavior and all, but I wasn't used to being betrayed.

Ginny was next as I reached Fox again.

"It was so nice to meet you Chastity, a real pleasure, please feel free to come and visit when you are in the Outer again."

She sounded sincere and I smiled, I even gave her a hug. She wasn't technically the one that lied to me, so it was easy to be kind back.

Margot rolled her eyes and disappeared after a 'heartfelt' goodbye of a grunt. Ginny just stared after her and shook her head.

"Sorry about that, she doesn't trust people easily."

I nodded. I wouldn't trust people either if I'd seen both my parents murdered in front of my eyes.

"Nice meeting you noodle, It was such a pleasure having you here, and please don't be a stranger. It's going to be so boring when Marge and Max leave the Compound." Stacey grabbed me into a tight hug. "Stay safe and kick some ass okay? Don't forget about me." She pushed me away at arm's length and I just blew out a breath.

"Okay, Stacey," I said and Ginny smiled.

Elliot was last. "Give this to Selene when you meet her Chastity." He handed me an envelope that had a crest pressed on top of a wax seal. "It's my report on your test results." He smiled but it didn't reach his eyes.

I took the envelope from him. It was thick and I put it into a backpack that Stacey had dropped off this morning with fresh clothes that were so not my style.

"I will," I said and smiled back at him. I walked past Fox and followed John down a couple of stairs opposite the front door. I could still hear Fox and Elliot speaking softly about me, saying that I would probably never forgive Elliot for what he put me through. To be honest, I didn't care what the man thought. Leigh said he was paranoid and I disliked people who carried that feature. They made people's lives unbearable and the other part was that I really just wanted to get away from the Outer.

Tom opened a door that led down more steps. The basement jumped into my mind as we entered a dark room.

A light close to John went on and there were four grey walls with a concrete floor.

Tom handed me Henry and he sat on my arm. A long thin line formed on his beak and I knew that the owl was enjoying every moment of it.

I glanced back at Tom and saw him drawing the

same markings as he had on the mirror against the wall.

When he was done, he stepped back and a door appeared.

"Is this going to be the same as when we entered the Outer?" I was referring to the fog and Henry just hooted.

Fox's giggle came from behind me. "No, but it's just as strange." She widened her eyes once which made me smile and I watched how Elliot, and Tom opened the heavy door.

colors streamed out of the opening. They were bright and blue, yellow, pink, all sorts of colors you could think of. It was everywhere around us.

Tom took Henry from me and nodded his head once in Elliot's direction and disappeared into the colors.

Fox nudged me to go next.

"See you soon Chas," Max said.

I looked at him and saw Ginny and Stacey with him. The first step I took was onto a floor that moved forward. It reminded me of an escalator I'd once seen in an airport when Mom and I went to pick up Tim after he returned from Afghanistan.

The colors never faded and were all around me moving all over the place. I couldn't stop looking around as they swirled everywhere as if a strong wind blew them in every direction. I lifted my hand up as orange came past us. I needed to know if I could touch it, to see what it felt like. A soft warm breeze blew over my skin and I pulled my hand back. It turned slightly orange and I lifted it back up when the yellow came past. My hand turned a brighter orange where the two colors collided but parts that hadn't carried color before, were yellow.

I did it with all the colors that passed by and found John and Fox just enjoying my little experience on our journey to Revera.

Henry stared at me too, sitting firmly on Tom's arm. The owl looked as if it was ready to take a nap and not as if it was surrounded by something out of this world, something that humans would only find in fairytales.

The colors eventually started to fade as we moved along but didn't disappear. A million doors rushed by so fast that it made my ponytail flip backwards. I felt Fox's hand clutching mine and after a couple of seconds the doors slowed down.

I gave Fox a look filled with horror as I knew what these doors were used for and I didn't see any platforms appearing in front of them.

"All of them lead to various parts of the world, just like the door we came from a couple of minutes ago."

"What, that door was moving just like those doors?"

Fox nodded with a smile plastered on her face. I knew she found this new astonishment of mine fascinating and entertaining, but never in a million years did I think anything like this actually existed in the real world.

A loud rushing noise appeared out of nowhere. I covered my ears, not knowing where it came from as nothing was remotely close to us that could make this sound. I felt Fox's hand on my arm again and I turned my head slightly toward hers.

"You see that door?" Fox pointed at a red one, standing right next to a green door.

"Which one, the red or green?"

"The yellow one, right there." I followed the direction Fox pointed at and saw a tiny yellow door coming into view. It was right behind the red and green door. "We are going to run, as we near it and then jump when we pass it, the door will suck us in."

"What?!"

"You'll be fine, Chastity, just follow my lead." Fox smiled again as my heartbeat felt as if it was running a race. I watched as Tom released Henry and the owl flew away in the door's direction. It opened as he neared and swallowed the owl. When it closed again Tom started to run. John was next. He took off his hat, which hid a bald spot on his head and folded it into a long tube and clutched it firmly in his grasp. He ran too. I returned my gaze to Tom who was very close to the yellow door. He picked up his pace and when the door seemed as if it was going to pass Tom, he took a dive and disappeared through it. It felt as if my heart was going to stop.

"Follow my lead, you'll be fine," Fox said again and started to run.

I had no choice, not unless I wanted to stay behind, and who knew where I would end up then?

It felt weird running on something that was moving in the same direction as the path you were taking. It made you feel extra fast.

When Fox started to sprint, I did the same.

This is a bad idea.

I watched with horror as Fox dove for the door and my heart sounded as if it was inside my ear as the door came nearer. Then I took that leap of faith, or dive.

The door swallowed Fox. Her feet were the last parts that vanished right in front of me.

The door was going to open and swallow me next. I waited for it.

The door opened but where I should have gone

forward, turbulence grabbed me and blew me back. The door vanished, and the wind took me further down the colored doors.

I found another door, it looked slightly blue, almost black. My insides twisted as the door came closer. It was cracked, old, and the surface looked like it was dripping sulphur. Then it opened and swallowed me inside.

THE SOUND OF LOUD DRUMS FILLED MY ears. It mimicked my heartbeat and with my eyes shut it resembled the darkness that was manifesting inside of me. Wind blew in my face so hard that I struggled to breathe. Another horrible sound filled my core, and the fear emerging from deep within me made me want to scream out, wanting this to stop.

I tumbled around in the air like a twig in a breeze.

When I landed on something, it wasn't a hard surface, the wind stopped and so did the sound. Air filled my lungs again, and I took deep breaths making sure that I got enough air to calm my beating heart. I opened my eyes and the only thing I could see was a soft golden glow shining from above. I looked up, but couldn't see where the light came from. It was so bright that I had to look away, yet it only lit up such a small surface.

I looked back down and couldn't see anything past the glow. It was pitch black.

I had absolutely no idea where I was or if I was going to ever get out of here. Then out of the darkness images of my life with Mom and Tim appeared. They emerged from blue, white and black dust, like I was watching a movie created by sand specks.

The scene played out a fight I had with Tim a couple of years ago. It happened in the kitchen.

"You're not my father!" I yelled, as I rushed up the stairs and slammed the door so hard that the windows rumbled. The look on his face wasn't anger or frustration, it resembled pain.

It faded and right across from that one another scene started. It was of a snow day, which was a good day, and I was about ten years old.

The scenes played for what seemed like hours. They showed me the good times and the not so good times when Tim lost his temper.

It was strange seeing it through another perspective. It looked dark and nothing like the way I remembered it. My heart beat more as the sound of something evil came again. When I started to run the golden light followed me. It led to a wall, a dead end and I started running next to the wall. I hit another wall, another dead end. There was no escape and I slid down in the corner as the sound came nearer. I covered my ears with both hands and hid my face.

Light flashing on the floor made me look up, and a scream left my mouth as a bright flaming hologram of a skull flew into me. The air vanished and I gasped frantically. Only when the skull vanished, could I breathe again.

The shape of an evil dragon was next. It wasn't on fire but I could make out a light around the darkness of it. Evil crept into my soul and I grunted and felt ice cold as the dragon hit me with force. It went straight through and all the darkness he brought with him flew through every organ inside of me.

I experienced being set on fire, and heard screaming

like I'd never experienced before. My heart felt as if it was going to explode.

When the dragon vanished, it felt as if I was going to lose my sanity.

The holograms of pure evil changed into more images of things, bad things.

Men hurting women, women hurting children, children hurting animals. I didn't want to watch anymore as their screams and cries made me want to lose my mind. I buried my head in my knees and started to pray, pray for this nightmare to end.

"Please, I need your help," a woman's tired voice said.

I looked up and saw a figure of a woman staring straight at me, created by blue and black sand. The woman looked oddly familiar but I couldn't recall where I'd seen her.

"I need to get out of here," the woman started to beg. "You need to help me get out of here."

"I...I....I don't know how," I whispered back. My fear meant I couldn't speak any louder. .

The woman turned around as if something was behind her, or coming for her and she disappeared with a scream that jolted through my being. The scream faded after the image was gone and I could still hear it echoing off the walls into silence. All the hair on my arms and back of my neck stood straight.

Another image appeared. It was a happy one. One that slightly resembled the images of my life with Mom and Tim. The woman inside of them was beautiful. Pure white blonde hair fell over her shoulders and bounced off her back as she was running and laughing. She was happy and I could feel happiness again. The emotion was that strong. The woman kept glancing over her shoulder back at me, as if I chased her.

A small chuckle escaped my lips and then the woman stopped running. She was on alert.

I felt fear again. Something was about to happen and neither of us liked it. The woman ran again, I followed, and then the image froze as the woman glanced around back at me.

I stared at her face and waited for what evil it was going to bring. The woman's face burned like a picture being lit with fire.

A dead body lying on the grass, the same woman screaming in agony. Men, all dressed in some exquisite type of robe emerged from all around her. She tried to explain but they didn't listen. They kept reading her some sort of law, judging her while she tried to explain. She saw a figure, I couldn't see who that figure was, it was blocked by the men; the figure said something to her, but I didn't hear a peep. I could tell by the woman's face that someone was speaking to her, making this beautiful woman realize what was happening, realize her fate as she just sat there with tears rolling over her betrayed face. I knew that look, I still carried it myself, and struggled to deal with it.

The emotion froze her face. I felt it too. She was innocent and these people weren't going to listen. Darkness filled my gut and it occupied my entire core as if this woman and I were connected and that they were reading me my rights.

I watched the woman standing up, as black sand emerged from her eyes, ears, mouth, and hands. It consumed me and I couldn't breathe again. It felt as if it wanted to coax out my own darkness inside of me.

I closed my eyes and remembered what Mom said about the darkness and what it was I had to do when I felt scared or angry. It was dark emotions that would make the black sand appear. Something I couldn't let happen as it would mean they would chuck me in Oblivion and throw away the key.

I was there once and if it hadn't been for Leigh, I would have never found my way home, back to reality.

"Breathe, Chastity!" Mom's voice ordered me. The command was so clear and so loud, it felt like it was going to break my skull.

The pain in my head made me scream again and I fell down onto my knees with my hands clutching my head.

"Calm down, baby. You can do this."

I tried to listen to Mom's soothing tone, a memory, as there was no way that Mom was inside this darkness.

My scream turned into a grunt. I ground on my teeth hard, while praying for this stab in my mind to vanish.

Everything suddenly stopped. I gasped as if the air in this darkness was gone. I tapped hard on my chest, with huge eyes, huge teary eyes and wondered when my life was going to flash by, or did that already happen?

Was I busy dying, or worse, was I already dead?

I fell over and hit my head hard on the surface.

The darkness crept all around me, sound became hollow and then everything became quiet. If it hadn't been clear a minute ago, it was crystal clear now. I was busy dying, this time for real and nobody was going to free me from this nightmare, I wasn't going to wake up and find myself back in some grey room, not this time. My life of seventeen short years was over.

The sound of footsteps rushed through the floor.

They were far off but they were coming for me. Whether they were going to get to me in time, I doubted that. My heartbeat started to slow down, doom, doom, doom, doom, . . . doom . . . doom . . . doom . . . . doom . . . . doom . . . . doom.

Everything went black.

IF THERE WAS AN AFTERLIFE IT WAS DARK. it was nothing and empty.

I didn't like this one bit, and the thought of Oblivion didn't sound so bad anymore. At least there were hounds created by shadows wanting to kill me and a dilapidated world with a sick rotting smell lingering in the air. It meant that I was still alive, even if it was in Oblivion, but this, this was different.

I wanted to go out of my mind, but couldn't. I didn't need air anymore, I couldn't smell, see or even feel anything, and the worst of it was I couldn't hear a sound.

It was a sickening place and one I really didn't want to be in for eternity.

Hours of nothing ticked by, no thoughts, no memories, I tried but it seemed I couldn't remember what memories or thoughts were. I'd never felt so invisible, never felt so unworthy.

Then a jolt of pain hit my chest. It was extremely painful but I welcomed it. It was better than the nothingness I'd been experiencing. Another jolt and then a voice shouted in the distance. It became louder and louder until I sucked in breath. My lungs burned as I jolted up right.

"Deep breaths, Chastity."

I looked at him crouching next to me. Tears were close as my stomach twisted and turned. I moved on all fours and a form of bile came from my mouth. It spilled on the floor. It was dark, and looked like tar.

A pair of hands held my hair back and I closed my eyes as a strong sulphur smell filled my nostrils.

"It's going to be okay. What the hell happened?" Leigh asked. I glanced at him from underneath my eyelashes and before I could help myself I flung my arms around him.

"Thank you."

Leigh's arm folded over my body. Being this close to him, feeling his warmth made whatever had happened, bearable.

"Chastity, what happened?" he asked again, using a gentle tone.

"I don't know," I muttered into his chest as I broke the hug. "The door was there but something blocked my path and it took me straight through another." My head turned sideways. We weren't in the same dark place anymore, but it was just as bad. It was a small room, slightly lit and a feeling of needing to cry out emerged in my chest. Leigh was here, at least that was some sort of reassurance and I took a huge breath trying to push the horrible feeling of never escaping whatever this was to the back of my mind. I looked back at Leigh, and our eyes found each other. I really liked his dark brown eyes, I felt safe whenever I looked at them, I felt hope.

He on the other hand, looked relieved and he blew out some air.

I squinted. "How....did you find me?"

"It's a long story and one we don't have time for right now. We've got to get you out of here."

I looked around again. There was no door or window. "Where are we?" My heart still beat fast but not as fast as it had been a couple of seconds ago.

"It's called the Guile. It's a world where all the bad things in Revera's history replay themselves. Some were unjust, where others, were simply horrifying. Usually Casters die, and Shadow Casters emerge from there stronger. You're lucky you almost died and not the other way around. The only way a Caster gets out of there is if they are dark, powerful or inside a body bag.

I remembered what Mom said about Leigh, needing to be powerful in order to appear inside my Initiation dream like he had. "We should leave, preferably now, if that is okay with you?"

"Sure, so what do we do, say a magic word and "poof" we're out of here? 'Cause I hate to break it to you, there is no door."

Leigh chuckled softly. "Watch and learn." He winked and cupped his hands in front of his chest. When he closed his eyes bright, golden dust emerged from his hands. It started to grow brighter and brighter, so much so that it hurt my eyes.

Then it reached a peak and a bright bluish white light exploded from his hands and filled the entire room. Figures of white birds flew in the colored mist. A unicorn galloped past me, and stood on his hind legs. His mane flew backwards as if in the path of a strong wind, and it whinnied. I jumped as a pack of white wolves howled softly in the distance and ran past me. It was simply breathtakingly gorgeous and something I would never be able to put into words. Not that I wanted to because it would surely win me a straitjacket and a white room.

Leigh nodded at the wall behind me. "There's your way out, take it."

I turned around and where there'd been just wall a couple of minutes ago, an old wooden door with a rusty knob stood in its place. My head jumped back to Leigh as I realized what he'd just said. "Wait, you're not coming?"

He smiled. "Another long story Chas, one I know you are dying to find out. Now go. The door isn't going to stay there for long."

I stared at him for a couple of seconds.

"Go!"

Shaking myself from the trance, I couldn't help but wonder why he kept showing up when I needed him, but I was grateful. "Thanks, again."

He smiled as I turned around and rushed to the door. I opened it, scared that it was going to disappear, and stepped through.

"Oh, don't forget to suck in your breath."

He shouted that advice a bit too late. The air was thin once more, and it felt as if someone had pulled the air from my lungs with a syringe. I didn't notice that there wasn't a floor and fell into nothing once again. The world around me twirled again and I was spinning literally out of control, tumbling and diving head first into whatever was down below, but it was the least of my problems. I couldn't breathe and found my hands clasped around my throat, wishing for a tinge of relief, but nothing came.

My lungs felt on fire and not being able to breathe brought out my worst fear once again: The Guile.

Dizziness clouded my mind, and just like that, everything stopped as I landed with a thud on the floor.

Air filled my lungs and I started to cough uncontrollably while trying to gasp for more.

"She's here!" Fox yelled with relief close by. The bottom of her white leather coat was moving fast toward where I lay. She crouched down as I still tried to regain myself. "What the hell happened?"

I coughed a couple more times before I could even think about speaking, which I didn't. My body was trembling from either shock or fear, I wasn't sure which.

I stared at Fox and I knew my nightmare was over. Tears filled my eyes. I didn't have to say anything other than that, the tears did the work and Fox understood. She wrapped her arms around me and covered me completely.

"Can I please just go home?"

Fox stared at me with concern. "Chas," her voice was gentle. "You are home."

Tom paced up and down a small smelly room that looked like it used to be some sort of cleaning closet that held supplies. He kept glaring at me, waiting for the answer he wanted to hear.

Clearly, lying about what had happened was not going to get me out of this mess I'd found myself in, once again, not by my doing.

"I told you taking the back road through the basement was a mistake," Fox said with a slight 'I-told-you-so' tone in her voice. Cowboy John leaned against the wall by the door with crossed arms, still chewing on a piece of straw. His hat almost covered his eyes as he just stared at the floor.

Tom gave Fox a look of warning and glanced back at me sceptically. "How did you get out of the Guile,

Chastity?"

"I wasn't alone." I didn't know if I was supposed to even mention Leigh.

"What do you mean, you weren't alone?" Fox asked.

"Do we really have to do this now?" John asked with irritation lacing his tone. "She just escaped the fucking Guile, alive. If you ask me, Leigh probably showed up or something." John turned around, opened the door and stepped through. I felt as if I could kiss him right now, except he was old, so not my type and I still felt like crap. But I was grateful that he'd mentioned Leigh's name.

"Leigh showed up?" Fox asked.

I nodded. "I wasn't sure if I should mention him or not."

Tom grunted, and Henry hooted as if he enjoyed Tom's foul mood. Tom turned on his heel and walked through the door Cowboy John had taken, with Henry still sitting on his arm.

Fox took me gently by the hand, which still shook slightly from what I'd just experienced and followed the men. We exited into another hallway, this time it looked like one of the hallways you would find in an old hotel. It had red carpet, walls with golden crests printed on them and old wooden wall frames that really needed some tender loving care. At least it wasn't dark anymore and a bright light lit up the entire hallway.

"So I take it that Leigh is not a figment of my imagination?"

Fox laughed. "No, he's not, but he's not entirely real either."

My head snapped up at Fox who was slightly taller than me. "He's not real?"

Fox smiled sweetly. "He's a Jumper."

"What's a Jumper?"

"Let me think of how to put this." Fox looked around her hoping the answer would somehow glide past us. It wouldn't surprise me. Considering what I'd just witnessed, that would be something normal in Revera. "You could say he is like a computer program. Jumpers, well, we are not entirely sure where they come from, we like to think of them as a piece of essence from very powerful Casters that died."

"How many Jumpers are there?"

Fox smiled again. "Leigh is the only one we know of. He somehow always finds a way to show up in the right place at the right time. He also helps with tutoring students in the Virtual Realm, something he created all by himself. You will see him again, especially in Defence."

I took a huge breath, a bit bummed out that he wasn't real. Still, it was extremely cool. A Jumper. Mom had never told me about those so Leigh must have been created while she went to the real world, not that this one wasn't real. I just never imagined that it could be this real.

Tom opened a door that led to who knows where and I was grateful for Cowboy John, once again, when he waited this time for Fox and I to walk through first. The light on the other side blinded me for a couple of seconds until my eyes adjusted.

I kept staring like an idiot, not because it was beautiful, but because once again it had no color. It was grey and white everywhere I looked, some places almost had a charcoal type of black where others where pure white fading to a deeper shade of white.

Fox giggled, and I looked at her. I glanced at Tom who just stared at me with the grey owl still clutching his arm. All of them had turned into a white and grey picture. I didn't understand any of this. A minute ago, I could still see colors, now they were gone. I even felt a bit disoriented from it and I knew it was evident on my face.

"Welcome home, Chastity," John said as he ran down a set of stairs made of stones.

"Yeah, sure…whatever…" The only good news was that there were no more doors, there were no more halls, just open white skies.

"Tell me Chas, what colors do you see?" Tom asked.

I was really getting annoyed with his demeanor. I knew he knew that I didn't belong here, and to be honest, I didn't really care anymore.

"None," I said and walked the down the steps.

"You see," he scolded Fox.

"It's normal. Maybe if you paid attention, you would know that it takes time for someone like her to get used to Revera's colors Tom. She wasn't born inside Revera," Fox snapped back. "Stop trying to see the bad in every situation and see things the way they are."

She skipped down the stairs past Tom. She touched my arm gently.

I wiped off a tear, a feeling of defeat lodged inside me. What if I was only wasting my time? If I was what Mom feared, then the black sand would come no matter how hard I tried to hide it.

Tom took off his jacket and revealed his bulky arms beneath a really tight t-shirt. John did the same and Henry, well the owl was gone.

"Is it truly normal, for me not to see colors?"

Fox nodded. "It will come, Chas. Just give it time and you will see. Your sight needs to get used to this world and the surroundings first."

A city emerged way up ahead, actually way down below, far in the distance, as the stone steps descended into the mist.

"Are you okay?" Fox asked and I nodded. She took the lead again and I followed her down what seemed to be a million steps.

I looked around. I wished that I could see everything the way I was supposed to. Mom said the little she'd seen was beautiful. Still, it was the total opposite of the Oblivion and that horrible blue room which Leigh had called the Guile.

I still didn't know who those people in those images were, but remembered what Leigh had said.

They were bad events that had happened in Revera's history. Things that were unjust. I kept seeing that woman's figure pleading for her life, but they didn't listen and then it hit me. Her hair was the same color as Mom's. What if that was Magdalene?

CHAPTER EIGHTEEN
DOMBEYA

WALKING DOWN THE STONE STEPS WAS A
journey all by itself. They curved around the wall, down
in another direction and curved again. The sun made me
extremely confused as it would be on one side and the
next minute we would turn around the corner and it
would then be on the other side.

I kept staring at the one in front of me, and tried to look
back where we'd just come from, but Tom blocked my
view.

Fox giggled again. "Revera has two suns. Your eyes
aren't playing tricks on you."

"Two suns?" I asked and Fox nodded again.

Tom passed us after half an hour or so and skidded
down the stairs with his jacket over his shoulder until he
reached John.

"So what's his deal?"

"He's a very private person, but he has a good reason
why he is the way he is. If we'd gone the route I begged
him to take this morning, well hopefully you would see

what I mean," Fox said.

For the next couple of hours Tom yelled a couple of times at us to keep up, and every time he did that, Fox let out a soft grunt and I would pull my face at his command.

I took off my blazer when Fox handed me a bottle of water and was a bit too eager bringing it to my mouth.

"Be careful Chas. We don't have time to stop for tinkles."

"Tinkles," I giggled and Fox scrunched up her nose with a small smile tugging at the corners of her lips.

I took a couple of gulps and handed the bottle back to Fox. For a dream world they should really think about adding a couple of make believe elevators or something. This walk was worse than my ballet classes.

When the first sun started to set, the temperature started to cool down to a heat that was more bearable. The two suns thing was something I needed to get used to if Revera was going to become my new home. Not to mention this grey and white affair.

Only when the second one started to descend did I put my blazer back on. It got dark pretty quickly and I was glad that Fox's white attire almost glowed.

A thousand small lights up ahead revealed the finishing line at the end of this journey.

Trees as big as giants hulked over the horizon and only when we got closer did I hear other voices coming from the distance. The trees were huge and if my eyes weren't deceiving me, they looked like they had doors and windows moulded into their trunks

Small lanterns hung from the trees, and in front of every one was a picket fence made from wood. Some were crooked, others were straight, and pointy and most of them were painted a different shade of black and grey.

I couldn't stop staring as a couple of kids ran to Tom. To my surprise he picked up a small girl and two boys.

Fox turned around and looked at me. "This is the village were Tom grew up as a kid. It is called Dombeya. As you can see their entire village is inside this forest." She smiled as one of the girls looked at her and gasped.

"Fox is here too, everyone!" she yelled. "Fox is here!" She wiggled from Tom's arms and ran as fast as she could into Fox's arms.

"Have you missed me, Grissy?" Fox asked.

"Very much. I made you something," she whispered the last part softly but not softly enough for me not to hear. The little girl's eyes locked onto mine. "Who is she?"

"That, is Chastity Blake. She's from the Domain."

Grissy gasped. "She's from the Domain!"

Fox giggled at her and nodded slightly. "That is what I said." She glanced around at me as they started to walk and put the little girl down. "She is a Dream Caster just like me."

"She's from the Domain and a Dream Caster?" Grissy's excitement was overpowering and I couldn't help but laugh with Fox.

Still, the way Grissy spoke about the Domain was enough to make me think of home; Chicago and Mom. A horrible ache lodged itself in my chest and I felt like I just wanted to be left alone. I had no idea if she was safe, back with Tim or whether my grandfather had her in Oblivion.

Another thought jumped into my mind, what in the

world had she told Tim about what had happened to me? But the thought vanished as quickly as it had come. No, Mom wouldn't have gone back home. She wouldn't have taken a chance like that and put Tim's life in danger as well.

I smiled as Grissy pulled me by the sleeve and forced me to squat in order to be at the same height as the four-year-old.

"Do you have Tulas in the Domain too?"

I looked at Fox, not knowing how to answer her question.

"They do, but what did Pappy Joe tell you about the Tulas inside the Domain?"

"They aren't as smart as they are in this one."

I giggled.

"That's my girl." Fox ruffled up the four-year-old's hair and when a woman in her mid-thirties called "Grizelda"'s name, she ran as fast as she could in the direction the voice had come from.

The woman waved at Fox as she waited for Grizelda to enter their home inside the tree.

Fox waved back and both the woman and the child disappeared back into the tree.

I followed Fox deeper into the forest. Even if there were no colors, I couldn't stop staring at each giant tree that was someone's home. Some of them only had one window where others had four or five. Birds still chirped from their perches as squirrels and chipmunks danced across the branches. I even saw a beautiful grey monkey climb down one of the branches and jump onto another man's shoulder as he walked past.

The people all greeted Fox and nodded their head toward me, which I returned with a slight nod as well. It was a weird feeling of awe and confusion. I hadn't expected the trees to be transformed into homes but, then again, I hadn't expected the people of this city to look ordinary like myself.

They wore normal clothes, and a part of me felt silly when the image of forest people with long pointy ears and leaves for clothes jumped into my mind. These people looked nothing like that.

We stopped at a huge tree which had to be in the middle of the forest. It had at least ten windows all the way up to the top of the trunk and the tree was the biggest of all the ones we had passed previously. Its branches flew into the other trees close by. There was a huge bonfire a couple of metres away. The ambience gave me the feeling they were celebrating something big.

"Here, Chas." Fox brought me back to reality and stood next to a door that led inside the tree.

I took a huge breath and entered the tree.

If Mom had told me five years ago that the dream world was real, I probably would've thought that she was delusional, but if she'd told me that people lived in giant ass trees, I would've called the nuthouse to come and take her away. Now I was literally inside one and it looked like any other house would. Except for the rough wooden walls.

I learned that Tom's grandfather was a big important figure in Dombeya. He was old, but extremely cool and he asked me so many questions about places in the Domain I'd never even known existed. We stayed with him for a few hours and he told me amazing stories about the places he used to visit when he was a Dream Caster. Paris and the Taj Mahal were amongst his favourite.

He'd even fallen in love with a human, which was completely forbidden as they never understood what it was Dream Casters did, or that he couldn't stay with her in the end. But I could see that he'd never regretted a thing in his life.

Grandpa Joe, or just Joe as he told me to call him so many times, was a Tula. That is why Tom had Henry. Henry had chosen Tom just as Abby had chosen Joe a long time ago.

Abby was a beautiful brown-haired fox, which wasn't such a beautiful brown anymore. She was old and mostly lay at Joe's feet while he fed her something that reminded me of beef jerky.

"Why don't you go and enjoy Cale's birthday tonight with the others?" Joe said, looking at me with soft eyes. I still couldn't believe that Tom was related to him, they were the total opposite of each other.

I smiled. "I don't know who Cale is."

Fox and everyone laughed.

"Come, I'll take you," Fox said and got up from her chair. I followed her out the tree and we found a fairytale celebration of people dancing around a huge bonfire. Still the black and white picture made me feel slightly disoriented.

"When do you think that I will be able to see Revera in techni-color?"

Fox laughed.

"When your eyes adjust."

I sighed as that answer didn't give me a definite date which I could mark off on the calendar. I could only imagine what everything would have looked like.

"Hi everyone. This is Chastity Blake. She is still very

new to all of this."

"Spending night and day with a team of Pursuers is not the way to show this lass what type of people we are," a big old guy said.

Everyone laughed as Fox went playfully for him. She wasn't scared of anything.

"Come, Chastity," a girl more or less my age with curls said as she grabbed my hand. "Do you dance?"

"What?" I asked with huge eyes. I loved ballet but hated performing in front of a crowd. Ever since I was little I had disliked it. She didn't pay me any attention and started pulling everyone up that loved to dance and we held hands as we skipped around the fire in a big circle.

I laughed because I felt like a lost boy in a Peter Pan story. I had never thought dancing around a fire could be so fun. The ones that didn't join us started to clap and play instruments. They were all laughing and having a great time while we just skipped and twirled around the fire.

I'd never felt so alive.

After our dance the girl introduced herself as Andrea. While we were talking, her mother shoved a big plate of roasted meat into my hand. We ate so much at Joe's that I was stuffed but the meat looked delicious and I dug in.

Andrea was really nice and asked me all sorts of things about the Domain. What people were like, what we wore and all sort of things that made Nomads, as Leigh called them, sound like we were living on a different planet.

"I've never been. My mother didn't want me to train as a Caster. She lost my father when I was little and since then we've just been trying to live a normal life as best we can. I'm bored out of my mind," she rambled.

"There's nothing wrong with normal."

Her entire body inflated. "Chas, you have no idea how badly I want to go to the Institution. I'm nothing like my mom and I guess got this free spirit from my dad. My sand appeared a couple of months ago and I can't stop experimenting with it. Mom doesn't like it so much, but a girl's got to do what a girl's got to do, don't you think?"

I felt sorry for her. She didn't want to be normal, it showed in her every gesture and I wished that I could just take her with me.

Andrea babbled on about her dreams that she felt were being crushed and I had to admit it was a bit of a mood damper but I had a feeling she had nobody around to rant and rave to about it.

The evening ended when Cale, a boy of about thirteen, went to bed and a very old man who was blind started preaching to us all. It wasn't really a preach, more of a warning.

He went to a couple of us, yelled that we had to be careful of the light, because it had shadows.

Andrea grunted softly. I figured she must know him.

Then he stared straight at me with those glossy eyes.

"Be careful!" he shouted. "The Light, the light has shadows."

It didn't make any sense but I didn't like how it felt as if those eyes saw things we couldn't.

"Come, Father. It's time for bed." Andrea's mom put a soft blanket over his shoulders. He was barely a man anymore.

Fox got up to help and when she touched him, the man said again, in a very disturbing, ranting way. "The light! The light has shadows."

"It's okay, Fox. I've got it," Andrea's mom said while the man still protested. He started to cry, it was sad to watch as she led him back to the tree."

"No, listen to me!" he begged. "The light, the light."

"Yes, Father. We know, it has shadows," she whispered softly as they disappeared into the tree.

The look on Fox's face said it all. She was worried about what he'd said, I guessed Guardians her age with years and years of experience looked at everything differently, even the things normal Casters would call lunacy.

"Andrea!" her mom yelled from the tree.

Andrea sighed. "I guess it's time for bed." She got up and smiled at me. "Nice to meet you Chas. Have fun for the both of us."

"Yeah, sure." I didn't know what else to say as I watched her figure retreat.

The conversing went on. A couple of men and women stayed and the booze started to flow. It was served in an old bottle that had deer skin around it. For a world where you could create anything, the people in this village sure like things primitive.

Fox sat down next to me on the log.

"You okay?" I asked.

She nodded. "I've known Geoff for a long time."

"Is that the old man?"

She nodded again. "He used to be one of the best Casters our world has ever seen. One of the famous ones too. He was the reason why so many of us joined. They still follow most of his techniques when it comes to overpowering the Shadow Casters. A really smart mind and look at it now. He doesn't even know what he's saying anymore."

"That is so sad. I can't imagine seeing someone I admired turning into someone I barely recognize anymore."

She smiled. "It's fine, it happens to the best of us."

She got up and went over to a couple of the men on the other side of the fire. The one that spoke to us earlier, warning me of spending way too much time with Pursuers laughed at something she said, and I smiled. She was a likable person.

I sighed and walked back to Joe's tree. It was quiet. Henry was sitting on a branch high up near the roof, and a small fire was the only thing that was still awake. I figured the rest must have gone to sleep or were still somewhere enjoying the party.

I climbed the stairs that led to the second level. Joe had shown us the rooms we would be sleeping in earlier tonight and I didn't mind the idea of Fox sharing one with me. I'd really become fond of her these past few weeks.

The room wasn't very big, but it was beautiful. It didn't have lights, at least not in the way I was used to back home.

A lantern shone a bright light filling the entire room. It was hanging from a root that grew through the top of the roof. Light danced over the walls and I really wished that I could see it in color.

Two small wooden beds with a dresser and a bathroom, which only had cold water, was enough for tonight.

It somehow reminded me of the secret cabin Mom had trained me in. Not that it was as primitive as the tree house, but it had the same ambience.

I found myself staring out the window. The stars shined through a couple of branches and I couldn't believe how much they resembled the ones from back home.

I couldn't get the old man, or what he'd been saying, out of my head. *The light, the light has shadows.* What did he mean by that? Could he see things none of our eyes could see?

I gasped. What if that warning was about me? I was light, as in Light Caster, and the light has shadows. What if the old man was trying to warn Fox and all the others that they'd transported a Shadow Caster into Revera?

My heart was beating so fast. What if I was really only fooling myself, thinking that I could hide what I really was? If there were people here that could sense I was dark, I was only wasting my time and should just give myself up, come clean and tell Fox who my mom really was. That I wasn't kidnapped, that it was her.

I rolled over onto my side when Leigh's voice popped into my head.

You can choose Chastity.

He had seen the black sand inside the mirror, clawing its way out of me. He knew and he still thought I had a choice.

The door opened up and Fox walked in, without making a peep. I turned around and she jumped slightly.

We giggled softly.

"Sorry," I said. "Didn't mean to scare you."

"Not many things do, Chas. Except being snuck up on. You can be glad I didn't pull out my sword."

I giggled again.

She disappeared into the bathroom while I just stared

at the stars shining through the trees.

Black and white or color. It didn't matter. It was still breathtaking.

When Fox came out she crawled back into bed.

"You should try to get some sleep Chastity. It's going to be a long day tomorrow."

Silence filled the room and I remembered another thing that had been bugging me since I walked through that mirror back in the lighthouse.

"Fox?" I asked.

"Uh-huh."

"Can I ask you a question?"

"Shoot," Fox said sleepy. She'd already lain down in her bed.

"Why is Tom the way he is and Joe's well you know, not like Tom?"

Fox laughed. "I know Tom is quite intimidating, but you need to understand where it is he came from Chastity. He lost both his parents when he was twelve. They were Light Casters that became Seekers. His father was one of the best to retrieve and his mother was one hell of a clever woman. One night, they were sent to retrieve someone like you, a boy that had no idea what he was and it ended up that the boy was a Shadow Caster, so halfway to Revera they were ambushed by Shadow Casters. His parent's crew put up an amazing fight, lost their Tulas and when his mother died, his father grew so bitter that he turned dark. Selene chucked his ass straight into the Oblivion. If it hadn't been for Joe, she'd have done the same with Tom."

"Why? Because his father turned dark?"

"She believes if one parent has the dark gene, the offspring has the gene too."

"That's a bit messed up, don't you think? I mean no disrespect, but people choose whether to be good or bad."

I couldn't see Fox's face but I could tell that she didn't have a problem with my comment, otherwise she would've been all over my ass.

"Go to bed, Chastity. It's been a long day and tomorrow is going to be even longer."

"Okay, sure." I stared back out the window and saw more bright stars as the forest started to quiet down. I didn't know how long I stared at those stars but I could swear that after a couple of hours I started to see a trail of light sand swimming through the sky. My eyelids became heavy and before I realized it, I was fast asleep.

CHAPTER NINETEEN
LIGHT AND SHADOW

I WAS AWOKEN BY A SCREAM. IT WAS SO loud and shrill it echoed through the entire village.
Fox jumped out of bed, and by sheer curiosity, I followed her lead.

I saw the backs of Tom and Joe disappearing through the front door as we reached the stairs.

All of us were wearing what we'd crawled into bed with.

When we exited the house there was a large crowd. There was a woman in the middle of a large circle of people whose screams were now turning into sobs.

"Chas, go back in the house, now," Fox commanded as she rushed toward the crowd.

I wished I had done what she'd told me to but I had to know what was going on, so I followed her after hanging back a couple of seconds.

When I reached the group I saw a very frail body lying on the ground. Huge men blocked my view and I pushed through gently until the entire scene was unveiled before me.

"Mary, Mary, he's dead," Fox said. "I'm so sorry."

"No, leave me alone," Mary yelled. I realized that the sobbing woman was Andrea's mom and the frail body was her grandfather. The blind man who'd given us a warning that night.

I gasped as I saw a huge wound on his torso. If you could call it a wound. It looked like an animal had seen him as an easy meal and had dug its teeth into him.

I immediately thought about the Shadow Hounds and about Fox's story. What if there were Shadow Casters and they'd come for me? I couldn't live in the Oblivion. I wouldn't make it.

I didn't know what else to do, so I let out a scream. Fox immediately got up from Mary and rushed over to me. "I told you to go back into the house. Why didn't you listen?" She sounded angry.

"What killed him?" I yelled at her.

"We don't know. By the looks of it a Shadow Hound."

"They're here?"

"We don't know Chastity. It's not safe out here."

"Are they coming for me?"

She stared at me with a huge frown. "Don't think like that okay? Nothing will harm you while I am here."

I nodded and Joe folded his arm gently around me, leading me back into the house.

I struggled to sleep after that. Why him? He was so old. He couldn't even see and his warning was plaguing me now more than ever. What if there were Shadow Casters inside Revera and retrieving me was their mission? It would mean that Fox and Tom, all of their team members were going to die.

THE NEXT MORNING THE SMELL OF BREAFAST WOKE me up. When I'd dozed off in the night, I couldn't remember. My blissful moment of early morning amnesia soon changed to fear once again. Fear of what I was hiding inside of me, fear of the Shadow Hounds lingering close by, fear of losing the only people I knew inside this new world.

I got up and found a middle aged woman, much younger than Joe but older than Tom, in the kitchen. The woman was making breakfast. Part of the course had been prepared the old fashioned way and another was done through her dust. It was weird to see a whisk beating itself and pouring the white liquid into a pan for pancakes. Small silver specks (which I knew were bright gold) sparkled off the whisk and pan as they prepared my favourite meal. Pancakes and maple syrup.

Tom and Joe were in a deep discussion, probably about last night's events. The ambience inside the tree was thick and smothering. The only one who didn't seem bothered about any of this was Henry, who was digging into a live mouse and sitting on a root that was way above our heads.

My stomach turned as I saw white fur with blood inside Henry's claws and his beak pulled away flesh. I didn't know how he could eat that.

"Morning, Chastity. I wish it was a good one, but after last night." Joe shook his head. "I hope you got some rest."

I nodded with a soft, unsure smile. "Do any of you know where Fox is?"

"She had to leave early this morning with John. Selene's orders. She heard about last night and wanted answers as soon as possible, so I'll be escorting you back to Atlas," Tom explained.

Just great. I nodded once and immediately wasn't looking forward to experiencing the rest of the journey with only Tom and Henry as my companions.

"Come, eat," Joe said and mustered the warmest smile he could while pointing at a chair right next to Tom.

I took it and the lady that was still preparing breakfast plopped a pancake with a bowl of fresh berries and cream right in front of me.

I really wasn't a berry type of person but I remembered my manners and smiled. "Thank you."

"You are welcome. My name is Trinity, you must be Chastity."

I nodded.

"It must be so horrible being taken from your home not even knowing who you are. That is what you said, right Tom?" She tried to desperately change the subject.

"Trinity," Joe said softly. "Let's give Chastity some space to eat her meal."

"Oh, sorry. I sometimes don't think before I speak. Forgive me, Chastity."

"It's fine, really."

I gave a soft smile. I hated that lie, I hadn't been taken at night and that horrible woman wasn't as horrible as they all thought. She was my mom and a damn good one too.

I devoured the pancakes as if I hadn't had breakfast in ages.

Well, if you didn't count the horse food with yoghurt every morning then I technically hadn't had breakfast for a long time.

Around ten we had to go say goodbye to everybody

and it was sad to leave in a crisis like this one.

Tom went to Mary's house while I was still packing. Probably promising her that he would find whoever did this to her father and make them pay.

When he came back, it was time to leave.

"Take care of my grandson on the way back home and try to rub off on him as much as you can," Joe said as he gave me a hug.

I giggled knowing that Tom would probably gag me with a bandage or something for being a smart mouth.

"I'll try my best not to work too much on his nerves."

Joe smiled. "It was such a pleasure to have met you Chastity Blake and I've got a pretty good feeling that we are going to see you again real soon."

"That would be nice. Thank you for letting us crash here last night."

"It was my pleasure."

Henry was hooting already and I knew it was probably at Tom's foul mood because I'd made him wait.

"Got to go, your grandson isn't anything like his old Pappy."

"No, he's not the most patient peanut in the bag."

I giggled as I walked with Joe to the front door. I bent down and scratched Abby's head softly as we passed. The fox was a pure delight and I couldn't believe how fond I'd become of her. It wasn't like I could've just gone up to a fox back home and scratched their fur, not unless I had some sort of a death wish or something. Abby was just like Joe, where Henry pulled at Tom's patience with every hoot he gave whenever the man seemed like he wanted to chip a tooth. Abby was relaxed and followed Joe wherever he went.

The crowd outside was somber.

"When are you coming back?" a big guy asked Tom.

"I'll be back before the funeral. Again, I will find whoever did this Chris."

"I don't want to think that it's a Shadow Caster, as you know what that would mean, Tom."

I knew they were referring to me, but pretended that I didn't know what the two men were talking about.

"You sure you don't want me to come with?"

"No, watching out for this one is more than enough."

"You wouldn't need to watch out for us. Have you forgotten? I used to be one of you guys not so long ago, cousin."

"Still, I'd hate to be the one to tell Sue that her husband died because I couldn't save him. I'll be fine Chris."

"Okay," the guy said and looked at me. "Take care of yourself Chastity. And be careful, okay. It's still a couple of miles until you reach the Inkas."

The Inkas?

"Don't worry, we'll be fine." Tom eased his fears. "Besides, they need you here."

Chris nodded as he grabbed Tom around the neck and slapped him hard on the back.

THE TRIP TO THE INKAS, WHEREVER THAT was, felt like it was taking forever. My nerves were tied up into a bundle and I wished I hadn't asked Fox what the deal was with Tom and his sparkling personality.

I couldn't help but scan the woods constantly. A small snap of a twig made me jump and then I would stop and stare in that direction which only annoyed

Tom more.

We walked past a gazillion trees and the only thing I saw was a snowy owl sitting on the branches of a huge oak. All the oaks looked the same and I took off my jacket again as the suns were streaming down on my skin, baking me as if I was a bun in an oven.

You need to calm down Chastity, I told myself after the fifteenth deep breath and I started to do the only thing that calmed me down. By the chorus, Tom stopped and I walked past him.

I came to a stop a few paces in front of him and saw the annoyed expression on his face. "What, I can't sing either?"

Tom huffed, shook his head and walked past me. "Teenagers."

The rest of the trip was extra torturous but to my surprise nothing happened. There were no Shadow Casters anywhere, no Shadow Hounds that were going to rip through Tom's flesh like they had through the old man's. I was certain that it would only be Tom's life they'd take as I knew they were going to take me to the Oblivion.

The trees still looked the same and when we passed the same tree with the same snow owl three times, I knew Tom was walking in circles, but I really didn't want to say anything, afraid that he would bite my head off, literally.

Small noises escaped my lips as I pondered whether or not to tell him.

Tom stopped again. "What is it Chastity?"

I rolled my eyes at the bark and walked fast again. "Nothing, just that we've passed the same snowy owl three times now."

"It's not the same one."

"I'm sure it is," I snapped and decided I wasn't going to walk another hour to prove that to Tom.

"It's not, they just look the same," Tom grunted. "It is not even alive to be honest with you, it was made to look like that."

"Made by whom? What's it doing…"

"Enough Chas. Just keep walking. We are almost there."

I zipped it, but couldn't stop thinking about the owls. Why would someone put it there if it wasn't even a real owl to begin with? What was its purpose?

I found another owl that looked pretty real but we didn't pass it this time. Tom stopped in front of another oak tree. It was nothing special but we stood there as a soft whisper left his mouth, so soft that I couldn't quite make out what he was saying.

A knob appeared out of nowhere and some of the veins that spiraled around the tree moved away from one another, forming what appeared to be a door.

I just gaped in awe and stared at it, guessing I would never get used to this world.

Tom opened the door when all was in place, and gestured with his head for me to walk inside.

I looked at him, scared about what was waiting on the other side and then glanced back at the door.

"For heaven's sake, it's a portal, unless you really would like to walk the entire way?"

"No, shortcuts are fine." I walked to the door and took a sigh. "Shortcuts are perfect."

"Just remember to hold your breath," Tom said and gently pushed me forward.

Not again.

Once inside, the air was extremely thin and I held the breath I'd taken when he'd asked me to. Then the twirling started, this time it wasn't me, but it was everywhere around me. As if the tree had started to spin around me faster and faster. I stood in one place with Tom opposite me with Henry on his arm. Different shades of white and grey appeared and I knew it was colorful again but that my eyes weren't ready to take all of it in.

This sucks so much.

My hair started to blow around my face and when my head swirled so much that my stomach started to turn, I closed my eyes.

My hair fell back over my shoulders and I opened my eyes. We were in some sort of closet. My legs felt weak and I fell to the ground, sitting on my bum.

A couple of seconds later Tom appeared out of nowhere, but he didn't look close to the state I was in. Henry was sitting on his arm and the owl hooted as if what we had gone through a couple of minutes ago was an everyday activity.

Tom stopped in front of me, fiddled for something in his jacket pocket and took out a piece of metallic foil, thrusting it into my palm. I realized quickly that the foil contained exactly what I needed. Chocolate.

"Eat, the sugar will help."

I knew that. Mom had given it to me once, I thought as I bit off a piece. At once I could feel warmth jolting through my legs and into my toes.

I took two more bites and finally had the strength to stand up.

"You ready?" Tom asked.

Not really, but I guessed I had no choice, and

nodded as he opened the door.

"Welcome to Lalouve."

CHAPTER TWENTY
FAIRIES ARE REAL

I HAD NO CLUE WHAT LALOUVE WAS BUT I did know it was breathtakingly beautiful, even without the colors. It was bright too and a million stars seemed to float around in between objects, objects that only existed in dreams. There were many things flying in the air above me. Pigs with really small wings. A boot, fishing rods, a grand piano, books, many books, and small objects that looked like pocket watches were among them.

Tom actually smiled and Henry, well the owl was twirling in between clocks and bicycles with three wheels. There were electronic objects which looked like animals. Some barked and mewed, and others chirped. There were plenty of doors too, but not like the ones that had flown past us yesterday, no these doors were moulded into what looked like a beautiful tree.

"Where are we?" I couldn't stop staring at this futuristic place.

"The Lalouve is a space created for pure inspiration. When a Dream Caster loses their touch, Selene sends them here."

"Who created this place? I mean the inspiration must come from somewhere."

"It does, the Inkas are responsible for this," Tom said as we started making our way forward.

"Inkas?"

Tom smiled. "You know them as fairies, I believe."

"They're real?"

"Everything that is myth and isn't, is real, Chastity."

"What does that mean?"

He just cocked his head, and smiled mysteriously as he ushered me forward.

The walk was a long one and we passed the Inkas' village, or Lalouve, as Tom called it, which was really just a big tree.

Further up we passed a semi-forest but didn't go any deeper into it.

Round and oddly-shaped fruit I'd never seen before hung from the trees, and berries of different shades filled the bushes.

I'd never seen fruit like that before or the beautiful leafy flowers that grew near the base of the trees. There was grass everywhere, but it looked dull and grey. Still the shadows between the trees looked so inviting that I wanted to take a breather, but Tom and Harry had no intention of stopping.

The dirt road we walked on was long and the only thing I could see on the horizon were hills upon hills. I really wasn't looking forward to this trip. We stopped and rested at a tree to have a break and Tom took out some sandwiches.

I looked at the fruit hanging from the branches above me. It appeared to be fruit I knew but they were mixed together and hanging from all the trees. Although I didn't like fruit, for some reason my mouth was watering for all of them.

"Can we eat the fruit?" I didn't know why I asked as I really didn't like the taste but my curiosity was begging me to just try it.

"Sure, it's for everyone's use." Tom put a piece of sandwich in his mouth and held out a piece for Henry who was sitting on his shoulder.

The owl picked at it with pinching movements before clutching the piece of bread in one claw.

I got up and picked the juiciest pear hanging close to my head and sat down, placing it in my jacket pocket for later, finally enjoying myself in this strange world. When Tom was finished with his sandwiches, he picked up his jacket and we moved on.

One sun was starting to set and the temperature cooled down immediately, just like it had yesterday.

When the other one started to set, I took out the pear. I bit into it and a thick juice, like liquid yoghurt squirted from it. It was sickeningly sweet but had a strawberry-slash-vanilla taste to it. I took a second bite and to my surprise I finished the entire fruit, as it turned out it wasn't a pear at all. Pears had been forced down my throat before, not literally, and they didn't taste like this.

My stomach started to make noises after an hour again and I knew that it was going to annoy Tom any minute.

The shadows the darkness created made my heartbeat rise slightly and then Tom just stopped. He held out his hand and for a second I just stared at him awkwardly, but then curiosity got the better of me, and I found myself reaching out too.

Before us was a low wall. I thought we were going to have to climb over as it looked as if there were many hills still up ahead.

We stood there until a knob finally appeared and Tom opened the door.

He let me go first and I took a deep breath but realized I didn't need it as we immediately stepped through to the other side. I felt as if I'd been transported back to the thirteenth century as I entered a long dark alley with cobblestones, paths and streetlamps molded against the walls.

One of the plates that hung above a door read The Lucky Windmill. I noticed there were a couple of bicycles parked in front of the tavern but we made our way to the alley to the left of the building. As we walked up Tom had to shove one of the drunken men that exited away from him which startled a sleeping Henry on Tom's arm, awake.

I put on my hoody again and closed it up. I was really getting tired now, my eyes burned and my stomach was still growling.

The alley felt long but when we finally found the end, it opened into a huge theme park. There were many attractions and people were everywhere. We started walking through and as much as I wanted to look around, I couldn't. I was too scared of losing Tom in the crowd.

I managed to keep up and we walked up the steps of what looked like a post office but when Tom knocked and a guy wearing the same clothes as Tom answered, I knew that the end of this long and tiring journey wasn't far off.

He signed his name in a black book as the guard just stared at me. It felt awkward after a few seconds and I tried to smile at him as our eyes met, but it didn't take.

When Tom was finally done, we moved on and went through another door, but it wasn't a wooden door. It was clear, and I could see what was happening on the other side. There were plenty of people wearing the same gear as Tom and Fox, and they were bustling around, rushing from front to back all in haste.

They didn't speak to anyone and I followed Tom as he led me to another room.

The room was completely white and it hurt my eyes after a couple of minutes.

It was too white, and I began to get worried that this was another test. One that would surely cause me to lose my mind and go crazy. I was sure this was how the patients felt at the nut house.

Tom just sat against the wall, as if this was everyday protocol while I paced up and down, trying not to let the white room get to me.

A soft pinging sound filled my ears and Tom got up, walked toward me, grabbing my arm as he went to stand in the middle of the room.

He didn't say anything.

"What's...."

"Shush," Tom said and gave me the raised eyebrow glare when I tried to speak again.

"Okay fine," I mumbled softly.

We just stood there, all huddled up like idiots. Then it happened.

The room changed right in front of me. First

windows appeared, then beautiful soft curtains and thick velvet drapes.

The white floor was now covered with a soft grey carpet. I couldn't stop staring at it and had no idea what the hell was happening.

When I looked up paintings appeared out of nowhere. They reminded me of Picasso's as the figures all swirled into one another and most of them were out of proportion.

The walls were richer now, more welcoming than the bright whiteness I'd stared at for the past half hour or so.

Couches appeared out of nowhere and they looked inviting, big. A small coffee table in the middle and a grand piano in the right corner also materialized. Bookshelves appeared against the wall, and before I knew it the room looked like the lounge of a very upscale apartment.

Tom cleared his throat, breaking my gaze from the unknown room as I looked at him. He tapped his chin and I closed my mouth.

When everything stopped appearing from nothing, Tom went over to the couch and sat down. He immediately picked up a magazine with a funny looking gadget on top of the cover, and started paging through it as if we hadn't just experienced something way out of this world.

I jumped slightly as a door behind me opened and a tall girl with short bobbed blonde hair with bangs walked in.

She looked elegant, with a tight skirt, high heels and a beautiful red top. Her makeup was laid on thick.

"Good day Tom. Selene will be with you in a few minutes."

"Thanks Donna," Tom said as the woman touched her ear softly and spoke as if she was answering a call.

She walked to the opposite side of the room, opened a door which hadn't been there a minute ago and disappeared, still busy talking into the device in her ear.

A couple of minutes later another woman appeared. She was really beautiful with friendly eyes. I thought she resembled a woman in her early forties. She wore a soft cashmere sweater and white pants with pumps. Her reddish brown hair was taken up into a chignon and she had small drop earrings hanging from her lobes. She walked straight to Tom, who stood straight, as she took both his hands in hers and gave him two kisses on the cheeks. "I'm truly sorry for your loss. If there is anything I can do to help, please don't hesitate to ask." She sounded so sincere.

She then turned her gaze to me and gave me a warm smile. When she reached me her arms folded around me. Personal space meant nothing to her at all, but for some reason it didn't bother me as much as I thought it would.

"I am so sorry about that test," she apologized.

"It's okay," I lied. I was sure I was going to have nightmares about that for a couple of days, if not weeks, to come.

I remembered the envelope Elliot had given me and I gave it to her. She opened it immediately and started to read. She read quite fast as she pushed one page behind the other. She sighed and put the paper back into its envelope. "Let me guess," Selene said over her shoulder to Tom, "You're still not sure where to put her?"

"Not entirely, Elliot thinks she would do well as a Guardian."

My mouth almost touched the floor. Tom was actually smiling and he sounded polite. *Wow.*

"Okay." Selene sighed and smiled as she looked back at me. "Come, Chastity, sit with me."

She led me to the sofa opposite where Tom had made himself comfortable and I sat right next to her. I had to admit, I hadn't expected any of this. I imagined her completely different, sitting on some throne with light emanating from above, with a scepter in one hand. Something that belonged in a *Lord of the Rings* novel, not this. She was warm, friendly and sounded sincere in her apology.

"So I heard that a Shadow Caster kidnapped you?"

I nodded and remembered the story that Mom drilled into me. "I had no idea what she wanted from me. I swear."

"Of course you didn't," Selene said in a very concerned way.

A cat jumped onto her lap and I froze. It was Shades. I couldn't believe it, the darn cat was here. I found Selene's eyes on me, squinting slightly.

Don't say a word when you see the cat. This must have been what Leigh meant.

"Do you like cats?"

I nodded and stroked Shades' head, just as I always used to do. I had to admit, a part of me was beyond excited that there was someone inside Revera I knew, and at that moment, everything started to make sense.

Shades pushed her head harder into my palm which made me giggle and everyone around me stared as if she was a sacred animal that shouldn't be touched or something.

"He's never done that before," Selene said and

giggled too.

"He?" I was sure Shades was a she.

"Mr. Grey. He isn't a regular cat either. He is an Anitule."

"You're a Tula?" I remembered what Fox had called them.

"Well, I wasn't at first, but then Mr. Grey kept following me around and I guess I sort of became one. Cats, animal or Tula are not very different from one another. They want to be petted when they want."

I giggled.

"You had a cat back home?"

"No, but I had a stray friend. She used to come in every night and I gave her some milk. My dad was allergic."

"So sorry to hear that. So tell me, who do you think the Caster was?"

I squinted at her, not understanding what she'd really asked.

"Your mother or father?"

"It had to be my father. My mother had no idea when those Seekers came for me. I didn't know my biological dad. Mom didn't speak about him that much and for a long time I thought that I was the daughter of some Chinese mob boss."

This made Selene laugh again.

"Far from it Chastity." She raised her eyes playfully at me.

"Is my mother okay?" I knew that she wouldn't be able to answer my question but I had to try to make all of this sound as convincing as possible.

"Your mother…" Selene sighed and I froze again. "She's fine, Chas, but Kyle told me that she was in such a state when they found her in your room, that they had no choice but to erase her memory of you. I'm so sorry, but it's for the best."

I nodded. Lucky for me, it wasn't really Mom. It was just a dummy and I knew Mom was somewhere, hopefully safe and sound, still knowing who I was.

We spoke about everything that had happened up to me meeting her today. Selene was the type of person I could tell anything to. She wanted to know as much as she could so I began at the beginning. I told her about the day my sand appeared and how all my friends, ex-friends who had turned into bullies, started to fall asleep. I didn't know what was going on and then I told her about the dream. I didn't mention the black sand or Leigh as I was still sure that he was not supposed to be in that dream with me.

"So the sand in this dream, what color was it Chastity?" Selene asked.

I stayed quiet for a couple of seconds, trying to rearrange my answer. "What do you mean by what color? It was the color it always is."

Mr. Grey made himself comfortable again on Selene's lap as she gave me a warm smile and stroked the cat's back. A soft purr came from his belly as I carried on telling Selene my story of how I'd woken up and still had the scars on my legs. Then about how I'd put bandages over them but they'd disappeared the next morning, and there was no sign of any blood whatsoever. I ended my story with a tear.

Selene wrapped her arms around me again.

"I know it's not easy to come to a new world where dreams are a reality, and to not know where you belong must be ten times worse," Selena said. "But I promise you Chastity, you are going to meet people, who I know cannot replace the old ones, but can make your new place feel like your home."

"So I can't go back home?"

"I'm so sorry, sweetheart, but it's not a possibility, besides, you will love Revera. The way I see it, you were taken from a world you were never supposed to leave. It does happen from time to time that my Light Casters stray, I mean they are beings too and have their weak spots. They find love in an ordinary human and the product of that love is sitting right here. You are not the first, but you were supposed to be given to your father when you were born. This was supposed to be your home, not the Domain."

I nodded and wiped my eyes.

"Hey, cheer up. From what I hear you are quite a feisty young lady."

I smiled

She looked at Tom. "So, Guardian it is. Dingle will be out of his element when he hears this," Selene said. "We will meet again in three months and we can chat some more then."

"Sounds like a plan," I said.

"We will get you some Guardian attire, everything you need and then take you to Fox's quarters."

"Fox is no longer a Pursuer?" Tom asked.

"She asked if she could be transferred," Selene said, "and I agreed, I think she has plenty to offer guiding our younger Guardians."

Tom didn't like this, but he nodded as if Selene's decision was law.

I, on the other hand, was relieved. She was another familiar face I would see every day.

I really hadn't expected Selene to be so warm and wonderful. She gave me another hug as her assistant came waltzing into the room with a stack of files in her arms. "Selene, the board is waiting," Donna said.

When I got up the cat was all over me, walking between my legs so much that I almost tripped over him.

"Sorry," I said softly.

"What is up with Mr. Grey?" Donna asked.

"Don't know. He's never acted like this before." Selena just looked at him, who I was still sure was a she.

The minute I bent down to say goodbye to Shades, the cat ran, as if something had scared him, to another part of the apartment.

"What did I tell you about cats?" Selene gave a small giggle which made me smile too. Still I had this horrible feeling that I wouldn't see that cat again. It was probably the darkness in me that he sensed and that really started to freak me out.

Selene stopped and hugged me again. "I really hope you are going to love Revera, Chastity. It's really a dream to live in."

"Thank you," I said.

"Tom, can we please speak in private? Donna will take Chastity to the institute.

He nodded as Donna led me toward a golden door.

"Goodbye Chastity, it was a real experience meeting you." He sounded so sincere that I just stared at him. Then he turned on his heels with Henry still lodged on his shoulder. The owl hooted a couple of times as if he too was saying his goodbye and I waved.

I was scared that whatever was behind that big silver door could be my last test, but something told me that the tests were finally over. I'd seen the cat, and the more I thought about it, the more I knew it was Leigh's sign.

Lost in thought, I ran to keep up with Donna. The door led down some stairs and another door appeared. We went through that one and I knew I was never going to know Revera like Donna did, but the sight made me gasp and I stopped in my tracks.

Color had finally come back. I now understood why I wasn't able to see it before as a rich brown color that almost sparkled made me squint. It was so vivid and so rich. The color was brown, but it was a brown I hadn't seen before, and the color was just the bricks on the wall. The steps were the same, a beautiful grey stone and I almost stumbled on them when red came through too.

Donna finally realized what was happening to me and she giggled. "You will get used to the colors, or so I've been told. I can't imagine a world where the colors aren't like these."

"Dull, you mean?"

"Dull?" She shook her head. "Nope, can't imagine that."

I was mesmerized every time a new color found its way into my life. The bright ones made me extremely happy, like giddy happy, which was something I'd never experienced before.

The hallway we were walking down led to the beautiful lobby of an enormous house. It had an old staircase going up and plenty of paintings of professors on the walls that almost looked like they were alive.

Another wall held lots of names on small brass plates. From what I could tell they belonged to important Casters that had graduated from the institute, or whatever this place was. The walls were covered from floor to ceiling with brass plates and I just hoped there wasn't a detention class that involved cleaning these walls.

As we stepped forward, the door opened and a very young, beautiful man, probably in his late twenties/early thirties walked in. He had blond hair, big shoulders and was extremely friendly. Confidence streamed from his body in waves.

"Donna, let me guess, this is the new Caster from the Domain?"

"It is, and Selene wants to see how she'll do as a Guardian."

"A Guardian, how exciting!" He smiled at me. I could feel my cheeks turning red and I had no idea why I had a stupid crush on the teacher, or whoever this man was.

Donna gave her beautiful smile and turned around to look at me. "This is where I have to leave you now, so good luck, Chastity."

"Thank you," I said, sounding like an idiot who only knew two words.

She turned around and started to walk into the direction we'd come from.

"Oh, before I forget," Donna said again. "Your clothes will be waiting at your house, so don't worry about that, okay?"

"Okay," I replied, "Thank you."

I took a deep breath. This place really sucked. I kept losing the people I was starting to know.

"I'm Mark, and it's nice to finally get another Guardian. We don't have many of them around here. For some reason everyone wants to become Designers, or Socialites."

I giggled. "I don't know what a Socialite is and I'm definitely not Designer material. I'm Chastity Blake, but everybody calls me Chas."

"Okay, Chas. Let's see what the Guardians are up to right now," he said. As the words left his perfect lips, a door with the word 'Guardians' appeared out of nowhere inside the walls.

PART III

CHAPTER TWENTY ONE
The Institute

THIS PLACE WOULD NEVER STOP TO AMAZE me. I'd thought my first day at the Institute would be like the first time I entered Revera with Fox and her team, but the two were nothing alike. We were still inside the learning center, but it sounded more like an institution the way everyone was talking about it.
The decor inside looked like it belonged at one of those posh, private schools my mother had shown me once.

They weren't shy about the use of color either. The walls were painted in a soft purple with a rich, darker charcoal black below. Big grey stone tiles lined the floor broken up by lush rugs. The walls were covered with pictures of famous people, like Mark Twain, Albert Einstein, a couple of American presidents, even some royals who lived in the Domain and many portraits I didn't know.

Mark seemed too young to be running an entire school or learning institute like this, but if I'd learned one thing in Revera, it was that age wasn't a factor here.

We walked to the edge of the hall and turned down another. Light seeped through big glass windows and I peeked outside.

I stopped and moved closer.

It was like I was looking through God's window.

Mountains were right in front of us and the drop to the surface was staggering.

Mark stood next to me and stared out the window too. "Beautiful, isn't it?"

"I don't understand. How can we be surrounded by mountains?

"Because the Institute is built on one and some of the floors are actually inside the mountain."

"Are you serious?"

He raised his eyebrows playfully. "Shall we?" he stretched out his arm and I followed him once more.

We turned another corner and the windows stopped as lights molded into the roof took their place. More doors filled the hallway. I couldn't stop looking around as various vibrant colors that you wouldn't typically find in a school welcomed me. It made the colors back home seem dull. There wasn't another word to explain it, except it seemed the Domain had gotten all the leftover colors.

We stopped in front of the last door and Mark knocked.

An older guy with a grey mustache opened the door. He had a friendly smile; grey highlighted his raven black hair and the bluest eyes I'd ever seen.

Mark smiled. "Good morning, Dingle. I have the new girl, Chastity Blake from the Domain; she's going to be a Guardian."

The guy looked at me and smiled. "A Guardian you say?" He looked at Mark, and back at me. "Well Chastity Blake, welcome to Guardian training." He stepped out of the way and stretched out his arm for me to enter.

"Fox will pick her up this afternoon."

"Fox is no longer a Pursuer?"

"Nope, she asked for a transfer, she's now the headmistress of the Guardians' home for girls." He looked back at me. "Chastity, if you need anything, please don't hesitate to ask," Mark said as he waved goodbye and flashed me his super gorgeous smile again.

I sighed as the door closed, and was quickly brought back to reality as I followed Dingle into a slightly dark classroom. There was absolutely nobody in sight.

"Please tell me I'm not the only Guardian?"

He gave a heartfelt, warm laugh and it lasted for almost a minute.

"Sorry, Chastity." He coughed to clear his throat and took a seat behind his desk.

I took a seat on the first open desk I could find.

"I was thinking we should get to know one another a bit before you join up with your other class members."

He opened a file and started to read from it. "It says here that a Shadow Caster kidnapped you." He stared at the file and his eyes rose as he read further. He slowly looked up and stared at me again, closed his eyes and shook his head softly.

"You know who Vinicola was?"

I shook my head. Lied again.

"She's an extremely dangerous Shadow Caster. One we thought was dead, until recently. It might, one day, be useful to know what she wanted from you."

I didn't like how he said that, like I was some sort of bait to lure my mother out of her hiding spot.

He kept reading further.

"You were in the Guile too?" he asked with slight admiration, or disbelief, I couldn't tell which, in his tone.

I nodded.

"What was it like?"

"Horrible," I answered with the first thing that came to my mind. "I thought I was going to die."

"You are definitely a Guardian if you survived the Guile." He smiled and carried on reading.

He read quickly and a couple of noises escaped his lips. He trailed off as pure shock filled the age lines of his eyes. "They only put you through one test?"

I nodded.

"How long were you inside the Virtual Realm?"

"About three weeks."

"Three weeks!" He looked at the file again and his eyes scanned through the report I assumed Elliot wrote.

"You know Max?" he asked again.

"Yes, they thought it was wise that someone was with me in the test. It really felt so real."

"They came early this morning, him and Margot and I have to say, the things the twins experienced is going to make this an exciting year."

"Max and Margot are already here?" I asked and he nodded.

"They're helping me with training. It was a wise decision to get sub-teachers to help with training the new guardians. I haven't been in the field for a long time, and I'm sure there are quite a few new things that I'm not familiar with."

I didn't like the fact that they were already here.

I let him finish reading my file and then he closed it.

"One thing I ask, Chastity, is you will soon discover that my methods are not entirely curriculum standard, but I do it for your own safety, to make you as strong as you can be. Facing real danger everyday is what Guardians do, and I'm the guy to help you learn how to deal with it. So there is a bit of discretion and loyalty when it comes to sharing my methods with others, that is all I'm asking."

A cold finger ran up my spine, I felt adrenaline rushing though my body just hearing those words leaving his mouth. I had no idea what was waiting for me or whether I was going to like it or not, but I nodded.

He smiled again, clapped his hands once and got up from behind the desk. "Great, excellent to have you in my class, Chastity," he said and walked past the tables and chairs to the wall at the back of the room. There wasn't a door or sign of another room. But as we got closer, the floor shifted and steps that led down to a lower level appeared before us.

The steps rumbled slightly and I could hear other voices coming from below. Someone shouted a command, others cried out, army-style, with a lot of yes and no sirs. I sighed. As if I hadn't had enough of that back home.

We walked in on at least a dozen kids standing in a circle inside a huge training room similar to the one my mom had trained me in. There were target boards and ropes dangling from the roof. A huge grey padded mat was in the middle where I saw two students fighting as the others cheered them on. The leader couldn't have been much older than any of the rest of us and then I gasped as I finally realized that it was Max. He'd cut his hair army-style short and was shouting commands at the two individuals fighting inside the ring. I looked around for Margot but didn't see her.

Everyone stopped when they saw Mr. Dingle, and Max blew his whistle. "Cadets, in line!"

They all moved into a perfect line and saluted Mr. Dingle. An urge to laugh out loud and shake my head filled my core. Clearly choosing to be a Guardian had been the biggest mistake of my life.

"At ease," Mr. Dingle said softly and they all, in perfect unison, took a step to the side with their arms behind their backs.

My gaze fell immediately on Margot. She was one of the girls in the ring, and I saw four others standing beside them. A parrot flew from nowhere and landed on a girl with bright, golden brown curls. She kissed his beak once and pretended to be a soldier again. Seven boys stood right next to the girls. All of them were big and masculine with broad shoulders. Max took his post next to Margot but I swore I saw a small smile tug at the corners of his mouth as he looked at me for a few seconds.

"I want you all to meet Chastity Blake. She came from the Domain a couple of days ago."

"Sir?" one guy asked.

"Yes Rudy."

"Is she the one that escaped Duke and Kyle?"

The class was extremely quiet waiting for Mr. Dingle's answer. He had a soft smile on his face.

He just nodded and all of them gave a small chuckle and giggled.

How many of them know about that day?

"Let's not spread it around, please," Mr. Dingle answered. "It's not good for the Seekers' status."

"Max, I need you to train a bit with Chastity one on one for the next couple of weeks so we can see where her strong and weak points are," he commanded.

Max smiled. "I'm sure I know where her strong points already lie, sir."

"Still, we need to make one hundred percent sure."

"Not a problem, sir," Max said.

"Welcome to Guardian training, Chastity." Mr. Dingle smiled and went to sit in a chair against the wall, observing us.

I sighed as Max gave the others the command to continue. They didn't cheer on Margot and her previous opponent anymore, but started forming groups of two and began fighting against each other. Some of the girls were fighting against the boys which made all of this feel so unreal.

"I told you that you would be seeing me again soon."

"Yes, you did." I sighed. "Too soon."

He smiled. "Are you ever going to forgive me for that stupid test?"

"Sure." I shrugged. "So what now? Are we going to fight too?" I looked at the others who all seemed as if they wanted to tear each other apart.

"Here." He threw a roll of duct tape at me which I barely caught. "Make sure you tie your fingers up."

I stared at the roll for a couple of seconds and back at his own hands and found duct tape taped around his knuckles and hands. I started to wrap my own hand with the tape slowly, and as tightly as I could manage without feeling as if I'd cut off all blood circulation to my hands.

It didn't look as neat as his and when he chuckled I looked at him again. He shook his head softly and took the hand that was already mummified, started ripping off the tape.

"Ouch," I yelled. "I actually need skin to cover my hand if you don't mind."

"The faster the less painful it is, Chas."

"I have to disagree on that." My hand burned and I contemplated giving it back to him, thinking that I had to go through all of this again when we were done.

"Give me your hand."

I did and he rolled it around my hand again.

"See, through the fingers, once, make sure that your knuckles are well protected so that the punches don't hurt."

"Punches? You mean we're going to fight?"

"Don't look so surprised Chas, this is Guardian training. Fighting is what we love to do and something you are quite good at."

I wanted to cringe. *Why, why, why do all my choices find a way to bite me in the ass?* Even if I was good at it, I still didn't like to fight.

When he was done with the other hand too, I had to admit, my hands felt well protected but I still didn't know if I was ready to fight against Max.

"Just go—"

His first punch was solid as it made contact with my face. I felt like one of those cartoon characters who got run over by a bus and started seeing stars floating around my head. I was slammed against the floor and grunted when my head touched the cold surface of the mat.

"There is no taking it easy in this class! You will

learn just like all the others did, Chas. Through fighting, the virtual lessons and weapons training." He paced in front of me, like someone that was ready to tear me apart. "Again," he said and came at me fast.

I ducked and avoided one of his punches but another hit me right in the stomach. I let out another groan and clutched my stomach. It felt as if he'd smashed the air out of my lungs. Still the minute I could breathe again he came for me once more.

I held my arms in front of my face, clenched my stomach muscles as hard as I could and just took each of his beatings. Back home, I was sure Mom would've flipped if we'd had classes like this, but this wasn't a world like home. In this one you had to fight strange objects regularly if you wanted to survive. Then again I remembered Mom's soft side and not the Shadow Caster side of her that was a platinum blonde with a reputation for being one of the nastiest Shadow Casters alive.

The punches carried on for what felt like forever and when I couldn't see through my left eye anymore the girl with the bright, golden brown curls took me to the nurse's office.

I felt defeated. There weren't any stepping stones in this class. It was chuck an ass in the deep end and watch it either drown or make its way to the edge type of class.

"You Guardians seriously don't know the meaning of the term first day, do you?" The nurse asked. Her voice sounded sweet and apologetic, I wanted to look at her but I couldn't see as my eye had swollen up so bad that it resembled the term beaten to a pulp. "Sit." She led me to the bed, the soft surface made me want to lie down but I chose to sit up.

Only when she pushed my body downwards did I

follow her gesture. My head ached and I cringed as she started dabbing an ice cold ointment on my face.

My lip pulsed and I flinched more as she dabbed some of it on there too. It carried a strong minty smell that burned my nostrils, but the deeper it entered my mind, the softer the pounding in my skull became.

She lifted my shirt up and I ached everywhere. I knew I was covered with bruises and the only thing I could think about was that Max was going to pay dearly for this. I would make him pay.

She rubbed some of it on my stomach and on the sides of my body. I winced every time she touched me and a part of me wished that I'd chosen another group, like the Designers. Then again, I would've sucked just as bad as a Designer.

A part of me knew that Dingle would never let me leave the Guardians now. There weren't many to begin with and I guess I knew the reason behind that now.

"I think we've covered every bruise. Try to sleep," the nurse said and I could hear her footsteps disappear.

The girl that'd walked me to the infirmary was gone. Or so I hoped. Whatever the case, she didn't make a peep.

I dozed off quickly and found myself walking through a maze of hallways. The bright walls made me squint.

There were students all around me, bumping against me as I tried to get to the other side of the hall, they seemed so real. But the faces belonged to strangers.

A whistle at my side made me look up and I found Leigh with a backpack slung over his shoulder.

I wanted to cry for making the stupid decision to become a Guardian.

"Not what you thought it was is it?"

I shook my head and rested my head against his shoulder. It was good to see one familiar face. "Please tell me that I'm still stuck somewhere in the Virtual Realm and that Guardian training is anything but this."

He chuckled. "I'm sorry to burst your bubble, Chas, but that was the real world."

I winced and gave an animated cry which made him chuckle. "Hey look on the bright side. One day you're going to be able to kick Max's butt for real."

"You can't do it for me?"

He laughed. "I do it on weekly, since the day he stepped into my world, but my punches have no effect on him whatsoever in reality. He wakes up unharmed."

I giggled. "That sucks so much."

"They aren't bad people Chas, but remember what I told you about being careful who you trust. Geoff's death..." He shook his head.

"You think it's the Shadow Casters?"

"If it was, they're getting really good at entering Revera."

"Do you think they're here for me?"

"Don't think like that, okay? The Institute is safe. Too many Guardians are teachers here."

I nodded and remembered seeing Shades.

"How did you know about the cat?"

Leigh gave me a smile. "The things I know, would raise the hair on your arms." He winked and started to walk in the opposite direction to the other kids.

My stomach flipped at his small gesture, and a giggle escaped my lips.

"See you later, Chas."

I woke up right before I could say 'see you' back and

found myself still on the bed in the nurse's office. I could see and squinted slightly as the white of the walls and other bed linen was too bright for my sight.

Both my eyes were in mint condition again and when I touched my lip, I felt that the swelling had gone down. The crack Max left was also gone.

"How do you feel?" the nurse whom I only heard before asked, as I got up. She was nearly a head shorter than I was and wore a white uniform with a little hat on her big red curly head.

For some weird reason I didn't ache as I had when I'd come in earlier.

I lifted up my shirt, the bruises on my stomach and sides were gone, like the past hour had never happened. I hopped off the bed and found the nearest mirror. My face was back to normal and didn't resemble a punching bag anymore.

"Is this for real?"

The nurse laughed.

"It's amazing stuff, isn't it?"

"I seriously need to get me some of that ointment."

She laughed at my reply but didn't say anything, like where I could buy some. I don't think she realized I was dead serious.

"I think what Dingle does is breaking the rules but it's for your own good. Nobody cares as much about you kids as Dingle does, especially when it comes to the Guardians. He isn't a bad guy, you'll see real soon."

I sighed and huffed, thinking it wasn't so bad getting beaten up one minute and having this wonderful nurse, whose name I still needed to get, with her wonderful ointment, erase all the pain.

"Okay. I'm Chastity, but everyone calls me Chas."

"I'm Leonara. I know it's not the Domain and I know Revera is a lot to take in, but welcome home Chastity."

"Thanks, I guess."

She smiled and stroked my back softly just as a knock on the door came. Fox entered with concern lacing her features. "What the hell happened? It's her first day and…"

"Relax, I fell down a rope. I'm fine. Just a precaution," I lied. I hated to lie but I promised discretion and that I wouldn't mention Dingle's methods.

"You sure? I can always speak to Dingle and ask him to ease up."

"Hell no! I want to be a Guardian. The only way I'll get there is to do whatever they are doing."

Fox shook her head. "Okay, whatever."

I laughed. "See you later Leonora."

"Please don't say that Chas. You're going to be careful tomorrow," Fox said.

"Bye Chas," Leonara sang as she went back to her paperwork.

"So apart from falling down the rope, how was your first day?" Fox asked as we walked down the hall.

"Selene is nice." I still couldn't believe she was the only Somnium, the one that kept order in Revera. "The rest was fun, really. Guardian training is not so bad."

I sort of believed that.

We walked down the hall and just like in the dream; I had to squint as the bright yellow was hurting my eyes.

Fox cleared her throat. "And Dingle?"

"What about Dingle?"

She gave me that look, the one where she knows I know exactly what she means. "What is he teaching you in that class?"

"What Guardians should be taught." I giggled and rolled my eyes slightly to the left.

"I'm just worried about him being offered this position."

"Why?"

"Chas." She blew out some air and I knew that what she was going to say next could get her fired and I felt all the hair on the back of my neck rise. "There are rumors that he almost went to the dark side...."

"So, Dingle was almost chucked out of Revera because...."

"By choice," Fox added before I could finish that thought.

"What?" I followed her down the steps.

"I wasn't impressed when Selene told me the news, but she makes the decisions around here. Be careful, please."

"Okay," I said. The thought about Dingle wanting to be dark kept playing around and around in my head as we walked.

When we turned the corner the walls were covered with royal blue tapestries and after passing through a huge main door, we stepped onto the greenest patch of grass that I'd ever seen with lots and lots of trees.

I had to admit, the scenery was something that could only exist inside a dream, with beautiful oak trees and blue open skies with no clouds blocking either sun.

Cobblestones with small white and purple flowers growing everywhere led us past the trees. Once we cleared the trees, buildings were outlined against the horizon.

About three to be exact.

When we got closer, I realized the buildings weren't buildings at all but mansions. Big, modern mansions with glass walls and plenty of space.

When I looked back the hulking building of the Institute barely showed from the top of the trees.

"So, we're still on top of a mountain?" I had to know.

"Yes, Chas," she said and laughed. "Don't worry, we are perfectly safe up here."

We walked to the mansion located on the far right and saw that there were about ten of these structures built inside a huge circle.

There was a huge swimming pool, tennis courts, basketball hoops and even a volleyball pit, surrounded by a long running track in the middle.

Fox gestured with her hand to follow her and we walked to the nearest house on our left.

It was big, really beautiful and reminded me of one of the houses back home we could never afford. It had glass walls that ran three stories up.

She stepped to the front door, which was actually a wooden door that had a huge welcome sign on the top, and a plate that read in Celtic letters, *House of Lords*.

"Welcome to your new home, Chastity. This is the House of Lords," Fox said. "I know it sounds cheesy, but hey, I didn't pick the name."

I giggled again as I followed Fox inside.

House of Lords. I liked it even if it sounded cheesy. At least I had a home now, and apart from all the people I'd had to say goodbye to, it was a beautiful home. *House of Lords, oh my.*

CHAPTER TWENTY TWO
CATS! WHAT MORE CAN I SAY

THE INSIDE OF THE HOUSE WAS ENORMOUS.
the walls were a soft beige and grey, lined with plenty of
abstract paintings. The lobby had a huge chandelier
hanging from the roof and a beautiful spiral staircase
welcomed us.

A lush, black carpet was strewn on the wooden floor
hiding the knotting in the oak floor boards.

"Your room is way at the top," Fox said. "But let me
show you the entire house first. I want you to feel
welcome, Chas."

I smiled as I followed her down the hall and into a
huge, open kitchen. There were so many cupboards and
a big walk-in fridge on our left.

At least three microwaves, from what I could see,
were spread over the kitchen on top of beautiful granite
countertops.

In the middle was an island with the stove and pots
and pans hanging from a rack mounted into the ceiling,
dangling right above.

As we passed through the kitchen Fox led me down two steps into the most beautiful open plan dining area I had ever seen. Complete with a huge glass table with soft semi-thrones that could seat almost twenty people.

There were no traditional walls, and light streamed into the room through huge glass panels. It highlighted the most beautiful orange and soft brown décor I'd ever seen. Even the flowers were orange and they complimented the dining room beautifully.

It was simply breathtaking.

Against one wall there was a big rule board that read, *In this house we forgive and forget, we support each other and think before we act. We give second chances and we never, ever have a dull moment.*

I smiled at the last part.

"Breakfast is served around seven thirty, lunch, one and dinner is at six."

"Got that."

I followed her back the way we'd come, past the lobby and down another hall that led to a different part of the house. Frames of uplifting quotes about how to reach one's dreams and how to treat each other lined the wall.

I stepped down more steps and found myself in what appeared to be a lounge-slash-game room.

"Here is what we call our entertaining area."

"It's a play room."

"Okay fine, a play room then. It's the Ping-Pong machines, right?"

I giggled and nodded.

"Oh, hi Natalie," Fox said and I didn't even see the girl who had taken me to the infirmary earlier hanging out in the lounge. She had her parrot lodged on her shoulder. "This is Chastity."

She waved. "We met, earlier in class."

I waved back.

"And this is Charlie. He is her Anitule."

"Hi Charlie," I said and I remembered what Henry was like.

"Hallo," Charlie said in a parrot voice. "Nice to meet you Chastity."

I giggled.

"He understands?"

"Yes, he does. He doesn't greet everyone like that, so he must like you," Natalie said and kissed him softly on the beak.

The parrot closed his eyes as if he loved her kisses.

My eyes caught the library through another set of double doors. It was huge and had books stacked right to the top.

I walked over and started scanning all the titles, some were unknown while others were books I'd grown up reading.

I found one open on a big round chair that could've easily been used as a bed.

My curiosity got the better of me and I reached out to pick it up.

"Chastity, don't touch that," Fox warned and I pulled my arm back as if it was a snake ready to strike.

She let out a giggle. "Sorry, it's just that books this side aren't like the kind you are used to back home."

"They're not?"

She shook her head. "Sure there are words written and everything but someone is actually busy reading it and if you close it she won't be able to get out."

I gasped. "Get out?"

Natalie laughed too. "I have no idea how you guys experience books inside the Domain but here, we actually get sucked into the story, literally, and become one of the characters."

"What?!"

"It's fun, we don't have to use our imagination but experience it on a much deeper level, the way the author meant it to be experienced."

"You're shitting me, right?"

"Language, Chas." Fox had that raised eyebrow kind of glare.

Natalie shook her head with a huge smile plastered on her face, as I made my apologies to Fox.

"So what you are saying, just to be on the same page, is if I open a book, I will literally go into the world the author created and become one of the characters?"

"Yep, that pretty much sums it up," Natalie said with a small giggle in her tone.

I looked at the book lying on the couch again. "And someone is actually reading that one now?"

They nodded again.

The book started to glow suddenly. A figure flew out of it and plopped onto the couch.

She was a brunette with shoulder length hair and big glasses resting on her nose.

"That one is not for the faint hearted," the girl said and saw me standing inches from the couch. "Oh, hi. I'm Sophia, you must be the new girl," she said as if she'd been waiting for me to show up the entire afternoon. She got up and held her hand out to shake mine. *No problem with her confidence either.*

I just stared at her with huge eyes.

"Sorry, this is seriously one of the best novels I've

ever read," she said as she walked past me and put it onto the shelf again.

"Chastity," I finally said and couldn't stop staring at the book she'd just been holding.

"So, you're the one from the Domain? For the past three days everyone has been chatting about you nonstop. I bet you never thought a place like Revera ever existed, right?"

I shook my head.

"Well, welcome home then. I hope you're going to love it here."

"Thanks."

Sophie smiled, picked out another book, right next to the one she'd just put back and skipped right past us and out of the lounge.

"Soph is a bit of a nerd but she is one of the smartest girls I know." Natalie smiled with Charlie still lodged on her shoulder. *A bit of a blabber too.* "Good to know, then I know who to ask for help if I struggle with something."

"I have no idea what that was though." Natalie pointed back at the direction Sophie had skipped. "She usually keeps to herself."

"It must be a really good book then." Fox walked to the shelf and glanced at the title too.

Natalie just giggled as Fox gave her the book. "You should read it, it's really good."

"Maybe not, if it does that to Soph, I'm afraid you will not be able to live with me."

Fox giggled. "Let me show you to your room, Chas."

I followed her up the stairs again, past the first and second floor. The staircase ended on the third floor in a cul-de-sac and there were only two doors.

"Sorry, all the others were taken and you're stuck on my floor."

"I don't mind. At least I'll feel safe."

Fox smiled and opened the door on the left. "This is your new room, Chas. Don't forget, dinner is served at six."

"Thanks," I said as she closed the door.

I had to admit, my anger with Fox had disappeared much faster than my feelings toward Elliot, Max and Margot.

My room was big, much bigger than the one I'd had back with Mom and Tim. It had big windows with beautiful, night blue curtains and a double bed. The linen matched the curtains and there were beautiful pictures made from sand hanging against the wall.

There was a small bookshelf but it didn't house any books. I was dying to try out a novel this side but realized that some of the stories that I'd loved to read would be a horrible experience in reality. Especially Crime Fiction.

A bathroom was on my right and I was grateful that I didn't have to share with all the other girls.

A small desk with a computer and a chair was against the wall opposite my bed and white cupboards that matched the carpet made the room complete.

I found heaps of clothes folded nicely on top of my bed.

They still had their tags on and I started to look at each garment carefully.

There were plenty of training clothes. A lot of tank tops, hoodies, and skinny pants of all colors. I was very glad when I found a good pair of training shoes at the bottom of the pile.

I put them away when I was finished and went on to the next which contained small bags of underwear.

The next pile was t-shirts, followed by slacks. Only a couple though. Two pairs, one black and one brown.

The next batch contained two pairs of jeans and long-sleeved shirts.

Thankfully, two pairs of nighties, the shorts and shirt type, were also in the last batch.

Someone had also gotten me a pair of pumps, boots and slops with a pair of slippers.

They'd bought everything and from the labels it looked like they were all my size. How they got that right was beyond my knowledge.

AT DINNER I MET ALL THE GIRLS THAT lived in the House of Lords.

I didn't remember all their names but the ones that stayed with me were called Amy and Tarryn. They reminded me a lot of Nicole and Clare and everyone loved them. I kept to myself even though Natalie tried her best to tell me all of the girls' names.

Then the door opened and a group of four girls entered. They were very masculine, with muscles most of the boys I knew could only dream of.

"Mila, I told you girls that dinner is at six," Fox said sternly.

"We were busy," the one I assumed was called Mila replied. I didn't like her demeanor as she sunk down onto a chair near me, followed by a girl with brown long hair and two others with light golden blonde hair. Mila had bright blue hair and had so much jewelry on her face that I was scared to look at her.

The entire table was silent as the girls started to grab

bowls of food to dish up.

"I know what it is you are trying to do, young lady, and I can tell you, you are only going to make it harder on yourself." Fox had a soft tone to her voice but her posture was yelling *Don't mess with me*.

"Please enlighten me as to what it is I'm trying to do?" she bit back.

"Seriously?" Natalie said. "You have to do this right now?"

I gawked at Natalie. *Does this girl have some sort of a death wish or something?*

"Eat your food, parrot face."

Natalie laughed. "Well at least I've finally got something in common with Charlie."

Some of the girls snickered, but stopped the minute Mila glared at them.

"Enough. I'm not going to be played with. This is my house now and if you don't like it I suggest you take it up with Selene. You will be on time for dinner, all of you, or you won't get any. Do I make myself clear?"

I'd never heard that tone coming from Fox before.

Mila just stared at her. "Fine, no need to get your panties in a twist," Mila said the other three girls snickered this time.

"And I will be treated with respect. I don't know who your previous Guardians were, but I promise you, I'm nothing like them."

"Good to know," Mila said and I saw Fox closing her eyes.

"Leave this table, right now."

"What?" The girl said.

"I said leave this table. Or do you want me to make you leave?"

"But I haven't had anything to eat."

"Go tell that to Selene. Now, leave."

Mila's jaw muscles pumped as all of us just stared at both of them.

She grunted, jumped from her chair, which fell over, and ran up the stairs.

"If anyone else would like to leave, be my guest." Fox looked at the other girls.

"You're not going to last," one of the girls with brown hair said and followed Mila. The other two just looked at their plates.

Forks clanged as everyone started to eat their supper again.

"If you can't follow simple rules, then you will learn to follow them the hard way. I refuse to be disrespected inside my own home. Do I make myself clear?"

"Yes, Ma'am!" All of us said and Fox nodded

"I'm not married either, so it's just Fox."

A couple of girls giggled and we all carried on with our food.

A knock came on the front door and Fox excused herself from the table, she reentered the dining room a few minutes later with Margot right behind her, luggage and all.

"I really am sorry, Fox. I didn't think it was going to take this long."

"Don't worry about it, I'll speak to Dingle in the morning. Now go sit down, have something to eat and I'll show you to your room later."

Margot smiled and took a seat at the end of the table. Our eyes met for one second and she looked away as if I was invisible to her. She started to twirl her pendant around in her hand before she finally let go of it and dished up.

After dinner Natalie walked me to my room. I invited her inside and we both sat on my bed.

"Nice room. I love the color."

"Thanks, me too."

Silence filled the room for a short while.

"Mila doesn't scare you?"

Natalie laughed. "She does but I've made a point of standing up to her. If I want to be a Guardian, I need to be able to confront egoistic bitches like her."

"That's a funny way to get over your fears."

"I'll probably get my ass kicked tomorrow. She doesn't like when people put her in her place. I'm just worried about Fox. Nobody speaks to Mila like that and gets away with it."

"Well, then you don't know Fox very well. She can handle anything."

Natalie giggled. "It will be nice. I'm sick and tired of Guardians giving up on this house because of the shit Mila does."

"I guess every household has its black sheep."

Natalie laughed again.

"Nice to have you here, Chas. Yell if you need anything. I have to dash, Charlie still needs his food."

She got up and left.

"Thanks."

"Good night, Chas," Charlie said and both Natalie and I shook our head at the parrot, as they left my room.

BY BEDTIME, I WAS EXHAUSTED BUT KEPT TOSSING and turning. The hours ticked by and it was too hot, but my eyes finally felt heavy, and I started to drift away. Someone tugging on my leg woke me up, and once I was fully awake, I realized it wasn't tugging, it was something kneading. I switched my night light on and was grateful that I didn't have to share a room with any of the other girls. I jumped as a ball of black fur and a flat face with circles around the eyes looked at me.

It was Shades, or Mr. Grey as they called him, not her, this side.

He just stared at me as if he was thinking, 'Chill, it's only me.'

Yeah, the voice in my head still belonged to a she though. I was sure the cat was female.

I scratched him behind the ear. It was a spot he liked and he pushed his head harder into my hand which made me giggle softly. "Selene is going to kill me if she finds you here."

"Selene doesn't have a say in this." a voice said and I jumped out of my bed and grabbed the lamp which made the light throw shadows on the walls.

"Who said that?" I asked a bit too loudly. The voice was quiet and I stroked the cat's head again when I passed him. My eyes scanned every inch of my room and my heart was beating wildly inside my chest.

"Put down the lamp Chas, you look ridiculous," the voice said again.

"Who said that? Show yourself!" I yelled. It was weird. I could clearly hear the voice, it was so loud, but I couldn't tell where it came from. I squinted in every direction trying to see where the person was hiding. It was male, that much I could tell but it was a voice I didn't recognize.

The next moment Fox stormed into my room and stared at me with hands held up in defense as she took in the sight of me standing with the lamp in my hand. "Chas, put the lamp down."

"No, there's somebody inside my room," I yelled and went back to searching for any sign of another person.

"There is nobody except the two of us…" Her eyes caught Mr. Grey. It was a wonder that the cat was still lying on the bed. I thought by now he would've ducked and run away. "What is Mr. Grey doing here?"

"I don't know. The cat has been following me for a long time."

She squinted, smiled, went over to my bed and scratched Mr. Grey's head while I still waited for whoever was going to attack us.

"Chas, put down the lamp you look ridiculous."

"No! I told you…"

"There is no one besides the three of us in your room."

"Fox, I heard him okay. Someone is here."

Fox laughed. "You hear him already? That's amazing Chas."

I stared at her, clearly confused why she was so jolly when I was so scared. "I don't understand."

Fox looked at Mr. Grey. "Stop scaring your Tula and introduce yourself properly, Mr. Grey."

"My what?"

"Tulas are the only ones that can hear their animals, Chas. Mr. Grey has chosen you."

"Mr. Grey….but he belongs to Selene."

"He doesn't belong to her. He just likes her leisure apartment and the warm milk she feeds him."

"I can hear…what? Cats don't talk."

"They don't in the Domain, but we aren't in the Domain anymore." She walked over to me and took the lamp and placed it next to my bed again. I didn't like this talking cat thing one bit. It was not natural.

Fox giggled again and started to walk to the door.

"You're just going to leave me now?" I whispered.

"He's a cat, make friends, Chas. He will be the best friend you've ever had in your entire life. Embrace it. And Mr. Grey knows plenty about what's going on in Revera, so it won't hurt you to give him a chance."

"Still, it's a talking cat."

"It's not really like that. I can't hear him, nobody except you can, Chas. You are not going crazy. Goodnight."

I stared at the cat that was still lying on my bed. "Yeah, fine. Go to sleep," I mumbled and could still hear her soft giggle as she closed the door.

"So this is for real?" I asked. He didn't answer me back, just stared at me as if this entire fiasco hurt his feelings.

I sighed and climbed back onto my bed. "Fine, don't speak to me then," I said and pulled the covers over me.

I waited for an hour to hear what the stupid cat had to say, but he was furious with me about my little outburst. How was I supposed to know that cats could talk in Revera?

I then started to remember what he'd done for me back home. How he'd led me back when I was lost in Chicago. It felt like months ago, but it had only been one.

I wished I'd never gotten scared that day, and wished that my sand had never appeared. Then I would still be back home with Mom, occasionally feeding a cat who I'd told so many things to, who had listened to my secrets.

Fox was right, he'd been my best friend for a long time, even though I'd never known it.

My heartbeat started to calm down and I closed my eyes when fatigue washed over me.

When I opened them, I found Leigh laughing at me.

I knew why he was laughing. Shit, news spread extremely fast inside Revera.

"I didn't know! You could've warned me that animals could talk!"

"I didn't know that you were a Tula."

"The stupid cat showed up about a year ago in the Domain."

"Don't call Mr. Grey stupid. The cat has feelings Chas, and the faster you learn that, the better it will be for both of you."

"He's a cat, Leigh."

"Not your average type. Mr. Grey is a very clever Anitule, Chas. He can help you a lot, but not if he is pissed at you all the time."

"So what, I should apologize for something I didn't know anything about?"

Leigh laughed. "You really grabbed the lamp?"

"Shut up," I said.

"Some Guardian you are," he joked and I finally started to see the humor in all of this.

"Still, a talking cat is a bit freaky."

"I think it's the coolest thing inside Revera. Look I've got to go." Leigh jumped up and waved back at me without looking.

"Sure, see you later."

"You bet."

I woke up and the first thing I did was see if Mr. Grey was still lying on my bed. He was gone. *Stupid cat*, I whispered to myself as I got out of bed.

Fox just smiled at me while all the other girls were grabbing cereal and sitting down around the table..

Natalie was taking to Charlie across the table. It was so weird hearing him speak softly back to her. I knew it was how things this side worked, still it was going to take a long time to get used to another voice only I could hear. At least Charlie had a voice.

Mila looked up and gave me a glare. I had a feeling she didn't like me very much either. The others chatted with one another happily as they ate.

"Here, grab yourself a bowl and some cereal before it's all gone." Fox handed me the bowl that was in her hand and started giggling again.

"I didn't know," I said in a playful tone and started to giggle too.

All of the other girls looked up at the two of us while I poured some cereal into my bowl.

"What's up?" a girl with blonde hair asked.

"Well, Iris, it turns out that Natalie isn't the only Tula in this house. We have another one." Fox started telling them about how comical I'd looked with the lamp in my hand as I sat down on the open chair and started to dig into my breakfast.

Mila laughed the hardest. Clearly a fake one as Fox just stared at her.

"Don't let them get under your skin, Chas," Natalie said. "They're just jealous that they aren't as cool as us."

"Ha," Mila started again and chirped from across the table. "I so don't want bird poop on my shoulder. Only Tulas are crazy enough to be okay with it."

"He doesn't poop on my shoulder. He actually flies away to go and do his business." She kissed Charlie on his beak and laughed softly.

"Oh, I agree one hundred percent on that one, Charlie," she said softly.

Mila just shot them both a look, got up and left.

"You shouldn't taunt Mila like that, Nats," Iris said.

"If she can do it, I can too," Natalie chirped back and smiled at Charlie. It was kind of creepy the way she looked at the bird.

"So what does Charlie have to say?" a girl with a pair of earphones hanging around her neck with a dark brown, pixie cut asked.

Natalie laughed. "Nothing, I just like to make him sound quirky."

All of us laughed, including Fox who just shook her head.

"So." Natalie broke her gaze from Charlie and looked at me, "Where is your Anitule?"

"I think I hurt his feelings last night," I said and she giggled.

"Yeah, they are quite sensitive with how you perceive them, but he'll be back. I can promise you that."

"Yay, me."

"Mr. Grey isn't that bad, Chas."

Everyone around the table gasped.

"Mr. Grey, as in Selene's Mr. Grey?" Isis asked.

"He's not Selene's cat. He chose Chastity."

"I wish he hadn't. I have so many things to deal with already, he's just going to work on my nerves."

"He won't, he's a gorgeous cat." Natalie smiled.

"Mr. Grey, wow. I bet Selene won't think it's too amazing," the girl with the earphones said.

"Andrea, she will understand. As soon as all of you

skedaddle out of here, I need to go and see her about something, and will mention that too. We need to make space for him inside the House of Lords."

"Just as long as he leaves Charlie in peace, the cat can do whatever the hell he wants."

I giggled again.

After breakfast all of us got ready for school. I walked with Natalie who couldn't stop talking about how amazing it was to be a Tula. Yeah, she was reminding me more and more of Clare. She had that same sparkle in her eyes when she talked about the things she liked and she yapped nonstop about the things she loved.

When we arrived, Mr. Dingle made a huge fuss about me being a Tula too.

I gave him a shy smile as I remembered what Fox said to me yesterday and how he wanted to go to the dark side. Why Selene hadn't chucked his ass into the Oblivion was beyond my knowledge and a story I was craving the details to.

The entire class, even Max, was in awe when they heard who my Anitule was. They saw Mr. Grey as some sort of sacred animal the way everyone was talking about him.

Still he was nowhere to be found and I was really starting to get annoyed with him. How long was he going to punish me for yesterday's meet and greet? Seriously, cats don't talk. He never had in the Domain when he was still a she, and how was I supposed to know he wasn't your regular Garfield but a supernova being that could actually tell you Revera's Queen's secrets.

That brought a knot to my stomach. How was Selene

going to take this?

He had been hers for I didn't know how long and she was so nice. I would just hate if that was going to ruin that wonderful first impression of me.

TRAINING WAS HARD AGAIN. I GOT
punched so many times in the stomach by Max, so much that I even blacked out. When they brought me back, my left eye was pounding and I could only see a small amount through it. This really sucked.
Still, Max did the gentlemanly thing, something I was positive he didn't know he had in him and took me to the nurse's office.

Half an hour later I was back to normal. Leigh didn't show up this time when I dosed off, and my biggest fear was waiting in the lounge when I got back home.

Selene.

"Hi Chas, come sit." Fox had a welcoming smile on her face.

"No, let her grab something to eat. She must be starving from all her training." Selene still sounded friendly.

"Sit, I'll go make a sandwich, you need to speak to Selene."

"She doesn't know?" I whispered softly.

Fox just smiled and walked away.

I took a deep breath and walked over to the lounge.

"So, Chastity, I heard something pretty amazing happened to you last night," Selene said as I sat in the chair opposite her.

I squinted as I saw the puffball on her lap.

"Yeah, apparently I'm a Tula."

She laughed. "A Guardian and a Tula, always a good

combination. My best Guardians are all Tulas, but don't tell Fox I said that." She looked around. "So, where is this special animal?"

I heard a laugh and saw the cat with closed eyes on her lap.

"Shut up," I whispered.

"Excuse me?" Selene asked, taken aback.

"Not you, sorry." I apologized and felt like an idiot. The cat laughed again, but it didn't show on his face.

"He's right here."

She looked again.

"On your lap, Selene." I spoke softly and hated every minute of taking something as precious as her cat from her. She looked at me, and then back at Mr. Grey.

"Is this true?" she asked Mr. Grey, who didn't pay any attention to her whatsoever.

"I think he's still upset about the way I reacted last night."

Selene looked at me again and then started to laugh.

"You're not mad?"

"No, Chastity. How could I be? He's finally found his Tula. You are one lucky girl though. He has been such a pleasure to have around and I'm sure going to miss him." She ruffled his face and made him look at her.

"Oh, yeah, I'm sure going to miss you too, Sunshine," Mr. Grey said in the grumpiest tone he could muster, jumping off her lap and onto mine.

"So that is it, I guess the trade is complete."

"He can visit whenever he likes," I said. I felt stupid saying that.

Selene smiled again. "He does whatever he wants, you are going to learn that the hard way, Chastity."

"I bet." I smiled back.

I picked up the cat and stood up as Selene picked up her jacket just when Fox entered with my sandwich and a glass of Coke. "Leaving already? Stay," she begged.

"I can't. Revera doesn't run itself." She looked back at Mr. Grey lying happily in my arms. "Take care of him Chas. He's not a bad cat."

"I'm sure he isn't," I said through clenched teeth, teasing him slightly.

"Don't start with that crap," he growled at me which made me giggle.

"You already hear him?" Selene's eyes were huge and I nodded.

"He's not one of the friendliest cats though."

She laughed. "Who could've known. I'd always wondered what sort of personality he had. Guess Grumpy was right."

We all laughed as Mr. Grey jumped out my arms and ran straight up the stairs to what I assumed was my room.

"Cats," Selene said and gave me a one-arm hug. "Take care of yourself, and please, I would love to know Mr. Grey better. So treasure all his snarky comments until we meet again, Chastity."

I giggled. "I will."

We said goodbye and she disappeared through a door that I'd thought was a broom closet.

Fox just stared at me as I tried to make sense of all of this. "I really thought she was going to be pissed."

Fox smiled. "Selene is extremely understanding when it comes to things like Tulas. She knows it doesn't matter what she says or does. Tulas this side, Chas, are extremely special and you will see, nothing can break them apart. Not even a Somnium."

I giggled. "You don't want to know what he said when she said goodbye."

"What?"

"He's seriously grumpy and extremely sarcastic." She laughed again.

"Cats."

I FOUND MR. GREY INSIDE MY ROOM sitting on the ledge when I entered.

"You don't have to stay here if you don't want to," I said and he turned his head and looked at me.

"House of Lords is not so bad. They've got a parrot who is just going to taste...mmm uh mmmm."

"Forget about Charlie." I scowled at him.

He chuckled. "I'm only kidding Chas, you need to learn how to lighten up."

"Yeah, practice what you preach, Grumpy." I giggled at the grunt he made. "Sorry about last night. I didn't know, okay? And I feel pretty stupid about everything. It's going to take a while to get used to you."

"Used to me? You've known me since the Domain, Chas."

"About that." I went to sit on my bed. "How did you find me?"

"Bond, I guess," he said and looked out the window again.

"She left through the door, the broom cupboard one, not the front."

"I don't care," he said grumpily, and if he was a human, I swear he would've pulled my curtain away to see more.

"Then what are you looking at?" I got up and went over to the sill to look out the window too.

"Made you look," he said and jumped off the sill and onto my bed.

"You really have a strange sense of humor, you know."

"Yeah, so I've been told."

I laughed. "By who, your mom?"

He chuckled too.

"Promise me one thing though," he asked.

"Sure, what?"

"Don't ever talk to me like Selene did again." He shivered and I giggled.

"She didn't know Mr. Grey?" I realized then that his name could be Dick for all I knew. "Hey what is your real name anyway?"

"Mr. Grey is fine."

"You sure? Now is the perfect time to change it if you want."

"And build up another reputation? No thanks. Mr. Grey is cool. I liked Shades too. You really thought I was a girl?"

"Well, you looked like one, so yeah. Sorry."

"It must be my beautiful shiny coat."

I giggled once more. Who could've guessed, a cat talking to a human, and one that had a sparkling personality too.

Only in Revera.

CHAPTER TWENTY THREE
Silly Little Pendants

TRAINING AT THE INSTITUTE WAS HECTIC
at least Natalie hung with me now that I was a Tula. The
fact that the Anitule was Mr. Grey made the news in the
Casting Times, Revera's daily paper. They did a huge
piece on Mr. Grey, the cat, and I was astonished at what
he was capable of. I scanned through a couple of things
and froze at one of the previous headlines about him.
He'd brought down one of Selene's advisors, a William
Withowzer, who was in fact a Shadow Caster.

If the cat could sense that, I was in deep shit.

He was about ten years old, and had won like three
bravery awards a couple of years ago.

They just mentioned my name. No picture, nothing.
Just a name.

On the third day of my new life here in Revera, my
classes changed. Natalie told me that the first two days
of each week, we just do Guardian training, the other
three days, they're mixed up with other subjects.

The classes were different from what I was used to
though. From wielding your sand into dreams, to how to

create enhanced objects out of trinkets. History, Math and all that other Domain subjects made it in there too, but it only lasts up to grade three, which is equivalent to a Level One Dream Caster. In third grade you can choose four subjects with Guardian and Casting Dreams as your main two subjects.

I knew one thing for sure, I wasn't cut out for any of this, except the fighting part.

My mom had been right. Fighting was in our blood and I thrived on the adrenaline.

Designing looked hard, but I was thrown off when I walked into the classroom with Sophie.

The teacher reminded me so much of Mom, the one I'd grown up with. She was a bit fruity, over excited about everything, and extremely eccentric with her hippie skirts and flower bands on her head. The classroom didn't have any tables but big fluffy pillows were strewn against the wall.

The woman smiled at me when her gaze locked on mine.

"Please, sit down. We have plenty to do today." She spoke kindly and Sophie led me to the pillow right in the corner and plonked down right next to me.

"Welcome to Designing, Chastity," the teacher said softly. "Would you like to introduce yourself to class?"

I stood up. I didn't really want to but I probably had no choice. Carpe diem.

"My name is Chastity Blake, I came from the Domain." I smiled softly and started again when the teacher cleared her throat. "My mother never told me what I was, and I guess she never knew as I have no idea who my real dad was. So yay me." Someone in the room laughed. "But here I am."

"Nice to meet you Chastity. Name's Sy," one of the guys, more or less my age, said. He had typical ass-and-abs, good looks and a sheepish grin on his face that would melt any other girl's heart. He lost about a gazillion points when he started to scan me up and down as if I was some product at a check out.

Still, I waved at him.

"That is so nice of you Siegfried," the teacher said and everyone started to laugh. "You can call me Mrs. Delvaga. Number One Dream Caster and Designer of Revera."

"Whoop, whoop," the class shouted and she curtseyed.

"Is she for real?"

"She's a bit eccentric, but you should see her dreams," Sophie said.

"I hope you all have done last week's assignment." Mrs. Delvaga asked the rest of the class, and scanned the entire class with her eyes rested on me. "Chas you can observe."

Thanks for that as I have no idea how to design anything, except once, a dagger, from my dreams.

The others started to take out devices, they were all different and looked like something that didn't belong to this world. All of them reminded me of kitchen appliances but they looked like nothing that should belong in any kitchen. Why a kitchen jumped into my mind, I didn't know.

Then the demonstration started.

Sy was first and I watched him get up and walk with a puffed up chest to the front where a table was stationed for all of us to see. He had scruffy light brown hair, huge blue eyes and very strong arms. I hadn't seen him in Guardian training before and he must be into enhancing gadgets, creating things. I thought Mark had said something about everybody wanting to be a designer, yep, that was it, so Sy must've been in that department.

As he began his demonstration, his thingamajig, made a horrible noise, which he apologized for as he turned a couple of knobs on the gadget. When the noise stopped it produced a creamy brown liquid that he put into a cup – see kitchen – and offered to Mrs. Delvaga.

She smelled it first, and by the sound escaping her lips and closed pink glittered eyes, I knew it must've smelled divine.

"Boring," Sophie yelled and the class laughed. I smiled at her. One thing Natalie had been right about was that she hardly said a word and disappeared when Mila and her gang came near.

Mrs. Delvaga lifted up her finger at Sophie and took a sip, followed by another one. I was sitting on the edge of my pillow waiting patiently. After a couple of minutes, I agreed with Sophie. I still had no idea what the glorified cappuccino maker did or how it was related to the dream world.

Then Mrs. Delvaga opened her eyes.

She looked around her, up to the ceiling and back down again. I followed her gaze and looked up too. Nothing happened.

The teacher smiled.

"This is amazing Siegfried. How on earth? An A+." She looked everywhere except at Sy. "Did everybody see the same thing?"

"No, my mom saw flying pigs." Everyone laughed.

So flying pigs was a myth, even in a place like

Revera.

"My father, well he was more of a blood, guts and war freak, so he found himself at a battlefield. He had so much fun and it was kind of funny to watch, a lot of stuff broke."

I knew more or less now what their homework was all about, to create their dream world through a gadget, and they'd created it in less than a week. I was so in over my head with all of this.

"Sophia," Mrs. Delvaga said and the girl next to me took a huge breath with a slight smile on her lips.

"Wish me luck," she whispered.

"I doubt that you'll need it."

She giggled, got up and took one of the contraptions that were stacked in a row with all the other masterpieces.

"So, I decided to make mine more visual, and share it with the entire class." She smirked at Sy.

"Hear, hear," Sy remarked and the entire class broke out in laughter. She didn't shy away this time and something told me that she was in her element.

Her small contraption had so many levers that I wondered if she knew how to even operate the thing.

She pulled the first one and I jumped in shock as a string of colors poured out of a nozzle and filled the entire classroom.

We all gasped.

Colors swam past me and just like the time I'd entered Revera, I had to find out if I could touch them. Soft sparkling granules prickled my palm as I held it in the orange mixed with pink and when I took my hand out, small orange and pink sparkles were all over my palm.

When I looked up the walls of the room and the roof had disappeared. The entire class was sitting on a rainbow that stretched as far as I could see.

It was simply amazing and I even had to pinch myself to know I was awake.

"I call this Rainbow Land," Sophie said.

"Extremely original Soph, like always," Sy chirped.

"Well at least everyone can experience mine, Siegfried," she said in a mocking tone and pulled the next lever.

Snow poured from the nozzle this time, and soft snowflakes drizzled on everyone. It fell everywhere on the rainbow covering all the colors.

It changed the scene from Rainbow Land to a snowy day. Trees appeared in the distance topped with snow and even a hulking mountain stood solid on the horizon. I reached out and touched the snow that was covering my feet. It felt so real, but it didn't feel cold.

"Let me guess this one," Sy said, "A Snow Day?"

Soph ignored him but picked up a snowball and it spattered all over Sy's face. All of us jumped from our pillows and started pelting each other with snowballs. Even Mrs. Delvaga got in a ball or two.

Laughter filled the entire class. Okay, so I had to admit, we'd never had a class like this back home.

When Mrs. Delvaga had enough, she quieted everyone down and we all took our seats on our pillows.

With a pull of the next lever a bunch of butterflies flew out. Thousands of them, not one alike, filled the classroom. The entire class snickered as for some reason half of them came to sit on me. I guessed it was a Tula thing.

The snow disappeared and we were left in a meadow

with millions of butterflies around us.

"Can you guess this one Sy?" Soph batted her eyes.

"Butterfly Cove?" The class laughed again as Soph had an annoyed glare on her face. She didn't say anything.

"I'm right, aren't' I?"

"Just shut up."

"She might not be original with choosing her names," Mrs. Delvaga said, "but I absolutely adore her creations."

Sophie smiled and pulled the last lever.

We all ducked as flying candy came our way and when it was all done, we were surrounded by candy houses and a road made from candy.

Mrs. Delvaga clapped her hands. It was simply amazing.

"Candy Land," we all sang and Soph just shook her head and took a bow.

All of us clapped as the candy land disappeared and we were back inside an extremely dull and normal classroom again.

Three more creations were shown and I had to admit that Sophie's was the best.

When the bell rang, class was over. I had no idea what time it was but by the two suns still shining brightly I knew that it was still a long time before lunch.

WE ENTERED MR. DINGLE'S CLASS AND took our seats when the bell rang.

He was sitting behind his desk and my eyes met Max's again as he got up and walked to Mr.Dingle's desk. Margot, who followed her brother, flashed me a

ADRIENNE WOODS

glare and I looked away.

Sometimes I could swear she knew that I was carrying dark sand, but then again, she would've said so a long time ago. She wasn't the type that kept things to herself.

Natalie fell into the seat next to me. "How was your first Designing class?"

"So awesome," I whispered back. "Sophie is really good."

"I know. She blows everyone's minds away. She should be in Designing."

"Why isn't she?"

"She chose to be a Guardian. Said there aren't enough Guardians to begin with…she has a good heart."

I liked Sophie more and more. She might be a geek, but they were my favorite kind of people anyway.

I admired her for her brilliant mind and hoped that one day I would be able to create something like that myself.

Mr. Dingle was speaking softly to Max and Margot. I could still hear today's events getting passed from teacher to sub-teachers but what they said specifically I didn't quite make out.

They each picked up a paper and took their seats.

"Good morning everyone." Mr. Dingle greeted the class. "I hope you had a good night's rest as today you will be spending time with Leigh."

"We will?" I looked at Nat who had this huge grin plastered on her face, she didn't reply.

"Yay us!"

We broke and walked over to another room at the back of the class. It reminded me so much of the one in the compound, the only difference was that this one had

310

a gazillion tables and chairs.

We all took a seat and Mr. Dingle left the room.

Nobody made a peep and Natalie lay back in her chair with eyes closed as if she was going to take a nap.

I started to think about Dingle again and what Fox had said. Had he really wanted to be a Shadow Caster and if so, why hadn't Leigh told me about this? He had warned me about everything else so far. Having a Shadow Caster for a professor fell in the danger category, sort of.

As I lay there, I yawned and my eyes started to close for no reason.

Bright light woke me and I found myself with the rest of the class inside a ruin structure. Part of the roof was still intact with lights seeping through the holes where the ceiling used to be. The floor was cement and the walls were partially dilapidated.

Birds made nests on the beams and some of them were cooing.

I looked around and found the entire class sleeping. I bumped Natalie softly and her eyes flew open.

"We're here!" she yelled and everyone stirred awake.

We all got up and followed Max outside.

"I was wondering where you were," Max said, and I knew who Max was speaking to. My heart beat a bit faster.

All the guys greeted Leigh with a slap shake, and most of the girls just smiled at him.

Margot actually gave him a hug, which I could tell was awkward for him as he tapped her slightly on the back and waited for her to let him go.

"Welcome to the Virtual world, Chastity." Leigh winked at me slightly which made me suck in my lips.

"What the hell is that about?" Nat spoke through gritted teeth.

I scrunched up my nose and shook my head as Leigh spoke about our lecture today.

"Today, we are going to go over taking your oaths. It will be a spiritual oath, so you all know what that means, right?" Leigh started.

"Oath day?" I asked.

"Oh yay us." Natalie didn't sound so ecstatic about this anymore.

"What is it?" I had to know.

"I've heard about these sorts of oaths. He's going to spring something on us, which will be huge and we're going to have to take an oath, which means that we won't be able to tell anyone about this, ever."

"What?!"

"Better listen up Chas."

The scenery changed while Leigh spoke and we found ourselves inside a museum. A guide was giving a tour to a group and we sort of mingled in.

"What is this?" Nat asked.

"I know," Max said. "It's the Basilisk Orb." He looked at Margot and then at Leigh. "What are we doing here?"

Leigh flicked his fingers together and the entire picture froze. The tour guide had his mouth still open as his sentence stopped in mid-air. The kids and adults around him froze like statues. We were the only ones that weren't frozen.

"A memory from a lie," Leigh carried on. "A lie that Selene thought was best at the time to keep from everyone."

"What do you mean, from a lie?"

"Easy Max. We're in front of the Basilisk Orb, what could it be? You're smarter than that, or has Chas finally found a way to beat you?"

"Haha" Max said sarcastically. "She wishes."

I rolled my eyes.

"Think." Leigh said again.

"I remember something like this," Natalie said and looked at Leigh. "The tour guide told us that the Basilisk Orb isn't needed anymore, that Selene is strong enough and doesn't need its powers to help sustain everything in Revera." She gasped and cupped her mouth. "That is the lie!"

Everyone gasped. I had no idea what they were talking about, just that it had something to do with that mother of a giant pearl-like object that was protected inside a glass box.

"It's not the real one, by the way," Leigh carried on. "The real Basilisk Orb is hidden inside the bell of the Cathedral on Wezington Avenue."

"That's the reason it doesn't ring anymore."

"Right you are, Isis."

"Why would they lie to us?" Andrea asked, with a slight hysteria in her voice.

"Because of exactly that." Leigh gestured toward Andrea's reaction. "To prevent Chaos."

"Do the Shadow Casters know about this?" Max sounded concerned too.

"They do," Leigh answered, "but they have no idea where it's hidden."

"What is it the Basilisk Orb does?" I had to know and I could hear a couple of bodies inflating as they were going to have to relive this history lesson again.

"Guys, Chas is new, she needs to know about

313

everything you do, so please, a bit of patience isn't going to kill anyone." Leigh spoke again. "Just listen Chas. It's why I thought it would be better to bring everyone here, to refresh their memories."

He snapped his fingers again and the picture unfroze.

"...the Basilisk Orb. Now I can see from all your curious little faces that you've heard of the Basilisk Orb but you have absolutely no idea what it does or did, a long, long, long time ago." The tour guide looked at the kids who were watching with huge eyes, like me, at the orb. "Selene and Darius Faline and Magdelena Sodivic used to live in the Domain, just like any regular Nomad. One day, they played a game in their garden and saw a trinket that was completely out of this world. All three of them picked it up, dusted it off and were sucked into another realm called Revera. Sand started to flow freely from their palms. They obviously had no idea what was happening to them, or how to stop it, and went back through the portal to their world on this trinket. But curiosity made them go back after a while.

The sand would appear again. Darius was the first to discover that it wasn't any ordinary sand, he could create anything he wanted. Coke, even food, would come from his sand." The kids laughed at the word Coke as I was sure they didn't had Coke back then.

"They went back to the Domain each and every night and after a while, Darius' sand followed him to the Domain. He wielded himself riches upon riches. They lived a wealthy life, but realized the more wealth he wielded, the faster his sand disappeared. So they had to return to Revera to get Darius his refill." The kids laughed with me.

"Each time they left with the next couple of months'

quota, but the Nomads in the Domain started to investigate Darius and his wealth, and when the authorities couldn't find the answers of where it came from, they started to follow him and witnessed how he wielded it from his sand. They ruled it out as some sort of witchcraft and wanted to burn him alive.

Magdalena and Seline helped him to escape and discovered that the sand they wield put Nomads to sleep. They fled back into the trinket, destroyed it, and had no choice but to live inside the Revera forever.

They started to explore this new world and found the Inkas who already lived here and some of the Anitules that bore a huge resemblance to the animals back home, but when Darius start hearing what the animals said, he knew they weren't just ordinary animals. He learned plenty from them and passed the knowledge of this world on to his sister Selene and to Magdalena since they couldn't hear a peep coming from the Animals.

Through the Anitules, they discovered the Orb's existence, how it empowers this realm and that without it, Revera would not exist anymore.

On their first visit to the Orb, they felt more powerful than what they had ever been and they started to create bigger things from their dust, but they soon discovered that when they were a certain distance from the Orb, they would lose this extra power and could no longer create bigger things. So they built the Manor right next to the Orb, the same building we know now as The Starlington where Selene still resides today.

They started to create more, built cities in a matter of months and areas where they could roam free. They created everything inside of Revera.

As the world and their magic grew, so did the Orb's

power, pulsating with the new creations.

One day, a Basilisk appeared and tried to take away the Orb. Sensing its power and connection to the magic of Revera, Darius fought the hulking beast. During the battle the Basilisk's fang pierced the Orb and it disappeared into the Orb's milky depths. The snake has never been seen again

Hence the name, Basilisk Orb. They say when the three of them picked up the Orb, small pieces of the light of the Orb started to fade and all that power transferred into them, becoming what we know as Somniums.

The three of them used this extra power and discovered that they could create a different kind of object, turning their dreams into a reality, but only they could explore their own dreams.

For centuries it was all they did. Each day enjoying a new dream. It was then that they realized that time didn't exist for them, that they didn't age like they used to.

They started changing more and more. They're dreams could be shared with one another and for the next few centuries, they did just that. They took turns in creating worlds and dreams to explore together.

Darius was the first to sense special beings back in the Domain and started recruiting them to come live in Revera. Selene and Magdalene helped.

Revera grew and grew, but not one single day passed when the three of them needed to go back to the Basilisk Orb, to regain more power.

It was said that after a long, long time, Magdalena wanted all the power and she became greedy. She tried to trick Darius and Selena, tried to kill them so that their power can come to her, but that her plan didn't work and the color of her sand changed.

Revera started to change too. Parts of the world exploded and the two siblings had no choice but to combine their power together, which cost Darius his life, which was how Selene gained the power to cast out Magdalena.

The Casters that shared Magdalena's traits witnessed their sand changing color as well. Selene was forced to cast them all out.

Because of Magdalena's act, she lost her immortality, but spent many years trying to get back into Revera. When she realized it was no use, that she was old and busy dying, she created her own world for her people, what we know now as the Oblivion, a world where all Shadow Casters belong."

A little boy put up his hand and the entire picture started to disappear until all of us were back in the field.

"You get what the Orb is, Chas?" Leigh asked.

"It empowered Selene and the other two a long time ago before it lost its power?"

"And that is the lie."

"All gasped."

"Selene is powerful, and yes, they did gain extra power the night the Basilisk disappeared into the milky depths of the Orb, but the Orb didn't lose its power.

"It became stronger, making them stronger but at a cost.

"They realized after a couple of years that their powers started to lose strength and the three of them went back to the Orb that had started to lose its light too. When pieces of Revera started to disappear, they decided to sacrifice themselves to empower the Orb, and because of that, the Orb gained its strength back and so did they.

"They did this once a month and as the years went by, they realized the Orb could go on much longer without their empowerment. Once a month became once every three months, every three months turned into every six months and now Selene only has to do it once a year.

"It was then that Magdalena has this bright idea and wanted more. She tried to trick Darius and Selene in order to gain all the power, but because of the dark in her, her sand changed. She tried changing the Orb to darkness with her sand and nearly destroyed Revera.

"Darius and Selene combined their abilities to destroy Magdalena, but instead of destroying Magdalena, it destroyed Darius and Selene got her brother's power, gaining more power to cast Magdalena out of Revera.

"So the Orb is still alive and it is still the main thing that keeps Revera sustained, but only through Selene, nobody else.

"If the Orb dies, her ability and Revera as we know it will die too. If a very powerful Shadow Caster, like Crane, got their hands on the Orb, they could change the Orb to darkness and Revera will become like the Oblivion. Shadow Casters will be able to live in Revera. As of now, Shadow Casters are only allowed a certain amount of time to live in Revera, before they disintegrate. The longest was seven days."

I stared at Leigh, but he didn't look at me. Was I going to disintegrate too?

"Why can only Selene—"

"Because of the power, Isis," Andrea cut her off

knowing exactly where she was going with this. "They were the only three that got this power from the Orb. It's only their bloodlines that can become Somniums. The only ones we know are all Shadow Casters, and if they get the Orb, they have the ability to reverse light to dark, meaning that Revera will change to the Oblivion." Leigh said, "And that is why Selene is so important to us, that is why we chose to become Guardians. Not just to protect Revera but Selene as well. Without Selene there is no Revera."

"And no Orb too," Max added.

"I know it sucks," Leigh said. "But Selene thought it was best to try and throw the Shadow Casters off and it worked. Selene tried to protect the innocents from more worry. And for that, we had to tell a little lie, to make Selene sound indestructible. Through that we didn't only protect Revera and its people but the Orb too."

"So now we're going to take an oath?" Nat still looked worried.

"I won't lie to you, it's painful, but it's more painful if you try to tell anyone about it."

"I don't keep secrets from Charlie."

"Anitules are clever. I'm sure Charlie already knows and that he's kept it from you. You can't discuss any of this, though. Or you will experience horrible pain, some even say that it can lead to death."

Everyone gasped again and started to look at one another.

"It's pretty serious, so do not mess with trying to break an oath."

The rundown structure with the trees started to ripple, I couldn't stop staring at it and didn't even pay attention to the procedure of taking the oath Leigh was speaking about. I was still worried about the seven day thing.

Everything around us rippled more and started to move around. It became a big blur, except for the class who'd just received the truth about the Orb.

I closed my eyes when the spinning around me got worse and when Natalie touched my arm softly we were inside a stone room.

Everything was made of stone; the walls, the benches, even the door. In the middle of the room was a huge stone altar with a stone bowl.

Leigh lit it with a blue spark that came from his hand.

The blue flame ran down the altar in a thin line, on both sides, across the floor to the walls of the room. It ran up the walls and shot out in a huge web pattern on the ceiling; it lit up everything.

I looked at Max who went up to the altar first and held out his hand.

Leigh grabbed something that looked like prayer beads and pressed them inside Max's palm. He grunted and clenched his jaw tight. His eyes were closed and from the pain on his face, I knew that it was real.

Leigh spoke in a language I'd never heard before and when the thirty second chant was over, Max dropped the beads.

He shook his palm a couple of times, probably trying to dispel the pain. A faint golden glow emanated from his palm where the blazing hot beads had left their mark and then it just disappeared.

Margot was next and the same happened with her, we each had to do this and I so didn't look forward to my turn.

"Chastity," Leigh spoke my name softly.

I looked up at him, his eyes were soft, begging me to

go through with this insanity.

The few steps I took toward him I didn't even realize, I just saw the altar coming closer to me and then I was standing opposite Leigh with my palm stretched open toward him.

"It's going to hurt…a lot." He'd barely said those last few words when a scorching pain burned the skin on my hand. Leigh closed my hand and I ground on my teeth as he said his little mantra.

I tried to block the words out, block the pain out, but nothing happened. It was still there and it became hotter each second I held the beads. I could feel the pain running up my arm, through my entire body and I became as warm as the beads that were inside my palm.

"Chastity, drop it," Leigh shouted. It felt as if I was about to pass out and automatically my hand dropped the beads. They fell on the altar and I stared at my hand. The ache was worse than a second ago when I was still holding the beads and I now had a burn mark that glowed a bright golden color. It started to disappear slightly and then it was gone. In its place was a completely different mark. It wasn't the print of the beads, it wasn't even blisters upon blisters as it should have been. The only thing that was on my palm was a black sign that resembled a three-leaf clover with sharp ends.

I couldn't stop looking at it.

"It's the mark of the oath. All guardians carry it and you'll see that none of those guardians have revealed the truth about the Orb for the past nine hundred years." Leigh looked at each and every one of us as he spoke.

"Nobody?" I asked again.

"Nobody, Chas," he said in a tone that had a double

meaning. I squinted and he raised his eyes slightly at me, like he wanted to tell me something and then looked back to the others.

It was probably just my imagination, why would he want to tell me anything that he wouldn't tell the entire class? I guess I really wanted Leigh to desperately share something with just me, I wanted to be that special to him.

I was really silly. My first crush ever and it was on somebody that wasn't even real. Someone that lived inside a virtual world.

The room rippled again and this time Leigh rippled with it. When everything spun again, I forced myself to look. I saw him disappear with his eyes staring into mine and then we found ourselves back in our seats in the room we entered an hour or so ago.

My head was still spinning and I was slightly tired but not as tired as everyone else around me looked. It looked like they'd worked for 24 hours straight. Their bodies were slumped in the chairs, their eyes barely staying open.

I got up, the only one to, and pressed the red buzzer. When Dingle came in, he just stared at me. His eyebrows knitted.

"Why aren't you tired, Chas?"

I shrug. "It's something I can't explain. It's like the opposite happens to me when I spend time in the Virtual Realm, I feel revived, not drained."

"I see. You're free to leave, since you don't need the tonic," he simply said, pushed me out of the grey room and closed the door behind him.

I went home as it was our last subject of the day and fell onto my bed. Mr. Grey was missing like usual.

I couldn't stop thinking about what Leigh had said. Would I really disintegrate after seven days? I needed to speak to him.

I closed my eyes and it felt like only ten minutes had passed when I found myself in the woods.

Leigh was sitting underneath one of the big oak trees with his back resting against the trunk. His eyes were closed with his glasses resting on top of his head. The picture of him just took my breath away. He was really so beautiful. For a second all my fears about what would happen in seven days disappeared, but they reappeared the second he opened his eyes and smiled at me.

It disappeared the minute he realized that I wasn't sharing his awesome mood.

"What is it Chastity?" he asked with a smile.

"It's almost seven days since I've been here," I said and he just stared at me to go on. "Am I going to go poof?"

He chuckled. "You are not a Shadow Caster, I told you that you can choose. Only Shadow Casters disintegrate. Does that answer your question?"

I nodded and looked at him, he still rested his back against the tree. I smiled. "I didn't know virtual people needed their rest too. What am I doing here?"

"Sit. We need to have a little chat."

"To be honest, I am seriously starting to fear our little chats. It's like you're the bearer of danger or something."

"It's nothing like that, Chas." He had a grin playing in the corner of his lips.

"Okay, fine." I sat down next to him and rested my back against the tree trunk too. I could still see part of his body. "Shoot."

"It's about the Basilisk Orb."

"What about it?"

"This is something I've never told anyone, so you have to keep your mouth shut, Chastity."

"What, no oath this time?"

"Just see it as me trusting you completely. Don't screw it up."

"I'm not the kind, I'm good with keeping secrets. Heck I even kept my best friend's secrets after she chose ass-and-abs above me."

He smiled. "The Basilisk Orb has a twin."

"What do you mean has a twin? Is there a second orb?"

He nodded.

"Remember when the tour guide said that they picked up the pieces that the basilisk broke off when he struck?"

I nodded.

"Those pieces form a smaller Orb which is a replica of the bigger one and has just as much power as Selene and the big Orb."

"So it makes it just as powerful?"

He nodded.

"Nobody knows about it, only Selene and I and now you. "

"Why are you telling me this?"

"I have my reasons," he simply said.

"Okay, so where is it?"

"I think it's in her vault."

"Wait, you don't know?"

He shook his head. "She used to carry it around her neck."

"Around her neck, like something you can insert into

a pendant?"

"Yes, Then one day, she didn't carry it around her neck anymore."

"Why do you think she took it off?"

"Fear, I guess. That's not the most important part, Chastity."

"What is the most important part?"

"If Shadow Casters find it, they'll need both Orbs to reverse this world and turn it into something as sinister and evil as the Oblivion."

"How do you know all of this?"

"If I tell you, I'd have to kill you."

"Haha." I punched him playfully on his shoulder, and he started to laugh. "I'm serious. How do you know?"

"I'm a good observer, Chastity."

"Fine, then don't tell me, but if you think I'm going to buy that crap, you're seriously mistaken."

I got up, ready to move back to reality, well my new reality that is.

I stopped, remembering one more thing I'd wanted to speak to Leigh about.

"You know plenty of things around here. Do you know what the deal is with Dingle?"

He squinted. "What do you mean, the deal with him?"

"Fox told me something on my first day here, that he wanted to become a Shadow Caster."

"Fox told you this?"

I nodded.

He squinted at a memory and then relaxed his eyes. "It is a misunderstanding Chas. Dingle isn't a bad guy. He's actually one of the few Guardians I would trust with my life."

My left eyebrow raised "You sure?"

"Yes, now forget what Fox said. It was a misunderstanding and the reason why he's still inside Revera and not parading somewhere in the Oblivion."

I smiled. "Thanks, I guess. Bye." And just like that my eyes opened and I found myself still lying on my bed, with drool running onto my covers.

I had no idea why I always fell into such a deep sleep when I met up with Leigh.

Still, why would he share something like that with me? If nobody knew about the twin Orb, why didn't he just keep it to himself?

I had to admit that I loved keeping his secrets and I would never do anything to betray Leigh like that, but my curiosity would eventually get the better of me and I would push to find out why he was sharing every little top secret detail with me.

THE NEXT DAY WE STARTED WITH ONE OF Dingle's lectures again. I found him staring at me, just as I jumped off the rope I had just climbed, his eyebrow slightly raised. A cold thumb traced down my back.

What if Fox was right about him? What if he was still dark and had just found a way to hide his sand? Could that even be possible?

We had another training session scheduled with Leigh for this morning and as I got up with Natalie to go to the grey room, Dingle spoke. "Chas, you will stay and train with Max," he said and then went back to explaining what the rest of the class was going to do.

"Okay, yay you, I guess," I whispered to Nat who just smiled.

We broke apart when he finished speaking about how the others were going to form two teams. One pretending to be Shadow Casters trying to enter Revera, the others needing to protect Revera.

All of them were ecstatic. A part of me wanted to go, because it was the virtual world but my black sand could easily appear. So I should have thanked my lucky stars that I wasn't going to have to pretend to be a Shadow Caster, it might have become my reality.

At nine, the class, except Max and I, left.

I followed Max to the training area where he wanted me to start experimenting with my dust.

It flowed freely now and I knew it would be gold, as I experimented with it every night, using all my different emotions. I even became angry, and my dust was still gold, which was a good sign. But fear of the dark was still inside of me. The mirror inside my Initiation dream had shown dark.

He really pushed me hard and my mom was right, the dagger came but the arrows didn't want to.

I looked kind of silly holding the bow and trying to hit a target board as nothing but sand emerged from my string. It would fly into the air and land in trails of sand aimed toward the target board.

"Come on, Chas. You can do it."

"I can't. We've been at this for two hours, Max. Please can we stop?"

"Chas, you need to learn how to fight with weapons."

"Then give me real ones."

"They are not…" He stopped and stared at me. "Okay, it might not be a bad idea. But you tell Dingle that we learned with your sand, okay?"

"Fine, whatever."

He smiled and opened the weapons chest. "So what will it be? They have no bats in here."

I smiled. "Are there real arrows?"

"Arrows it is then."

He handed me a quiver filled with old dusty arrows.

"Why are they here when Dingle doesn't want us to practice with weapons other than our sand?"

"Sometimes our sand doesn't take the right course so well, so he lets new students practice their technique first with the real weapons."

"Makes sense." I took out one of the arrows and it wobbled in my hand as I tried to connect the tip with the string.

Max started to laugh.

"What are you doing, Chas?"

"I don't know. I've never practiced with a bow and arrow before."

"Here, let me show you."

He took a position behind me and turned the bow around. "You pull the string back until the arrow is in line with the bow, and then release."

I released the bow at his command and the arrow shot out, but didn't come close to the target board.

"It's harder than I thought."

"It's easier with your sand. Again."

The second arrow went a bit further, and we practiced shooting arrows until my shoulders and arms ached.

The arrow didn't hit the target board once, which was a bummer.

"The stronger your core gets, the easier you will handle your bow and I promise you will hit the target board, Chas."

"Okay." I sighed as I put the arrows back inside the chest. "Can I ask you something?"

"Shoot."

"Do you think my weapons in Revera might be as effective as the bat in the Virtual Realm?"

"I have no idea, Chas. But for some reason you trust a real weapon more than your sand. You should really learn to trust your sand, Chas. It's your only weapon in Revera."

.

AT LUNCH I MET NAT BACK HOME WHERE A cooked meal was waiting for us.

When we entered the front door, Margot pushed me hard against the wall.

"Where is it?" she spat.

"Where's what, you crazy loon? Let me go!" I tried to push her hands away from me but she was really strong.

"Fight, fight." Mila and her gang egged Margot on to hit me.

"I know you took it, Chastity. Where is it?"

"Where's what? I don't know what you're talking about."

"Oh, don't play dumb with me you little thief. Since the first day I met you, you've been staring at it as if it was some sort of drug. Why do you want it Chas, what are you hiding?"

"I don't know what you're talking about. Let go of me!"

"Enough!" Fox's voice filled the room. "For goodness' sake, what is going on in here?"

Margot finally let go of me.

"She took it. I know she did."

"Chas?" Fox looked at me.

"I have no idea what she is talking about."

"My crystal!" Margot yelled. "The one that can tell me when a Shadow Caster is near."

CHAPTER TWENTY FOUR
Dream A Little Dream of Me

EVERYONE GASPED. I JUST STARED AT HER. so she did know what I was.

I looked at Fox. No, she didn't.

Fox said that it was a stupid pendant Margot believed that had the ability to show her if a Shadow Caster was near or not.

My nostrils flared as I stared at Margot.

"Chastity?" Fox spoke.

"I never took the stupid thing. I don't even know what it looks like."

Margot started to laugh. "It's been around my neck ever since you met me, now it isn't."

"Your necklace?" I gave a sarcastic laugh. "This is serious bullshit." I looked back at Fox. "I'm no thief. I never took it I swear."

"Okay, I believe you."

"Are you shitting me?" Margot yelled.

"Margot! Your language," Fox yelled, but took a

deep breath. "Do you have proof that she took it?"

"No, but I know she's hiding something."

"That's not enough. If you don't have real proof that she took it, this case is closed."

"Un-freak'n-believable!" Margot yelled and ran up the stairs.

Everyone just stared at me. They'd heard what her pendant could do and I saw it on all their judgmental faces.

"Everyone is free to leave. This doesn't concern any of you," Fox said and all of them disappeared.

I didn't eat any lunch and went straight to my room.

Shades was lying on his basket that Selene had dropped off a few hours ago to make him more comfortable.

"Chastity?" the cat said.

"Not now, okay."

"What happened, you look as if you are about to kill someone."

"I am: Margot." I told him the story of how she'd accused me of taking her stupid pendant. Shades just stared at me with his flat face and I swore if a cat could roll his eyes, Shades just did. "You want me to sniff around?"

"No, please, you'll just get me into more shit if you go sniffing around."

"Whatever," he said and went back to lying in his basket.

I knew he meant well, but it wasn't a good idea, trying to find who took her stupid pendant.

My first Tula class, with a Mrs. Mios was right after lunch.

I entered her classroom which looked like any other

classroom, except every student had their Anitule with them, everyone stared at me again. Tulas and their Anitules. I didn't have to read other animal minds to know what it was they were thinking, it was evident on their faces.

Hell, news travels fast.

"Good day, Chastity," a short, rather big, woman with curly dark hair said. "Please take a seat." She showed to the very first table that was vacant.

I felt like the only idiot without her Anitule. She introduced her Anitule, a lizard, as Greta.

The class was interesting but it still felt weird not having Shades there with me.

MEOW! a cried call, and to my surprise, Shades made his graceful entry through an open window and jumped into my lap.

"A bit late, aren't we?"

"Shush, I had better things to do with my time but felt it was probably necessary for me to make my appearance."

"Thank you so much Your Highness for showing me this courtesy."

"Chas," Mrs. Mios said, and both of us looked at her. "Please tell Mr. Grey that class started 15 minutes ago and that next time there won't be an open window for him."

"Okay," I said as her lizard, sprawled on his log behind her desk staring at both of us.

"He looks absolutely yummy," Shades said and I had to suppress my laughter.

"It's a she," I whispered.

"Doesn't matter, it will make my stomach full."

"Way too much info, dude."

"I'm a cat, not a dude, Chas."

"Whatever."

"And to be quiet." Mrs. Mios interrupted our conversation.

"Sorry," I apologized.

"Who spat in her milk this morning? I'm out of here."

"Don't you dare," I whispered at him but was too late to grab him. He walked out the way he'd entered.

"Cats," Mrs. Mios said and everyone laughed.

"Sorry about that," I said and wished that I was a bird that could just fly away.

I felt left out with the assignment. Nat and Charlie won as they knew each other really well plus she could hear him the way I hear Shades.

He was her eyes when they blindfolded her, everyone was in awe at how she got the answers right to everything Mrs. Mios asked her to point out.

Not a lot of Tulas could hear their Anitules the way we did and these exercises were supposed to help make that connection.

I guess Shades wasn't wrong when he said it was a waste of his time. We heard each other perfectly and he would've probably told me the wrong answers anyway for that very first night.

I walked alone through another hallway, far from my classmates so as not to see the judgmental stares or hear the gossip about what I was.

I looked up and couldn't remember ever being in this hallway. A set of stairs were to my left and I took them, but paused as I heard harsh whispers below.

It was a quarrel between two people.

"I have my eye on you Dingle. You might have

fooled Selene but you don't fool me. I know what you are and it's only a matter of time before it will show. My advice, bring back Margot's pendant."

Dingle laughed and I knew that Leigh was wrong about him. If Fox could still sense the dark in him, then that was good enough for me.

I found another route out of the Institute and back to the House of Lords. I guessed now that everyone had made up their minds about me, Natalie wouldn't want to be my friend anymore.

When I got back home I was attacked again the second I took my first step through the door.

"Really, Chas." Margot was five inches from me. "What is..."

"If it isn't your long fingers that take my stuff it's your cat!" She had one of her tops in her hand covered with thick long grey fluff. Mr. Grey.

"How do you know it's him? And I didn't take anything from you."

She gave me a sarcastic laugh. "Don't even try to deny it. WHAT ARE YOU HIDING?"

"I'm not hiding anything, you crazy lunatic!" I yelled back.

"Enough!" Fox barged into the lobby. "What is it now, Margot?"

"It's Chastity's cat. Look at what he did!" She pushed her top into Fox's face.

"It's just hair, Margot. We can deal with it."

"No, she put him up to it. What are you looking for this time, Shadow Caster?"

"Enough Margot, now go to your room."

Everyone was in the lobby now, thanks to Margot's little outburst and was staring at me again. If it wasn't clear before, it was clear now.

"All of you, go to your rooms."

Margot glared at Fox before she stormed off in the direction of her room. I couldn't help but stand there. I knew that Margot would figure out why I never wanted to show my sand inside the Virtual Realm. Even if I never knew that it was the Virtual Realm. Still, to blurt it out like that, she had no right.

"Chastity…" Fox looked at me.

"I never took her stupid pendant," I replied.

"I know, but please, you need to try and keep Mr. Grey out of the other students' rooms."

"It's Mr. Grey, Fox. The cat never even listened to Selene, why on earth would he listen to me?"

"Just try, please."

"Fine, I'll speak to him tonight."

"Tonight? He's not here?" she asked, worry lacing her tone.

"No, he only comes back from his rendezvous at night. Who knows what mischief he does? I can't be held responsible for his actions Fox."

"Then let him know that his actions reflect badly on you."

I nodded and went straight to my room.

Dinner was quiet and Nat kept to herself. I knew that she didn't want to be my friend anymore.

Even if that wasn't true, all of them would label me as the girl that had an agenda and that I might be hiding something, which I was, but they didn't know that for sure.

I didn't ask to be a Shadow Caster. Heck my mother tried her best to guard me from this world, and I knew if my Grandfather found her, which I was pretty sure had already happened, she would pay with her life for what she did.

By nine, my eyes didn't want to stay open anymore and I'd tried so hard to stay awake to speak to the stupid cat about making everything even worse. Why had he gone and messed around in Margot's room? He knew how much she had it in for me, why go and make things worse? I told him not to.

I still thought he had another agenda, one that was going to get me into more trouble.

The pendant would come back when she was tired of searching for it. That was what lost things did and then she would feel guilty for saying all those awful things about me.

When I couldn't open my eyes anymore, I got up, and went to sit on the sill of my window. I opened the window more, trying to get the cold breeze to wake me up.

I'd seen many nights in my life but none of them were quite as gorgeous as Revera's. The huge moon with its million stars was simply lovely. Then right before you fell asleep, the evening sky became filled with golden beams, like the northern lights. They flew in every direction and believe me, I didn't think anybody saw how it ended as one breath of sleeping dust was enough to knock you out.

My dreams were filled with Leigh, lately.

I knew why too, I would die if he ever found out how I felt about him. He didn't look like the type of guy that would go for a girl like me. He was more of ....Margot's type.

Still, dreams were there for the impossible, and I knew Leigh fell under that category.

I wished that I could share this with Mom. I remembered how she used to scan guys at my school and ask plenty of questions to find out if there was one that I liked, but I always gave her the raised eyebrow or lip, which made her laugh every time.

She would've liked Leigh. I was glad that I'd told her about him, still she would never know that he was my first real crush. Well secretly in my case.

A girl could dream, even in a dream world. I lay my head on my knees and slowly my eyes started to close. It was dark for a few seconds and then a meow made them fly open.

I found myself staring at a plastic horse, not my stupid grey cat.

It was a weird feeling.

At first it was just the plastic horse and then the entire picture came to life and expand. The horse was moving, followed by more horses turning around in a carousel, until all the other plastic pieces of a carousel with an old eerie tune played, was fully in my view. I turned to my left and saw other rides. Hot dog stands and people, plenty of people that moved around.

I place my hands in my hoody's pockets as a cold finger traced up my back. I knew I'd been here before, in my Initiation dream, with Leigh. But the only difference was that this fair wasn't in ruins like the one inside that dream.

A part of me felt uneasy, even though I knew the tests were over, I still felt like this dream tried to betray me, to show what I really was.

I started to walk away from the carousel and past a vendor who sold popcorn, cotton candy and other treats. A hot dog stand was across from him and something about those two vendors looked familiar. I just couldn't put my finger on it.

Their heads shot up and they stared at me. A pair of black eyes, the same kind I'd seen once on Mom when she'd turned back into a Shadow Caster.

I knew what these men were and why they were in this dream. They wanted me and were probably searching for me as I dreamt. I didn't stay to find out if my instincts were right. Instead I ran as fast as my legs could carry me.

Screams filled the entire theme park as objects near me exploded before dark sand took their place and fell in heaps to the ground. For some stupid, unknown reason the only escape route I could find was the House of Horrors.

Who would've thought that I would become the bimbo who chose the House of Horrors to lose her dark pursuers?

I jumped as a skeleton with a long sword fell on me with teeth chattering inches from my face. Adrenaline flowed through my veins and black sand formed in my hand. I didn't care if it was not natural anymore and destroyed all the art created to scare the living jeepers out of a human.

One horror after the other came. A cat, spiked on a steel beam appeared next and the only thing I could make out was its bushy grey tail. I screamed, and wanted to get him off the spike but the barrel inches from me exploded.

It connected hard with my leg and a grunt left my mouth as a stabbing pain seared through my leg and up into my torso.

One of the wooden splinters was sticking out from

my leg. There was blood everywhere.

I had no way of escaping them now and I crawled into the only dark secluded spot I saw, leaving a trail of blood behind me.

More black sand flew from my hands. It was stronger than my golden sand and it flowed more freely. Its powers awakened a darkness inside of me I never knew I had.

I waited for the first figure I saw and willed a weapon to appear with all the concentration I had.

It took shape real fast, the shape of my baseball bat, and I used it first to get myself back onto my feet.

I balanced myself on my good leg and took hold of the bat in my right hand.

When the first figure walked around the corner, I swung as hard as I could and I felt my bat connect with his face.

He fell down immediately as I pulled the bat back for the second blow, only to find that the body lying in front of me was Leigh.

CHAPTER TWENTY-SIX
Just plain Freaky

I WOKE UP WITH A START AND FELL OFF
the windowsill.

My leg still ached, but it wasn't gashed open with
blood seeping out. It was aching because I'd fallen with
all my weight on top of it.

Still, I didn't think it was broken and I pushed myself
from the floor and fell onto my bed.

Why was I dreaming about this shit? Had I really hit
Leigh?

I hated this not knowing. The dreams always felt so
real, and dreams in Revera, well, they weren't your
average dreams.

"Did I interrupt something?" I heard the voice before
I saw its owner.

"Would you stop doing that?" I growled at the cat.

"Sorry," he said in a sarcastic voice. "What happened
to you?"

He must have seen the dread look on my face.

"Chas?" He jumped on top of the bed. "Are you okay?"

It was the first time he'd actually asked me that.

"No, I'm not okay. I keep having nightmares."

He gave me a funny stare, yep, even cats have those and Mr. Grey's was open for anyone to read. "Don't look at me as if I'm insane."

"Okay, what was this dream about?"

I told him about the theme park I'd experienced inside my Initiation dream but I didn't tell him about Leigh or about my dark sand. The cat already avoided me most of the time and only pretended that I was his favorite Caster at night. If he ever discovered that I was a Shadow Caster, and of royal blood, he would certainly avoid me forever. Still I told him about the Shadow Casters chasing me through the House of Horrors and he even chuckled when I told him about the cat I thought was him, dead on the spike.

"It's not funny, it felt so real."

"If it's any consolation, I care about you too, Chas."

"You do?" I raised my left eyebrow. "You have a funny way of showing it, like getting me into trouble and shedding all over Margot's top."

"Blah, blah, blah. I can't help it."

"What were you doing in her room? I told you not to go and sniff around."

"I'm trying to find the person who stole her amulet for real."

"You made it worse. She called me all sorts of things today because of it and now the entire house thinks it's the truth."

"What, that you are a Shadow Caster?"

"It's not funny, Shades."

"Chas, why are you so worried about what people think about you? Unless it's true?"

"Don't. I don't have the strength to argue with you tonight."

He chuckled. "Is that why you don't like to experiment with your sand?"

"Shades."

"Hey, I'm on your side. Well, just as long as you don't expect me to follow you into the Oblivion. Those Shadow Pups...they don't work for me."

"It's not funny."

"Chastity, your sand is golden."

"What if it changes?"

"Do you want it to change?"

"No!"

"Then why do you worry about it?"

"Because..."

"Because what, Chas?"

"What if I have the gene? What if Margot is right, Shades, and those Shadow Casters in the dream were some sort of sign?" I told him about everything that'd happened in the Outer. We'd shared a couple of stories since he claimed me as his Tula.

"Then you will change. It won't be right now or tomorrow, but down the line, if that is what you want, Chas."

"You know that's not true, Shades. I will turn and it doesn't matter if I want it or not."

"It does, more than you know, Chas. I can tell you of dark Light Casters living inside of Revera. They still have their golden sand, even though I'm pretty sure they are destined for the Oblivion."

"What do you mean?"

"You can choose, Chas. You don't have to be so afraid. You are a Light Caster because you are fighting to be one."

"It can't be that simple. They say Shadow Casters are *born* Shadow Casters."

Shades laughed again. "Nothing is born dark, Chas. It's made."

He yawned and curled up on my bed. I knew that our conversation was over. He knew that I was a Shadow Caster and he hadn't jumped out of my window and run back to Selene.

"Believe me, I would rather take my chances with a Shadow Caster than go back to Selene."

"You can read…"

"I'm your Anitule, Chas. You read my mind, it works both ways."

I felt pretty stupid all of a sudden. All the things I thought in his presence. Leigh….

"Yeah, know about that too."

"Just shush."

He chuckled one more time and fell asleep.

MY SECOND DREAM OF THE NIGHT WAS IN the forest. It reminded me so much of the one I'd spent three wonderful weeks with Mom in. Finding out what and who she really was.

I missed her so much.

A twig behind me snapped and I turned around and found Leigh.

He was laughing. "Sorry, didn't mean to scare you."

"I thought I killed you."

"When?"

"Urgh! It doesn't matter." I walked past him, pissed that he would sneak up on me like that and pissed...I don't know at what, I was just really pissed at him.

"Hey?" He ran to catch up and grabbed my arm softly. "What is up with you lately?"

"Nothing. What are you doing here anyway?"

"I needed to talk and I like your company," he said.

"My foul mood you mean," I said in a quirky way and he laughed again.

"Yes, that one. So, you going to tell me what is really bugging you?"

"I had a dream. A stupid dream where these two Shadow Casters were trying to...." I didn't know what they were trying to do as they looked like they were really going for me and not in a good way.

"Trying to what?"

"To kill me."

"Chas, that is absurd. Shadow Casters won't kill if they sense the dark in another Caster. They would welcome you in a heartbeat."

"Yeah, well my dreams disagree."

"And I showed up in this dream?"

"Yes, your face connected with my bat."

"Ouch, how so?"

"I thought you were one of them."

He chuckled.

"It's not funny. I didn't know if it was real like now, or not. I really got scared."

"I'm fine. It's nice to know you dream about me."

"Hahahaha."

"Don't need to be sassy about that. Miss Chicago."

I giggled, this time for real.

"So how's Shades?"

"You knew before I came to Revera?"

"What, that the cat belongs to you?"

I waited for his answer.

"Yes, I've always sensed him close to you. I bet you Selene didn't take it well."

"She was okay, I guess. If she wasn't, she sure hid it well." We started to walk deeper into the woods. "You still haven't given me a proper answer as to why you are here, for real. What danger do I have to look out for next?"

"Busted."

I giggled. "Spit it out."

"It's about Shades. Don't misjudge the cat so much, Chas. He's onto something. I can feel it."

"What do you mean, he is on to something?"

"Something is wrong with Revera. The Virtual Realm is starting to change but I can't pin-point it. It has something to do with Margot's pendant."

"It's just a stupid pendant."

He shook his head and I just stared at him. "It's not?"

"No, it's the real deal. I don't think she knew how real, but it does show when a Shadow Caster is near."

"I didn't take it."

"I didn't mean you. Whoever took it, Shades is onto that person. All I'm asking is, give him some credit Chas. He knows about a lot of things in Revera."

"You think he's close to finding out who stole the pendant?" My mind automatically went to Dingle and the conversation I'd walked in on between him and Fox. He must've known that Margot's pendant could show a Shadow Caster being near, and he could've taken it easily from her as they exited that last virtual test with

Leigh, the one I'd had to sit out.

"Maybe, but I'm not his Tula and I sure as hell don't read kitty minds."

I rolled my eyes and kept walking on. "So what, I need to be the middle man now?"

"If you don't mind. I'm not as useless as you think, Chas. I can do some things inside my world that could save Revera if it comes to that."

"I'm sure you can." Okay that came out totally wrong but was so right at the same time.

He just chuckled.

"Keep your eyes and ears open."

"You're leaving already?"

His mouth opened but the weirdest sound came out of it. I just looked at him and then my eyes opened for real. The sound from Leigh's mouth still rang inside my ear. It was my stupid alarm clock.

When I looked around, Shades was MIA like usual.

Okay, so I should trust the cat, give him more credit and find out what the hell someone wants with Margot's pendant.

THE NEXT DAY I WAS RELIEVED WHEN Natalie poked her head into my room.

"Hey," I said a bit confused about what she was doing here.

"You weren't at the table, you okay?"

"I'll be fine, it's just Margot and now everyone thinking what she said is the truth."

"Not everyone, okay. I know yesterday was hard on you, but I also know it's not the truth. So stop whining and let's go, otherwise you are going to be late for school."

I smiled. "I'll be there in a sec." I looked at Shades who was lying on my bed. The cat came back while I was in the shower, exhausted and I found him curled up on my bed. "Guess I'll see you later."

"Yeah, sure, whatever," he said, closed his eyes and fell back asleep. I ruffled his head which made him growl from deep within. He hated that, but I didn't care.

Our relationship was the reverse of what Tom had with Henry. Henry was the giddy one, and Shades shared Tom's foul mood. The cat was always grumpy.

I didn't have time to eat breakfast as I'd overslept. An apple flew in my direction and I caught it.

"An apple a day keeps the doctor away." Fox stood in the kitchen.

"Really, they use that saying even in Revera?"

She laughed. "We have healers."

I giggled and ran to catch up to Nat and Charlie who were waiting at the front door.

"So, he's not coming?"

I huffed. "That cat is the spitting image of Sleeping Beauty."

She giggled. "Still, he is your Anitule, Chas. It's not good for him to just stay cooped up in your room the whole day."

"He's not cooped up, he just feels that school isn't for him."

She giggled again.

"Charlie loves school," she said and kissed him on his beak. "Even helps me when it comes to the difficult tests."

"He helps you cheat?"

"It's not cheating Chas. It's a perk of being a Tula."

"Okay, that just sucks even more that mine is useless."

She giggled again.

"He'll come too. Just give him some time. Mr. Grey always followed his own path anyway."

"Yeah, I guess. Still it would be awesome if he could help me out with tests."

We both laughed and walked to the entrance of the school.

Max caught up with us which I thought it was strange because I was sure that his sister would eventually tell him her theory and he would put two and two together about why I didn't want to use my dust in the Virtual Realm. But he wasn't running away.

"Hey Nat," he greeted her and she gave him a super smile. Something told me she had a huge crush on Max. It was clear on her face. "Chas."

I nodded once and saw him sigh.

"Charlie wants a cracker," he said and Nat laughed.

"Not cool, Max," Charlie said which made us laugh.

"Charlie isn't your cracker type of parrot." Natalie stroked the bird softly with her lips. "He has feelings and he doesn't like crackers either."

Max pulled his face, smiled and ran toward Sy and a couple of guys in class that were a couple of paces in front of us.

"You still haven't forgiven him yet?"

"You wouldn't either if it was you, Nat."

"Probably. Still, he's not a bad guy, Chas. He's cute too."

"Please, don't go there."

"You don't think he's cute?"

"No, he's … I don't know. He was different at the

Compound. Reserved. Here he's all personality and stuff."

"The Outer does that to people. Still it's good to have both of them here to help with teaching the class their skills."

"I guess."

"You really didn't know that you were inside the Virtual Realm?"

"Nope," I said.

"I wonder what those tests are like. I mean we know every single time we go into the Virtual Realm."

"You do?"

"Leigh sums it up pretty much."

I looked down as she said his name. "It would be awesome seeing him, other than in my dreams."

"Ahhhh, you like Leigh!"

"Oh stop it. I know he's not real."

"He is, he just doesn't exist in this world."

"Still, it could never be real."

"I can see why you like him, you have to be careful though. Margot once admitted her undying love for him and for some reason he's kept his distance from her, so don't let him know the way you truly feel, Chas."

"Believe me, I won't."

THE FIRST CLASS OF THE DAY WAS WITH Mrs. Delvaga again. It was hard as I still didn't know how it all worked. It was the other subject she taught too, Dream Wielding. The type you needed your sand for.

Today she sort of taught us, or me, how to connect with my sand in order to create dreams. Just like the dagger, I had to conjure things from it. The only difference was that you must somehow connect your thoughts with your sand, and let it create what is inside your mind.

It was easier said than done, as my sand created part of a hoof, when it should've been a full unicorn.

Sophie was really good at this, and created a small airplane that could actually carry her own weight. We watched in awe as she took a ride inside the thing around the class room.

When she misjudged a turn, it exploded and she fell on top of a heap of her sand.

The entire class doubled over and we just couldn't stop laughing, including Mrs. Delvaga who was a legend when it came to creating dreams. Still Soph was the only one that could wield her sand to take a form that was strong and real.

She couldn't stop talking as we walked to our next class

She just babbled about what it was I needed to control to make my sand take form like hers.

"Really Chas, it's not that hard. You should just connect with your creative side and voilà. Your creation will come to life."

"What if I don't have a creative side?" I mocked her and she bumped me playfully.

"All Casters have them, you just need to find yours and start with the small stuff. That unicorn you tried to wield is very difficult to do."

"How did…"

"The hoof, it said it all."

I shook my head with a small grin on my face as we entered Mr. Dingle's class.

We met up with Natalie again and Mr. Dingle started

immediately after he greeted us.

"You all need to split into two teams. Max take Chastity with you."

"Yay me," I said to Nat and she laughed and bumped me playfully.

"Easy task, Leigh will give you a map and you need to get to your point of target first, do the task which, if I know Leigh, will probably be something hard, something physical which surely involves a Shadow Hound or two, retrieve the missing object which will be given when you receive your map, and find a Celestial with your team's color on and get back."

"Yay us."

"Whoever finishes their task first will win a day free from the ring."

Everyone was up for that as none of us wanted to get beaten to a pulp.

"So who will go first?"

"Chas, what do you say?"

"Fine, not pleased that it has to be with your mug again," I joked and Max laughed. Nobody else knew what I meant as I didn't tell anyone about spending almost a month inside the Virtual Realm, except for Natalie.

We were taken into the grey room.

Dingle closed the door and we just stared at one another for what felt like an eternity.

The room started to change. The chairs disappeared and I fell on my ass. Max laughed. He knew what was going to happen and I found his hand in front of my face, offering to help me up.

He lift me up with no effort and we found ourselves standing on top of a roof.

I touched the ledge and couldn't believe how real it felt.

"You expected something different?"

I shook my head. "It's hard to think that this isn't really here."

"It's real, Chas, just not in the way you think."

"Try to explain that to me? I know what virtual means."

He chuckled. "Leigh is making all this real. It's why nobody can really tell whether they are in the Virtual Realm or not, only the grey room tells you the truth."

"Amazing."

"Sure is."

I looked around. The building we were on was tall. It soared through the sky and more buildings with tiny cars below were making my heart bounce a bit faster.

"Don't worry, it's just like last time. You won't die if you fall, you will just wake up in the room again."

"Thanks for the heads up."

He chuckled. "Where the hell is Leigh? He's plenty of things but never late."

I chuckled as I remembered Leigh telling me that he used to kick Max's ass on a daily basis inside the Virtual Realm back at the compound.

Natalie and Margot appeared next.

The look on his sister's face told me that tardiness wasn't Leigh behavior at all.

"What's going on? What are you still doing here?" Natalie asked.

"Still waiting for Leigh."

"He hasn't come yet?" Margot asked and Max shook his head.

She started to go and investigate, looking over all the

edges as if he was hiding somewhere from all of us. "Leigh!" she yelled. No answer.

Nat rolled her eyes and I smiled, remembering what she'd told me about how Margot felt about him. It must suck for her that she wasn't going to see him. It also sucked for me because it meant I wouldn't see him either.

The next team came and the same thing happened. Everyone wanted to know where Leigh was.

Margot kept searching like a crazy person who'd lost her pendant all over again.

"Give it a rest. He's not coming."

"But he has a class to lecture. He needs to be here."

"Maybe he didn't get the memo. Chill, Mar. You will see lover boy again real soon."

She squinted at her brother but a small smile appeared on her lips.

"So that's why our real boys aren't good enough for you? You've got a thing for the virtual nerd."

"The virtual nerd will kick your ass ten times over Sy. I'd be careful which names you call him."

I had to admit, it was a good answer.

"Well if Leigh isn't going to show, I guess this is a waste of our time." Max walked over to the ledge.

"What are you doing?" Margot scolded her brother.

"The mission is over when we do whatever the hell he set us up to do. No Lover Boy, no mission."

He winked and climbed on the ledge.

"You're seriously just going to opt out?"

Max turned around, winked and fell backwards off the building. We all ran to look at him and a bright light swallowed him whole.

That is so freak'n cool.

"He's crazy!" Natalie yelled. "I'm not doing that," she growled at Margot.

"Chill scare-dy pants, I'm sure there is another way."

"Well, maybe there isn't," I said and climbed on the ledge too. "Besides I've always wanted to know what it feels like to fall off a building."

"Chas, you're insane. Get away. Dingle will...."

I fell before she could finish her sentence and just closed my eyes as the wind blew against my back.

A white light engulfed me and I landed with a thud inside the gray room.

"....mean he didn't show?" Dingle roared.

Max didn't answer and I could tell he was a bit out of it.

Why I didn't feel like that was beyond my knowledge. "He didn't show," I said.

"Chastity, he's never done this before."

"Please tell me how you do it," Max finally said.

"Do what?"

"Deal with the effects. I feel as if I've trained for hours."

Dingle just stared at me again and I shrugged.

"That's quite remarkable, Chastity."

"Thanks, I'll be here all day. So are the others going to be called for?"

Dingle chuckled. "There is only one way to get back. It seems this lesson wasn't wasted after all."

Max laughed. "Face your fears."

Margot landed with a thud, followed by Natalie.

Both of them experienced the Virtual Realm's effects the same way as Max. They were drained.

I helped Nat up. "Never again. Don't make me do that again." She looked at me as I was grinning at her.

"How on earth did you enjoy that? It was horrible.
"Guess I like adrenaline."
"Urgh, crazy. You are both insane."

THAT ENTIRE DAY WAS OFF. SOMETHING was definitely wrong and I couldn't help but worry about Leigh. He'd said when Margot's pendant vanished that something was starting to change inside the Virtual Realm. What if something happened to him and that was why he hadn't shown?

Class with Mios was just as strange. Greta was missing. I feared that my Anitule had gotten to her; I would kill him if he was in my room, with her inside his belly.

She couldn't stop crying and we all helped search for Greta in trees and gardens, but she was gone, really gone. She didn't even reply to Mios' thoughts.

The third strange occurrence was finding Fox's room destroyed. She was gone too, just like Greta, taken, and I had a really bad feeling inside my gut.

A group of Seekers came, thank heavens Beavis and Butthead weren't among them. I thought about that day again. *What if I'd told Mom, would we still be together?*

There were also a couple of dogs, probably Anitules, sniffing through all her stuff and two of the Seekers, a woman with short dark hair and a man in his late forties, had some sort of scanning device that replayed more or less what had happened.

I peeked outside my room and could see a holograph of two bodies, but couldn't make out their faces, wrestling in Fox's room.

Why would anyone take her? My thoughts

immediately went to Dingle again.

She didn't like him, that much I knew, and if he knew it too...

As I stood there, the woman looked over her shoulder and saw me standing at the door. She walked over to Fox's bedroom door and shut it.

Later that night, Natalie came over to my room with Charlie on her shoulder. She looked distraught, it was written all over her face, her entire body was on alert. She even jumped when Mr. Grey entered gracefully through my window.

"It's just Mr. Grey, relax." I looked at him through narrow eyes. *I swear if he ate Greta he will be getting a spanking.*

"I didn't eat the stupid lizard, it was just a joke." He snorted and went over to his basket and crawled up.

Natalie's hand rested on her chest. "I'm just not myself today. We've only heard of things like this, we've never experienced people going missing and danger lurking around every corner."

"Do you think this is why Leigh wasn't at our training session?"

"It has to be, Chas. He's never been late for a lecture before. Something's not right." She looked at me with huge eyes. "I can feel it, and Charlie feels it too."

A knock on the door made both of us jump this time.

Outside was Sophie. "They're calling us all to the dining room."

I looked at Nat and cocked my head once and we left.

Tom was standing by the window with Henry sitting on top of a coat stand. John sat in one of the chairs off to the side.

Almost all the girls were around the table and I

couldn't help but notice the stupid grin on Mila's face. She was dark and I was sure she was on that list of Light Casters Mr. Grey had warned me about.

I took a chair between Sophie and Nat and looked at John who stared at the table in thought.

Tom cleared his voice. "When was the last time any of you saw Fox?"

"This morning," Iris said. "She was here at breakfast, everything seemed fine."

"She didn't look as if anything weighed heavily on her mind?" Tom squinted and she shook her head. He looked at all of us.

"Chas?"

"She looked just like she did every other day, Tom. Nothing out of the ordinary. Why are you asking?"

"Just answer the question."

"I just did."

A couple of girls giggled softly but when Tom looked at them they immediately went quiet. "It's not a joke, Fox could be in real danger."

"Do you have any thoughts about who could be behind this?"

"We have our suspicions but it's nothing for you girls to worry about. Fox's replacement will be here shortly while we try to find her." He held out his hand and Henry flew from the coat stand and landed on his arm. "I suggest you girls go to your rooms while dinner is being prepared. Try to stay inside tonight, please."

John got up too and our eyes met for a few seconds. He gave me a soft smile and both of them left.

That night I struggled to sleep. There were so many questions on my mind and Mr. Grey wasn't in the mood to talk.

The replacement that came was nothing like Fox. She reminded me of an Italian grandma that knew how to make a mean pasta sauce.

I was worried about Fox. Was she okay? Who took her? Was Dingle behind this?

The next day no one made a peep around the breakfast table, until Mila had to open her big mouth.

"I told you she wouldn't last."

My eyes shot up and I saw gloating reflecting off her. "She's been taken, Mila. Probably lying somewhere in a ditch for all we know without a heartbeat. Have some sympathy and if you don't know how then keep your mouth shut."

Mila's smile vanished as I got up. I didn't care what she was going to do. I could take her if I used everything my mom had taught me, and maybe bring her back down to earth. I hated bullies. I ran up the three steps and through the kitchen, back to my room to get my backpack.

"You seriously have a death wish or something." Sophie was right behind me. I didn't even see her get up or hear her footsteps.

"She just pissed me off so much."

"Still, Chas. She is going to make you regret that, it's what Mila does best."

"Well, then maybe it's time someone other than Natalie stood up to her, Sophie."

We left for first period and said goodbye to Natalie right in front of Delvaga's class.

It was another lesson that didn't fit the past couple of days.

Something was seriously wrong and it could be felt in most of the lectures.

Mrs. Delvaga wasn't her giddy self. She had a huge migraine and was snapping our heads off whenever we made a peep. It was the most horrible lesson ever.

Dingle was missing from his class too and Max and Margot took over. It was physical training and no time in the ring, still it didn't stop Mila from trying to go after me.

She shoved me from behind and I fell on the floor.

"What was it that you said this morning, mix-breed?"

"Mila, back off." Natalie was the first one to react.

"What's going on here?" Max seconded.

"Stay out of this, parrot face and don't make me hurt you, pretty boy," Mila snapped at both of them.

"Mila this is enough, you were out of order this morning." Margot came to my defense too, but the only thing that kept rolling in my mind was what she'd called me, mix -breed. It felt dirty. *'Don't cast your sand if you are not in the right mood, Chas. The dark will show.'* My mother's voice replayed inside my head.

Mila was going at Margot now as I got up. "That the best you can do, ogre?"

Mila's head snapped to me. Her nostrils flared.

"Chas, enough!" Margot yelled.

I could see Max had a grin on his face.

"Do something you idiot," Margot yelled at her brother.

"This is Guardian class, maybe it's something that needs to happen, Mar. Chill, I'll step in before they kill one another."

"Oh, I'll be the one doing the killing, don't you worry," Mila said through clenched teeth and came at me.

I kicked her once, just once, right in the gut and we

all heard how the air in her lungs escaped with an *umph*. She fell backwards, and gasped for air.

I found myself standing over her body and I cupped my hand underneath her chin and lifted it up softly. "If you ever call me mix-breed again, you will regret it. This is over."

I let her go and walked up the stairs.

Suddenly, I was grabbed from behind and chucked hard onto the ground.

Some girls just never knew when to give up. When I looked up she was busy doing a somersault and was about to land on me with a kick, but I moved out just in time and she found nothing below her. She grunt as her leg connected hard with the floor.

Next I found myself on top of her, punching left, right and center; she somehow blocked my fists and got the upper hand again.

Mom had taught me a lock grip, and as she was ready to give me a punch I saw the surprise on her face when she was once again on her back, with her massive boy thighs still around my waist. I knew that this was far from over.

Plenty of the girls yelled on the side lines. Margot tried to break us up, but Mila got in a punch and she fell backward.

The only word I heard was *hooligans* as Margot ran up the stairs.

I took a good few beats, but Mila got a couple of really hard punches and kicks from me too. She just didn't know when to give up and without realizing I'd grabbed a bat, I swung and the bat connected with her body. She fell backwards.

Everything in my body was aching.

"You have enough? Margot's right. We are a bunch of hooligans!" I yelled at Mila who was lying in a fetal position, cradling her body.

I chucked the bat down next to Mila. "If you know what's good for you, you will back off, Mila. This is over," I said again and felt sorry for her as she just lay there, defeated.

She sure was one angry girl, but this had to stop.

"Let me see." Max touched my face and I slapped his hand away.

"Your sister was right, you should've stopped this, Max."

"And miss how you beat up someone twice your size? I knew you had it in you, Chas."

"It's not funny."

I walked away as some of the girls crouched beside Mila to check if she was okay, others just stared at me with huge eyes. I reached the stairs and ran up toward the infirmary.

Later that afternoon, we entered the house for lunch, and Selene was waiting for all of us in the lounge.

"Sit, please," she said with a kind tone.

Mila didn't even look my way and from the way she still looked, something told me that her pride was way too big to let her get help from the Leonora.

"What happened to you?" Selene asked and I slid into in my chair.

"It's nothing, Dingle's class."

"He's making you fight against one another?"

Everyone was staring at Mila. She was such a bitch.

"You put him there. What? You thought he was going to teach us history or something?"

"Mind your tone, Mila," Selene said and Mila

cowered away. "I'll deal with him later."

She looked at all of us. "I'm sure all of you know that Fox isn't here anymore. But I assure you she is perfectly safe. The Seekers found her early in the wee small hours and she is busy recovering. Still it will take a few days for her to come back home. So Mrs. Pottermeyer will stay on for a few days longer. I thought you all should know that your Guardian is well and safe and we are dealing with what happened to her."

I knew it, Dingle was behind this and Leigh was wrong about him. I was glad that she was safe, that they found her and I hoped that Selene's eyes would open this time and that she'd chuck his ass into the Oblivion where he deserved to be.

We broke and Selene laid her hands on me as she passed. "Don't look so worried, Chastity. Fox will return soon."

"I'm just glad that she's safe."

After dinner I went straight to my room, waiting for Shades to see if he had any answers about what was going on.

The cat finally came home but something was wrong. He looked tired.

"Shades?" I asked.

He collapsed on my carpet and I bent down next to him.

"What is it?" I asked, worried that he was going to breathe his last breath.

"The air," he thought. "I can't breathe."

I took a deep breath, and the air smelled fine, but whatever my cat was experiencing I had to make it stop.

A shield jumped into my head and I wielded my sand without any thought.

I closed my eyes when a big enough heap was lying on my carpet and started to concentrate on a bubble contraption that would have oxygen flowing freely into it.

When I opened my eyes it was right in front of me. It was a big plastic bubble, something that belonged on a space craft. It had small pods attached to the inside and I could see that air was releasing through. The contraption in front of me was just like the picture inside my head.

I'd never conjured anything other than the dagger before and guessed Mom was right. Your will for something had to be strong.

I put his pillow from his basket inside and put him in gently and closed the door of the bubble.

All I could do was wait and pray that it would work and wait for him to wake up and find out what it was he knew and who did this to him. I knew he had the answers as there was someone here that didn't want him to speak, but whoever it was hadn't bargained on the connection we shared and that someone had the ability to save him.

If there is one Anitule that figured everything out on his nightly strolls, it was the cat lying in that bubble. My cat.

CHAPTER TWENTY SIX
MAKE OR BREAK

I DOZED OFF SOMEHWERE IN BETWEEN MY worrying about my cat and what was happening. I awoke with a start and found Margot's face inches from mine.

"What the hell…"

Margot pressed her palm over my mouth while Natalie stood like a ghost by the door, or where my door used to be. It was just a wall now.

The Compound jumped into my mind.

Shadow Casters were here.

I took Margot's hand and whispered, "What's going on?"

Both girls' eyes looked bewildered. Okay Natalie was downright losing it? sitting on the floor with her hands cradling her head. Her eyes were red from crying, and then I realized why. Charlie wasn't on her shoulder.

"It's happening," Shades said in my head and I jumped on all fours, crawled off my bed at the speed of light and opened the ledge of his bubble.

"What the hell is that?" Margot stared at the bubble.

"Someone attacked Mr. Grey and he couldn't breathe so I had to think fast."

I took him out, he was still a bit weak but at least he was speaking again, and laid him on my bed. "Thanks Chas. I think that bubble just saved my life."

I didn't care whether he liked it or not, I grabbed the cat and hugged him tight against my chest.

"What is happening?" I asked out loud, remembering what he said when he woke up.

"What is Mr. Grey saying?" Margot grabbed Shades from my arms and held the cat up to meet her gaze. "Speak fast."

"Leave him alone." I pushed Margot hard as Shades scratched her hands. She dropped him.

"Guys, don't fight please. They've got Charlie and I can't deal with this going on as well."

"If the cat knows something, Natalie, he needs to speak," Margot said.

"He's a cat, he won't talk if you try to squeeze it out of him and he just woke up from a near-death experience."

"Deranged girl, lunatic, psycho…" Shades babbled a lot more words but I only caught the last three. "It's going to take forever to get her smell off of me." Okay, that manhandling from Margot actually worked for some reason and Mr. Grey was sitting on my desk, licking his fur fiercely.

"Calm down," I said to the cat. "What happened?" I asked Natalie.

"They came out of nowhere." Her lower lip trembled. "Sophie is dead, Chas."

A jolt of shock mixed with numbness rolled over my

body. "What?"

"We found her body, blood was pouring from her ears and eyes," Margot said. "She's dead, Chas."

I started to pace up and down with my hands clutching my hair. Soph couldn't be dead, she just couldn't.

"If it hadn't been for Margot killing one of them…" Nat spoke again. "Grabbing my hand, I would be dead too. They must have Charlie. I have to get him." She turned around to face the wall where my door used to be and started to feel for a knob. "Open this, now!" She hit with her fists hard as tears rolled over her cheeks.

I just stared at her and then looked at Shades who was staring at her too.

"Are you insane? I'm not risking my life for a bird." Margot grabbed both her hands and shoved her toward the bed. "And keep your voice down. They might still be in the house."

"It's not just any bird, Margot. It's my Anitule, please we've got to go get him."

"Calm down Natalie. I'm sure Charlie knew danger was near and he got away."

"How?" The girl had more tears streaming down her face. "I didn't leave a window open for him to fly away. They've got him, Chas." She started to sob.

I wrapped my arms around her. I could only imagine how she must feel as mine was still safe with me. Even though he was still ranting about what Margot said about Charlie, that I could not possibly say out loud.

"Tell your cat to speak, and fast too," Margot barked.

"Mr. Grey?"

"Tell her to apologize first. And she needs to make it

sound sincere."

"We don't have time for this."

"Apologize!"

"Fine! He wants you to apologize."

"What? He's a cat."

"Apologize or you can forget about the cat saying a word."

"Fine, I'm sorry."

"Not sincere enough," Shades said.

"For what are you sorry?" I translated.

She gave me the *huh* look. "You're shitting me, right? My brother could be dead for all I know and he wants to know in detail why I'm sorry."

"You want him to speak, make it sound as if you mean it."

"Fine, I'm sorry that I manhandled you and that your ego is bruised."

"Margot!" Natalie yelled. "You will never get it. Anitules aren't just animals. They have feelings and I know you think that we are psychos for hearing them, but they are more than just animals. Now, apologize as if he was your brother."

"Fine, Mr. Grey. I'm sorry, okay?"

"Better," the cat spat and jumped onto my bed again.

"So, what's going on?"

"It was someone in this house that stole Margot's pendant but it wasn't you. I tried to get their scent that was why I was in her room."

"Dingle."

"It's not him, Chastity."

"Are you sure about that?"

"Yes, now translate."

I started to translate, and Margot just stared at me

and the cat. "That's why your top was ruined but he said that it was the only thing that had two scents on it, he couldn't make out the other scent clearly."

"It still doesn't answer what is going on."

"You still owe me an apology."

"Chas, we don't have time, please. Max could be dead."

"What else?" I asked and listened again. "He said that over the past couple of weeks things in Revera have started to change." Leigh had said that too, that he could feel it inside the Virtual Realm. "They needed your pendant so that nobody would be alerted when they entered." I looked at Margot. "Margot's pendant is real." Natalie asked.

"Why is this happening?" I had to know.

"Why do Shadow Casters always try to get into Revera? They want to eliminate us." Shades' voice sounded grave, but his facial expressions were still those of a grumpy cat. I translated again.

"So they're out to kill all of us?" Natalie asked him.

"Pretty much and they're trying to destroy Revera." I spoke Shades' words.

"If Revera no longer exists, it will become like the Oblivion. I can't stay inside the Oblivion, men or no men, I'm going to find my brother."

"Not so fast Terminator," Mr. Grey ordered and I had to translate fast.

"Mr. Grey knows of another way," I said and the cat jumped off my bed and ran toward my closet.

"Tell the war freak to draw what I tell you, Chastity, precise translation this time."

"Got it. He wants you to draw what he says on the door."

She didn't say a word and took her marker out of her pocket.

"What about Charlie?"

"Natalie, we will find him later, I promise. Right now we need to get out of here, safely." I put my hand on her shoulder and gave her a pleading look.

She nodded and Mr. Grey grunted annoyingly.

"Okay, shoot." I said.

"On the left top corner of the closet, draw a triangle with two diagonal stripes running through it." I translated and Margot drew fast.

"Mark a circle with a pie sign in the center. Right corner and square with a circle around. Another triangle right below in the middle with diagonal stripes in the opposite direction. Right corner below a circle with a square sign around, next to it another square with the same pie inside and left corner below an infinity sign with the sign of a crow's beak right on top of it.

She finished and Mr. Grey put his paw on the infinity sign.

My cupboard door started to turn into a mirror but it wasn't like the one in the lighthouse.

It was bright, like the Celestial, and we all jumped through it.

I fell with a thud on top of Margot, right behind a thick set of bushes right behind our house.

"Tell the girl to remember those signs, and when you find others alive, go back to any door, Chas. Draw it again and tap on the crow's beak. above the one I just did. It will take you to your lover boy. He can help."

"He's not…" I wanted to finish but the cat ran away. "Where are you going?" I hissed.

"I have something else to do."

I shook my head. Stupid cat.

"I heard that."

I shook my head again as I watched his bushy tail disappear inside another thick set of bushes.

Voices that made my skin crawl filled the air and it felt as if my heart was going to stop.

They were walking in the opposite direction away from the house, toward the school, and I poked my head out from one of the bushes and saw a couple of men leaving the house with the rest of the girls. Mila was in the front, her ogre body was just as big as the guy walking in the front but he was at least a head taller than her. Her trio of friends were a couple of paces behind and I saw how one pushed Tarryn to walk faster. Iris and Andrea were there too.

Why did they kill Sophie if they took the rest?

Where the hell were all the Guardians, the lecturers and Seekers? I didn't see Mrs. Pottermeyer at all and got a flash in my mind of her body lying somewhere next to Sophie's.

Maybe it was part of the plan to lure them away so that they would succeed. Still someone had stolen Margot's pendant, someone close to all of us and I don't care what Shades or Leigh said, Dingle was still my number one suspect.

When they were out of view, Margot made a run for the boys' house where Max stayed.

We had no choice but to go with her. We needed her to get into the Virtual Realm.

The House of Knights had been raided just like ours, still standing but abandoned.

"Max," Margot said softly.

We found a body that belonged to Sy and I

swallowed hard.

Margot shook her head with her eyes closed as she felt for his pulse and carried on walking through the pieces of ceiling that had fallen through the floor. The boys had put up a fight, that was for sure.

"Max," Margot said a bit louder and a cough from the stairs made all of us jump.

We rushed to the stairs and found Max in bad shape. Blood lingered on the edges of his mouth and Margot took off her hoody and cleaned his mouth.

"You are going to be fine," she said hurriedly. Her voice broke a couple of times.

"There are little kids upstairs, I locked them in with the protection charm, Matt brought them here minutes before the attack came," he coughed.

"They attacked the house of Squires?" Margot had tears in her eyes.

I could put two and two together that the house was filled with little kids.

"You need…"

"No, I'm not leaving without you," she said.

"I'm as good as dead, Mar, I'm not going to make it."

"Bullshit, you've been through much worse. We got a charm from the cat that will take us to the Virtual Realm. Leigh will know what to do with you."

She started to lift her brother, and he let out a loud grunt.

"Get up."

"I can't."

"Oh, for crying out loud," I said and bent down to help Margot. "Your sister is right, Max, you've been through worse. Now stop being a girl and get the hell up."

He chuckled and grabbed me around the neck. His weight was heavy even with both of us sharing it. But we managed to get him onto his feet.

Natalie walked in front, up the stairs with the three of us stumbling as we followed her.

We put Max back down on the floor near the wall and Margot drew the protection charm that would open the doorway to the room of the kids on the wall. The door appeared and we found five boys and one girl between the ages of seven and eleven hiding inside.

"It's okay." Natalie spoke sweetly and bent down to comfort the seven-year-old boy with big blue eyes and ginger hair. "Get Max in here, we can use the closet door to go to the Virtual Realm."

"You ready?" Margot asked and I nodded. "Just one more time, Max. I promise you can do whatever the hell you want in the Virtual Realm, just don't die."

He chuckled again and we picked him up and helped him into the room.

"Natalie, I need to draw the signs again. Keep my brother up, please."

Nat took Margot's place, but she wasn't as strong as her and it felt as if my back was going to break with the extra weight.

Margot drew the signs again with my help. She was really smart and remembered most of them. She reached out to tap the infinity sign.

"No, the crow's beak," I said and she changed her direction real fast.

The door rippled and it showed a beautiful starry night on the other side.

Margot took Natalie's position as she guided the

kids through the door. We were last and once we stepped through the door, it disappeared.

We found ourselves on a hill. Below the hill was a farm house.

"You've got to be shitting me," Margot said.

"Put him down, I'll look for help," I said and we put Max down gently against the nearest tree.

"Keep them safe." I looked at the kids and gave them my super smile. "It's going to be okay." I crouched down in front of the girl. "Help Natalie okay? She lost a really good friend today." The girl nodded and grabbed Natalie around the waist.

"If you see a bat, grab it." Max joked.

"Hahaha, just stay alive." I looked at Max and then at Margot. "I promise I'll be back in a few."

She nodded and I started to climb down the hill. "Chas," Margot called back. "I'm sorry for thinking that it was you that stole my pendant."

"It's fine, Margot. See you later."

The farmhouse seemed far but it came close sooner than I thought. Why I couldn't tell that I was inside the Virtual Realm the first time I did that test was beyond me. The colors were all wrong and even the grass was way too hard. It was something Leigh needed to work on.

That thought made the corners of my mouth curve slightly.

Lights were on but they weren't bright enough.

I reached the back door and just as I was about to knock, it opened slightly.

I walked inside. It was quiet as if nobody was home and I took my first step into the house.

Don't speak, my gut said. It was Mr. Grey's voice

and for a second I thought the cat was here, but he wasn't.

Voices and loud footsteps from above made me hide behind the kitchen counter.

I knew those voices, every time I heard them my skin tingled and the hair on my arms rose. They belonged to Shadow Casters and although this was the Virtual Realm, they were just as strong and deadly as the real ones. Leigh had made sure of that.

"That was easy. Did you hear how the old man cried out?"

The other one laughed as one guy mocked the old man's pleading.

"We need to get back, there's plenty to do."

Their footsteps on the stairs stopped and I heard one of them inhale deeply.

My heart was jumping inside my chest fast.

"We have company."

Shit, crap. I almost thought about the "f" word too, but my mind was redirected to find something I could fight with.

My sand would be black in the Virtual Realm and useless against these Casters.

I opened the drawer and found a couple of things I could throw at them.

Their footsteps came nearer and I focused in on where exactly they were going, just like Max taught me the first time.

One was at my nine o'clock and the other moved in the direction of my three. Their hearts gave it away, but the fact that they were steady and not beating as fast as mine made me wish that I could be as confident as they were.

I grabbed a couple of normal knives and a sharp steak knife and rolled from my hiding place, letting three of the blunt knives leave my hands so quickly that the Caster only had time to block two. The third one, with my ability to think happy thoughts, hit him straight in the chest. He immediately started to glow, and began grunting, which turned into a scream, right before disintegrating into black dust. The other one was aiming arrows at me and I ducked all of them. I rolled towards him quickly. I got up, took a leap and grabbed him with my legs around his chest. I brought him to the ground with me and used the steak knife and stabbed him in the eye.

He screamed and pulled it out, but it was too late, my sand was already glowing inside of him and it was starting to pull him apart. He screamed more and exploded like he'd swallowed some sort of a bomb. I covered my face and rolled myself up in a ball.

Dark sand covered my entire body, and when it was all done, I took a couple of breaths.

The sand clung onto everything, the walls, the curtains, part of the kitchen counter and even the couch.

I shook off the sand and ran up the stairs.

In the first room I found the body of the old man they were making fun of.

He had white hair and was barely alive.

I crouched beside him and he opened his eyes. "It's okay. I'm not here to harm you."

He whispered something but I couldn't hear and I bent my head back down.

"The light has shadows inside them."

I frowned. It was exactly what the old man in the woods had said before he got killed. What did it mean?

Could he see what the other old man saw? That no matter how hard I tried, nothing I did to stay good would be enough.

He blew out his last breath and fell backward with his eyes open.

I closed them for him and swallowed hard. Virtual Realm or no Virtual Realm, he was alive and now he wasn't anymore.

I went back down the stairs. I raided the cupboards for anything that might help Max and his wounds and found a couple of bandages, some medicine, a needle and a Celestial orb. Why did the old man have a celestial orb? And why didn't he use it? Nevertheless, I took it and put it all inside my hoody and tied the arms so that I could carry all of them.

A voice, not from inside the house but over a radio, started to speak. It belonged to one of the Shadow Casters and I knew if they didn't hear anything from their comrades soon, they would come running.

We were not safe hiding on that hill. I had to get out now and back to my friends to warn them. We had the orb, but where we should go, was a different question.

I rushed out the house and sprinted to where they were hiding. My legs ached and my lungs burned slightly.

On the hill, Margot was the first to meet me. They'd moved everyone behind the trees. "We need to go. The owner of the house was ambushed by Shadow Casters."

"No, we need help," she said and wanted to go back to the house.

"Margot, he's dead. More are coming. We have to go."

I showed her the Celestial orb and she put two and

two together.

"Max is not going to make it. The fall. He would die for sure."

"It's a chance we have to take. We're dead if we stay."

"Then go, I'm not leaving him."

"Margot."

"Chas, take Nat and the kids and go, we'll be fine. If you find Leigh, please tell him where we are."

"I promise." I grabbed her around the neck and gave her my hoody. "Here's what I could find. Hope it helps. I'll see you again, promise."

She nodded.

"Take care of your sister, Max. Don't you dare die, you hear."

"Go, Chas," he said in a tired voice.

I gave him a soft hug. It felt just like the previous time we'd been in the Virtual Realm and I hated leaving them there.

I left and took Nat and the kids with, found the closest tree and slammed the Celestial orb on the trunk.

"Do you have any idea where he might be?"

Nat nodded. "But it's not safe for them."

"Then the closets. You can hide with them, keep them safe and I will try to find him."

"Backerwood theme park," she yelled and I closed my eyes.

I knew which theme park she was referring to. *More Shadow Casters would be hanging out there*, I thought as the orb turned a bright color. I grabbed the youngest boy with the ginger hair and jumped with him through the light. We came to a hard landing, followed by the other four boys and last was Natalie and the girl.

The little ones were crying. The fall wasn't nice but it wasn't as bad as it had been the first time. I remembered my head was spinning like mad.

"Can you wield some chocolate?" I asked Natalie and she nodded.

She paused as she was about to give each a piece.

"How did you know about the chocolate?"

"Max, in my virtual test. He said chocolate helps."

"Really, they're that real?"

"We're in the Virtual Realm now, Natalie."

"Oh, right." She shook her head and started giving the boys each some chocolate.

The eerie song of the carousel and the sound of a huge crowd played softly in the background.

"Do you have any idea which is his favorite ride?"

"Nope, just that he has a thing for theme parks."

"I hate that so much."

Natalie huffed. I knew she wanted to giggle but it wasn't the time for laughter.

"Will you be fine?"

She nodded. "I've got Stan to protect me." She ruffled up a blond kid's hair.

"Okay, keep her and all your friends safe, okay Stan? And if you see a bad caster, you run."

He nodded.

"Leave no one behind."

"Promise," he said with a puffed up chest.

"Be good." I smiled and left.

The wind felt cold and I hated how all of this felt so real. Why didn't he like to hang out in normal places like hotel pools or a club? Why a stupid theme park, with stupid eerie carousel and a House of Horrors?

I remembered my dream, the one where I'd smacked

Leigh in the face with a baseball bat.

I made a mental note of not going into the House of Horrors.

I took a deep breath as I reached the entrance. Paid the dollar and smiled politely, as if I was one of Leigh's creations.

These people felt so real, all of them. There were plenty of kids around, laughing, playing the games they had at the booths. A drunken man started a fight with another. A couple of punches flew and I took a couple of side steps, not to be in their way. I took the opposite direction to the men and their vendor carts selling cotton candy and popcorn and walked toward the big Ferris wheel.

I scanned the crowds, wishing that a dark-haired guy with glasses would pop up any time, but nothing came.

I passed a crowd that was busy watching a freak show. I'd never had any desire to watch them, they would only end up giving me more nightmares. I already had enough to deal with.

A tall man wearing a pair of slacks and a Bob Marley shirt turned his head and our eyes met for a second.

Smile, Chas.

I did, but the guy narrowed his eyes and my strides widened a bit and I walked faster.

I glanced around at the guy, which was a huge mistake, and I saw him walking with huge strides toward me.

I ran as fast as I could.

I knew who that guy was, he had to be a Shadow Caster and could clearly see Light Caster written over my entire body.

The carousel with horses and carriages was on my left and I jumped over the barrier that blocked the crowds from the ones enjoying the ride.

Someone yelled and the sound escaping his lips with a couple of other expressions of disbelief was a good warning that he wasn't far behind.

I didn't think twice and jumped onto the revolving floor and made my way as quickly as possible toward the middle. I opened the door, but didn't go in, rushing off to the other side, hoping that I would lose him, making him think that I went and hid inside.

I jumped off the carousel again, and left on the opposite side I'd entered.

Glancing back one more time, I found that my pursuer was gone.

I started to scan the rides again. *Leigh, where the hell are you?*

I started to search the rides, one by one, but couldn't see Leigh either enjoying one or standing in line.

Running off to the next ride, I bumped into another man. Only when his hands gripped me hard, did I look up to see who it was.

The smile with yellowish teeth and dark eyes was enough to tell me who it was.

"Got you, little bird."

I pulled hard from his grip and when that didn't work, I brought my knee up and collided hard with his groin. When he crouched and grunted, my hand thrust up into his face, and another kick made him fall backward. I ran again as fast as I could and the only attraction in front of me was the House of Horrors.

Urgh! I couldn't believe that I was back where I said I didn't want to be, and that this time I literally had no choice.

CHAPTER TWENTY SEVEN
EMBRACE

I RAN AND DUCKED PAST ALL THE PUPPETS and art that was meant to give you a slight heart attack without blinking an eye and hid behind the corpse bride that was floating with a mechanical laughter mechanism molded inside of her.

The thing was creepy with her torn wedding dress and hair that was slightly showing bits of her skull.

Flesh still hung from her body and the weapon that'd killed her was still lodged inside of her. Cobwebs were everywhere and with the fog that a machine created it sure felt like everything was real.

A couple of men ran fast past a couple in the next cart who screamed when the laughter went off.

I watched from behind her skeleton how they stopped and searched. I lowered my head back down, praying for the cart to just pass so that the light would go off.

When that happened, I crawled from my space and crawl-walked in the opposite direction back out of the House of Horrors.

Another cart was coming in my direction and I made myself small against the wall, off the tracks.

The teenagers inside were making jokes.

"It's a walk in the park, man. Buff up."

"I bet fifty dollars that Tiff is the first one that screams her head off."

They all started to make bets as the cart passed.

I walked back onto the tracks and ran up toward the next attraction which was a scarecrow killing people.

I had to say, Leigh was surely one talented guy, and scary all at the same time.

When the cart passed me again, I walked further until I saw the entrance.

"Hey, you. Stop. What are you doing here?" the conductor selling tickets asked and I jumped over the ledge and fell about two feet, landed on my feet and started running again.

"You, stop!" He yelled again. I didn't like the attention he was drawing toward me and the security officer running behind me made it worse.

I needed something to hide my face and I spotted a grey hoody that was lying over one of the barriers next to a ride. I grabbed it, pulled it on and put the hoody over my head and started walking again.

The security guard ran past me and I walked in the opposite direction again.

I passed a couple of the Shadow Casters too, pretty annoyed that they'd lost me.

"Are you sure it was her?"

"Yes," the other one growled.

I lowered my head and walked on. What did the guy mean by was it me? How did he know me? My mother would never have told them what I looked like if she was with them, so why on earth were they looking for me? What was it that they wanted from me?

I turned the corner and walked faster, back to the entrance. If Leigh was here, he would've found me.

Screams filled the place and I was ready to run when I looked back, sure there was a Shadow Caster. There wasn't. It was much worse than a Shadow Caster.

It was something invisible, something that started to suck up the entire theme park.

Rides broke from their sockets, some still had people inside. They rattled like mad and then would get sucked into an invisible vortex.

People screamed everywhere and a strong wind was coming in my direction.

Plenty of people ran in all directions and I thought that it was the best idea for now.

It moved really fast and I ran as fast as I could, bumping against people, trying to make my way back to Nat and the kids.

"Chastity." I heard Leigh's voice.

"Leigh!"

I saw him on my left a couple of yards away and we ran toward each other.

"What the hell is going on?"

"I can't stop it, we have to leave."

"Natalie, and the kids...."

"Don't worry, they are safe. I found Max and Margot and they told me where you went. It wasn't hard to find Natalie and the kids, but you were a different story."

"I was looking for you."

"I know. We need to get out of here."

"How?" I asked, still gazing back to see how far the

invisible vortex was.

Leigh pulled me to the side and we started to run.

A couple of steel pipes flew past us and we had to duck and dive, changing direction a couple of times in order to get away from the force.

It was a hard run and my hand was inside of his. My legs ached with the pace he was keeping.

We started to outrun the screaming and it was dying out really fast. Still, I didn't look over my shoulder to see what was behind me.

I saw Leigh take something from his pocket as we reached the trees where Natalie and the kids had been hiding. My legs burned as we ran up the hill, and my feet even slipped a couple of times, but Leigh just pulled once and I was back on my feet, pushing forward.

He slammed something onto the tree perfectly and grabbed me as we dove into the bright light.

"CHASTITY," I HEARD NATALIE'S VOICE. I was still lodged inside Leigh's arms when I looked up.

The look on Margot's face said it all. She didn't like it one bit that Leigh's arms were around me and didn't even care that he'd just saved my life – for the gazillion time.

"What happened?" Nat asked Leigh.

"The same thing as the farm house."

"Wait, you mean it's going to destroy the entire Virtual Realm?" Margot asked Leigh.

He nodded.

"What was that?" I had to know and didn't care if speaking to Leigh was going to give Margot more insecurities.

"At first it was only in small places. A little at a time so that I wouldn't pick up on it. It progressed in the past couple of hours and now it's like a vacuum cleaner, wiping everything I created clean." He sounded worried. "I don't know how to stop it."

"Are we going to die if it reaches this place?"

"I don't know. You might not. There's a loophole created in the Virtual Realm. If you die in this one, it will transport you back to where you came from."

"So we'll go back to Revera?" Natalie asked.

"We opt out," Max said at the same time Natalie asked her question. He was leaning against a pillar that was right in the middle of the room, which reminded me of a basement.

"As easy as that," Leigh said, "and yes, you guys will go back to Revera." He looked at Natalie.

"We don't know what's in Revera. They'll kill Max if we go back now." Margot started to freak out.

"What will happen to you?" I had to know.

Leigh just looked at me.

I knew the answer. He was part of the Virtual Realm and he would die. I didn't like it and looked around. The room was dark with only a dim light that illuminated the place. There were no windows. "Where are we?"

Leigh looked over his shoulder and I saw a bed. "The safest place at the moment but I don't know for how long."

"Guess?" I said.

"Two hours maximum."

I set my watch to count down two hours. "That's all we need."

"Need for what?" Natalie asked.

"Chastity?" Leigh squinted.

"I'm not going to sit here and wait for the entire Virtual Realm to be destroyed. Are they here for what I think they are?"

"Yes, and it's a terrible idea."

"Leigh, help me and stop wasting time."

He took a deep breath.

"Is there a way we can stop this from spreading?"

"There might be. But I still think you are going to waste your time.."

"How?"

"The only thing I can think of is that they must have reached the Basilisk Orb."

I looked at him with raised eyes. "It has the power to do all of this, Chas."

"But you said…"

"I know, if they find it, they'll wipe out the entire Revera and change it into the second Oblivion."

"What are you talking about?" Margot asked. "If they're already at the Basilisk Orb, we're screwed."

"Not entirely," Leigh said and gave a huge sigh.

I knew he was going to tell them about the twin that Selene used to carry and was hiding now for safekeeping.

"There's a twin Orb that is just as powerful as the Basilisk Orb."

"What?" all three of them yelled in unison.

"It's small, and Selene used to carry it around her neck." He looked at me. "It's in the form of an angel, Chas. The angel's carrying the Orb. It resembles a pearl, if the Shadow Casters find it, they'll use their power to change it into the dark."

"Where is it, Leigh?" I glanced at my watch. Ten minutes had passed.

"In her vault."

"How do we get into her vault?"

"It's a waste of time, Chastity."

"You said nobody knows about it." I didn't care anymore about our secret meetings in my dream.

"One does, Lord Crane." My grandfather.

"How?"

"I don't know that part. He'll tell the Shadow Casters, but they need a Light Caster to open Revera for them.

Dingle.

"I told you before, Chas, it's not him."

"I didn't say anything."

"That look on your face spoke a thousand words, one in particular."

"You have a suspicion of who it is?" Margot asked.

"No, she doesn't."

"Then tell me the reason why it isn't him?"

"He's not what you think he is, okay. He is fighting for the greater good Chastity. It's someone else."

"Who, Leigh?"

"I don't know."

"We're wasting time," Margot grunted.

"What do I do when I get the pendant?"

He shook his head.

"Leigh, please."

"Light Casters won't be able to save the Orb anymore. Only a Shadow Caster can revert it back to the light."

"So we're going to die," Margot said.

The children started to whimper, they were scared.

The Oblivion was no place for them.

I felt Leigh's eyes on me but I couldn't look at him. I knew what he was thinking. I was thinking it too and they would repay me with everlasting darkness.

I looked at the children again and Shades' voice from the day Margot accused me of stealing her pendant jumped into my mind. It was a hopeless case from the beginning to be honest.

The Oblivion was no place for any of them.

I took a deep breath and looked at Leigh.

"No." Leigh shook his head and stared at me.

"It's going to be okay. If it's to save Revera, I can do that."

"What are you talking about?" Margot and Natalie asked at the same time.

"Chas, it's a one way ticket straight to Oblivion."

"I'm going to be fine. After all it's where I really belong Leigh."

"What?" Margot yelled. "You are a Shadow Caster?"

"Easy, Margot. Right now Chas is the only one that can save your ass." Leigh spoke through clenched teeth and she backed off. "I can't let you do this."

"It's not your choice Leigh. I can't let Revera turn into the Oblivion. Think about the children, about everyone you care about."

"I am."

My eyebrows knitted as the butterflies in my stomach went wild. Still, he could mean it in a friendly way.

"No," Max said. "I saw your dust, it's gold, Chas."

"It'll change, Max. Sooner or later. It will change," I said.

"You can choose, Chastity," Leigh reminded me.

"Not anymore. I have to revert the twin Orb back to light. I can do that."

He shook his head again and looked away.

"What do I need to do?" I asked. He didn't answer, just stared at the floor.

"Leigh, what do I need to do?" I asked again.

"Please, if Chastity can stop this, we need to give it a try, Leigh," Natalie whispered.

"I'll go with you." Max started to push himself up against the wall.

"Are you insane? You can't even walk properly."

"She's going to need help. I'm the best fighter against Shadow Casters. She can't do it alone." He looked at me. "It'll be just like old times."

"No," Margot interrupted. "You can't. She's a Shadow Caster, Max."

"Not yet. She needs help," Max said through gritted teeth.

Margot looked away. I felt like I could punch her in the face. "Fine, I'll do it."

"Hell no. I know how you feel about Shadow Casters. She wouldn't get a chance if she left the Virtual Realm."

"I promise I'll help her. I swear it on Mom and Dad's grave. If you think I want to live inside the Oblivion, you've made a huge mistake," she said.

Max and Margot stared at one another. "Okay."

"Now what do we need to do, Leigh?" Margot asked.

"Do you have a pen and paper?"

Natalie took some paper from her back pocket and handed it to him. None of us had a pen so he took a piece of twig and the ash from the fires he stoked at night and started to scribble something on it.

He drew a map too. It was Selene's quarters and where we could find the safe. He even put the combination of the safe onto the piece of paper. *How the hell did he know all of this?*

Then when he was done, he told us about all the secret passages into her quarters. There was a passageway that was built behind the walls. All of this information was crazy and I couldn't stop wondering how he knew about it.

He mostly spoke to Margot and she kept nodding her head as he carried on.

"Once they get to the Basilisk Orb, they have to break the enchantment that is protecting the Orb, hiding it's light. So you will see the tower engulfed in light from Selene's room. If no light emanates from the tower, then come back. It's a lost cause because someone will already have the twin Orb, and it will be too late. But if light still emanates from the tower then go to the safe. It has to be inside her vault."

"You're not sure?"

"90% sure." The corners of his lips tugged slightly upwards. "If you find the pendant with the twin Orb, you can revert it back to light with your dark sand. All you have to do is think about the things that made you the happiest and turn the dark, Chas."

"What?"

"It's not so hard, but it's crucial that you have to make every happy thought a sad one."

I didn't understand what he meant, but I knew when the time came, it would make sense.

"It's the only way it will work."

"What if Selene has it with her?" I had to know.

"She doesn't. I promise you that. She'll be at the cathedral with the Basilisk Orb as the Shadow Casters will have taken her already."

"How do you know this? And don't give me that sappy story of, *I'd tell you but then I'd have to kill you.*"

He smiled.

"I needed her help to create the Virtual Realm and I saw plenty of things, especially around the Basilisk. So you can trust me."

I nodded. "I do."

"Okay, I'll draw the gateway back to Revera. Remember what I said, Margot, and be safe."

She smiled and nodded.

He took more ash in his fingers and started drawing symbols on the wall. I didn't know that walls could work too, but this was the Virtual Realm.

Natalie got up and wrapped her arms around me. "You are seriously one insane girl and whatever reason you are doing this for, thank you."

I smiled at her. She knew that it was because of Leigh. I couldn't let him die, be wiped out, not exist. Even if he wasn't real, he was real to me.

"If I don't see you again, know that you're the bravest girl I've ever met."

"I hope you find Charlie."

She giggled.

"I'll keep my eye out for him, I'm sure he's okay, Nat."

She nodded and hugged me again. "Be safe."

For what that was worth, it felt good hearing it. Even though she knew what I was, she still wanted me to be safe.

"Hey, little Nightmare," Max said as he steadied himself against the wall. "She promised that she won't attack, but if she does I won't hunt you down for the first three years okay."

"Max," Margot said.

"It was a joke," he said and Margot rolled her eyes. "She promised. She'll fight with you to the end. I can promise you that."

"Okay, just stay alive. You'll get help soon. I promise."

He chuckled and slid back down the wall.

"It's time," Leigh said and I looked at Margot.

"After you," Margot said.

Guess I'll have to take my chances. One thing was sure, she didn't want her brother to die or live inside the Oblivion, and we shared the same feelings for Leigh, even though he didn't share hers.

"Remember what I said, make sure your dust is dark."

I nodded. I had no idea how I was going to master that one. My dark dust never flowed, and to do it on the first try, while having good thoughts, just didn't make sense. But I needed to find a way to save Revera – and the guy that made my knees weak whenever he was near.

"Got it, happy thoughts, dark dust. If I don't…"

He put his finger on my mouth making my heart beat faster. "Shhhh, you'll do it, I know you will." He wrapped his arms around me and I could feel his lips brushing my hair. "Just stay safe, okay?"

I nodded.

I broke the hug and walked through the opening fast.

I knew that it could be the last time we would ever see each other, but I just couldn't look back. I would've done something stupid like kiss him or something and then he could reject me.

A couple of seconds later Margot walked through the opening too with the piece of paper in her hands.

Neither of us said a word about my departure from Leigh, or hers for that matter.

I looked around and saw we were inside the building that had Selene's private quarters on the top floor.

None of us knew where the twin Basilisk Orb was, but I prayed that she didn't have it with her.

The entrance to the building was empty. The lights were dimmed and the colors seemed all wrong. Revera's colors were bright, made you think of magic, and this was just so ordinary, like the colors I'd grown up with.

"We need to hurry, the light is already going out."

"Lead the way," I said as we ran up the stairs.

"First, the cathedral."

She watched out the window and we could see the cathedral. Light still streamed from the tower. The light was faint, but it was there. We could still do this.

When we made it to the room down the hallway to the left, she looked at the map again and the sketch of the room Leigh had told us about.

There was no opening like he'd said, only paintings, so we started lifting them.

"This one is molded to the wall," Margot said.

It was one of the last ones and I helped her tear the canvas apart.

To our surprise there was an opening, but it was so small that I didn't think either of us would be able to fit.

"You ever experience the dislocated transformation?"

"The what?" I asked.

"Time for a crash course. You need to put your golden sand to the test, one last time."

I sighed. "Okay, what is it I have to do?"

"Think…..small." Her golden dust flowed from her hands and she sprinkled it all over herself. She smiled and at first nothing happened. She just looked like a girl having fun in her golden dust. Then she started to shrink, and shrink.

I had to close and open my eyes a couple of times as I watched. She stopped when she was the height of my knee.

"Your turn Chas," she said in a squeaky voice. I sucked in my lips trying not to burst out laughing and thought the word "small" over and over in my mind. My sand accumulated inside my palm and I sprinkled it over me, while concentrating on the word. When I opened my hands, I hadn't shrunk one bit.

"What am I doing wrong?"

"Did you think about being small?"

"Yes, over and over inside my mind."

"The word or the size?"

"Is there a difference?"

"Yes, Chas. The word will not do anything." She sounded hilarious as if she'd sucked in some helium. "You need to think about what you would look like small, and stop thinking about it when you reach the size you want to be."

"Okay, let's try this again."

I thought about this room but bigger. In my mind the paintings were huge, what they would look like to a toddler.

My dust started to flow once more and I sprinkled it on top of my head with thoughts of the big painting.

My body shifted and I grew a head smaller. A yelp left my lips and there was another pull. I was now another head shorter. With the third shift, I was Margot's size and I dusted off all the sand that was still on my body. I stopped shrinking and we immediately removed the shredded canvas from the painting that covered the opening and climbed inside.

Margot lit up the passage with her sand as we crawled forward.

She took a left as she gazed down at the paper and crawled again to a dead end. She gazed down at the paper again and took a right.

We even had to climb upwards through one of the tunnels which was hard, my hands and legs ached when we reached the top.

We reached a turn, and a huge furry body blocked the middle of the duct and a low grunting sound came from his core.

"Shades?" I asked and he laughed inside my head. "Now is not the time. What are you doing here?"

"I hid, the minute the Casters came for Selene. I was trying to help her escape but it didn't work."

"Is she still inside her quarters?" I whispered.

"No, they took her and the Basilisk Orb to the cathedral's tower."

Margot gave me a look.

"She's not here?" I tried to push Shades out of the way.

"Not so fast tiny tots. There are two Shadow Casters guarding her safe. Why do you think I'm still hiding?

They have orders to destroy Anitules on sight if they find them."

"Charlie?"

"The bird is fine. He's hiding with all the other smaller animals up there." His gaze went up above us and I wished I could see through the pipes at what he meant, but I was tiny girl, not super girl, and didn't have x-ray vision.

"There are two Casters guarding the safe."

"GREAT!"

"So what, we attack their shins?"

"We need to get out of here, before we can grow big again, so I suggest someone acts as a distraction while the other one transforms back to their normal size."

"Urgh, you two are going to give me a headache. I'll distract." Shades sounded annoyed.

"You sure?"

"No, but it's the only way to shut the two of you and those ridiculous voices up."

"Mr. Grey will distract," I translated.

The cat didn't think twice and jumped back down into the room.

"Catch me if you can," I heard him say and the two idiots ran after him. They weren't very smart.

Margot jumped down first and I followed. I had to admit, being this small had its perks, but this wasn't one of those times. The landing was hard and I cried out.

Margot was almost back to her original size.

"Chas, are you okay?"

I sucked in a breath and tried to damper my grunts. "I think I hurt my ankle."

"Can you get up? You still need to transform back.

You can't fight at this ridiculous size."

I tried but the minute I put weight on my ankle, my entire body gave in and I landed flat on my butt again.

"Here." She held out her hand and pulled me up with one pull. I thought about getting big again. It was hard not knowing how big all the objects should have been but it did the trick. Three shifts and I was back to my original size. The pain was ten times worse but Margot didn't waste any time. She'd already started to punch in some numbers to open Selene's safe.

I looked toward the passage that Shades had taken. I hoped he was safe and for some idiotic reason, I didn't want to imagine what this life would be like without my talking cat.

A whooshing sound emerged from the vault and the door opened slightly.

Margot had to put her back into it, to open the door and then she flew backwards as a bright light hit her straight in the chest.

Her body hit the wall and she landed on her stomach.

I had no choice but to hop on one foot and hide behind the door.

I didn't know who was inside that safe. But I knew it was someone that had knowledge about the Orb, just like Leigh had discovered. Someone that was close to Selene. Dingle's face still entered my mind and sure as hell as we stood there he came strutting out of the vault.

Quickly I conjured my sand and it glowed a bright gold, just like my father's.

He saw Margot against the wall and turned around just as I released the sand.

I watched him fly through the air and hit the same

wall Margot had a couple of minutes ago.

As I stood over him, I heard a cough from behind the vault door and found Fox locked in a fetal position on the floor.

She was hurt, had blood on her lips and was coughing up more.

"Chastity, wait." Dingle had gotten up and Fox let her sand flow freely. Dingle's mouth locked up and he began mumbling frantically.

I was beyond mad. Mad at Leigh for not seeing what I had, mad at what he had done to Margot, mad that he'd found a way to stay here in Revera, when my mother would never be able to. I was furious at everything and that I'd almost turned Shadow Caster myself in order to save Revera.

Fox crouched down next to Margot.

"Is she okay?"

Fox nodded. "She'll be fine."

"What happened?"

"I saw how they took Selene, and found the scumbag inside her room. Pushing buttons on the wall."

Dingle grunted again.

"Oh give it a rest," Fox said. "There's no way Selene is going to believe you this time." She hit him with her golden sand and his body collapsed again next to Margot's.

"Was it him that stole Margot's pendant?"

Fox nodded.

"He also let the Shadow Casters in to Revera."

I jumped up and looked back at the cathedral. The light was still fading.

"I don't understand." If the twin Orb was safe from Shadow Casters then why was the light still growing dimmer by the second?

"Chas, we have to find the twin Orb now or we can forget about saving Revera."

"Yeah, sure," I said and took Fox's arm, hopping toward the vault.

Then it hit me. *She just said what Leigh had said.*

I stopped and Fox stared at me. "Chas, are you okay, are you hurt?"

I looked over at Dingle's form, lying lifeless close to Margot. *It wasn't Dingle, it was someone else.*

Other images filled my mind. The old man's death. The way he looked at me when he said the *light has shadows*. The way he looked at Fox a second before. Then he'd died.

"He was warning me," I said.

"What?"

"You killed him, because he knew."

"What are you talking about, Chastity?"

"He said the light has shadows. He was talking about you and you knew that. You killed that old man." I looked at Dingle again. "He was here to stop you."

"What are you talking about?"

"Nobody knew about the twin Orb except Lord Crane."

Fox looked at me, let out a breath and closed her eyes. Realization that she had been caught red-handed washed over her body.

"Is it too late to make a deal with you?" She spoke in a voice that made my skin crawl.

"How could you? I trusted you. It was you that took Margot's pendant, wasn't it? And you let me take the blame for it."

"Think Chastity. I told her it wasn't you. I had no

choice, that pendant would've shown her that a Shadow Caster was near."

"You are not a Shadow Caster, Fox."

"I know. I didn't want it to end this way."

"Yet, here you are."

She started to laugh and sucked her lips, looking at me again.

I just shook my head. *How could she do this?*

"The question is, how did you know about the twin Orb, Chas?"

"Leigh told me."

"Leigh….that idiot. Well I'm sure he won't be a thorn in our boots anymore."

"Tom and John are with you on this?" I had to know.

"No, they are all for the greater good. Tried to explain why I'd done it, but they didn't want to listen."

I gasped. "What did you do, Fox?"

"I silenced them. Forever."

"They were a part of your team!"

"No Chastity, they left me to the dogs. If I didn't make a deal with them, they would've killed me."

"What are you talking about?"

"The last mission, the one where I lost my rank. We were overpowered by Shadow Casters and I did what I thought anyone in my position would do. But they just left me. Nobody even tried to send out a search party, Chas. Nobody. It was as if I was replaceable. Not worth saving. I had to make a deal with Crane, told him that I would become whatever he needed. He set me free, but it wasn't as easy as I thought it would be. When I got back, Selene didn't trust me anymore. After everything I'd done for her. That was how she betrayed me. Gave my team to that idiot of a man with his stupid owl.

Henry. My heart contracted as I thought about him. *Had she killed him too?*

"She didn't believe that I'd escaped with my life after Tom told her how many Casters we were fighting against. Had me locked up for observation to make sure my sand was still light. It was, brighter than before, which only helped me gain her trust again."

She gave a sweet smile.

"Still you were safe, why didn't you just stop?"

"I never wanted to be a Caster, Chas. They made me forget about all the heartache they'd caused me when they brought me here, made me start loving everything I stood for. Well that couple of weeks in the Oblivion made me remember all that pain they'd caused." She took a couple of steps toward me. "You want to know why I liked you so much? We were so much alike, you and I. I used to live in the Domain too. Grew up there. My mom was the Caster, my father the Nomad. When she had me, she didn't want this life for me, so she gave me to my dad. We had everything. A beautiful home on almost every continent. I was normal, rode horses, swam in the bluest oceans. Anything I could possibly want, I got it. Then on my sixteenth birthday, a guy wanted to have sex with me. I didn't, so he thought he could just take it, that was when my sand came and he screamed. The next thing I knew Seekers showed up on my doorstep forcing my father to give me up and then they just erased me from his memory. I had no choice but to go with them. They had no right to do that to me. The deal the Shadow Casters made with me is everything I've ever wanted. They'll reverse everything. Make me human again so that I can go back home."

"You can't. Nobody will see you."

"They can reverse it, Chas. We could live among humans like normal people. Have a good life without these psychos intervening. Don't you want to go back home?"

"No, I am home, remember? That's what you said."

Her lips got thinner and thinner and her blue eyes turned darker. Her nostrils flared slightly. "Then you give me no choice, but to destroy you, Chas."

The sand in her hands appeared. It was bright, like my father's. I knew I didn't have the experience to fight Fox. She was a Level Four Caster and I knew I would die.

I blocked my face with my arms and waited for her sand to blow me apart, but it never came.

Did she have second thoughts?

When I opened my eyes I was surrounded by dark sand. It protected me and I could see light trying to seep through.

When the light stopped, the dark faded slowly.

Fox just stared at me, she was drained, and heaving like she'd just run a hundred meters.

"What did you just do?" she asked through deep breaths. She looked at her hands again. Nothing came. "What did you do to me?" she yelled.

I had no idea, but the time had finally come. "I have a secret of my own, you know."

She squinted and rested with her hands on her knees. "The woman that kidnapped me. She didn't. She was my mother."

"Your mother?" She stared at the carpet, probably reliving a memory that was inside her mind somewhere.

"You wondered why she disappeared and why she

suddenly showed up with me. They wanted to take me away, but she had other plans."

"She's your mother, which means Crane is your grandfather." Her face lit up again as if she'd just found a huge bargain. "I can take you to him. He would be so happy to have you, Chas."

"You freak. I would rather die than spend the rest of my life in the Oblivion. You only think about yourself, Fox. What about the millions of kids that will have to live in the Oblivion once Revera is destroyed? What about Grissy?" I huffed. "Guess you don't really care about her."

"Chas, the Shadow Casters aren't what you think they are. They have no choice about living in the Oblivion. They only want things to be equal."

"Bullshit. That's what they want you to believe."

"It's not. I'm telling you the truth."

"You would say anything to get yourself out of this one. Like you said, you had everything, and you will do anything to get it back. You should've never taken me from my mother."

My sand flew, this time it was dark and I was angry. I hit Fox in the chest and she flew against the wall, landing on the other side of Margot.

I fell down on my knees and started to cry as everything just overwhelmed me.

A huge cracking sound coming from the cathedral's tower made me stop. I got up and went to investigate.

The light was almost gone.

I looked back at Fox again and I had to tie her up, if she woke up…

I hopped to the drawers, and searched like hell.. There was nothing.

Then, my eyes landed on the tie backs that held beautiful draped curtains back. I took both and rushed over to Fox, tying her hands behind her back. I pulled at her feet and tied them together too, attaching them to her hands with the second rope.

When I was sure that she wouldn't get out the ropes, I hopped on one leg to Selene's vault and locked myself inside.

Margot was the only one who knew the code and she would let me out, even if it was to hand me over to Selene once Revera and the Virtual Realm were safe.

The lights flickered again and it turned darker.

I started to search for the pendant. Selene used to carry it with her and I looked in the spots Fox hadn't searched yet.

I found it in one of her jewelry boxes. This meant that Fox had no idea what it looked like.

It was a beautiful pendant, the twin Orb was dark blue and resembled a round pearl.

A stone angel with long hair held it in her hands.

I took it out of her grip and held it inside my own palms.

Happy thoughts, Chas.

I closed my eyes.

The first memory that jumped into my head was my mother's face. We were laughing, like we used to and I could speak to her about anything. It got replaced with a bit of dark, anger. I was angry at her for not telling me what I was. For her ending up leaving me, even if she had no choice.

Next my friendship I'd had with Clare, both of them. The time she'd been my best friend and the time she was upset with me, even if it wasn't my fault. I thought about Shades, when I was still under the impression she was a girl, and the day I discovered she was actually Mr. Grey and that she was indeed male. That he never tried to tell me the truth.

Natalie came next and the relationship she shared with her parrot. Speaking to him, laughing at his silent jokes. It would be a reunion that I wished I would be able to see and how she looked at me when Margot yell that I was a Shadow Caster.

Max and Margot jumped in there too. Even though I thought Max's friendship came first, and the fact that he wanted to fight, even though he was broken, then the dark came, he was a douchebag for not telling me the truth a couple of months ago, and for beating me up.

Leigh was last. I wouldn't be able to live in a world where he wasn't. Whether that world was Revera or the Oblivion, I didn't care. I had to save him, and the dark part was that he wasn't real. He was a character in a very realistic game.

Then my mind did something on its own, it was as if I succeeded and a memory of what was going to happen, or what would've happened, flashed through my mind.

It was the memory of my dream with me as an adult walking hand in hand with someone filled my head again.

It had been a winter's evening. I wore a coat and I laughed. The hand in mine was warm. This time I looked up and smiled in awe as I saw the face of the person that would treasure me the way my father had treasured my mother, even if she wasn't the right one for him. He loved her nonetheless and couldn't live his life without her.

I knew now what she'd felt – to love someone that you shouldn't be with – as I was staring at Leigh, watching his lips moving as he spoke to me. I didn't hear what he said, but I knew he loved me. I could feel that.

My hands burned and I opened my eyes. A bright light—even brighter than the one Fox carried in her hands when she wanted to kill me, even brighter than Leigh's—shone from my hands.

I flew backwards in the air and hit the wall of the vault hard before I crashed to the floor.

My ears rang loudly and images of fire and burning ashes fell onto the floor. Then everything blurred out and my world went dark.

THE RINGING FINALLY STOPPED BUT I struggled to open my eyes. When they finally opened I was staring at a ceiling with lights flashing by.
The air that filled my lungs burned so much that I didn't want to breathe.

People wearing masks hovered over me and I realized where I was. I was at the hospital and I knew my mother was going to lose her mind.

I tried to remember what Clare had done this time to make me end up in the hospital, but nothing came. I was so tired and I closed my eyes again.

Leigh...it was the last thing that entered my mind before the darkness consumed me again.

"SHE'S WAKING UP?" I HEARD A FAMILIAR voice I opened my eyes and found a grumpy-looking face inches from my own. "Welcome back, Chas."

I lifted up my hand and scratched his ears softly.

Natalie slept in the chair next to my bed with Charlie on her shoulder.

I blinked around the room suddenly confused. *Damn it!* I was color-blind again. It was as if I was stuffed inside an old black and white TV once again and all the beautiful color I had just started to love had been sucked away.

I felt like crying, suddenly remembering that I would not see my mom barge through the hospital door demanding the doctors tell her what happened.

I would never see her again, or maybe I would, but she wouldn't see me.

I was sure that by now Selene would know what I was and that she would wait until I was better to chuck my ass into the Oblivion.

To be honest I didn't care as I had one thing on my mind, and it was something I had to know immediately.

I cleared my throat and Natalie jumped in her chair. Charlie fell off her shoulder and his wings flapped as he landed on the floor gracefully.

"You okay?" She came closer and I nodded.

"Can I have some water please?"

"Yes, of course." She poured a glass half full and handed it to me. "Here."

I shifted myself upright with my arms. She kept the glass close to my mouth so I could take a couple of sips and when I'd had enough she put it back on the table.

"Did I save Revera?"

She nodded with a soft smile, but it disappeared. I could feel my heart breaking as I knew what that meant. I hadn't saved the Virtual Realm in time.

"He's gone, isn't he?"

"I'm so sorry Chas," she said softly. "I remember telling the kids not to be afraid, that there was a loophole. Even Leigh told them that. He didn't show any fear– not even for a second. Then it came. It hurt like hell and I could hear all of our screams. When I opened my eyes, we were back in Revera. Max is fine, the kids are fine too. Margot woke up yesterday. She said that Dingle hit her with his sand."

"It wasn't Dingle."

"Told you it wasn't him," Shades said.

"It was Fox."

"Yes, Dingle told us that, but not everything. What happened, Chas?"

"It's a long story and from that question something tells me that she got away."

She shook her head. "She's dead Chas."

I gasped. My heart stopped beating for a few seconds.

"Don't you dare feel bad. Fox chose to betray us all. If you didn't …Revera would've been lost. We owe you our lives for what you did."

I killed Fox. And I killed Leigh.

The tears started to flow. I couldn't hide it anymore and I didn't care if they were a sign of weakness or not. I would never see Leigh again. He was gone and I killed Fox, even if she turned out to be the bad guy, I killed her..

Natalie folded her arms around me. "It's going to be okay, Chas. When they found you inside Selene's vault, your sand was gold again. There is no trace of you being a Shadow Caster. Max made Margot promise to not say anything, she's agreed to it. You can stay in

Revera. Think of it as your reward for saving us."

As much as that part should be amazing, it wasn't. I would just have to hide my dark sand again, find new ways to not let it show. Margot would eventually tell. She hated Shadow Casters and she would blame me for Leigh's death.

"Selene is getting the best technicians in to try and reboot the Virtual Realm again. Maybe he would still be there?"

I nodded.

I could only hope.

I turned around, trying not to be rude to Natalie. But I wanted to be alone.

I had to be alone to find a way to deal with all of this, and hopefully to sleep.

If Leigh wasn't going to be in the Virtual Realm anymore, I knew where he would turn up.

Inside my dream

CHAPTER TWENTY EIGHT
LOVE AND LOSS

A MONTH HAD PASSED SINCE THE SHADOW CASTERS invaded Revera.

They held a huge funeral for all the Casters that had died in battle. Tom and John were among them.

I was super glad that Shades was still alive. The stupid cat had found a way to dodge the Casters and they found him and all the other animals inside the vent.

I wasn't awake to see the reunion between Charlie and Natalie but Max told me it was amazing to witness. She cried and laughed all at once when she saw that parrot.

Selene asked me so many times how I'd reversed the shadows in the Orb to light and I just told her I'd used my happy thoughts and the other question I didn't want to answer, I told her I didn't know.

She let me stay close to her after I got out from the

hospital.

I wasn't in lock up the way Fox had said she was. I saw it as a well-deserved rest, being waited on and pampered for a couple of weeks, occasionally showing Selene my sand.

It was a bright gold every time. At least that is what they told me as colors still hadn't come back and my world was all shades of grey. All I saw was this white bright light.

She let me go after three weeks, the day all of Revera was going to find out if the Virtual Realm still existed. They'd only picked a couple of people to enter the reboot, not many were chosen and I wished that I could say I was one of them, but I wasn't.

Still I was able to watch on a special screen inside a special room that looked onto the lab where the technicians worked. Once they got into the Virtual Realm to find out if Leigh was still alive or not, the screen would show us what they saw.

Three men were chosen. Two technicians and a Guardian.

It was a loss to Revera, knowing how long it'd taken Leigh to create the Virtual Realm and how quickly it had been destroyed.

If he was gone, the Virtual Realm would never be the same again.

Shades rubbed against my legs before he jumped onto my lap. How he'd gotten in... *I'm not even going to ask.*

"So, did I miss anything?" he asked.

"Nope, haven't started yet. They are still getting there."

"Getting gassed you mean?"

413

I giggled. The cat had a wicked sense of humor but he was just as brave as any of the Casters walking Revera's halls.

My heart started to beat frantically as I looked down from the gallery onto the three dentist chairs where the three men had started to fall asleep.

It was the easiest way to get into the Virtual Realm.

Deep breaths, he just needs to be alive.

"He's going to be fine, Chas."

"Shush, Shades you don't know that."

I opened my eyes and looked at the big screen.

It reminded me of a dilapidated world. Everything was gone. The buildings, the people.

Tears filled my eyes as the three of them walked and walked for miles.

They entered what was left of homes and walked out again, just shaking their heads.

It carried on like that for hours, and not even in one of those seconds was there any sign of Leigh.

Hope was relatively high when the first day was over and there was still no sign of Leigh. The Virtual Realm was huge, but when they reached the third day, I couldn't watch anymore. I got up and went straight to my room and fell on my bed.

He'd never even known how I really felt about him. He would never know, and that hurt the most.

"Meow." Shades jumped onto my bed and lay right next to me. His long fur brushed against my skin and I was mad that when he was finally being there for me when I needed him, I really just wanted to be alone.

"Tears are not a sign of weakness, Chas. They're a sign of caring and love. They're also a sign of strength, because if you cannot cry, it means you don't have a soul to cleanse."

I looked up at the cat.

"I can't do this."

"Okay, now that is the stupidest thing I've ever heard," he said. "You saved Revera, and I don't care how much help you had. You saved Revera and still decided to be good, otherwise your sand wouldn't have turned back to gold. If anyone can do it, you can. Remember, the Virtual Realm is big. That boy had plenty of time to create the world, and he doesn't do things half-ass."

I giggled. It sounded like Leigh.

"He's going to be fine, you'll see. They just haven't found him yet."

"I hope you're right."

"So I guess you will tell lover boy how you really feel if you see him, right?"

"He would probably think I'm a silly Caster having feelings for something that isn't real."

"He is real, well not the way we want him to be, but if he's real to you, he's real."

"Thanks Shades."

"And he won't laugh."

I rolled my eyes. "You know that cats don't know everything and that they are not always right. You could be wrong about that."

"I'm not about this. Just tell him how you feel when you see him, please."

I giggled. "Thanks, Shades."

"You are most welcome. My job is done, see you later."

"Yep, see you later."

He left and I felt better. But whether the cat was

speaking the truth or not, I would probably never know.

Fatigue finally came.

I hadn't dreamed of Leigh once in the past month which told me that he didn't exist anymore.

Darkness consumed me and I drifted away.

When I opened my eyes I was inside the woods. The vibrant colors of the brown bark and green leaves assaulted me as I took in my surroundings. I could still see in color in my dreams. I always searched for him in the woods, but I never found him.

I tried to dream about theme parks but it never happened that way.

I walked and walked, the trees looked the same. They were dull and lifeless, it wasn't the colors of Revera anymore, it was the same colors in the Domain; another sign that he wasn't here.

The tops of the trees moved slightly. I could see it, the wind. It blew small pieces of leaves from their branches and they descended toward me.

They brushed my face gently, leaving a million goose bumps on my arms and blew through my hair. I closed my eyes not knowing what caused this and when it left, I followed it with my eyes. I looked behind me as it blew more leaves in its wake.

I didn't want the wind to leave my sight as it was the first dream where anything had happened.

The wind picked up again and started to blow orange leaves that had fallen to the ground, twirling them round and round.

A figure started to appear in the leaves and I squinted. It was vague at first, but they were definitely forming a figure. Then the picture got better. First the color of dark hair with broad shoulders appeared. Then his arms, torso and hips. It shifted down to his legs and lastly a pair of glasses rested on his nose.

I cupped my mouth as tears welled up in my eyes.

It was really him.

When the wind finally found its resting place, leaving Leigh standing on the leaves, I didn't think twice. I ran and my arms wrapped around his neck.

He smelled the same. A bit of musk, mixed with danger and something sweet.

His arms folded around me too.

"Please tell me that you are okay?" I said into his shoulder.

"I'm here, aren't I?"

"It's not the same. This is a figment of my imagination. My dream."

He chuckled. "Chas, I was always just a figment of someone's imagination."

I looked at him, confused. "No, you weren't. You were real."

"I'm not. I'm a virtual creation, that's it and...." He looked down to the leaves. "You must know that this isn't a healthy relationship."

He'd said it, the word. Relationship. "My parents didn't have a healthy relationship either. I don't care."

"Chas, your dad was real. There is a huge difference."

"I don't care!" I said, a bit louder which made me look away. I knew what was going to come next. The cat was wrong. He was going to reject me like he'd done to Margot.

"Yeah." He sighed. He lifted up my chin to look at him. I hated the tears of betrayal, but it hurt, and I finally understood why Clare had been so upset with me. If she'd hurt this much too, I could finally relate.

"You aren't the crying type, why the tears?"

"I just wanted you to be okay."

"I am, I'm here." He kept saying it over and over.

"It's not the same, Leigh. I'll never see you again, other than in my dreams, which are my doing. I want you to be okay inside the Virtual Realm."

"Why? Why aren't your dreams enough?"

"You know why. I don't know if this is your or my doing. I want it to be you."

His lips curved slightly.

"Why?"

"You know why." I looked at him again.

"Chastity?"

"I really don't care, Leigh, and you might not feel…."

I couldn't finish my sentence as his lips were planted firmly on mine. He kissed me gently and my stomach did a million flops with the knowledge that he felt the same way, even if it wasn't real.

I wrapped my arms around his neck again and he pulled me harder into him.

He was slightly out of breath when he finished and gave me a smile.

"What?"

"You worry too much Chas, and Mr. Grey, you should trust him more."

I giggled. "You have to say that because this is my dream."

"No," he spoke through laughter. "Cats are always right."

I giggled.

The wind blew and he looked up at the sky again.

His eyes became sullen, with his smile. Something was wrong.

"What is it?"

"It's time, Chas."

"For what."

"For me to go."

"No." I grabbed him again and could feel his mouth on my head. "Shhh, it will be fine. It will be fine." His voice became softer and softer saying it will be fine over and over until my eyes opened and I was back in my room, lying on my bed.

Shades was purring loudly and was lying close to me. I scratched his head.

Whether Leigh was alive or not, I didn't know but at least I was dreaming about him again. Which was altogether a really good sign.

I guess only time would tell if there was anything left in the Virtual Realm or not. Only time would tell.

DREAM CASTERS
SHADOW

BY

ADRIENNE WOODS

CHAPTER ONE
HAPPILY EVER AFTER DOESN'T EXIST

IT HAD BEEN FOUR MONTHS, FIVE DAYS, six hours and twenty-odd minutes since the night the Virtual Realm was lost to us.

The night that the one person I'd looked up to had betrayed us all. Fox, a brilliant Guardian who'd made a deal with the Shadow Casters and then she died by my hands.

The night that Sophie, a sweet, smart, curly-headed girl died. The night that the only guy I would ever love was tossed into the unknown.

They'd given up on the search and today was the day that they were going to switch off the machine. It didn't matter to them whether he still existed or not, but he existed inside my dreams. My beautiful, colorful dreams.

I was lucky that my cat Shades, or Mr. Grey as the Reverians knew him, a talking cat who only I could hear, hadn't died.

He was alive and still as grumpy as ever with his snarky comments but he truly had become one of my best friends.

He said that the Virtual Realm was huge, and that Lover Boy might still be alive. Well sort of, as Leigh was part of the Virtual Realm. Technically he didn't exist, he was like a computer program, just way more advanced, or what Reverians would call, a Jumper.

He gave me hope and now they were just going to plunder it, killing the only guy that I would ever love.

It was also four months, five days, six hours and now seven minutes that I'd been living a lie.

I dreamt of Leigh every night, it was the one place he still existed, and in these dreams, well we'd gotten to know one another pretty well.

I'd crushed deeply for him, and the worst part of it was that I had no idea whether it was my imagination or whether he was really there.

Dreams inside Revera were not like the dreams that the humans in the Domain were used to. Here they could be used by someone like Leigh to have a private conversation or they could be used for a silly girl's fantasy of a boy she could never really have, but they were real, you experienced the full dose and not just twenty percent the way my mother, Vinicola Sodivic, a name the Light Casters feared, and one of the best Shadow Casters alive, told me.

Leigh and I kissed many times in my dreams and each one felt so real, but again, it could be all my doing and have nothing to do with Leigh whatsoever. Like I'd said, a big lie, which didn't matter one bit because whichever way I looked at it, it was going to be over.

Footsteps rushed up the stairs and a head with blonde scruffy hair peeked into my room with a huge grin on his face. I hadn't recalled ever seeing Max grin like that before.

"What?"

He just smiled and stared at me like an idiot. "They found him."

I sucked in a breath. "What?"

"It's just a voice, but they think it's Leigh."

I ran out of my room and down the stairs with Max right behind me. "A voice. How?"

"It was when they just exited the Virtual Realm, they were about to make it final, to shut down the entire world and then his voice just popped through."

We ran back toward the science building that housed all the people who were hard at work trying to save anything that had been destroyed inside the Virtual Realm when we finally entered.

"The frequency was not clear and we couldn't make out a single word, but it's him Chas."

I sprinted up the steps. I'd never run so hard, just to hear his gibberish for myself. If his voice was there, he was fine. It was the sign that I'd been praying for these past four months.

We'd spoken about this day so many times, which always led to my insecurities about all of this. How it was only my imagination.

He'd just laughed at me.

The gallery windows were blocked by everyone standing against them to see better. The scratching while they tried to find the right frequency was all over the speakers.

"Leigh, can you hear me?" One of the scientists said.

There was no response and more scratching began as they tried to find a better frequency. It drove me insane every time they spoke and there was no answer.

After the umpteenth time I got up; I seriously could not do this – go through this again. He wasn't there. He was gone.

"Chas," Max said softly.

I couldn't look at him and touched the knob of the door.

The scratching noise stopped and a voice came through. My stomach flipped as I knew that voice. It was him. It was really him. I ran to the window and didn't care who I had to shove aside to get a better look at how the technicians were working.

One word was said and then scratching again, another half of a word, more scratching. I started to giggle. It was Leigh, it was really him. What he said wasn't clear as they tried to tune into the frequency to hear him better. But none of that mattered as I knew he still existed.

Then he spoke again.

"Tell Chas…" The voice disappeared.

Everyone stared at me, even Margot. I didn't like her look at all, the way her lips thinned and the soft muscles alongside her jaw started to pull slightly.

I looked away and back to the technicians. *Tell me what?*

They fine-tuned the frequency, trying hard not to lose him. My heart was pounding. *Tell me what?*

His voice came again. "…cat is always right."

The cat is always right. I started to giggle and knew that somehow my dream wasn't a figment of my imagination. He was really there and the past four months had been real, even though it was only in my dreams. It *was* real and he really did feel the same for me.

ABOUT THE AUTHOR

Adrienne Woods was born and raised in South Africa, where she still resides on the East side of Johannesburg with her husband and two little girls. She's been writing for the past four years and in her free time she likes to review books of new and upcoming authors.

WWW.AUTHORADRIENNEWOODS.COM

www.ingramcontent.com/pod-product-compliance
Lightning Source LLC
Chambersburg PA
CBHW021213260626
47172CB00002B/407